# OF EDEN

by George Moakley

Paperclip Publishing, LLC
Chandler, Arizona

*Tides of Eden*

Copyright © 2025 by George Moakley

Published by: Paperclip Publishing LLC




Editor: Abigail T. Matteson
Cover Illustration: Shaun Cochran
Cover Design and Interior Typography: Hannah Thigpen

Library of Congress Control Number: 2024943756

ISBN: 979-8-9891077-8-0 (paperback)
ISBN: 979-8-9891077-9-7 (hardcover)
ISBN: 979-8-9891077-7-3 (eBook)

Printed in Rephen Printing, Co. LTD in Guangzhou and the United States of America

First Printing: 2024

Paperclip Publishing LLC
3800 W Ray Road Suite 5
Chandler, AZ 85226

www.paperclippublishing.com

To Diana, for believing in me.
To my kids, for sharing my love of monster stories.

# CONTENTS

# FORWARD

If you've read and (hopefully) enjoyed *Kraken of Eden*, you may confidently skip this forward and begin reading *Tides of Eden*. But, if you're new to the Deep Space Exodus series, or if you want a bit more insight into the foundation of the series (or maybe you're just a compulsive reader like me), then please read on.

I love science, which was an unlikely love given my upbringing. I grew up in a blue collar neighborhood in Queens, NY, where completing high school was notable and "wilderness" was a weed-filled lot or the unmaintained section of the neighborhood cemetery. While the other kids were choosing sides for pick-up games (no organized sports), I was carrying a rinsed out pickle jar with holes punched in the lid hunting for bugs.

Somehow, in all of that, I fell in love with nature; as nerdy as any TV caricature, I was unable to explain to the other kids why the habits of local insects or birds should interest them. Fiction didn't hold my attention until I found stories that involved discovery, that took place in a reality other than my own, that were imbued with an education about other conceptual frameworks whether it be other planets, organized crime, or feudal Japan.

I'm often asked why I write. My reply is that I write what I want to read. I read a *lot* and I read a wide variety of things, but the books I truly love to read are more than great stories. They're great stories that take place in alternate realities. Other planets, sure, but it's about more than science fiction. I love anything that's richly detailed, thoroughly researched, and realistically presented in such a way that the story is enriched with discovery of that alternate reality. If I come away from the story with new insight into my own world, *that's* what I want to read. I started writing because I wanted a monster story that fits that bill.

I originally envisioned *Kraken of Eden* as a standalone novel. When I started the project, I wondered whether I would really be able to produce a full-length book. When I finished writing, I had over 120,000 words and a number of additional plot ideas that would have made the novel prohibitively long. But after publishing, I found myself missing characters I'd grown fond of, wondering about their future. As reviews were posted, it became clear readers felt the same way.

So, what to do? Keep writing, obviously!

As I began storyboarding *Tides of Eden*, I realized there would be a (as yet untitled) third novel, and probably a fourth. I also realized that there were a number of plots that would work as novellas. I'm resistant to thinking in terms of sequels or trilogies, especially with more than three books in mind. Plus, in most (but not all) trilogies, the second story often feels more like a "bridge" than a complete story, and I really hoped this would *not* be the case with *Tides of Eden*. Instead, I thought in terms of stories set in the same future history that I (and hopefully my readers) find plausible and compelling. Clearly, stories set in that future history should not contradict each other, but they should not need to be read in any particular order.

In *Kraken of Eden,* the reader discovers Eden with the colonists as they explore their new world. *Tides of Eden* takes place fifteen years later. Do I risk boring the returning readers by re-discovering what they discovered in *Kraken of Eden*? Do I risk leaving new readers confused? Or do I just write a forward?

Obviously, I chose to write a brief forward.

The Deep Space Exodus novels take place in the 26th century. By the 26th century, Earth's population declined to a sustainable level through migration. Some two billion humans now live elsewhere in our solar system (Moon, Mars, asteroids, etc.), and seventy-five million more live on colonies across forty-nine star systems. I envisioned the formation of an International Deep Space Cooperative to share the costs and profits of interstellar exploration, including an incentive program monitoring colonial gene pools and incentivizing migration to other worlds.

I gave a great deal of thought to the implications of humanity aspiring to spread among the stars without faster than light travel, thinking of our previous journeys. One such example is humanity spreading through Oceania. If people could spread one land mass at a time, through islands, archipelagoes and the Australian continent, then surely we could someday spread one star system to another?

I also gave a great deal of thought about xenobiology. As a fan of hard science fiction, I wanted an alien world that might evolve a monster that could munch on our colonists. What would be different about alien life? What would be the same? Humans haven't discovered alien life…yet. Many experiments have recreated primordial conditions and demonstrated that the basic building blocks of carbon-based life form naturally. From this, I believe it is reasonable to extrapolate that, given sufficient time and the right conditions, such organic compounds would combine to form simple cells comparable to earthly bacteria that would in turn evolve to more complex cells and multicellular life.

So, in our stories, as humanity spreads through and settles nearby star systems, we encounter many worlds with organic chemicals of scientific and commercial interest as well as a smaller number that have simple cells.

So, we're back to delightful thought experiments about what alien life would be like, both in terms of what must be analogous and what could be completely different. Much of the appeal of these novels, for me, has been the challenge of imagining alien life forms, especially given the diversity of earthly life. And please bear in mind, as our colonists learn about the denizens of their new home and our xenobiologists cite earthly analogs, that all of the earthly creatures offered as examples are real!

I hope you enjoy reading *Tides of Eden* as much as I've enjoyed writing it, and I hope that, if you haven't already, you're intrigued enough to read *Kraken of Eden*, as well as the forthcoming novels set in this future timeline.

Thank you!

# PART 1:
# ALIGNMENT

# ▪ DAY 1: 11:47
## THE HUNT

Ronnie stood in awe.

She'd lived her entire life under pressurized domes. As a child, she watched videos and dreamt of seeing the kinds of natural wonders her distant ancestors took for granted. As she matured, she had sadly accepted she never would.

Then, she got her shot, the opportunity to be among the first Eden colonists! The first alien world with a complex biosphere, rich with biodiversity and unspoiled wilderness. Finally she would see, for herself, the stuff of dreams.

But gradually, familiarity replaced wonder as Ronnie spent her days escorting teams of xenobiologists and planetologists across the surface of Eden. She too began to take it all for granted. She'd almost become jaded after seeing so many beautiful, pristine environments on Eden. Oceans. Mountains. Deserts. Forests.

*But this…*

Somehow, she knew this moment would stay with her the rest of her life.

They'd been climbing for hours, trudging along a misty, muddy game trail. Sounds were muffled. Light was dim. Even in their environmental suits, they could feel the oppressive weight of the fog. Then, as they approached the crest, the trees thinned, and mud gave way to rock. Ronnie focused her attention on the placement of her feet until she reached a relatively smooth, level surface.

She sighed deeply, slung her rifle and stretched, eyes closed, arms extended, arching her back.

As she opened her eyes, she gasped.

Before Ronnie stretched a broad valley of unrelenting green beneath a clear, blue, endless sky. Green gently ruffled where random breezes touched the forest canopy. Green interrupted only by a ridge of sheer red rock to the west and the pure blue of a river meandering eastward towards the sea, sparkling in the sunlight as it drained this spectacular valley.

She turned her head to drink it all in. As she turned, she could see the gray clouds they'd spent the morning plodding through fall back into the canyon behind them. The analytical part of her mind worked through the meteorology. Air on this side of the crest, warmed by the sun, rose and tumbled back the cooler clouds into the basin from whence they came.

But understanding what she was seeing did not, could not, detract from the majesty of this moment.

Her reverie was interrupted by the sounds, or perhaps more to the point, the silence of her team. They'd followed Ronnie's footsteps, looking up as she had once they reached the smooth rock surface and no longer worried about where they placed their feet. She hadn't been paying attention to their chatter, but she noticed when it stopped.

*Movement.*

In the distance to her left, as if on cue, perfection. A large creature soared above the valley, high above the canopy yet below her vantage point, affording her a peer's view of the majestic beast as it stretched its long, broad leathery wings to ride thermals from the valley below.

It was clearly from the trilaterally symmetrical super-kingdom of Eden. Its clawed forelimbs and stout hindlimbs folded against its body as the six elongated fingers of each mid limb stretched wings to harvest every bit of lift from the sun warmed air. Its sensory cluster extended over its long, thin beak. Two eyestalks aimed forward as it flew, two scanned the canopy below, and two pivoted to monitor the airspace above and around it. Two long, thin tails trailed behind it. From above, its coloring matched the forest canopy. From below, Ronnie assumed it would match the sky above.

She sighed. Ronnie could not imagine anything more perfect. But she had a job to do, so she turned to count heads. As she looked at each member of her team, she checked their vital signs on her heads-up display. They were winded but recovering. They'd only burned through about half their oxygen, but given the rugged terrain, they were consuming the nutritional supplementation of their reclaimed water at a faster than average rate. Still, a quick analysis confirmed they'd be able to hold to their original plan as long as they boarded their EAGLE within four hours.

As an original colonist, Ronnie remembered supporting field expeditions from the orbiting platform via landing craft. As field expeditions shifted to the growing surface settlement, the engineering team designed a new aircraft favoring versatility and agility over the ability to reach orbit. The design was relatively straightforward, using the same versatile platform as landing craft and orbital shuttles, but with thrusters rather than wings.

A lively naming contest was held, then easily won as the judges realized a partial acronym for the otherwise ungainly "Efficient Agile Ground Limited Extended Range Craft" spelled EAGLE. The following year a smaller, faster, and even more agile aircraft was introduced. The name "Falcon" was deemed such an obvious counterpart for EAGLE that nobody felt the need for another contest. There was, instead, an art contest for the "eagle" and "falcon" symbol that would be emblazoned on the craft. Not that anyone had actually *seen* a falcon or eagle. The few species that survived the mass extinctions of the 21st and 22nd centuries were only found on Earth, and none of the colonists had ever been to Earth.

Like most field expeditions, the tracking team's EAGLE was outfitted as a mobile base. A break from environmental suits and a bit of solid food would be most welcome! Ronnie brought up a map on her heads-up display. At some point, perhaps soon, they would need to abandon their quest and head for the beach. It would depend on which direction their quarry chose from here. The alternative would be to move the EAGLE closer to them, if they could find a clearing large enough. That might be challenging, given the mountains and rainforest. Yet another alternative would be to have a Falcon ferry them to the EAGLE.

*Too many variables.* She'd need to keep re-evaluating.

"My god, that's beautiful!"

Vivek, one of the trackers, stood arms akimbo, turning right and left to take it all in.

The xenobiologists pointed at the creature soaring over the valley and held a lively debate about it. It was completely new, of course. Their best estimate was that, after fifteen years, they might have cataloged some 10-15% of Eden's biodiversity. In fact, the rate at which they were still discovering new life forms suggested their initial biodiversity estimates had been far too low.

Most of the animals and plants cataloged thus far were those small enough to find their way into sample containers borne on suspensor pallets. Encounters with larger creatures were common but limited to recorded observations. They'd only recently launched expeditions, like this one, to learn more about Eden's larger animals.

Well, they really weren't animals. Or plants.

These "animals" were as alien as they could be. Colloquially, Eden scientists had taken to calling the green growth around them "plants" because of their superficial resemblance to Earth plants. The growth was green because that was the most efficient color for photosynthesis, but their phytochemical was not the chlorophyll of Earth. The green had structures that lifted broad, thin surfaces to the sun because that was the most efficient way to compete for sunlight, but those structures were not made of wood and the green surfaces were not leaves. They were as different from earthly leaves and branches as they could be within the constraints of what evolutionary competition compelled them to be.

Similarly, they commonly referred to the creatures that moved through the green growth as "animals," but the creatures were not animals. Eden's life forms moving through water or over land faced the same physical challenges as their earthly counterparts and evolved structures superficially resembling the fins, limbs, and wings of their earthly analogs. But these structures had completely different evolutionary heritages and therefore completely different internal structures. The creatures that bore them were also as alien as could be.

Throughout known space, life is common but complex life is not. Dozens of colonies grew on worlds inhabited by life forms no more advanced than Earth's bacteria. Only Eden bore rich ecosystems populated with complex, multicellular life, offering for the first time an opportunity to discover and explore what aspects of life might be universal. What forms are inevitably driven by evolutionary processes acting within the constraints of biochemistry and biomechanics against the permutations of random mutations?

Ronnie shook her head, catching herself in her daydreaming and pondering.

She swept her eyes across the valley for one last time, then barked, "don't bunch up! Trackers! Let's follow the trail!"

Vivek and Ahmed led the way, as they were among the most experienced wildlife biologists. They each learned their trade as junior staff at mature and expansive inner colony zoological parks, then accepted migration opportunities to be part of a new zoological park planned for one of the outer colonies. It was these migration opportunities that put them in the right place at the right time to be part of the initial colonization runs to Eden. Now, they were faculty at Eden's Deep Space Service Academy (DSSA), whose xenobiology program had direct access to the only complex ecology in known space other than what was left of Earth's.

They'd started their quest early that morning. Their EAGLE carried them to a clearing in the coastal rainforest east of the surface settlement. Ronnie and the scientists wandered about until Ahmed found a game trail, which they followed searching for signs of larger creatures. Eventually, they found evidence of a large herbivore. At least they believed it to be an herbivore, based on an analysis of its droppings. They also believed it to be from Eden's bilateral super-kingdom. The xenobiologists said it was new, something they'd never seen before.

The only thing Ronnie knew for sure, based on the size of the droppings, was that it was *big*.

They tracked the herbivore as it headed west through the foggy canyon and now over this crest. Ronnie and Ivan took point. Ben and Omar brought up the rear. Their drones circled above them, patrolling for anything large enough to be a potential threat.

Ronnie scanned the trail and monitored the group nervously. She wasn't supposed to be in charge. She, like Ivan, Ben, and Omar, were security/medics, or secmeds. They were supposed to be support personnel, only taking charge in emergencies. And emergencies did happen. They were in true wilderness, and Eden had her share of predators. Attacks were rare, thankfully. The group was, after all, just alien beings clad in environmental suits that denied potential predators any scent. But some of Eden's predators were more aggressive and less discriminant than others; some were equipped with sensory capabilities not thwarted by environmental suits. Most secmeds had more than enough harrowing cautionary tales to quash the initial skepticism of new arrivals.

This expedition's leader, Deirdre, realizing she was easily distracted like the rest of their flock of xenobiologists, was self-aware enough to ask Ronnie to take point. Ronnie's compromise was to follow Deirdre's increasingly rare directives while keeping them on track. She did so by periodically interrupting whatever new species discovery was diverting their attention to ask their trackers for updates on their quarry. She also had to remind them to drink their reclaimed water from their environmental suit's reservoirs. "Carry your body's reclaimed water in your body," she'd chastise them. "Don't deprive your body of the nutritional supplements your environmental packs are adding to your water."

She smiled and shook her head. It was like herding toddlers, so easily distracted. She had to keep reminding them it was their insistence on moving quickly that kept them from bringing suspensor pallets of sample containers for all their discoveries. They had to satisfy themselves with imagery, and precious little of that, if they were ever going to catch up with whatever it is that they were tracking.

Vivek and Ahmed disagreed briefly about the implications of a print and a bent branch. They eventually reached the consensus that, after cresting the ridge, the creature moved generally downhill, through the rainforest and back towards the coast.

*Good.* They would be heading, at least generally, in the right direction of the EAGLE. That would buy them a little more time and improve their odds of finding the creature before being forced to abandon their quest to recharge environmental packs.

Ronnie let them lead the way. The rest of the troop followed. Movement was easier on this side of the ridge. The ground along the game trail was dry and firm. But now, descending rather than ascending, their knees were starting to complain.

At least their quarry was moving slowly; they were gradually catching up with it. The trackers said the signs were increasingly fresh. They hadn't seen it yet, nor had the patrol drones circling one and 2 km about them. They believed they were getting close, but the drones couldn't see it through the rainforest canopy.

Ronnie was anxious for the drones to get a glimpse of it. If Earth's life forms were any guide, even an herbivore could be dangerous. And carnivores also followed game trails, including, possibly, something capable of bringing down whatever it was that they were tracking.

Their mission parameters were clear. They were to get close enough to try their latest megafauna research prototypes, but they could not take unnecessary risks. No xenobiologist came to Eden with real field experience dealing with truly wild megafauna. Those with zoological park experience honed their skills under controlled conditions. Animals were tagged with devices that continuously collected, processed, and forwarded detailed information. This generally preempted any need to track and subdue them. When it *did* become necessary to capture them, methodologies were clear and trackers always had detailed physiological information about the animals, down to precise tranquilizer dosages.

And, sadly, Earth's larger animals were simply impractical to transport between stars. Nothing larger than a dog roamed an interstellar zoological park. The few larger species that survived the ecological collapse of the 21st century lived out their lives in Earth's zoological parks. Perhaps, someday, when Earth's biosphere finally recovered sufficiently, open preserves could be created to let them roam freely.

*Here?*

Ronnie pondered the potential. Large creatures are plentiful here; some were substantially larger than anything encountered by humans on Earth. These are novel life forms with unknown physiologies. But the scientists were *years* away from being able to use tranquilizer darts to subdue anything safely and effectively. For now, the plan was to track their quarry and get close enough to observe it before deciding how best to proceed.

There were, of course, obvious possibilities. One would be to observe their quarry only, but that would have limited value. Another would be to kill a few specimens to learn what they could through necropsies, hoping to gather enough information to enable future, less obtrusive sampling techniques. They also brought nets that might be able to physically subdue the creature.

But this troop was betting on something experimental: a shell carrying a mesh network of minuscule autonomous devices that would be fired at the creature. As they approached a target, they would spread tiny, mechanical legs to create enough drag to slow themselves and, hopefully, not be felt as they made contact. The devices would distribute themselves over the external surface of the creature and conduct internal scans to produce and transmit detailed internal imagery, not unlike sick bay diagnostic scanners. The devices also had a piercing structure that would allow them to take minute tissue samples from and through the creature's hide. It was this piercing structure that inspired the xenobiologists to refer to them as "ticks." On hearing this, the engineering team feigned enough offense to amuse the xenobiologists and reinforce the nickname.

The ticks were small enough, Ronnie hoped, to not affect their hosts' behaviors. It wasn't clear how long the devices would be able to stay with said host. They had a limited ability to recharge themselves from the kinetic energy of their host's movements, but the devices would eventually fall away and, being made from Eden materials, safely decompose.

*Movement.*

Ronnie stopped and raised her left fist to halt the troup from advancing. She heard the others come to a stop. She lowered her hand, pointing where she'd seen the movement.

A distant noise confirmed the direction.

As they'd climbed the ridge, the canopy thinned until they reached the edge of the forest. As they descended, the canopy thickened again, stealing most of the sun's light, leaving them in dim gloom interrupted by trunks and sparse undergrowth. Their drones could detect and report the movement of large things, but beyond that, they were blind.

Ronnie let her arm fall to her side as she peered in the direction of the noise. Vivek slowly approached to stand beside her. Through her headset, she heard him say, "that sounded *big.*"

She nodded, then realized he couldn't see her nodding. She answered quickly, "indeed. I saw movement. Did you?"

"Briefly. Somewhere over there. But I've lost it now."

*Silence.*

Something rustled in the canopy above them. Deirdre, looking upward, said "we really need to explore these canopies. We have *no* idea what's up there!"

"Not today."

*Movement.*

Ronnie slowly raised her arm again, pointing through the gloom towards what appeared to be a relatively illuminated space.

"There!"

It was indeed big. Perhaps 3500 kilos. Bigger than anything any of them had ever seen before reaching Eden. It was as big as an elephant.

She could see it, vaguely, in the distance. One of the mature trees must have fallen, leaving a gap in the canopy. A few saplings desperately raced to fill that gap, yearning for the chance to raise their photosynthetic surfaces to unobstructed sunlight. But, for now, they were still vulnerable to browsing.

Cautiously, the group moved closer, their quarry becoming increasingly visible as they approached. When Ronnie saw it pause, she gestured to keep a safe distance. After a moment, the creature resumed feeding. It was generally gray in color with a disruptive pattern that made it hard to see in subdued light. It was a member of the bilaterally symmetrical super-kingdom. Unlike Earth's land vertebrates, each of its four limbs had two articulation points rather than one. The hind limbs were stout, ending in broad, round, bony feet balanced by a short, thick tail. This allowed the creature to extend heavily clawed forelimbs up to the leaves of one of the saplings. It pulled leaves and branches toward its vertically oriented mouth, which ended in rounded, symmetrical plates that effortlessly cut through even the thickest branches. Behind the mouth, under the eyes, was a large, pulsating bulge. One of the xenobiologists explained it must be a throat mill, similar to what they'd found in smaller Edenic species. It ground the snipped leaves and branches to pulp before progressing to the gut to complete the digestive process.

"Ideas?" Ronnie asked.

She heard a long exhalation, then Ahmed spoke. "We can try to surround it, then cast a net over it and try to hold it down to take measurements. But I don't think that'll work. Those limbs look strong to me. I think it'd put up a fight, and I don't think our net would last long against those claws. I mean, look at those claws! I don't think it needs them for feeding. I think they're for defending itself against a predator, a *big* one."

Ronnie paused. "I do *not* want to meet what it fights with those claws! But, yeah, I think it would shred our nets. What do you think, Deirdre? Want to try the ticks?"

"Yes, I think that's our best bet. We need to test them, and, as you say, I have little confidence in our ability to subdue it with our nets. I don't want anyone hurt."

Ahmed cleared his throat. "You all stay here, and I'll try to get close enough for a shot."

Ronnie laughed. "You think you're stealthier than me? Or a better shot?"

Ahmed, feigning offense, leaned back and answered, "who won our last marksmanship challenge?"

Ronnie paused, momentarily distracted. She suddenly received a message from Guido Hideko, Commander of Eden's Security Forces. It was flagged as "priority" but not "critical," so she didn't take the time to open it just yet. She returned her attention to Ahmed and gave a delayed laugh. "Oh, all right. Go ahead."

Ahmed detached his shotgun from his pack. He broke the gun, then reached into his right thigh pouch to pull two tick cartridges. After loading, he closed the breach and activated his environmental suit's camouflage to match their surroundings. He crouched as he started moving slowly through the underbrush towards the creature. Ronnie's visor highlighted him with a yellow glow as he circled around and moved closer. She held her breath watching him move stealthily forward. She raised her rifle, loaded with explosive rounds, and set it to burst mode, ready to protect him should the creature charge. But it remained oblivious to his approach.

Finally, when he was within a few meters of his quarry, he paused, stood slowly, aimed carefully, and fired. The sound, muted by the design of the barrel, was still loud enough to alert the creature.

It didn't bolt.

It was a new noise for the creature, inspiring curiosity more than alarm. It stopped feeding to scan the environment, turning its head left and right, as a frill of bright orange raised around its neck.

One of the xenobiologists abruptly stood and pointed. "Ah! See that? See that frill? We've seen that on some of its smaller relatives. The body is covered with little fringed dermatological flaps. Closest thing on Earth would be feathers, I suppose, but structurally, very different. The ones around the neck carry assorted colors. We think they raise different colors to communicate."

One of her peers shot back. "Maybe, but that's just speculation for now. Personally, I think…"

"Hush!" Ronnie snapped. "It may not be able to hear us talking, but it can see you moving. Don't spook it!"

The team held still. Those standing slowly returned to crouching.

After a few minutes, the creature, satisfied that nothing was threatening it, resumed browsing. From her perspective, Ronnie couldn't tell whether Ahmed had missed his target until she heard Deirdre exclaim "yes!"

Ahmed walked slowly back, pumping a fist, obviously pleased with himself. Eventually, as he deactivated his camouflage, his environmental suit returned to bright yellow. Then he paused, resumed walking, then paused again. Ronnie assumed he was watching his heads-up display, too enthralled with the data stream to continue gloating.

"Did it work?" she asked.

Deirdre responded. "Oh, my goodness, yes! I don't think the creature felt the sensors at all, but they're spreading over it, collecting and reporting data. This is amazing!"

Ronnie could hear the other xenobiologists chattering back and forth as the data poured in. Then she observed them absentmindedly stand up and gesture as they focused on their heads-up displays and began to debate the information they were receiving.

Ronnie saw the herbivore pause again as their movements caught its attention.

"Stay down!" she snapped. "Don't startle our friend!"

The admonishment worked. The scientists crouched, and, after a few minutes, the herbivore resumed browsing.

The situation seemed relatively stable, so she opened Guido's message. Ronnie's eyes widened. She blinked, then reread the message. She quickly opened a sidebar channel with Ivan, Ben, and Omar, saying, "Deirdre and I need to go. Let's give them a few minutes to enjoy the data, then we need to get ourselves to an extraction point. They're sending a Falcon."

After a moment, Omar whistled, then asked, "problem?"

She sighed, "yes. One of the construction crews reported a casualty. A predator. Or predators. Either way, Deirdre and I are being reassigned. Omar, you'll take charge with Ben. Same plan. Now that we've found our friend, get the rest of the team to our EAGLE on the beach. It's been outfitted to serve as our mobile base camp. The scientists want to observe the predicted tsunami from that offshore quake when the alignment peaks. We'll catch up with you when we've sorted out whatever needs to be sorted out. Meanwhile, Ivan, Guido's sending a newbie to help you bring up the rear."

# ▪ DAY 1: 13:09
## WU CITY

Rajiv Patterson stood by one of the east-facing windows of his conference room, watching the shadow of the space elevator base station begin its daily pilgrimage towards the dome stem wall. It was more than a conference room really, taking up so much of the top floor of the base station, a massive structure whose foundation extended deep into the planet's largest, thickest, and most stable equatorial tectonic plate.

The base station was the tallest building on the planet, and would remain so until and unless another space elevator was built to link a new surface settlement to another orbiting platform. But no such structure was currently planned, leaving those who walked the periphery of the top floor unparalleled views of the rest of the settlement and the surrounding landscape. This view was reserved for the poshest venues, the most senior government officials. Rajiv's conference room, with adjacent private offices and quarters, offered a spectacular view of the immense mountain range that separated the surrounding desert from the coastal rainforest.

He shifted his gaze upwards, as he often did, through transparent roof panels to see the cables of the space elevator ascending to the heavens. Somewhere, thousands of kilometers above him, beyond the blue sky, those cables terminated within the rotating drum of the orbiting platform. The drum wasn't visible by day, but by night, the colonial drum and the "stalk" came alive with a spectacular display of lights.

As he looked upwards, a gondola slowly left its airlock to begin its ascension. Once clear, it would rapidly accelerate to 600 km/hr to reach the drum in about two days. The framework surrounding the gondola airlocks served as the central support for this, the primary dome. It was a modest 2 km in diameter, a concession to Eden's seismic restlessness driven by the tidal forces of her four moons. Even here, in this tectonic island of relative stability, there were occasional quakes. Despite the latest materials and techniques, their domes would be limited in size. Outpost domes, subjected to even more seismic activity, had to be even smaller.

It was simply beautiful, the capstone of his career.

Rajiv was Chief Construction Engineer for the surface settlement, christened Wu City in honor of Daniela Wu. She'd been the initial security chief for the colony, but she had not survived the kraken. He never met her. He arrived the year after she was lost.

He oversaw several teams planning concurrent projects. Every year, another colony ship brought another 1,000 new colonists, some of whom joined his growing army of construction teams. But he missed the initial planning. Working alone was challenging, but there was something wonderfully satisfying about it, about being *the* engineer designing a space elevator and its base station. This project was monumental, a linkage between a new surface settlement and its orbiting space port, a bridge bringing a new world into the ever-growing interstellar community of humanity.

The heart of Wu City, like any colonial surface settlement, was the base station. It was everything: the anchor of the space elevator, the tallest structure on the planet, the seat of the colonial government, the growing community's transportation hub, and the central support of its surrounding dome. All Wu City domes would match the base station dome's 2 km diameter, but none would be as tall.

Completing the base station was a turning point. It took nearly three years, but they no longer needed to use landing craft to ferry work crews from the orbiting platform every morning. Crews could sleep in the pressurized base station with weekly breaks to fly back to the orbiting platform to spend time with their families.

Completing the base station dome also provided living and working space for some 2,500 people. Besides temporary housing for construction crews and their families, the station supplied a diversifying economy of supporting services like stores, restaurants, and pubs. As the first residential dome was completed, residents moved in, opening the base station dome to public spaces, government offices, and surface facilities for their Deep Space Service Academy.

The skeleton of each dome was a set of graceful arches stretching from a central tower to stem walls supporting a skin of transparent panels. Each central tower housed the dome's transportation hub, connected via subterranean shuttles to the settlement's transportation hub in the base station of the central dome and with other residential domes. Agricultural and industrial domes were also connected with the central dome, as were the smaller domes supporting the landing fields used by the EAGLEs and Falcons for transportation across the planetary surface and used by landing craft for reaching the orbiting platform.

The central towers also housed stores, professional offices, and municipal services. The first (and thus far, only) residential dome enclosed an apartment building. The building, now a growing arc, expanded with every inbound colony ship and would, eventually, form a circle enclosing parks, athletic fields, and other recreational spaces. Agricultural domes were divided into slices, with farming residences surrounding their central tower.

Eden's challenges weren't confined to seismic restlessness. Eden's economic and scientific importance meant an accelerated growth rate. An unprecedented pace of inbound colony ships compounded by the typical high fecundity of human colonists brought Wu City's rapidly growing population to nearly 18,000. The first residential dome's planned capacity was 100,000. The city's current strategic plan reserved space for nine more such domes for the first million colonists. Long range planning for fifty million was, at least for now, presuming structural integrity breakthroughs, or additional cities.

For now, their most pressing need was agricultural space. After centuries of advancement, most of their crops and livestock were compact and high yield; but, as populations grew, space became available for crops and livestock still requiring large, open spaces. A number of agricultural domes were already in service, with an aggressive construction schedule for more. Fortunately, in addition to scientists, shopkeepers, farmers, and so forth, each vessel also brought more construction workers and engineers that allowed Rajiv to expand and accelerate the construction projects.

To the east, the Garcia Mountains dramatically framed the city in contrast with the broad, flat desert stretching endlessly towards the western horizon. To the north and south, a distant, raised berm built from material displaced by construction shielded the city from flash floods when rare clouds cleared the eastern mountains. To the west rose up the necessary but unaesthetic infrastructure: fusion energy plants, waste reclamation, storage silos interconnected by subterranean rail with the space elevator. Some silos held materials from extraction projects around the planet ready to be loaded into ascending gondolas; other silos held bulk construction material from elsewhere in the system brought down by descending gondolas to be loaded into their fabricators. Landing pads for landing craft and their growing fleet of EAGLEs and Falcons spread out across the western edge, large and small craft supporting their transportation needs beyond the bounds of Wu City.

*Beautiful.*

Rajiv sighed and returned his gaze to the horizon.

His day started normally, with a quick breakfast in his quarters. He sipped his first cup of coffee just as dawn broke. He paused to admire a beautiful sunrise before heading to the command center to review progress reports from the night shift teams. As he tapped his wrist computer to highlight those reports, the model shifted to the structures involved, projections appearing above them to provide extensive details.

He was still reviewing reports when his lead construction foreman, Nur Okeke, interrupted him to say there'd been an incident. Earlier that morning, one of the line supervisors had dispatched two workers to survey a rock formation that needed removal before building an agriculture dome, and they were overdue. Per standard operating procedure, when she couldn't reach them through their security drone, she requested a security team be dispatched to look for the missing workers.

The security team was new. They'd just arrived on the *Mother Lode*. They weren't field specialists; all their field specialists were committed to escorting various xenobiological and planetological expeditions across the planet. Settlement security personnel usually spent their time settling minor disputes between colonists and escorting people that overindulged back to their quarters. Occasionally, security went looking for overdue workers.

Nur wasn't particularly concerned. The situation wasn't common, but it wasn't unheard of. She presumed the security team would encounter a routine disciplinary problem.

What they found wasn't pretty.

It wasn't clear who, or what, attacked the workers. At least, it wasn't clear to the security team. They had little forensic experience and no wildlife experience. Before Eden, only Earth had wildlife, and precious little of it. For people in the colonies, the only animals they encountered were livestock, pets, vermin, and the denizens of zoos.

As surface construction expanded, especially to the east, wildlife encounters became more frequent. Eden's lifeforms had no reason to fear humans, and prospective predators weren't tempted by humans in environmental suits. The encounters had not, to date, been a cause for concern. Indeed, these encounters thrilled those lucky enough to have them, and the onlookers eagerly shared their attempts to capture images with xenobiologists who often graciously named new species after photo-happy discoverers.

Things gradually changed as expansion encroached the eastern mountains. Survey teams and work crews reported sightings of larger creatures. Debates began regarding whether they needed to assign secmeds to survey teams. Some expressed anxiety and a strong desire for protection. Others dismissed the notion as an overreaction and wholly unnecessary, almost resentfully, in fact, which Rajiv found odd the more he pondered it.

In any case, it was all academic until they trained more secmeds.

Until Nur told Rajiv what the security team reported was left of the workers. He briefly considered sending a medical team, then decided it wouldn't make a difference. Instead, he asked Nur to tell the security team to not disturb the scene and called Bhavia Harkins to join him in the Governor's main conference room. Bhavia, another recent arrival, had been Security Chief for the *Mother Lode* and was now Wu City's Security Chief. The security team dispatched by Nur worked for Bhavia.

Rajiv went to the main conference room. Glad to see it was unoccupied, he directed the display. "Connect me with Guido Hideko."

As he waited, Bhavia entered the room, and they exchanged greetings. Bhavia was new to the colony and Rajiv was still getting to know him. He found Bhavia somewhat brusque, polite and pleasant enough, projecting competence and confidence, but not particularly chatty. A few moments later, a projection of Guido Hideko appeared, seeming to stand beside the conference table. Given the rate at which the colony was growing, Guido was thrilled with Bhavia's arrival. Although all security matters fell under Guido's perview, Bhavia took over responsibility for security of the surface settlement, allowing Guido to focus on the orbiting platform and spaceport.

"Rajiv!" Guido said, "good to see you. Bhavia, I'd say good to see you, too, but I have a feeling that your presence means we have a problem."

Rajiv sighed, "Guido, I'm afraid I'm in need of your services." He relayed the situation as Guido listened intently.

Guido asked a few clarifying questions, then nodded and turned aside for a moment. They watched idly as he briefly consulted a display they could not see. He nodded again, turned back to them, and said, "my best security/

medic specialist is in the field with a xenobiology team not too far from you. They're tracking megafauna. I'll contact her and have her brought to you as soon as possible. Give me a moment…"

Guido's image dissolved as they waited.

"The security team is back," Bhavia interjected. "They left a patrol drone to monitor the site. They're here, now, waiting to meet with the secmed."

Rajiv nodded and thanked him.

After a few minutes, Guido reappeared. "Ronnie Verchesky and Deirdre Sun are hiking to an extraction point and a Falcon will bring them here."

Rajiv hesitated. "Why a Falcon? An EAGLE would support telepresence so I could bring them up to speed."

"I understand," Guido nodded, "but they're in a dense rainforest east of you. The Falcon will get them here before they could reach a clearing large enough for an EAGLE. Should be there within an hour."

It was Rajiv's turn to nod. "Understood and thank you. We'll be standing by."

# ■DAY 1: 13:44

## FERNANDO'S RESTAURANT AND BAR

"What am I doing wrong?"

Fernando vented to one of his regular customers, Pete something, a smallish guy and kind of average looking. Pleasant, though, and easy to talk to. Pete's blue coveralls bore an insignia indicating he had something to do with gondola operations at the base station.

"I mean, this location is perfect. PERFECT!"

He pointed at the base station. "There's the base station, right there. The transportation hub for the whole city is *right there*. You can't enter or leave this dome without walking by my place."

Indeed, now that the primary dome was fully converted to public spaces, there was an endless stream of people walking by as they arrived from or departed for their homes under the other domes. He could immediately tell which ones worked in colonial government by their coveralls. Others wore a broad range of styles. Recent immigrants tended to wear whatever was fashionable before they made their crossing to Eden. More established colonists updated their wardrobes to reflect what they saw on subspace entertainment.

Regardless of their attire, they were, indeed, walking by. Perhaps more to the point, they were not coming in.

"You got people here!" Pete's compliment fell flat.

"Not enough. Don't get me wrong; I really appreciate the folks that come in, especially regulars like you! But it's just not enough. I'm losing money. You open a place, you expect to lose money for a while, but you also expect to see improvement. It's not getting better, and there's a limit on how long I can keep my doors open without at least breaking even!"

Fernando sighed. He offered good food at reasonable prices. It was a nice place. Most of the bar and many of the tables had a nice view of the park across the way and the base station. Watching gondolas ascend and descend the stalk was compelling; as they continued to add cables to the stalk, there'd be more and more gondolas to watch. And at night, when the stalk lit up at dusk? It was a beautiful scene!

What was he doing wrong?

He wasn't new to the business. Fernando had worked at a very successful pub before making the crossing to Eden. But he always dreamed of having his own place! So he scrimped and saved to build a modest portfolio that would compound nicely while he made a crossing. When he had enough, he volunteered his name and his genome to PIP (the Panmictic Incentive Program) as part of the effort to keep the human gene pool churning, especially in the smaller, outer colonies. He'd never heard of Eden, of course, but when he was offered a chance to make the crossing, he jumped at it. It would be three years for him, but fifteen years for his portfolio!

Fernando arrived, found himself wealthy, and managed to secure this location, this *perfect* location, right in the primary dome, right by the base station! But, if he couldn't think of a way to get people to actually walk in, rather than walk by, his place, it wouldn't last very long. Fernando stared out the window, thinking about the pub where he'd learned the business.

"I need a draw!"

Pete raised a curious brow. "What do you mean?"

He paused for a moment, then leaned on the counter. "I learned this business at a place I used to work. Nice spot at an established colony. Owner was a friend of mine. Behind the bar, he had this big terrarium with a big lizard. A monitor lizard. Thing slept all day until feeding time. Then oh, man! He'd drop a few rats, different colored rats, in there, and this thing went absolutely nuts! Ran around the cage, grabbing the rats, shaking them, *hard*! Killed them, of course, then ate them. Folks at the bar would go nuts, too, betting on which rat would be next, how long they'd last. Buying drinks, of course, lots of drinks! And the lizard didn't mind at all!"

"How'd the rats feel?"

Fernando barked a short, hard laugh and shrugged. "Didn't know; didn't care. All I know is, people loved that lizard. They never talked about the restaurant by name; they called it 'the place with the lizard'. Maybe I need a lizard! But here? Where the hell am I going to get a big lizard?"

His customer smiled slyly, then leaned forward. "Maybe I got something better!"

TIDES OF EDEN

# ▪ DAY 1: 13:56
## SKY ISLAND

Ronnie stared at the passing terrain through the Falcon's transparent floor panels as they flew over the mountain range separating the coastal rainforest from the desert surrounding the settlement. The mountains were tall and lush with growth occasionally interrupted by sheer, red rock faces.

She usually found Falcons cramped, but with only two passengers, she took advantage of the opportunity to spread out. She'd even managed a power nap despite wearing her environmental suit. Deirdre, on the other hand, was unconsciously sprawled across the opposite bench. She'd fallen asleep as soon as the Falcon lifted off.

Ronnie envied her. She didn't mind, really. Spared her having to make small talk. Not that she didn't get along with Deirdre, but Deirdre tended to be chatty, and Ronnie tended to be quiet.

As they cleared the range, the relatively flat, brown desert stretched towards the horizon. Ronnie could see Wu City sprawling outward from the central dome and space elevator. She crouched and craned her neck as she always did when approaching the settlement, following the stalk upward through the transparent wall panels. It was a captivating sight, seemingly infinite, disappearing into an endless sky. She couldn't be sure, but Ronnie saw what might be a gondola ascending towards the heavens.

The growing city was still largely open space reserved for growth around the primary dome. The residential dome that would eventually be home to 100,000 residents was still only sparsely populated, but more would eventually need to be built.

Ronnie could see a number of new structures under construction. Some, presumably industrial, were deeper, suggesting plans for extensive subterranean layers. Others, Ronnie guessed, were agricultural. The Eden colony wouldn't need another residential dome for a while, but every year another inbound colony ship brought another 1,000 colonists, on top of their very healthy birth rate. They were always in need of more agricultural domes, especially given dome size limitations.

She'd recently enjoyed a documentary on the construction process. Every dome was lined with a thick layer that served as an impenetrable barrier between the dome's earthly microcosm and Eden's alien biodiversity. At the center of each dome was a tower that would house the dome's transportation hub and serve as the central support for the dome's ribs. One such rib was being built as she watched; swarms of suspensor drones hovered to position arch sections between a central tower and its dome stem wall.

Under optimal conditions, the potential size of a dome was determined by the tensile strength and weight of the supporting members that would serve as the dome skeleton and the precision with which they could be placed. The precision of the placement was, in turn, determined by the collective intelligence of the suspensor drone clouds. As they self-organized they coordinated between lifting the members and holding them in place between the central support tower and stem wall until the supports were firmly set.

She continued watching until she felt the Falcon slowing as the pilot shifted the orientation of the thrusters in preparation for landing. She smiled in appreciation as they descended; the pilot was executing a perfectly vertical descent to a spot directly in front of one of the central dome's airlocks rather than the nearby landing pad. She was impressed with his skill, and nerve.

A gentle nudge followed by a less gentle one stirred Deirdre. They stepped out of the Falcon and Ronnie waved to the pilot as he lifted off. They turned and walked to the airlock. On entry, Ronnie and Deirdre were subjected to decontamination, and their suits underwent pressure tests to ensure they had not been compromised. They exited the airlock and found an operations tech ready to assist them. Grateful to save time, they let him deal with refreshing their life support packs and putting their environmental suits in a locker.

Deirdre, standing in her undergarment with its various reclamation systems and environmental suit interfaces, checked her wrist computer before addressing Ronnie.

"If you don't mind, I'll let you deal with the briefing. I need to stop by my lab before we head out. Sound good?"

After a quick nod from Ronnie, Deirdre thanked the tech and made her way towards the door.

The tech looked appraisingly at Ronnie. He could see she was tall and strongly built. She was a typical outer colonist, the result of generation upon generation of genetic churning as her ancestors capitalized on migration opportunities between colonies. In her case, the tech marveled at her attractive combination of olive skin, close cropped blond hair, bright blue eyes, high cheekbones, flattened nose, and full lips.

She was briefly flustered by his lingering gaze, then returned his smile as he offered her a set of coveralls not unlike her usual daily attire. She stepped into the changing room and set the entry to opaque. She was pleasantly surprised to find the coveralls fit perfectly. Stepping out, Ronnie thanked the tech as he took her undergarments and promised it would be serviced and cleaned when she returned.

They chatted as he led her to a transport cart, agreeing to meet for a drink when she returned from her assignment. The tech flicked his wrist computer once to program the cart to take her to the space elevator base station, then again to send her navigation instructions to the construction command center on the seventy-fifth floor.

Ronnie, following guidance from her computer, made her way through corridors filled with colonists. Eventually, she found the conference room and met a wiry, energetic man in his mid-sixties. He was fair skinned, with short dark hair and close-cropped beard, wearing a coverall not unlike her own. He was younger than she'd expected. He turned from the window, looked at her, extended his hand and asked tentatively, "Ronnie Verchesky?"

She nodded, shaking his hand. "Rajiv Patterson?"

He nodded back, then asked, "how much do you know?"

She tilted her head slightly before responding. "Not much. I understand you've had a casualty involving a predator. I'm guessing you want to understand what happened and how to keep it from happening again."

He nodded again, then turned and pointed through the window towards the mountain range she'd just flown over. "We're in a broad, level plain separated from the eastern rainforest you were exploring this morning by that mountain range. It's massive; in fact, it's a sky island."

He turned from the window and waved his arm across the model on his conference table. "It's the best place to build the city; we're on the broadest, thickest tectonic plate along the equator. The placement of the space elevator base station was determined by the relative geologic stability of that tectonic plate. It *had* to be built right here. It's closer to the Garcia Mountains than I would have liked. Not that I'm worried about stability. Yes, these mountains were formed by the collision of two plates, but the planetologists tell me these two plates are now fused together and about as stable as anything gets on Eden. But the mountains constrain our potential growth to the east. They're surrounded by smaller formations, some of which we can remove to make room for more pressurized structures. They've been superficially surveyed with drones. But now that we're planning an agricultural dome over there, we need to better understand our options. We dispatched a survey team. They didn't come back, so my foreman sent a security team looking for them. They didn't find much, just enough to suggest we needed you."

Ronnie, staring out at the formation, zoned out during his long speech about the city's placement. But she snapped back when he finally addressed the concerning deaths. "Understood. As soon as we have a team assembled, I'll go review the scene." She paused, then asked, "I've spent a lot of time in the Garcias, but I've never heard them described as a 'sky island'. What's a 'sky island'?"

Rajiv smiled eagerly. He loved talking about his city and its surrounding environment. "An important concept you'll need to understand. A 'sky island' is a mountain range big enough to create its own climate distinct from surrounding ecosystems."

He raised his hands over the table, then brought them slowly together as the model shrank to include the surrounding area.

"We're on the equator. We have to be. We're tethered by the space elevator to the orbiting platform, which is in a geosynchronous orbit."

He paused for a moment, saw her nod, then continued.

"Clouds form here over the ocean and are then carried towards us by prevailing equatorial winds. The coastal area gets a lot of rain. But, as these clouds reach these mountains, they're trapped and wrung dry, subjecting the eastern face of the mountain range to even more rain than the coastal rainforest and creating our semi-arid desert. There are different kinds of deserts on Eden just as there were on Earth. They differ according to altitude, latitude, total rainfall, and rainfall patterns. Our desert is relatively wet overall, but we only get our rains seasonally. Eden's declination creates seasonal wind patterns, including the seasonal rains we get when the wind shifts and sneaks a few clouds around the mountains.

So, where does that leave us? We have this massive mountain range that creates its own climate. Earth had sky islands, too. For example, in North America, in the Sonoran Desert, there are mountain ranges like the Chiricahuas that catch clouds from summer monsoon rains, resulting in far more biodiversity and productivity than the surrounding deserts. Many species in those mountains were endemic to those mountains. Many years ago, before human encroachment, those mountains supported populations of large predators, including big cats like puma and jaguar, that would range into the surrounding deserts."

He turned to her and smiled. "I know all of this because the xenobiologists have been explaining it all to me. They tell me they're years away from any comprehensive understanding of the life forms in those mountains or this desert, but that we should expect, given the productivity and biodiversity of those mountains, to see life forms beyond what we might otherwise expect the desert to support. Particularly where water makes its way to the formations in the foothills of those mountains. Most of the rain falling on those mountains flows down through the basins and, eventually, through the coastal rainforest to the sea. But there are places where water finds its way to form relatively lush pockets in the smaller formations, either percolating through to emerge as springs, or flowing to cut passes."

Ronnie nodded along. "I think I understand. You think whatever attacked the survey team came from those mountains and probably returned to them. Possibly through one of these passes."

"Precisely. We've had a lot of wildlife sightings. We've seen nothing roaming the desert big enough to be a threat, but we have seen some larger creatures near those mountains, and, as we build, we're encroaching those mountains. So, did something come out of those mountains? Did it, or they, attack our survey team? How likely is it to happen again? How should we respond? Better security measures? Hunt them down and kill them? Or constrain our plans with respect to the mountains?"

"Can I review the recording from their patrol drone?"

He paused. "Well…you're welcome to review the recording, but it doesn't include the attack. The drone stopped working before that happened."

It was her turn to pause. "Really? How'd that happen?"

"I have no idea."

Ronnie looked at him for a moment, then sighed. "Well that complicates things a bit. In any case, I've been working with Guido to pull together a team. We need to move fast, so we'll keep it small. More secmeds, of course. Top notch trackers. I brought Deirdre Sun with me, but we'll need another xenobiologist that knows the mountains. I need an EAGLE outfitted as a mobile base camp. Provisions, life support pack recharging, and a full weapons locker."

"Of course. Guido's been communicating with me as well. Some of your people are already down here, and the rest of your team is flying down as we speak. Nikko's people are prepping an EAGLE the way you want it. You and your team will meet at the landing pad." Rajiv paused, then interjected, "it *is* getting late…"

Ronnie waved off his concern. "I know, but I want to get there as soon as we can. We'll scout the area, recover the bodies, then spend the night aboard the EAGLE to get an early start."

Rajiv started tapping at his wrist computer. "Then we'd better send a Falcon, too. It'll follow you to the site, then bring the bodies back to the lab."

She thanked him and started to turn, then stopped. "Do I understand correctly that the security team that found the bodies is here?"

He looked up from his computer. "Yes, they're waiting in one of the break rooms. You should have time to debrief them before heading to the pad."

# ■ DAY 1: 14:30
## DEBRIEFING

Bhavia stepped through the portal into the security team breakroom.

There'd never been any effort to designate any particular breakroom for any particular group of colonists, but over time (and as usually happened) people self-sorted. Otherwise identical breakrooms became the unofficial homes of the xenobiologists, planetologists, construction workers, engineers, pilots, and so forth. Most of the people in this room wore the red coveralls of his security team.

He scanned the room, looking for Harry and Bob. He nodded to those that met his gaze as they stood at serving stations or clustered around tables. They'd been part of his security team on the *Mother Lode* and were now part of his team here. Harry and Bob were not his best people. Good enough to be eligible to make the crossing to a new colony, a high bar indeed, but not his best people. If Bhavia had known the assignment would be anything but routine, he would have overridden the rotation to dispatch someone else.

Bhavia spotted the two chatting alone at a table with empty snack plates before them, glasses partially full and napkins crumpled on the plates amongst assorted crumbs. He walked over and took one of the two empty seats at their table, trying not to notice that many of the conversations in the room had slowed or ceased.

After exchanging greetings, Bob asked Bhavia whether he wanted anything. Bhavia shook his head, then observed, "your first outing was interesting!"

Harry smiled weakly. "I prefer boring."

Bob nodded, then added, "so, what happens now?"

Bhavia leaned back in his chair. "They're pulling together a team. It'll be led by one of their top secmeds. She was out babysitting an expedition. She's one of the original colonists and she's dealt with some of Eden's little monsters before. She's on her way here to talk with you two, then she'll take her team to the site."

Harry raised an eyebrow. "This 'secmed' thing's a little weird."

Bhavia briefly held out his hands as he responded. "Makes sense to me. Remember, they had a wildlife incident right after they got here. Lost 143 of the original 1,000 colonists. Left them particularly short of field medics and security people, so they trained a team to do both until the next colony ship arrived a year later. Worked out well for them, so they've stuck with it. You two ought to look into it. Pays better than straight security. And you get to go on expeditions, see the planet a little. They're still running the secmeds out of the orbiting platform, but will be moving them here as the settlement grows."

Bhavia frowned as he looked at his computer clock. "Where the hell is she? Ah; she's getting close…"

Bob leaned back. "I'm still not clear about this 'wildlife incident'. The reports say they weren't expecting anything. Why not?"

"I talked to one of the xenobiologists about it," Bhavia responded. "Aliens aren't supposed to be able to eat people any more than we can eat any of the alien plants or animals. That's why we're living under domes. Earth crops can't grow in Eden soil, Earth livestock can't eat Eden grass, etc. Anyway, they figured some weird alien beastie might be able to physically hurt somebody, but they shouldn't be able to eat anybody. So, they were careful on the planet but not as much on the orbiting platform. They had protocols in place to make sure nothing could escape, of course, but, hey, if anything did? Should starve in no time, right? But these kraken things start as some kind of spores, and somebody got infected with one, and that led to a kraken that could eat people. A *lot* of people. And that's why we wear environmental suits when we're out and about. The guy that explained it to me sent a link to a report about it. Gets technical, but worth reviewing, especially if you're thinking of applying for a secmed spot. I'll send the link to you both."

He looked up and saw a tall woman standing in the doorway and scanning the room. "That must be her!" Bhavia stood and raised his hand to get Ronnie's attention. Ronnie nodded and strode towards them.

"I'm Bhavia. Nice to meet you; I've heard good things." Bhavia tilted his head towards the serving stations as he spoke. " Need anything?"

Ronnie shook her head. "No, thank you. Nice to meet you as well."

Bhavia turned toward Harry and Bob. "These are the two we sent out to look for the survey team."

Ronnie nodded to them and settled into her seat as Bhavia returned to his. "Harry and Bob, right?"

Harry raised a finger and said, "I'm Harry. He's Bob."

She smiled cordially. "Nice to meet you. Tell me what you saw."

Harry shrugged. "Not much to tell, really. The foreman submitted a request for someone to look for her missing survey team. Kind of an unusual request, right? Usually, if you're overdue, they can just check your patrol drone, right? But their patrol drone wasn't answering, so we got the call to go check on them. Thought we'd find them either busy working or slacking off. Either way, we figured they just didn't realize their drone wasn't working."

Bob hummed along. "Hmm yeah, we had a rough idea where they were based on the last uplink from their drone; it wasn't too far from the rocks they were sent to survey. We took a Falcon, and the pilot set us down as close as he could. We deployed a drone to look for them and started hiking towards the rocks."

Bob paused, so Harry continued. "Right…we were hiking towards the rocks when the drone found them and relayed imagery. They were actually further into the rocks than they were supposed to be. We could see they were down. Not moving. Pretty clear they were dead."

Ronnie leaned forward. "Why? What made that so clear?"

Bob shuddered. Harry's eyes glazed over, clearly remembering a scene he was struggling to *not* remember. It was a look Ronnie had seen before, from kraken survivors. Finally Bob spoke up.

"Even from the drone's altitude, we could see that their faces were gone, and their guts were ripped out. I've never seen anything like that. Never."

"That's when I told them to come back," Bhavia interjected. "No point going any further and risk disturbing the site. Just leave the drone over the site and come back here."

Ronnie paused, then asked, "did you see any signs of how it happened?"

Bob leaned forward, almost anxious to address the very point Ronnie brought up. "No, we couldn't see *anything*. At least, not anything that meant… anything to us. We could see their equipment scattered all over the place. But no sign of any critters, if that's what you're asking."

Bob paused, and Harry did not add anything, still lost in his memory, so Bhavia spoke up. "That's it. We flew them back and notified Nur. She told Patterson. He called Hideko. And now you're here."

"Can you send me the link to your drone?"

Harry snapped out of it and nodded. He tapped at his wrist computer, then flicked it as he said, "there you go."

Ronnie stood abruptly. "Thank you."

Bhavia stood as well. "Do you need them to accompany you to the site?"

Ronnie thought for a moment, then shook her head slowly. "No…no, I don't think that'll be necessary. But I'd like them to be on hand if we have any questions."

"Of course." Bhavia paused, contemplating the appropriateness of his question. Ronnie gave a puzzled look at his awkward pause, so he asked, "were you here? For the kraken?"

Ronnie looked away, turned back, and met Bhavia's eyes. "Yes. Yes, I was here. I lost a lot of friends."

He held Ronnie's gaze, then held out his hand. As Ronnie took it, Bhavia said, "You go, go do your job. When you get back, I'd like to buy you a drink and hear about your friends."

# REAL CORN

"I'll bet five."

Katy grunted, threw her cards down in disgust, and started to stand.

Jenny laughed and looked at her. "Already?"

"I got nothing, and he's got jacks or better. I'm getting another drink. Don't worry; I'll be back!"

Jenny shook her head and muttered, "ye of little faith!" She paused, studying her hand. She put in five, then smirked. "I'm in."

Don pursed his lips, nodded, and put in five. Katy, watching, rapped the table with a knuckle, then turned towards the bar. She scanned the bottles on the counter until she saw what she wanted. Smiling, she poured herself a bourbon. Next to the bar, there were a few bowls of different kinds of chips, nuts, pretzels, and such. She walked over and paused, tilting her head side to side as she weighed her options.

The bowls were arranged around a strange thing in a pot. It was generally round, sorta stubby, and yellowish green. It looked like it had a thick rind, almost armored, with broad green leaves on short branches with a red blossom on the top.

It was kinda pretty, in a weird sort of way. Didn't seem real, somehow…

Katy shrugged, then used a pair of tongs to serve herself a bowl of chips to go with her bourbon. She popped one of the chips in her mouth before turning to return to the table. A broad smile spread across Katy's face as she crunched the chip and walked back to her seat, talking while chewing.

"Wow; have you tried these chips? They're amazing! Real corn! Or damned good synthetics, but I'm betting that it's real corn! Finally! Did you know you can't grow decent corn in orbit? One of the domes must have finally planted some real corn!"

Sandy ignored her and put in five as well, then turned to Alex. "Ok…cards?"

Alex discarded two cards and held up two fingers. She dealt him replacements, then continued around the table.

Katy crunched another chip, savoring as she chewed, and sighed. "Real corn! Damn. About time. You guys just don't appreciate the finer things!"

Don snorted. "Finer things? Chips? How about a decent porter or stout?"

Alex, deadpan, said, "five more."

Jenny responded, "call and raise." She turned to Don. "That's ten to you."

Katy leaned back, looked up at the ceiling, and meshed her fingers behind her head. "Does it ever strike you as ironic? I mean, we pilot EAGLEs and Falcons. None of us have ever actually *seen* an eagle or a falcon!"

Jenny glared at her. "Not this again! Please…"

Don pursed his lips, shuffled his cards, leaned back to look at them again, and grunted. "Hah." He put his cards down and took one of Katy's chips. "Hey, these *are* good!"

"I know! Right?" Katy leaned forward and put her palms on the table as she smiled broadly, her commentary gradually getting louder. "I'm telling you, when we started the crossing here, I had NO idea how much I was going to miss real corn! I know, I know, I go on too much about food, AND drink! But now that the agricultural domes are producing? Life's just getting better and BETTER!"

Sandy stared at Alex. She leaned in, pointed a finger at him, and declared, "you're bluffing, and it's gonna cost you!" She put in ten, then ten more.

Don tilted his head towards the break table. "You think the corn chips are good? I'm guessing we're gonna see some fresh pineapple on the menu soon!"

Katy turned to look at the thing by the chips. "Is that what that is? I've never seen a real one. Why's it with the chips?"

Don looked over at it and shrugged. "Dunno. The operations kid that set out the snacks put it there. Called it a pineapple. Said it eats bugs."

Alex smiled and put in his ten, as did Jenny. Alex laid out his cards to reveal a full house, aces over sevens. He leaned back and smiled.

Sandy swore and threw down her cards. She looked over at the pineapple and said, "yeah, they eat bugs. We keep ours near the air vent. Haven't seen a bug since."

Katy stared at it, then shrugged. "Never heard they ate bugs." She pondered a moment, then shrugged again. Anything that kept flies off the snacks was okay with her. She'd love to try fresh pineapple, though. She couldn't recall ever tasting anything but algal synthetics, and she was from a well-established colony! Katy looked at it again, frowning. She couldn't remember even seeing a picture of a real pineapple; usually, there's just a stylized image on the synthetic stuff. She shook it off and turned back. "Ok…another hand. Raise the stakes?"

Everyone muttered in agreement and looked at Jenny, who was due to deal. Jenny was staring at her wrist computer.

Don stared impatiently. "Well?"

"Oh! I'm sorry." She looked at Alex's cards and frowned. She dropped her cards and started collecting her things.

"Going somewhere?"

She shrugged nonchalantly. "I'm on call, or I'd have joined you for a drink. Well, they called. I'm to report to the landing pad. They're configuring my EAGLE as a base station for an expedition."

Don laughed. "Well, better you than…" He looked at his wrist computer. "Hey, I'm to report to the landing pad, too!"

Katy looked at Don quizzically. "Huh? I wonder if this has anything to do with that secmed you brought over the mountains this morning?"

Sandy cleared her throat dramatically, as she placed her cards on the table, one at a time. "Don't know; don't care. Know what I care about? I care about my four queens." She smiled and stretched forward to collect her winnings.

# ▪ DAY 1: 15:27
## THE CALYPSO

George cruised through pristine waters over a sandy expanse surrounded by rock formations encrusted with vibrantly colored life from every super-kingdom of Eden. Most were sculpted by evolutionary forces for efficient movement through the beautifully clear water, while others, prioritizing stealth or specializations, were shaped so bizarrely as to defy categorization without structural and genetic analyses.

He'd gradually descended to 22 m, then leveled off to cruise over the substrate. As he descended, his environmental suit added air volume to help him maintain neutral buoyancy and adjusted his breathing mix to manage his nitrogen exposure. Now, with fingers meshed and elbows out, George let his legs do the work, swimming slowly less than half a meter from the sea floor. He breathed gently, using his lung volume to fine tune his buoyancy, scanning the riot of life forms beneath him.

By contrast, his graduate student and dive buddy Bernard was working much harder. He struggled to keep up, struggled to maintain his depth, and occasionally flailed his arms to avoid damaging structures. George slowed, then moved a couple of meters upward. He turned to face his dive buddy.

"Relax, Bernard, relax! You're working too hard; you're going to use up all your breathing gas! Let your legs do the work. Keep your arms folded, like this. Long, slow breaths so you don't move up and down so much in the water column."

"Easy for you to say!"

Their secmed escort, Diego, laughed. He was swimming a couple of meters above them. He divided his time between monitoring their patrol drone and scanning the area with his own eyes.

George tutted at Diego's laughter to reassure Bernard. "Fair enough. I've been doing this a long time. But, Bernard, if you're serious about studying large predators, you're going to need to improve your dive skills. Let's do more buoyancy management practice later, closer to the surface. Meanwhile, don't swim so close to the bottom. You don't want to crash into anything! And keep your eyes open!"

Diego laughed again. "One of us has to!"

George laughed with him, gave Bernard a reassuring 'ok' sign, and turned to resume his transect.

George absolutely loved being underwater. He never had an opportunity to visit Earth, let alone scuba dive any of her few remaining reefs. Videos and immersive virtual realities, created centuries before to record biodiversity now lost forever, were no substitute for the real thing!

Eden was fascinating. Fascinating, and beautiful.

Here, he could be a true scientist! Here, he could make discoveries! Here, as an ecologist, he could strive to make sense of the interplay of new species and their environments!

George sighed; he didn't see his dive buddy. Must have fallen behind again. Not that he minded an excuse to pause and scan a nearby outcropping. He never got enough of the brilliant colors and fascinating shapes.

"What did you find now?"

George yelped slightly, as Bernard was actually hovering right over him. "Bernard, you nearly gave me a heart attack! I'm getting too old for surprises!" He immediately regretted his tone.

"Sorry, Bernard. That's on me. This is why I need a dive buddy. Even when I program my instrumentation to sound alarms, I get so focused I lose track of everything."

"No worries. Just curious what you're studying so intently."

George turned back to the rock outcropping and Bernard, thinking George had seen something specific of interest, realized he was about to get another lecture. But Bernard didn't mind. He knew what he signed up for when he became one of George's graduate students.

"Just look at this rock surface! It's a riot of colors and shapes. You have, I'm sure, seen images of the biodiversity of Earth's oceans. Even in the areas of greatest biodiversity, like the Indo-Pacific. Yet everything on Earth shares the same fundamental building blocks, all built on the magic of carbon. Carbon, whose covalent properties facilitate the formation of carbohydrates, lipids, amino acids, and nucleic acids. All life, everywhere, is built on such compounds, but every world has its own unique set of them."

Bernard waited patiently. He knew all of this, but he also knew George was simply laying a foundation for the points he wanted to make.

"Such compounds have proven to be common on worlds with liquid water. Not surprising; experimentation demonstrates that, under the right conditions, such carbon compounds form naturally. But only a few such worlds have such compounds organized into replicating forms roughly analogous to Earth's bacteria. Only Earth, and now Eden, have complex life."

He turned back to Bernard and hovered effortlessly in the water column, hands outstretched.

"Why, Bernard? Why has this only happened on Earth and here? What is different about Earth and Eden? What 'spark', what quality of these fundamental building blocks or environmental conditions resulted in the development of eukaryotic cells, colonies of cells, specialization of cells, organization into tissues and organs and creatures and ecosystems and a complete, rich, and oh! so beautiful biosphere?"

As he spoke, George rose slightly in the water column, orienting himself vertically and pointing an index finger towards Bernard.

"Bernard, I know you've been struggling to choose a dissertation topic. And, perhaps, there's something else that you'd rather work on. But I've been watching you, and I think this is a puzzle you can wrestle with!"

Bernard was taken aback. It hadn't occurred to him that George would have such faith in him. George turned, looking out across the sea floor. Mouths were everywhere. Sessile creatures reached out with finely bristled appendages to capture and consume minute life. Tiny creatures abruptly darted away or pulled back into their burrows, while others ignored them as they slowly swam by. Occasionally, something larger, something so precisely matching the substrate as to be invisible would suddenly jet away, making him wonder what other wonders he might have missed. Beautifully colored, free-swimming creatures sifted mouthfuls of sand for food, used long, specialized mouths or appendages to find morsels in nooks and crannies, or shot forward to snatch insufficiently wary prey.

"Why here? What do Earth and Eden have in common that's different from anywhere else we've explored? And, what's different about Eden? All life on Earth shares the same biochemistry, indicating one common ancestry. But Eden has five distinct biochemistries! Five different, distinct origins! Why?"

George continued looking outwards as Bernard pondered what he'd heard. Most of the creatures swimming through the area bore a superficial resemblance to earthly fish. Torpedo-shaped bodies and brilliant colors helped them identify prospective mates from their own species. Others more concerned with concealment bore neutral hues. Their flattened appendages were indistinguishable from fins to the casual observer.

As George looked about, he could see the signature structural aspects of Eden's super-kingdoms: bilateral versus trilateral body symmetry. Beaks and vertically oriented mouths, throat mills and fin configurations, eye-stalks and so, so much more. And still, as much as they'd learned, George fully appreciated how very little they really understood, how many life forms remained unknown, how limited their understanding was of life cycles and food chains and behaviors and physiology and…

"You know, Bernard, that I'm a man of faith. That's not a prerequisite to undertake such questions. But it does add something, at least for me. The exploration of an unspoiled creation, for me, is an opportunity to experience the mind of God."

After a moment of silence, George turned back and, sheepishly, added, "forgive an old man's preaching. As I said, faith, or the lack of faith, is not directly relevant to our work here. But I do hope that you can appreciate how my faith colors my passions with regard to not only the exploration but also the preservation of what we've found here."

George turned to resume his transect, adding, "and stop dawdling! You really need to learn to keep up without burning through all your breathing gas!"

George returned his attention to the task at hand. His heads-up display presented him a navigation line in addition to a wealth of data about his vitals, gas mix and levels, and remaining no-decompression time. He was following the line, a transect, letting his environmental suit's cameras record life forms as he passed over them. Sure, George could deploy drones to run these transects as they quantified the biodiversity and productivity of this environment; but, occasionally, he preferred to swim the transects himself. It gave him a feel for the environment, and, well, he absolutely loved diving and observing myriad life forms.

George sighed. He'd love it more with an experienced dive buddy! But every experienced diver was a newbie once, and Bernard was a promising student. George loved going into the field as much as he loved teaching. He loved sharing his passion for xenobiology with wave after wave of graduate students, instilling in each of them an appreciation, a reverence, a protective passion for Eden's biodiversity. And he had the positional authority to protect Eden from excessive development.

But some days, he had days like today. Opportunities to swim through Eden's oceans, conducting research and, slowly but surely, expand humanity's understanding of creation. He rolled, gently, to look towards the surface. The water was so gloriously clear! Even from this depth, he could see the hull of the *Calypso*.

George sighed, rolled again to face the bottom, and resumed his transect.

An alarm disturbed his revery. His first thought was the drone was warning of an approaching predator large enough to be a concern, but that wasn't it. He checked his displays. He was nearing his no-decompression limit, but he still had nine minutes at this depth. Plenty of breathing gas.

*What was it?*

Ah, a message! After opening it, he groaned. "Bernard, Diego, we need to ascend. I need to join a meeting. We'll let the drone complete the transect."

# ■ DAY 1: 16:00
## DEPLOYMENT

Governor Elke Lubandi ducked to enter her conference room. At 2.2 meters tall, she couldn't help it. Raised in a low-g environment, she exceeded Deep Space Service (DSS) standards for height. But her aptitude was off the charts, so she had been recruited and provided corrective therapies for gravity tolerance. And of course, she learned to duck. Like most of her direct staff, she divided her time between the surface settlement and the orbiting platform. Her quarters occupied the northeast corner of the building, with views of the Garcia Mountains to the east and the open desert stretching north beyond the residential dome. She loved that view, glancing towards the mountains as she took her seat at the head of the table.

Subdued greetings were exchanged as the others took their seats. Physically present were Chief Medical Officer John Schmitt, Chief Engineer Dieter Jian, Operations Chief Nikko Harris, Chief Construction Engineer Rajiv Patterson, and Security Chief Bhavia Harkins. Commander Guido Hideko was virtually present from his office aboard the orbiting platform.

Elke was happy to see Dieter already in his seat; he was often late. It mystified her that someone who lived a professional life committed to timeliness so often lost track of time. Elke didn't know why it didn't bother her; she usually found tardiness irritating. But he had an infectious, almost child-like enthusiasm for his work that, somehow, made his tardiness tolerable. And, truthfully, she knew what she was getting into when she and Moira selected Dieter to take Moira's place. He'd arrived a few years before, rising through the ranks of Moira's organization. When Moira decided it was time to return to space and signed on for an outbound vessel, he was the clear choice.

"How long before they reach the site?" Elke asked.

Guido checked his wrist computer. "Five, maybe ten minutes."

She nodded, then asked, "Where's George?"

Nikko answered. "He should be here any moment. They're at sea. He and his team were doing some field work near a reef structure, and they needed some time to surface and board."

Dieter brightened slightly. "How's the *Calypso* performing?"

Visibly relieved to have something pleasant to discuss, Nikko answered. "The science teams are thrilled with it, and we're collecting ideas for improvements as they live on it. Of course, implementing those improvements would involve returning to the shipyard, and I don't see them giving up their toy any time soon!"

The *Calypso* was the culmination of a massive engineering program. A long-range research vessel designed for teams of scientists, their equipment, and support staff, the *Calypso* was equipped with life support pack charging stations, a diving platform, a submarine, and landing pads for EAGLEs and landing craft. It was George that suggested naming her after the research vessel of explorer Jacques Cousteau, the inventor of the self-contained underwater breathing apparatus (SCUBA).

Building the *Calypso* required building a shipyard on the coast, and building a shipyard required building their first domed outpost to support it. It was the largest dome outside Wu City, albeit constrained by a less geologically stable location. It was a town in its own right, providing living space, working space, housing fabricators and raw materials, and a landing field. There were plans to eventually link the outpost with the settlement by rail, but the prospect of tunneling through the Garcia Mountains was daunting. In any case, construction of another research vessel was underway.

"Anything we should cover while we're waiting?" Elke asked. "Rajiv, did you get the alignment projections from David?

Rajiv looked up and said, "not yet. Not surprised; I'm really not expecting them until tomorrow."

"Why is that?"

Nikko raised a finger. "David and his team are revising their models with the latest round of sensor placements." He tilted his head towards Dieter. "Dieter's people finished the last of the new sensor probes yesterday and my team has been installing them as they've become available. The last of them were installed this morning. Hundreds of them in various locations around the planet."

Dieter nodded along, then added, "they're big devices, too, and they need to be precisely placed if they're going to work. They're really interesting! David got the designs from a research team on…"

He was interrupted as a projection of George appeared at the table.

Elke brightened; she was fond of their lead xenobiologist. "George! So good to see you. It's been a while!"

George smiled and gave a little wave as he looked about the room. "It *has* been a while! We've been busy! All sorts of things happening with the alignment building! New life forms are emerging that we haven't seen before, and a number of plant equivalents are producing what may be reproductive structures. We've been stumped trying to figure out how they reproduce, and it looks like we're about to find out!

We knew, when we arrived, that the four moons would impose complex tidal cycles. We know a number of Earth species synchronized aspects of their life cycles to Earth's tidal cycles, so it stood to reason we'd see something analogous, but richer, here."

Leaning forward, George continued. "So, a few years after arrival, when we had our first dual alignment, we weren't surprised to see it triggered the reproductive cycles of various organisms. We also weren't surprised to see previously unobserved species emerge. But what *did* surprise us, when we had our triple alignment, was that there were species that ignored the dual alignment but responded to the triple alignment!"

He leaned back and added, "my personal favorites are the squirts. Think of it, a diverse group of species, none of which we'd seen before. They're the only creatures we've seen from that super-kingdom big enough to see with the naked eye. Some were as big as a dog! And beautifully colored. They emerge from somewhere deep, millions of them, to spawn on beaches after alignments!"

Elke raised a hand as John opened his mouth to ask a question. Everyone was fascinated with Eden's life forms, but she needed to finish the conversation about the alignment projections. She turned back to Dieter and folded her hands. "You were saying?"

Dieter blushed briefly. They had gathered in response to the loss of the survey team, and it seemed disrespectful, somehow, to go on about mundane things. "I…uh…I was about to tell you much more than you'd ever want or need to know about these new sensors. The important thing is that they'll provide David and his team a broad range of new, precise sensory capabilities as they monitor the alignment."

Rajiv jumped in. "And that is why I'm happy to wait for the new projections. We're on a tight schedule, and I don't want to interrupt any construction projects until it's absolutely necessary. We're already seeing increased seismic activity. The last round of projections suggested we have at least another day before the alignment of the four moons exerts enough tidal forces to interrupt anything. If the next round of projections buys me a few more hours of productive work, I want them!"

Elke smiled again. "I gather our Chief Planetologist and his team are enjoying themselves?"

Nikko laughed. "I don't think they've left their lab in weeks. Remember how excited they got with the alignment of two moons a couple of years ago? Well, they tell me alignments of all four moons only happens every thirty to forty years, so they're…"

Guido raised his hand. "They're landing!"

■ ■ ■

Ronnie sat next to their pilot, Jenny, and stared at the outcropping as their landing pads touched the surface and gradually assumed the weight of the settling EAGLE.

"Jenny, thank you. We'll make our way to the site, then return with the bodies. We'll load them into the Falcon to send back to the settlement. We'll spend the night here, then set out in the morning. Questions?"

"Nope; I'll make myself comfortable. You take care out there, okay?"

Ronnie nodded, then stood and turned her attention to the team rising from their seats behind the cockpit.

EAGLEs supported the surface settlement and outposts in a number of standard configurations. This unit was configured as a mobile base. The upper level's back rows were removed to make room for sleeping pads and rest rooms. A lift provided access to a lower level divided by an airlock. On one side of the level was environmental suit maintenance, life pack recharge station, a kitchenette, a well-stocked weapons locker, and a limited emergency medical bay. The remainder of the lower level contained lab facilities and storage for suspensor pallets.

Ronnie nodded to herself, then spoke. "We're here. Let's get below and prep to examine the site. Sasha, please distribute handguns to everyone and rifles to you, me, Pablo, and Badru. Nijaz, we'll need a suspensor pallet for bringing back the bodies. Let's take two of the smaller ones; they'll be easier to maneuver through tight places. Pascal, I want five drones up and patrolling. We already have one hovering over the bodies, courtesy of the first security team. I also want one hovering directly above our team and three more circling at one, two, and three kilometers. Remember, people, this isn't an expedition. We're not talking about potential dangers; something out there killed two of our people, so stay alert!"

As she walked towards the lift, she shouted, "let's suit up!"

■ ■ ■

Elke tapped her wrist computer and a detailed projection of the site appeared on the conference room table.

The Garcia Mountains were among the tallest and broadest on the planet. The mountains and surrounding formations were folds formed millennia ago by the collision of two plates that fused together and now moved as one. The same folds thickened the plate, making it the best available place to build the surface settlement anchoring the space elevator, now that it straddled the equator. The tallest fold formed the spectacular ridge that scraped clouds from the sky to feed lush eastern growth and starve the western desert.

Lesser folds to the east formed a series of ridges and valleys. The valleys cached rainwater in lakes that eventually continued on through streams, then rivers, to the eastern sea. These folds were patiently, relentlessly attacked by the flowing water, wearing them down to form soils that nurtured growth to join the campaign against the rock. Only the tallest, most severe ridges remained unclothed, a harsh testament to the violence of the range's birth.

Comparable folds to the west remained starker. Some water percolated through the rocks to emerge as springs feeding pockets of relatively lush growth. Other water, following random inclinations amongst the folds, found its way west, whittling the rock to expand slopes into passes. These passes swelled during rainy seasons, allowing torrents to rush through the folds, swirling to carve clearings from the rock and channels between them. Life moved freely through the passes, roaming between different worlds. These passes created opportunities for specialists adapting to the resources, threats, and the competitive pressures of both worlds.

The projection, based on their most recent survey data, was depicted in monochrome because the imagery was stale. As each drone flew into position, its field of view displayed in full color. Objects appeared, changed, or disappeared, reflecting changes since the survey or even the last pass of each drone. As patrol drones began their circuits, they responded to movements by widening or narrowing their points of view, prioritizing scope or detail as needed. Nothing they detected raised any alarms.

One drone hovered above the two bodies discovered by the security team, the awful image appearing at the center of the table in full color. The bodies were in one of the irregular clearings, surrounded by weathered vertical walls.

As the projection coalesced, Rajiv frowned, then stood, looking at the clearing with the bodies.

Elke noticed his unease. "Rajiv, what is it?"

He shook his head, then pointed at the bodies. "Why are they so far into the formation? We're tentatively planning an agricultural dome that would impinge on the western edge of this formation. They were supposed to be surveying that area to assess how much of the formation we'd need to remove. They're quite a distance from where they were supposed to be working!"

He returned to his seat. "They shouldn't be that far into the formation. Let me check with Nur…"

Another drone hovered over the EAGLE and a much smaller Falcon settled beside it. The image of the EAGLE was near the edge of the table, surrounded by the reddish-brown desert soil and sparse, scrubby green growth. It cast a long shadow, reminding everyone that the day was nearing its end.

As its door lowered, eleven bright yellow environmental suits emerged, and their respective points of view added more detail to the projection. Each yellow suit was tagged with a name that was color coded by role. The first to emerge were the secmeds, Sasha and Pablo, walking cautiously down the ramp and assuming defensive positions on either side. Ronnie and Badru followed, leading the rest of the team out of the EAGLE. They walked in the general direction of the bodies as Sasha and Pablo brought up the rear and the EAGLE door lifted back into place.

Nikko stood and held his hands, palms together, over the team, then spread his hands, zooming in on the western foothills of the range. He pointed to a small clearing near the rock. "You can see, here, where a Falcon set down briefly to deploy the survey team. There's no mistaking the debris displaced by the thrusters. The security team's Falcon set down in the same place." He pointed again, this time by the EAGLE. "The EAGLE is bigger, so it needed more room and set down over here, as close as possible to where the Falcons set down." He pointed at the secmeds. "They're carrying Dieter's latest rifle design. Selective, supports semi-automatic, fully automatic, and a burst mode. Armor piercing rounds with an explosive charge. Everyone else is carrying our standard issue handguns. All ammunition is made from Eden materials that will, eventually, degrade."

Elke furrowed her brows and placed her fingers over her lips. Only John noticed she did so to hide her anxiety. She turned to Dieter. "Any progress on energy-based weapons?"

Dieter sighed. "No, not really. Energy storage is the challenge. Projectile weapons and ammunition are effective, portable, easy to fabricate. We haven't been able to come up with a comparable energy weapon."

Elke then turned to George. "I don't know these xenobiologists. Who are they?"

"Deirdre Sun is one of my doctoral students," George responded. "Absolutely brilliant and almost ready to defend her thesis regarding the biodiversity of that mountain range. Nobody knows those mountains, or its inhabitants, better than she does. Though I must remind you that there's still a lot we don't know. Marta Gertrud is another doctoral student. She's new, and she's been assisting Deirdre while coming up with her own thesis proposal."

Her next question was interrupted.

"Governor? Can you hear me?"

"Yes, Ronnie, we hear you loud and clear. In the room with me are John, Dieter, Nikko, Bhavia, and Rajiv. Virtually, we also have Guido and George."

"Very good. We're walking to the site." She pointed to their trackers, then said, "Finn, Edana, and Kalyan, we're near where the survey team was deployed. Should be over there. I need you to find where they entered the rocks. Badru and I will stay with you in the lead. Sasha and Pablo, please bring up the rear. Pascal and Nijaz, you have the drones and the suspensor pallet. Everyone, keep your eyes open."

Elke could see Guido nodding his approval.

They moved towards where the previous Falcon landed, adjusting their course slightly when Kalyan called out that he could see the disturbance from their thrusters. The trackers quickly found boot prints from the survey; the security teams followed them to a trail leading up and into the rock formation.

The trail was more challenging than the desert, the grade variable but generally increasing as they progressed. They knew roughly where they needed to go, based on the drone hovering over the bodies, but they wanted to retrace the steps of the survey team. They were making pretty good time but occasionally paused as the trackers conferred to interpret what they were seeing.

The trail broadened and narrowed, sometimes bounded by gentle inclines and sometimes caged in by sheer, vertical rock walls. A variety of green growths sprouted from the soils at their feet or from cracks in the rock, working with the elements to further break down the formation. Deirdre pointed out that periodic flash floods limited lower levels to small, fast-growing forms, while larger, more established plants could be found higher up, above the scouring water. Most of the team were more focused on the relative pliability of these growths. Some were abrasive, testing the tensile strength of their environmental suits.

"Ronnie? You need to see this."

The team stopped as Ronnie stepped forward to see what caught Finn's attention.

"Governor? Are you seeing this?"

Elke held her hands over Ronnie and spread them apart, enlarging the projection. On a rock, neatly folded, were two environmental suits and undergarments. She could hear Rajiv swear and John mutter under his breath.

"Kraken deniers."

Nikko began tapping at his wrist computer as he muttered, "should have guessed when we saw the bodies weren't in environmental suits."

Bhavia looked around, confused and disturbed by the resounding frustration. "What's going on?"

Without looking up, Nikko answered him. "Happens when we get new colonists. There are always a few that, despite all the briefings, just don't believe the kraken spores are real."

"Invariably," John added, "some idiot will take off their helmet, breathe Eden air, and, because they don't immediately suffer any consequences, think the whole thing's been exaggerated or it's some kind of hoax. And, of course, you don't get infected every time. And, even when you do get infected, you don't feel anything right away. This reinforces the idea that we're all just a bunch of overprotective nannies. But, given enough exposures, they will get infected. And once you're infected, you'll be dead in a matter of days without surgical intervention."

Nikko looked up from his computer. "There aren't any Eden proteins in the waste treatment for the surface settlement, which is not surprising. We'd have seen an alarm. But I checked anyway, and there's no sign anyone's been infected with kraken spores. Yet."

John leaned back, hands out, and said, "*yet*. That's the right word." He turned back to Bhavia and added, "actually, I think it's getting worse every year, as the population grows, because there are always holdouts that continue to believe it's a hoax. The problem is, the better we get at screening, the longer we go without losing anyone to kraken infection. We do the surgery with nanobots now. It's routine, but still hard on the body, especially as the infection advances. Which, of course, it does. *Rapidly*. But the better we get at screening, the earlier we're able to detect and respond, the less awful infection seems to be. It's been a few years now, since we've seen an advanced kraken infection, and even longer since anyone died from one. I swear, sometimes I think we should let one of the idiots succumb for the good of the rest."

Bhavia shrugged. "Help me out here. I've read what I can find, but I'm struggling with how the spores fit in."

Nikko sighed, but not out of exasperation. "When a kraken spore comes into contact with your skin, it infects you with parasitic worms. Or tries to, anyway. In theory, we are biochemically incompatible, so they shouldn't be able to infect us. But remember that Eden, unlike Earth, has five completely different organochemical suites just as alien from each other as any of them are from us. Kraken are highly adaptable, and their spores are designed to infect anything they land on."

He leaned back, running his left fingers through his hair while gesturing with his right. "So, when they *are* successful, the worms spread through your body, feeding on your tissues as they grow and reproduce. After a few days, they get big enough to emerge and metamorphose into kraken. They form a…cocoon, like a butterfly, but what comes out isn't pretty. At that point, the victim is so weakened they can't move, and the kraken eat them alive. It's a miserable death."

He grimaced. "Anyway, once you're infected, as they grow, they release waste products with Eden proteins. Your body passes those proteins with your urine and feces, so we monitor our waste treatment for those proteins. If we detect them, we know someone's infected, so we conduct screenings until we find them. We must find them fast, though. Infections progress rapidly; you can be dead in as little as five days."

He turned to Guido. "We'll need to reinforce environmental suit discipline for work crews, especially involving recent arrivals."

Guido, already tapping at his wrist computer, nodded.

"They went this way!" It was Edana's voice, one of the trackers, pointing to a partial human footprint.

Attention returned to the projection as the team made their way along a trail that wound through the rocks. Eventually, they came to an open area, then stopped.

"Oh, my…"

Ronnie and Badru stepped between the stunned trackers.

Ronnie's voice came through sternly. "Nobody touches anything until everything's been recorded. Governor, are you seeing this?"

Badru directed the trackers and the rest of the team to keep to the edges of the clearing as they entered the space. As they entered the space, their environmental suits uploaded their perspectives, adding awful detail to the projection of the grisly scene.

It was a broad, open area. The substrate was uneven, mostly rock, with some soil and some rock shards from the weathering of the walls surrounding the area. A few small green shapes struggled to maintain a foothold while others sprouted from cracks in the rocks above and around them. Strewn among the rocks and struggling greenery were bits and pieces of destroyed equipment and a slightly damaged but still functioning suspensor pallet. There were other gaps leading to other trails, and Badru, Sasha, and Pablo quietly moved to cover them.

In the middle lay two nude bodies. One, male, was on its left side. The face was crushed beyond recognition, compressed from the sides, the back of the head shredded. The right forearm was detached and lying behind the body. The chest and abdomen were torn open with viscera spilling onto blood-soaked rock and sand, moving randomly as small scavengers searched for anything they might recognize as edible. The other, female, was supine. Her face was similarly destroyed, the chest and belly similarly shredded, the limbs broken and torn.

Ronnie stepped forward and crouched to examine the body, then called to Deirdre. "What are these things moving in the gore?"

Deirdre crouched next to Ronnie, using a probe to sift through the gore. "I recognize many of these scavengers. They're common to the area. I'm seeing representatives from all the super-kingdoms. All invertebrates, roughly equivalent to Earth insects. Everything I'm seeing would have traveled here; I'm not seeing anything that hatched here. You know, like maggots, fly larva if this were Earth." She stood and looked around as she spoke. "I wouldn't be surprised to find such things in there, but they wouldn't be big enough to see, yet. And they might not grow at all." She looked down and pointed. "They don't seem to be consuming anything. They're attracted to the viscera, but they don't seem to be recognizing anything as edible."

Ronnie stood as well. "I admire your ability to be so…analytical." She paused, then, looking down, added, "but that's what you'd expect, right? They can't digest earthly tissues?"

Deirdre was still looking down at the body. "It's been an ongoing area of research since the kraken incident. You're right, though. All life on Earth descends from the same ancestry, so everything on Earth shares so much biochemistry that digestive processes don't need to break things down very far. We all use the same carbohydrates, lipids, and amino acids. We came here expecting all Eden life would share a common biochemistry, too."

She looked up before continuing. "What we didn't expect was to discover that, unlike Earth, Eden life descends from multiple, distinct origins. There are at least five distinct sets of organic chemicals on Eden. Most Eden life forms have digestive systems tailored to their own lineage, like us. They can't digest anything from the other Eden life lineages any more than we can. But a few, like the kraken, favor plasticity over efficiency. They break their food down completely, then rebuild organic chemicals from raw materials. It costs them dearly physiologically, but it allows them to feed on anything. Including, unfortunately, earthly life like us.

Anyway, some Eden scavengers, like the ones we're seeing here, specialize in specific life lineages. They tend to be the first to arrive and, if they can't feed on the carrion, they move on. If we were to leave these bodies here, though, the generalists would arrive. Once they did, they'd be able to feed."

Ronnie wrinkled her nose, watching the critters worm around in the two carcasses. "Okay…that's interesting…but right now? Right now, I want to know what did this to them. Ideas?"

Deirdre paused, then looked up and turned to face Ronnie. "Not yet."

Ronnie turned to the trackers and said, "Finn, Kalyan, Edana, what are you seeing?"

Finn, who'd been conferring with Edana as they crouched near one of the gaps, stood. "It looks like they came in from this direction. We're seeing prints from a number of individuals. Maybe a dozen, can't be sure. They're about the size of a really big dog, maybe 50 kilos. I'm thinking bilateral super-kingdom. Looks like four legged gaits, not six. Can't be completely sure, though; some of the trilateral critters only use four of their legs. Anyway, we don't recognize the prints; nothing we've seen before."

Kalyan examined some droppings by the gap. "I've got scat over here. Different size droppings, so I'm thinking they paused and voided their waste before attacking. Genetic analysis of the dung confirms the bilateral super-kingdom."

"We haven't seen much pack behavior from the vertebrates in the bilateral super-kingdom," Deirdre chimed in, clearly concerned. "Usually, it's the diploid phase of trilateral predators, like the diploid phase of the kraken. But there were pack hunting animals on Earth, so I don't see why we wouldn't expect some pack behaviors from the other super-kingdoms."

Deirdre paused, then continued. "Ronnie? There's no feasting. There's no missing tissue. I mean, I get that they might not have been able to digest anything they ate, but there's no sign that they even tried to feed on them. There's no missing tissue as far as I can tell, other than from their heads. We won't know for sure until we track them and find more droppings, but I don't think we'll find that they passed any undigested tissue from our...victims. They were attacked, clearly, torn apart, but not eaten, in the sense of feeding "

Marta looked at the suspensor pallet. "And look at how they destroyed the equipment. Why would predators destroy equipment?"

There was a long pause. They heard Elke clear her throat and ask, "so, what are we seeing? If not predation, then, what?"

"That's the question, isn't it?" Deirdre echoed. "If not hunting, then, what? Did they see the survey team as a threat? A territorial incursion? Did they come between a parent and its offspring?"

George weighed in. "We need to figure this out. When you consider our ancestors' experiences with predators, we've been pretty lucky with respect to wildlife incidents. Kraken aside, we haven't seen many attacks on humans by anything on Eden. Mostly, I think, because our environmental suits limit their sensory experience of us. But roaming packs that see humans as territorial incursions? If that's the case, we're going to have more incidents. And I don't think keeping their environmental suits on would have saved them."

# ▪DAY 1: 18:03
## SUNSET

Eden's sunsets never disappoint.

Don could not have asked for a better vantage point. He sat in the transparent bubble of the Falcon's cockpit atop the boxy craft, watching the sky erupt in outrage as the horizon nibbled at the sun. He'd never seen a sunset before reaching Eden, never even heard of them. Sunsets simply weren't a thing among the other colonies.

He'd arrived last year and moved to the surface settlement right away. That first evening, as the sun descended, the sky bloomed with color, and he was mesmerized. Now he had a number of favorite perches around Wu City from which to enjoy sunsets. Sometimes he watched alone, sometimes he gazed at the night sky with an attractive guest. But, tonight? Tonight would be a rare opportunity. Tonight, as the sky darkened, from here in the foothills of the eastern mountains, Wu City would be part of that horizon.

The sun continued its descent, setting the sky aflame as it gradually lost its battle with the glow of Wu City. The lights of the space elevator gleamed against the darkening sky, a jeweled chain erupting from the central dome leading up to infinity. Don craned his neck hoping to see the orbiting platform but was thwarted by the aggregate light of the aligning moons.

"Don? They're back!"

He turned to the east and saw the team making its way back to the EAGLE The secmeds, rifles ready, were at the corners, environmental suit headlamps illuminating the area around them.

Don sighed. He'd been looking forward to the night sky. It was completely different from his home world. An amateur astronomer, Don loved picking out new constellations and a few of his submissions were now officially recognized. He didn't get many opportunities to observe the night sky away from the settlement's lights, and he'd hoped he might see something new from this vantage point. But, as the team approached, Jenny activated the EAGLE's lights.

*Ah, well. The light from the moons would've been a problem, anyway. Another time.*

"Thanks, Jenny, I see them. I'll be ready."

He sighed again, took a final glance at the setting sun, then focused on his control panel. He isolated his cockpit from the cargo bay. Then, as the team approached, he lowered the door.

"Ronnie? You can just push the suspensor pallets up the ramp and then deactivate them. I'll take it from there."

"Thank you, Don."

As he watched, two environmental suit-clad figures, presumably Nijaz and Pascal, took turns guiding their burdens up the ramp and into the bay. When he could see them stepping back, he looked down through the observation panel at his feet to verify that the loaded pallets were resting on the floor.

"Anything else you need to load before I take off?"

"No, that's all, Don. Thank you."

He operated the controls to raise the cargo bay door, absentmindedly nodding as he began his preflight check. Satisfied that all was in order, he said, "I need you to step back a few meters so I can take off."

Most of the team was already heading towards the EAGLE. One figure, presumably Ronnie, stepped back and waved.

With that, he activated his thrusters, reached his cruising altitude, and turned towards the city.

■ ■ ■

Ronnie watched the Falcon take off, then turned towards the EAGLE.

It had been a quiet walk. Seeing the bodies was hard enough. Loading the bodies onto the suspensor pallets had not been a pleasant task and sifting through the site to pick up every potentially interesting artifact was tedious. It all took longer than she liked, but they needed to be thorough.

"Jenny? We're ready to board. Nijaz, I'd like the patrol drones to keep circling through the night. Same one, two, and three kilometer circuits. I'd like the drone over where we collected the bodies to hover there in case something comes back, and I'd like our drone stationed over the EAGLE."

"Will do."

The EAGLE door lowered. Ronnie and Badru led the way, Sasha and Pablo brought up the rear.

Once the door closed, Ronnie said, "Pablo, please collect weapons and restore them to the locker. Pascal and Nijaz, please work with Jenny to recharge our packs, then get everyone fed. I need to talk with the Governor."

■ ■ ■

Elke leaned forward. "Ronnie, anything we need to cover before you call it a night?"

"Thank you, no, Governor. It's been a long day, and we have an early start in the morning. We'll be heading out by 06:00."

Elke hummed in approval. She looked about the room, eyebrows raised, wordlessly asking whether anyone had anything else that needed to be addressed. In the absence of responses, she said, "Ronnie, thank you and thank your team. We'll reconvene at 06:00 to review autopsy results before you set out. Now, go get some sleep."

She broke the connection and the projection disappeared. She looked across the table at John.

"Your team will see to the autopsies?"

"Yes; the Falcon should be arriving shortly. I have a team waiting and we'll have a report in the morning."

"Very good." Elke stood up. "People, we'll reconvene at 06:00. Get some rest."

# ▪ DAY 2: 05:27
## THE LAB REPORT

Ronnie woke gradually to the gentle buzzing of her wrist computer. It took her a moment to remember where she was. Swinging her legs over the side of her bunk, she sat up and yawned. She could hear someone moving in the kitchenette on the lower level. She looked about the upper level, sorting through who was still asleep, stirring, or stretching, and realized it must be Pablo. She didn't know him well, but she'd heard he was an early riser. She stood and stretched, hoping he had the decency to make enough coffee to share. Ronnie glanced at Jenny's empty bunk and realized she, too, must be down below, fueling Ronnie's hope that she'd find coffee waiting when she made her way down.

Before heading to her bunk last night, Ronnie had asked Jenny to set the EAGLE's lights to gradually increase starting at 05:00 to help everyone wake up. She had no trouble navigating the sleeping area and making her way below.

Ronnie was pleased to smell a variety of breakfast options as well as coffee. She'd advised everyone to plan on a hearty breakfast. Once they donned their environmental suits, they'd be hiking for twelve hours and be limited to the nutritional supplements their life support packs would add to their reclaimed water.

Greetings were quietly exchanged as the team sat to eat. A few discussed the previous night's tremors. None were intense enough to disturb anyone's sleep, but Jenny informed them that, according to their instruments, seismic activity was continuing to intensify. There'd also been a large seismic event in the southern hemisphere, but not near any of their observation outposts or extraction projects.

As Ronnie took her seat, her wrist computer buzzed with an incoming message.

"Sorry to interrupt your breakfast, folks, but we need to join the governor's meeting. The autopsy results should be ready. I hope nobody's squeamish."

She took another bite, sipped her coffee, and tapped her wrist computer. "Good morning, Governor. We're finishing our breakfasts and we're on schedule."

"Very good. While you slept, the medical team examined the bodies you retrieved, and they're ready to deliver their report. Dr. Chen, the floor is yours."

A young man appeared over the table, his white lab coveralls contrasting with his dark skin. He appeared a bit disheveled, unsurprising given that he and his team had worked through the night.

"Thank you, Governor. I understand the team is preparing for their expedition and that the secmeds had an opportunity to thoroughly examine the bodies before retrieval. Therefore, I'll spare you the full clinical detail and confine myself to what I believe are the salient points. Please do not hesitate to ask questions."

He bent to tap his wrist computer, then disappeared as an image of the bodies appeared above the EAGLE's kitchenette table and, presumably, in front of the other attendees, wherever they might be.

"I apologize for the imagery; I know this is unpleasant.

We have two young adults, one male and one female, both deceased. Naked, as you can see, and her reproductive system contained his semen. Both were violently attacked, killed by the damage inflicted on their heads. You can see here that there are three deep, conical puncture wounds in roughly matching arcs on either side of the head, suggesting their heads were gripped with two appendages each bearing three clawed digits strong enough to puncture their skulls. As their skulls were gripped, their faces were removed by the lateral application of two sharp, curved blades. These blades cut into the sides of their heads in front of the ears and were then drawn forward, destroying their orbits, and removing their mandibles, or lower jaws, along with the eyes, skin, and much of the musculature of their faces. This tissue is missing from both bodies but not found in the surrounding area, suggesting it was consumed by whatever attacked them."

The images mercifully disappeared, but the voice continued.

"These were mortal wounds, but, unfortunately for them, they were not killed immediately. They were also both disemboweled and the male's forearm was forcibly detached pre-mortem, not severed, torn. The humerus is still in place, but muscles, tendons, and ligaments are stretched or irregularly severed. This would require considerable strength. The blood spatter from their wounds indicates that their hearts were still beating, and the imagery you captured suggested some thrashing, so, unfortunately, we estimate their time of death at some 5 minutes after the attacks began."

A heavy pause lingered.

"We were able to account for all the tissue except the missing faces, which, as I mentioned, we believe were consumed by whatever killed them. Given that no other tissue is missing, we don't believe the attack was predatory. I believe that your trackers, after examining the site, suggested the attacking creatures were approximately 50 kg. That's consistent with the size of the creature we believe inflicted these wounds. We were able to take tissue samples from the wounds and provided them to the xenobiology team."

A new image appeared as another voice was heard.

"Good morning. This is Hasani Owens. I'm a wildlife biologist. We analyzed the DNA sample provided by Dr. Chen. It is clearly from one of the endothermic, or warm blooded, classes of the vertebrate phylum of the bilaterally symmetric super-kingdom, but not a species we've seen before. The closest match we could find, and I caution you that it's not a close match, would be this creature."

A new image appeared as the voice continued.

"This is a bilaterally symmetric quadruped relatively common to the rainforest east of you. Note the vertically oriented mouth typical of the vertebrates of the bilaterally symmetric super-kingdom. This creature's mouth has a broad, vertical beak consistent with the wounds inflicted on the victims' faces but bear in mind this is an herbivore and weighs less than a kilo, about the size of a rat. It uses that beak to sever branches, which are then passed to this throat mill to be ground before progressing to its gut. Note that the hind limbs allow it to raise the forward part of the body to use the forelimbs to manipulate the branches upon which it feeds. Note also that the forelimbs have an elongated paw with five digits. The three middle digits are strong and the outer two are, to a limited degree, opposable, like our thumbs. It's an interesting arrangement that combines strength with delicate manipulation. We suspect that whatever killed the survey team had a similar arrangement given the skull punctures reported by Dr. Chen."

Dr. Chen's voice returned.

"Thank you, Hasani. We also consulted with our colleagues from the operations side to examine the other artifacts you collected. The environmental suits and undergarments were intact; their folding suggested they were voluntarily removed before the attack, presumably to facilitate their sexual behavior. Their drone was in perfect working order but manually deactivated, presumably to avoid recording their coupling. Their suspensor pallet was not significantly damaged, but their kits were torn open, and their surveying equipment was destroyed. Our operations colleagues were able to identify all of the artifacts as parts of the typical equipment complement carried by any of our survey teams with one notable exception."

Shards of clear material appeared over the table. They were curved with sharp, jagged edges.

"Nobody we consulted has any idea what these are. We found a number of similar pieces but not enough to reassemble into anything we recognize as part of a typical surveyor's kit. Assuming you collected everything at the site, and I'm sure that you did, we can only assume the other pieces were distributed beyond the site of the attack or carried away by the creatures. We did note that one of the shards bore a residue that our analyses revealed to be blood from something in the trilateral super-kingdom but not closely related to anything we've seen before."

The shard disappeared as well.

"Questions?"

After a few moments of silence, Elke cleared her throat.

"Apparently not. Thank you. Ronnie, everyone here will remain ready to reconvene immediately should the need arise. Until then, please keep us posted and we'll individually monitor your progress. Good hunting!"

# ▪DAY 2: 06:09
## TRACKING

The Garcia Mountains were engulfed in the glowing red and yellow of the sunrise behind them. The eastern slopes and the rainforest they nurtured hungrily drank the morning sunlight, keeping the western slopes and the desert they shielded in cool shadow for a few more hours. As the team emerged, their environmental suits kept them comfortably warm in the early morning chill.

They were traveling light. Everyone was fully armed, but they weren't bringing sample containers. Their mission was to find the pack that attacked the survey team. All other considerations were secondary. Ronnie, Badru, Sasha, and Pablo stood watch as Pascal and Nijaz dispatched additional drones. Ronnie looked towards the mountains, thinking about how, just yesterday, they were forced to rely on trackers given the density of the rainforest canopy. But here, in the open, drones should be able to manage much of the tracking.

As they walked towards the clearing where they'd retrieved the bodies, Nijaz reported, "the drones found two sets of tracks. They're following both sets to resolve which leads to, and which leads away from, the clearing. Shouldn't take too long…"

They reached the rocks, then the clearing. Ronnie glanced about, then said, "we'll take a short break as the drones resolve the tracks."

Finn laughed as he walked towards one of the gaps in the surrounding rocks. "You can wait. Bet I can figure out which set is the outbound set before the drones do!"

As everyone else relaxed, Deirdre crouched to watch a small creature plodding across an exposed stretch of rock.

"Something interesting?" Badru asked.

Deirdre laughed, stood, then raised her arms. "Everything is interesting!" She let her arms fall back to her sides. "I've spent most of the last three years exploring these mountains and, let me tell you, I still find new species every time I come out here. Especially here, on the western slopes. I've spent most of my time on the eastern slopes or in the rainforest beyond them. The biodiversity isn't as rich on this side, but that doesn't mean there aren't thousands of as yet undescribed life forms. I'm expecting to find new things all day." She pointed at the small creature. "That's a completely new species, one of the insect-like forms from the bilateral super-kingdom. I took some images, but I wish I could take a sample. I understand why we're traveling light, but I still wish I could pop that little guy into a sample container!"

Sasha laughed. "I'm pretty sure that little guy is thankful you don't have a sample container." She paused, then asked, almost sheepishly, "what do you mean by 'insect-like'?"

"Everything on Eden is completely alien to us, right? Down to the biochemistry. Sure, all life involves sugars and fats and proteins, but they're completely different from any of their earthly equivalents. But there's no escaping physics or evolutionary pressures. That's why there's so much green around us, right? Once biology came up with green, green won the evolutionary competition and now, it's everywhere on the planet. On Earth, the most successful body design is an exoskeleton with jointed legs. Crabs, spiders, insects. Most especially insects. There are more kinds of insects than anything else. In fact, there are more kinds of beetles than anything else! The great taxonomist, Haldane, was once asked what his study of God's creation taught him about God, and he answered that God had an inordinate fondness for beetles!"

She chuckled, then felt awkward when she realized the others hadn't joined her. She hesitated, then continued. "Ah so, anyway, it's not surprising that, as life evolved on Eden, as evolution experimented, once that body design happened, it just exploded. And, not just once! Remember, there are five super-kingdoms on Eden. On Earth, everything's related. Everything shares biochemistry because life originated there only once. Here, life originated five separate times and we have five distinct lineages with five distinct biochemistries, but this kind of body design evolved and proliferated in each of those five lineages! Someday, when we find another planet with complex life, I'm telling you, the one thing we can count on finding there will be something resembling insects!"

"So, you're essentially saying there are roaches everywhere?"

Deirdre laughed. "No, no, not at all. That little guy…" she looked around, then, "…wherever he's gotten to, well, I can tell at a glance he's alien. Definitely not a real insect. The body's completely different, too many legs, too many eyes. Nothing remotely like him on Earth. But I know a bit more about insects than your average colonist, so I can tell the difference."

She paused, embarrassed, and said, "sorry, I find this all fascinating."

Sasha laughed. "It shows. I appreciate the enthusiasm, and, until the trackers find something, we don't have much else to talk about anyway."

Pablo snorted. "Just keep your eyes open!"

Sasha nodded. "Absolutely." After a moment, she asked, "what about bigger animals? Why haven't we seen any giant bugs?"

Marta jumped in. "There's a size limit for this body design. Here or on Earth, in water environments, you can get big creatures. Eden's answers to Earth's lobsters and crabs and such. But, on land? Without water to help carry their weight? At some point, the muscle mass required to lift the body just won't fit inside the shells. The bigger they get, the slower they get. There are very few forms as big as your hand. Bigger creatures have internal skeletons, just like on Earth. The skeletons are completely different, right down to different bone tissue, but they're recognizable as internal skeletons."

After a pause, Sasha said, "interesting."

"I prefer the little stuff anyway." Marta thought out loud. "The little animals, the little plants. The tiny things everybody else walks right by without a thought."

Pablo laughed. "There's no shortage of them! This place is crawling with your fancy bugs."

"Truth! The pack we're tracking aside, the life forms in these rocks tend to be small. Plentiful, but small. If you pay attention, you'll see a splendid quantity and diversity of life in the area. It's interesting, really; we need to learn how this ecosystem works. What are all these creatures feeding on, and what's preying on them?"

She looked up at the glow of the sun rising behind the Garcia Mountains. "Did you know the guy they named these mountains after?"

Pablo said, "no, before my time. I think Ronnie might've known him."

"Yes, I knew him." Ronnie responded to the comment made about her, slightly annoyed to be spoken of but not spoken to. "Not well, but I knew him. Sam Garcia, one of the original xenobiologists. Nice guy. The first casualty on

Eden. They were on a deep dive, an ocean dive, and something came up from the deep and grabbed him. Never found him."

There was an awkward silence. Badru, sensing the unresolved tension, weighed in. "We should have pressed on last night. Trail's cold now. Bad enough they had, what, ten maybe twelve hours head start? Now it's more like twenty hours. I'll be surprised if we can catch up with them before our life support packs run out."

"You may be right," Ronnie responded, "but I didn't like the idea of catching up with them in the dark. Let's see how fresh the trail looks this afternoon. Remember, we can reposition the EAGLE when our packs are running low and have a Falcon ferry us to our EAGLE. Fair?"

"Fair enough."

Finn called out. "Here! This is the outbound track! They spent some time here, maybe exploring the area a bit. There's a lot of signs to sort through, but this is clearly the outbound track."

Ronnie turned and spotted him standing to the east, arm raised, looking down. Edana crouched, using a probe to examine something. Kalyan was a few steps further along the trail.

"Great. Pablo, you're with me. We'll keep up with them. Sasha and Badru, please bring up the rear. Let's go!"

Nijaz chimed in. "I'll redirect the rest of our drones to join the one following what you say is the outbound trail."

# ■ DAY 2: 06:42
## ELKE'S DILEMMA

John stepped into the café nearest the governor's conference room. As he expected, he found Elke sitting alone at a table near one of the windows, staring at the mountains.

She'd just received word that the *Lucky Strike* reached Alexandria.

Eden's initial colonists arrived aboard the *Lucky Strike*, with Elke as their captain. After a couple of weeks, with her Executive Officer Sridharan Rizzo promoted to Captain and a crew of twenty-five, the *Lucky Strike* was refit to carry cargo and departed to return to Alexandria.

Then they faced the kraken.

Elke and her crew hadn't known, when the *Lucky Strike* departed, that young kraken were already prowling the orbiting platform. By the time they began to understand the threat, the *Lucky Strike* had already accelerated beyond the ability to exchange messages. As Elke and her staff's understanding grew, as they began to realize that a member of the *Lucky Strike* crew might be infected, there was simply no way to warn the ship.

A few days ago, after a fifteen-year crossing, the *Lucky Strike*, on autopilot, reached Alexandria. Elke's worst fears were realized. There were no survivors.

She took it hard, of course. In typical Elke fashion, she assumed responsibility for the loss. She had not shared their former shipmates' fate with anyone but him, yet. She asked that the news be withheld for a few days so she could inform the rest of the *Lucky Strike* alumni privately before they heard it through the media. But she was running out of time.

She'd been aboard the orbiting platform at the time. John strongly encouraged her to rearrange her schedule and join him on the surface. He knew Elke vastly preferred being on the surface and loved the views from their quarters. He told her to think of it as a "prescription."

Here, alone in the café, John assumed she was sorting through how to break the news.

He hesitated, collecting his thoughts. He paused to look at her, her cropped blond hair, bright green eyes, and soft ebony skin. He caught himself smiling. Finding the right balance between respecting her privacy and being a supportive partner was complicated enough. The fact that she was technically his boss didn't make it any easier.

At least they were alone. *For the moment, anyway.*

He sighed, then walked to the counter. He picked up a tray and briefly studied the options displayed around a weird potted plant, absentmindedly humming as made his selections. He poured a cup of coffee and walked towards her table.

"Pardon me, Governor, is this seat taken?"

It took her a moment to look up, but, when she did, she gave him one of those wry, little smiles that made his heart skip a beat.

"No, love; that seat's not taken. Please join me."

He placed his tray on the table. He bowed extravagantly, then swept a hand over the table. "Can I get you anything? Coffee?"

She looked down at her still steaming coffee, smiled again, and looked up to meet his eyes. She shook her head. "No, love; I'm fine."

"Well, for the record, I offered!" John sat, then sipped his coffee. "As always, I strive for the appearance of gallantry without all the fuss and bother required of being *actually* gallant!"

He looked out the window and sighed, then turned back. "Beautiful. The view, too!"

She smiled again. "Flattery will get you everywhere…"

He nodded, then sipped his coffee again. He folded his hands on the table and leaned forward. "Alright, love. Let's talk about what you're feeling. Thinking about the *Lucky Strike*?"

She wrapped her hands around her mug and tilted her head slightly as she looked at her coffee. "My mother's hands."

He paused. "Excuse me?"

She glanced back at her mug and her hands, then looked towards the window and, catching her faint reflection there, smiled awkwardly. "Every so often, I catch a glimpse of my hands, and I ask myself how it could be that my mother is holding my mug? Or, these days, my grandmother?"

John nodded, understanding her meaning. "Sometimes I see my hands, or I look in the mirror, and I expect to see what I saw when I was a kid. What the hell happened?"

Elke turned towards him and huffed. "Beats the alternative! Seriously, we're not getting any younger. We're living longer, a *lot* longer, and we're staying active and healthy a lot longer, but, at some point, however long you live, you still, eventually, get old." She turned to look through the window again. "I should be thinking about retirement."

He leaned forward, taking her hands. Her eyes came slowly up to meet his, and he spoke softly yet earnestly. "Elke, love, you're only 122."

She held his gaze, then smiled and laughed. "Biologically. Chronologically, I'm 392." She shook her head. "John, you're eight years older than me biologically, but you haven't made as many crossings. You haven't spent as many years at relativistic speeds. I was born, what…" She shook her head, trying to remember dates and do the arithmetic in her head. "…200 years before you were? Already in my sixties biologically when you were born?"

He leaned back, cocked his head, and smirked. "I have always been attracted to older women!"

She laughed again. He loved that laugh.

He leaned forward again. "Elke, my love, I understand what you're saying. I have moments like that, too. And I really don't think this is what's been weighing on you."

She cast her eyes downward; her brow furrowed from stress. "I'm losing an important argument."

John was confused. "Losing what argument?"

She glanced around the café. They were still alone, but she leaned forward and lowered her voice. "I'm not supposed to discuss this with anyone, not even senior staff."

He held up crossed fingers and whispered dramatically. "I won't tell a soul."

Elke's eyes became sullen and the lines on her forehead increased. "Thank you; I appreciate that." John dropped his overly cheerful act; he could tell by the look in her eye, she was serious and stressed.

She leaned back. "A big debate is raging at the senior levels of the Deep Space Service."

He waited, then prodded. "Yes? And?"

Elke propped her elbow up on the table and nestled her chin into her hand to gaze out the window.

"When we first arrived, the plan was to be yet another outer colony. The only colony on a world with a complex ecology, yes, but, otherwise, just another colony. Faster than usual growth, topping out, someday, at some fifty million people. Wu City, the orbiting platform, and some outposts elsewhere on the planet and among the other bodies in the system."

He nodded encouragingly. "Go on."

"We've had tensions, as you know, balancing development and conservation. The planet's even richer with mineral deposits than we expected. David's discovered superheavy elements, and thinks that, if they're extractable anywhere, it'll be on Eden given the tectonic activity. Then there's the biochemical potential. So many complex organic chemicals for plastics and pharmaceuticals."

John nodded along. He knew all this.

"The latest discoveries are hydrocarbon deposits. Having a complex ecology means the planet's supported a lot of biomass over the millennia, and David's team was sure that some of that biomass would have become petroleum. They've now confirmed massive reserves. Cecilia's modeling extraction options. Preliminary numbers suggest that, even with interstellar transport costs, some of the potential refinement products would be cheaper than locally sourced algal synthetics. And some of the hydrocarbons they're finding are new and can't be synthesized yet at any cost. They're already excited about some of the new plastics they'll be able to make."

He laughed and held out his hands. "So, we're all rich beyond our wildest dreams!"

She smiled wryly and nodded. "Well, yes, there's that. But remember, we consumed all of Earth's petroleum reserves years ago. Centuries ago. We've found lots of hydrocarbons across known space, but not like this. Not petroleum. Cecilia's doing her best to come up with minimal impact extraction methods, but we have a long way to go and a great deal of demand."

"Hard to believe we ever burned the stuff."

Elke shrugged. "Once upon a time, it was cheap. A seemingly endless supply. And a gallon of fuel refined from petroleum was a very convenient way to carry an awful lot of energy compared to anything else available at the time."

"I know, but the damage…"

"I know. Humans have an amazing capacity for denial. To our detriment! Here, at least, nobody's going to burn it. Too valuable to burn. But it's still messy, and awfully risky to extract, store, and transport."

John pursed his lips in thought. "Ok, so, that's what's been stressing you? They're ratcheting up the pressure to develop Eden's resources?"

She snorted. "I wish. No, I mean, that's an ongoing struggle, sure. But, no, this is bigger." Elke leaned in. "They're talking about making Eden a second hub."

He stared at her. "What do you mean?"

"Okay…given life spans and interstellar distances, we're not starting any colonies more than thirty light years from Earth, right? Without faster than light travel, it takes us years to make a crossing. Sure, we're improving our drive systems, getting closer to the speed of light. That shaves off a little of the actual crossing time. But, at best, if you're almost at the speed of light, it still takes a bit more than a year to travel a light-year, and stars are light-years apart. Relativistic time dilation makes a ten year crossing feel like a couple of years for those aboard, but it's still a ten year crossing."

John nodded. He understood all this. Not the intricacies of relativity, but the practical implications of time dilation. He also understood the context. Every child's education covered the ecological devastation of the 21st century. Climate change, famine, drought, and pandemics were only followed by horrific wars as humanity spread through the solar system, re-inventing tribalism as the Moon, Mars, and Belt colonies fought for their independence.

The nations forming the DSS learned from this, and realized how much worse if could be given interstellar differences. They responded with PIP, monitoring colonial gene pools and encouraging migration between planets. Pippers, usually young adults, but really anyone wanting a fresh start, was offered a free education at another colony. They'd earn degrees, pair off with other migrants, and start families, thereby churning the interstellar gene pool.

But PIP modelers recognized that even the greatest incentives wouldn't motivate people to make crossings that meant losing all track of anyone they'd ever known, resulting in the current practical limitation of colonies within thirty light years of Earth.

"Right…" John waved his hand casually. "But we still have a lot of colonies. That's a lot of room for growth."

"Between PIP migrations and local birth rates, it takes us about 200 years to get a seed colony of about a million people. Do you realize that some of the earliest interstellar colonies have over ten million people now? Assuming we don't develop faster than light travel or find a way to make us live a lot longer, even the outermost colonies will be getting crowded in a couple of centuries. Remember, we're talking about an organization that has to incorporate ten to fifteen year interstellar flights into their strategic planning. They take a long view!"

"Okay, so what are you so concerned about?" "

Elke continued to gaze out the window "There's a faction that thinks Eden could be a second hub. They've modeled an interstellar population with Eden becoming a peer of Earth's, with a billion or more people, and PIP migrations churning the gene pools of Earth, Eden, and colonies within thirty light years of either system. It would be a huge expansion and buy us a lot more time."

"Huh. I can see that. I don't like it. But I can see it."

She leaned back and folded her arms. "Let's think about what that would mean. We planned to constrain Eden's colonial population to protect her ecosystems. We're designing Wu City to support a million people or so. Now picture a thousand such settlements around the planet, some of them tethered with space elevators to orbiting platforms to expand space port capacity."

She leaned in again. "We can work to reduce our ecological footprint. Surviving the 21$^{st}$ century required reducing our per capita ecological footprint. But there were just too many of us! We cannot limit the ecological impact of our biomass. Every kilogram of human biomass is one less kilogram of Eden biomass. And they're not talking about domed cities. The more extreme voices are talking about doing whatever it takes to allow us to roam the surface without environmental suits."

"So, what, exterminating kraken so there's no spores?"

"More than that." Elke spoke in a harsh whisper. "No domes. Treating Eden soil to grow Earth crops in the open. Terraforming, essentially. Converting Eden to another Earth."

John stared at her a moment.

"Wow! That would be…catastrophic!"

Elke tapped the table a few times anxiously. She pushed her coffee away in frustration and folded her hands.

"Makes me wonder about the next 'Eden'. It's out there, you know? Has to be. We have two planets with complex ecologies now, which gives us at least some basis from which to extrapolate how common such worlds are.

Or how rare. If we make Eden a second hub, extending 'known space', then I figure we're likely, eventually, to find another Eden. Will we make that a third hub? Will we terraform every alien ecology we find? Will that be humanity's legacy? What if the next one has intelligent life?"

She looked at John in exasperation. " As Europeans spread across the globe, what did they do? They brought their familiars. Crops and weeds, livestock and vermin, contaminating every earthly ecology with alien invaders. Hell, we've brought them all here! Despite centuries of interstellar colonization, we still have to put out vermin traps to keep the roaches and rats under control!"

Elke's back stiffened with frustration, her eyes glazed over, fingers tapping nervously on the table again. Finally, John saw her relax, her shoulders stooping with an invisible weight.

"I know." Elke addressed John unprompted. "I'm worrying about things that are a long way out. But that's part of my job, right? So, I've been arguing the importance of preserving Eden. I'm thinking, even if we decide to embrace this dual hub model, can't we still preserve Eden? Do we really want to bequeath to our children a reality in which we've only found two worlds with complex ecologies, and we've destroyed them both?"

John nodded with serious concern. "Have you talked with George about this?"

She tilted her head side to side, clearly uncomfortable. "No, not yet. I mean, I'm not supposed to talk to anyone about this, not even you! But, yes, George would be a passionate voice in the discussion. I'm thinking about how to bring him into the debate."

After a moment, she sighed heavily. "John, I can't even think about retirement. Not now, not with this at stake." She leaned forward, took his hands, and looked deeply into his eyes.

"This is extremely confidential. Don't discuss it with anyone else, ok?"

# DAY 2: 09:16
## PUZZLE PIECES

Bhavia looked towards the mountains. It was midmorning, and the sun was clearing the peaks.

He left the conference room after the autopsy report. He knew he needed to stay nearby, which blew up his plans for the day. He'd planned to personally inspect the security infrastructure in one of the new domes. Bhavia preferred to see things for himself, get a feeling for how the final schematics deviated from engineering plans. Since he'd arrived and taken charge, he'd found enough problems with new construction to inspire retroactive inspections of completed projects, as his schedule permitted. He'd found a few issues which required a bit of finesse to address without embarrassing anyone.

But Bhavia didn't want to impact construction schedules, so he sent someone from his team and promised himself he'd make the time to visit the site later in the week.

He tried waiting in a breakroom, but that was awkward. People wanted to ask about the situation, and he didn't have much to offer. That left him with going back to his quarters. Nur should be at work, so he could have their quarters to himself, but he really wanted to focus. Bhavia smiled. Nur could be…distracting.

He sighed. Nur could be distracting for less pleasant reasons, too. Things were progressing awfully fast. Bhavia hadn't arrived that long ago, after all, and here they were, living together already. Recently, they'd started talking about starting a family someday, and Nur suddenly informed him that "someday" wasn't as far away as Bhavia seemed to be thinking. As much as he loved Nur, Bhavia was still sorting through his feelings about starting a family.

This wasn't always conducive to focusing on work. He made a cup of coffee and a quick breakfast. A bit of small talk about their respective plans for the day was followed by a quick embrace.

Bhavia stopped for a quick coffee refill at one of the breakrooms, then headed to a picnic table with a nice view of the mountains at the park near the base station. People moved randomly around the park: individuals, couples, clusters of adolescents, families with children. He sighed again, trying to put aside thoughts about children.

*I really should not be dwelling on this so much…*

It was quite pleasant there. The park had a broad, green lawn with a number of young trees, seeds brought from another colony and planted a few years ago. They didn't offer much shade yet, which wasn't a problem under the climate-controlled dome. Still, Bhavia knew, from the last colony he called home, even when the temperatures are artificially maintained at a comfortable level, there was something pleasant about sitting in the shade of a tree on a sunny morning. And, here on Eden, "sunny" was very real.

Beyond the trees, Bhavia could see where the dome met the stem wall. Beyond that, the mountains loomed in the distance. He took any excuse to get outside and look at them.

Unlike Nur, Bhavia's role did not take him outside the settlement's domes. His entire life, he'd lived under domes. Nur's construction work sometimes took her to the outskirts of the settlement, where she could see the desert and the mountains. There she could see, in the distance, unobstructed by a dome's frame and stem wall, a horizon. Bhavia envied her for this, and frequently asked her to describe it over dinner.

He leaned forward, rested his left arm on the table, and brought up a projection of a death scene shard floating above his wrist computer. The forensic team let him examine the shard after he'd left the breakroom. He was, after all, the head of security for the surface settlement. But they wouldn't let him take it. Instead, they provided Bhavia with digital representations of each shard, and he had spent the last hour or so reviewing them as he sat and pondered.

Nobody else seemed particularly interested in them. They were much more interested in finding the pack that killed the survey team. Which was understandable, of course. Elke and the senior staff needed to know what they were dealing with and whether to worry about more attacks.

But there was something about these shards that bugged him. An intense fixation tickled his brain.

*Why the hell did they turn off their patrol drone?*

Bhavia leaned back and sighed.

*They said there weren't enough pieces to reassemble them into anything recognizable…*

He brought up a simple, virtual puzzle game. It was a trick he learned years ago. Solving simple puzzles helped him think. Never understood how or why, but it never failed him.

Bhavia lost count of the puzzles and the passage of time when it hit him.

He had come across a report of a case some time back. There was a critical piece of evidence that had been destroyed, leaving a few small pieces. They built a modeling tool that took the pieces and iteratively came up with a series of possible recreations of the original object. It was a long list, with lots of junk, but the modeling tool was smart enough to prioritize shapes that were potentially useful, and one of them turned out to be right!

Surely that modeling tool was still out there, somewhere. He could search for the report to figure out which colony, then see if he could find the modeling tool.

Bhavia leaned forward and started tapping furiously at his computer.

# ■ DAY 2: 10:41
## REST BREAK

Ronnie checked everyone's vitals. *So far, so good.* They'd been hiking some four hours with only one break thus far. She knew the secmeds and the trackers were up to it, and it sounded like the xenobiologists were spending a lot of their time on expeditions, but she wasn't as sure of their operational support. She smiled ruefully as she thought that they were either in better shape than she'd expected or remarkably stoic.

Ronnie could see that their life support packs were responding to their bodies' demands with an above average consumption rate for their nutritional supplements. She thought about that for a moment, then dispatched a request to their EAGLE pilot Jenny that she add more supplements to their packs this evening.

Ronnie swept the vital signs from her heads-up display and brought up a terrain map from the drones circling them. The track they were following was highlighted, going through another clearing like the one where they'd found the bodies. According to the drones, the pack spent some time in that clearing as well. Beyond that, they'd be doing some climbing. That would slow their pace.

A few minutes later, as they entered the clearing, she called for a break. "Fifteen minutes, people. Pablo, Sasha, Badru, keep your eyes open!"

She heard groans as people stretched and milled about, looking for anything that might serve as a seat. But there weren't many options. After a few minutes, Pascal asked Deirdre whether she'd ever seen the pack hunters before.

"No, I haven't. I have seen the smaller, related species mentioned in this morning's report, but, no, these things are apparently new to science."

"But you've been researching this range for years, right? How could you miss creatures this big?"

"Have you *looked* at this range?" Deirdre raised her eyebrow, slightly insulted. "It's 50,000 hectares! And the topology!"

"I know, but still…"

"Wait. Here's a map of the Garcia Mountains"

Deirdre pulled up a topological map of the mountains and shared it with Pascal. As she continued speaking, others pulled up the map as well.

"See this ridge? It's so tall, clouds can't pass over it, so they dump their moisture. Keeps the eastern part of the range intensely wet and this part, where we currently are, very dry. Now, look at all these other ridges, forming basins. The rain falls on them and the water collects in lakes, then overflows and runs mostly east to the sea. There are a few exceptions, a few that run west, into what would otherwise be desert, but most, almost all, run east. Some of these basins are so wet and lush, it's like they're in perpetual fog!"

Ronnie laughed, interrupting her. "I know. I hiked out of one of those basins yesterday. Thick, thick fog, and, when we crested, you could see the fog rising up and falling back into the basin while looking at clear skies all the way to the coast! Just beautiful!"

"I know! There are a few basins like that, absolutely stunning. And every basin is huge and highly productive, supporting a stunning level of biodiversity. And the ridges are high, isolating the basins from each other. There are life forms unique to each basin. It's an evolutionary laboratory, just an amazing richness and diversity of life! I've spent three years working the range, cataloged thousands of new species, and, I mean, I don't think I've scratched the surface!"

"I know, but these things are *big*!"

Marta laughed and chimed in. "Well, would it surprise you to learn that, on Earth, they were still discovering large animals in the 20th century? Among smaller species, we believe thousands were lost without ever being discovered."

"Seriously?"

"Absolutely. We've learned a lot, don't get me wrong, but there's just so, so much to learn." Marta sighed, then added, "gives you an appreciation for what we lost on Earth. Makes you wonder what life forms we drove into extinction without ever discovering them."

Ronnie stopped the reverie. "Okay, people, time to get moving!"

# ▪ DAY 2: 11:14
## DRONE FOOTAGE

Bhavia's coffee cup was long empty, and he'd completed all the tasks he could address sitting in the park. He found the modeling tool he'd been looking for. Bhavia loaded the digital representations of the shards, then spent some time working with the tool to provide additional information. There was a lot he didn't know about whatever the pieces came from; but, for example, he had a rough idea as to the upper size limit given that the survey team carried the pieces to the site with a compact suspensor pallet.

Still, the modeling tool generated a *lot* of possibilities and showed no signs of slowing. He needed to narrow it further. Bhavia tapped the picnic table idly, staring off into space, when he realized that he had an opportunity to collect more information that might help the modeling tool.

*The survey team turned off their drone, but wouldn't the drone have caught any images of whatever the shards were from before they turned it off?*

He was the Security Chief; he would have no trouble accessing drone footage.

Bhavia started to tap his wrist computer, then thought better of it. It would be easier, and more effective, to review the footage from the workspace in his quarters. There was a slight chance Nur would be home. A very slight chance. But he needed to do this from his quarters.

*And I guess I could grab lunch on the way...*

# ■ DAY 2: 14:45
## THE PINEAPPLE

Pete was back, with a package. It looked heavy. Fernando raised a hand in greeting.

"Welcome back! Here for a late lunch?"

"Yes, but not by choice," Pete grunted. He was clearly struggling to carry the item but trying very hard to hide that fact. "We were busy and I couldn't get away."

"No problem at all. Plenty of tables and plenty of food. Sit anywhere you want."

Pete looked around. The place was empty. *Perfect.*

"How about I sit at the end of the bar?"

"Anywhere you want."

He expected Pete to pick a table with a view or at least the end of the bar with a view. But, for some reason, Pete went to the other end of the bar, plunked his package on the counter with a sigh of relief, and sat down. Fernando groaned slightly and walked behind the bar to serve his only customer.

"What can I get you?"

Pete smiled smugly, clearly pleased with himself and with Fernando's question. "Today, it's not about what *you* can get *me*. It's about what *I* can offer *you!*"

Fernando cocked his head. "What are you talking about?"

Pete tilted his head towards the package. "Got something for you."

Pete started unwrapping the package. Slowly, carefully, he revealed a shallow flower pot bearing a large, greenish yellow object with a rough, scaly texture. It was roughly egg shaped and about the size of a human head. From the sides sprouted four short branches ending in broad, green leaves. The top bore a crown of bright, red, feathery petals that unfurled as he removed packing material. Each petal was tipped with a sharp thorn. They extended outward, almost horizontally. At their center was a conical depression.

"What is *that*?"

"This, my friend, is a pineapple!"

Fernando stared. He'd never seen a real pineapple. Pictures, sure, but not recently. It kind of looked like what he remembered seeing in the pictures. Not exactly, maybe, but kind of…

"A pineapple? A *real* pineapple? I didn't know there were any pineapples in any of the outer colonies. Where'd you get it?? Can you get more??"

Pete shook his head quickly. "Oh no no no. Not *that* kind of pineapple. You're right; there are no Earth pineapples out here. This is an Eden pineapple!"

Fernando's shoulders slumped. "Oh. You had me going for a minute. I was starting to think about putting real pineapples on the menu. I had *real* pineapple once, a long, long time ago at one of the inner colonies. Just amazing! Folks love pineapple, and the simulated stuff we get from the algae farms just isn't the same. Yeah, real pineapple on the menu, now, that'd be a draw…" He realized that he was babbling, and Pete was starting to scowl at the lack of appreciation for his gift. Fernando shrugged.

"Ok, so, it's an Eden pineapple. What does that do for me?"

Pete smiled again. "Get me some raw meat."

Fernando blinked at Pete a moment, then shrugged again and went into the kitchen. He came back a few minutes later with a raw chicken breast on a plate. He put it on the counter between Pete and the pineapple. Pete reached into his back pocket and pulled out a pocket knife. He quickly diced the chicken breast into 1 cm cubes.

"Watch this!"

Pete moved the pot to the middle of the counter, under one of the lights. He picked up a piece of chicken breast and laid it gently on one of the petals.

Fernando looked at the petal, then at Pete. Nothing was happening.

"What's supposed to…"

Something came out of the depression at the center of the petals. A small opening appeared in the bottom of the depression. From that opening, a long, thin tendril slowly and deliberately stretched out along the petal. When it neared the piece of chicken, the tendril suddenly shot out and curled around the chicken, then slowly pulled it into the opening, which then disappeared within the depression.

"Whoa!"

"Think that's cool? Watch this!"

Pete reached back into the remnants of the package and pulled out a small, opaque plastic box. He lifted the box over the red petals, opened the top, and flipped it over. A cricket fell from the box and landed on a petal. It didn't move right away. It tried to explore the petal with its antennae, but, when the cricket touched its antennae to the red surface, the antennae stuck. It began to struggle, slowly at first, then increasingly until it was kicking violently. But the cricket couldn't move.

"The petals are sticky, and they'll sting you. Don't ever touch them!"

Fernando looked at Pete, then looked back. The tendril came back out of the opening in the depression again. It stretched steadily towards the struggling cricket. Suddenly, it lashed out, wrapping itself about the cricket, tightening as the cricket struggled. It began to pull and, as it did so, temporarily freed the cricket from the sticky petal. The cricket jumped and kicked, landing on another petal, and got stuck again. The tendril never loosened its grip. Every time it pulled the cricket free, the cricket would jump and land closer to the center; the tendril withdrew, relentlessly drawing the struggling cricket towards the center until, finally, the cricket disappeared into the hole in the depression.

Fernando smiled. "Amazing! That was cool!"

Pete raised his eyebrows and said, "now, watch this!"

Pete reached into the package again and pulled out a larger box. He could hear something moving in the box.

Pete held the box over the petals, then, as he turned the box upside down, pressed a button on the box with his index finger. The lid retracted and a small, white mouse fell on the petals, then squealed as it struggled to right itself.

Suddenly, the petals flew upward, wrapping themselves around the mouse. The thorns at the end of each petal turned inward, and each petal bent at the same set of articulation points, pushing the thorns down towards the mouse.

The petals blocked Pete's and Fernando's view as the petals contained the violent struggles of the mouse screaming in fear, then pain. After a few moments, the petals slowly opened and splayed, their thorny tips red with blood stretching outward once more. The mouse was gone.

Fernando started, then swore, then smiled.

Pete was smiling too. "Here's the deal. It's a plant, but you don't have to feed it at all. You forget for a day or two or a week? Don't worry; it'll be fine. But, if you want it to grow, then feed it. Feed it as much as you want. You can't over feed it; it'll just grow faster. Plus, you can feed it *anything*. Table scraps, bugs, anything. Any of the pet shops that cater to people that keep snakes and lizards will have crickets, mealworms, mice, stuff like that. When it gets big enough, you can switch to rats. The more you feed it, the faster it'll grow. And it'll get big. BIG! I've seen them as big as a barrel, taking full sized rats. Remember that lizard you were telling me about? Well, this is better! You can put more than one bug on the petals, then let folks bet on which one it'll take first!"

Pete leaned forward. "And it gets even better. The petals aren't just sticky. They attract bugs, too. If there's a fly around, it won't be able to resist. It'll land on one of the petals and get stuck, and then eaten. You not only get a draw like that big lizard you were talking about. You'll never see another bug in your restaurant!"

Fernando stared at the pineapple, thinking about where to put it.

"What else does it need? I have to water it, right? What about, you know, fertilizers and such?"

Pete waved his hand and snorted. "No, no, none of that. It's *so* easy. These things are tough. As long as you're feeding it, it gets all the moisture and fertilizer it needs. It doesn't need a lot of light, either. I wouldn't put it in a dark closet, mind you, but if there's enough light for you to see, it'll get all the light it needs. And don't worry about the size of the pot. When it outgrows this one, you just call me, and I'll come by with one of my guys to transplant it to something bigger."

Fernando liked this deal, but something wasn't right. "Wait, you said it's from Eden? I didn't know you could bring anything in from outside." He switched his gaze from the pineapple to Pete, looked around, then lowered his voice. "Is it legal?"

Pete waved his hand again nonchalantly. "Do you have any idea how many of these things I've sold? You'll be the first bar to have one on display, sure, but that's not a problem. People have been buying them for their homes. Hell, *I* have one myself! Like I said, they attract and consume vermin. No bugs, no mice. And they're pretty, right? Look at those petals!"

He nodded. Pete's argument won him over. This was *perfect* for his place!

They started haggling over the price.

# ▪DAY 2: 15:07
## LUNAR ALIGNMENT BRIEFING

Elke sat at the head of her conference room table. Nikko, Dieter, and Rajiv were in the room with George present virtually. They were waiting for David to brief them on the latest alignment modeling. Elke, ever a stickler for punctuality, exhaled with frustration. She knew David and his team were spread thin preparing the colony for the alignment, but her patience had limits.

"I haven't heard anything from David; hopefully he will be here any minute. We can put the time to good use. Are you all following Ronnie's updates?"

She summoned a projection of the formation and mountains appeared on the table, with the team's route highlighted. They were now in the foothills of the mountains, and Ronnie's latest report said the trackers were confident the team was catching up with the pack.

Nikko piped up. "I review every update as she posts them. I also get updates from their pilot, Jenny, and their support staff, Pascal and Nijaz. They concur that they're making good progress and the trackers believe they're closing the gap, but the drones haven't spotted the pack yet. Their life support packs are good for another three hours or so. Their pilot already flew their EAGLE to the nearest clearing we could find. At 17:00 hours, we'll find their nearest extraction point and send a couple of Falcons to carry them to the EAGLE for the night." He laughed, then continued. "I expect they'll be exhausted! Jenny's expecting a quiet night. Fortunately, the kitchenette is fully stocked!"

Elke was about to ask a question when David barged through the door, nearly flying into the table. She briefly considered chastising him, but reminded herself his punctuality track record was, overall, quite good. Besides, he was clearly having the time of his life. She opted for a gentle reminder.

"David! So glad you could join us…"

"I am SO sorry to be late! Nikko, Dieter, the new probes are now all online, and we are just drowning in data!"

The projection of Ronnie's progress disappeared. A large model of Eden formed over the conference table. Surface features were richly detailed but transparent, revealing a network of irregular shapes.

"Here's our home with an overlay of the outlines of the tectonic plates. I doubt any of you have spent enough time staring at these shapes to notice the changes, but we've just finished revising these outlines based on what we've learned from these new probes…"

He smoothed his disheveled hair with one hand and pointed at the shapes with the other. "Eden's tectonic plates are unusual. Most worlds, like Earth, have a variety of plate sizes. Mostly large, with a few smaller ones here and there. Well, Eden has many small plates, reflecting the intensity and complexity of the tidal forces of her four moons. These probes have really helped us improve our understanding of Eden's plates, and that, in turn, is really helping us improve our seismic forecasting!"

The model grew smaller, and Eden's four moons appeared.

"You can see the moons are reaching alignment, and their combined tidal forces are already affecting the planet. Normally, Eden's coastlines experience a tidal cycle based on the interplay of the moons' gravities, but, as the alignment progresses, those cycles are coalescing as extremely high and low tides. We can also see movement of the plates in response to the alignment, which is already leading to a number of seismic events around the planet."

David turned and asked, "oh! Did anyone feel the midmorning tremor in Wu City? No? Not surprised. It was a big quake, but the epicenter was quite a distance from here. I can't even be sure I would have noticed it if I wasn't watching our instruments!"

He cleared his throat and continued. "We know, from the deep space probes that preceded us here and the modeling we've done that alignments of all four moons occur every 37.3 years or so. And this one will be even more intense than usual because of the relative position of the aligned moons and the sun. In short, we're expecting a lot of activity.

Here's what we believe the next couple of days will be like. Peak alignment will be over the desert west of Wu City tomorrow evening, uh, 23:07. We're expecting a number of quakes, ranging from moderate to severe around the planet. I'll distribute those predictions. For this conversation, I'll confine myself to events we believe will have direct implications for the colony.

First, we're expecting a divergence of these plates on the opposite side of the planet. A gap will appear between these plates exposing the mantle, leading to a series of volcanic eruptions on the seafloor, with a strong possibility that, here, closer to the continent, we may see some new islands. That divergence will lead to plates moving relative to each other in these areas."

A number of red circles appeared on the model. "We'll see these plates sliding by each other, and, here, on the sea floor east of Wu City, we expect a subduction, um, a pushing of one plate under the other. The subduction will generate a substantial tsunami that will hit the coastlines late tomorrow night. Nikko, as we ran our models this morning and it became clearer that a tsunami was likely, we advised the *Calypso* to move further out to sea to ride out the tsunami. She'll be safely away from shorelines in plenty of time."

Nikko nodded, "yes, they kept me in the loop. Thank you!"

David tapped his wrist computer and a number of blue circles appeared around the planet. "Here are our current extraction projects. As you can see, a number of them are near places we expect activity. Not surprising, such stresses are how desirable materials get concentrated. In any case, they were designed with such events in mind and will lock down until we're through the alignment."

Nikko interjected, "and we'll be prepared to offer assistance or even evacuations should the need arise."

David, nodding, tapped his wrist computer again. A number of green circles appeared on the model.

"Thank you, Nikko. And you've worked with George regarding his requests for field observations?"

Nikko nodded and turned to George, who responded. "Yes, we're expecting to see a number of organisms respond to the alignment. Nikko has a number of EAGLEs configured as mobile base camps. Much better than setting up blinds, really, as they can take off in an emergency."

Elke nodded her approval. "I appreciate you two working together!"

"And finally," David resumed, "Rajiv, you've been asking me about your construction schedules. We'll experience some quakes here, and they'll be more intense than the one we had this morning, but not that bad. We'll all definitely feel it, maybe to the extent of some people reporting things falling from shelves, but I'm not anticipating significant damage. I'm sending you a detailed projection…" He tapped his wrist computer a couple of times, "now. I think you'll find that only a very few kinds of projects will need to be held. Wouldn't be a great time to try to set dome support arches, for example."

Elke turned from the model. "David, it sounds like you're predicting a lot of activity, but with preparations guided by your modeling, we should be fine. Minimal injuries and damage, but we may have a few scared people, am I right?"

"Exactly. And! And this will be a very productive time for the planetological team. We'll be collecting data that will keep us busy for a very long while. Maybe until the next alignment!" He grinned broadly. "But we've built our structures in the right places, we've designed them properly, and we're taking the necessary steps to lock everything down. Of course, we can't predict everything, but we hope for nothing dramatic." "

Elke turned to Nikko. "We should still issue an alert. Do you have any kind of standard advisory for this sort of thing?"

Nikko nodded his head confidently. "Yes, yes we do. We prepared one a few years ago in preparation for a two-moon alignment. I'll forward it to you. Would you like the advisory to come from your office or operations?"

Elke paused for a moment, then said, "we'll issue the advisory, but we'll refer questions to you. Acceptable?"

Nikko nodded his head in acknowledgement.

George spoke up. "We've suspended our research while the *Calypso* repositions to ride out the tsunami. We're already in water far too deep for diving, and we can't effectively deploy the sub while the ship's cruising, so we're deploying drones for remote observations. The megafauna team, the one Ronnie was supporting before she was plucked away, is now on the beach with an EAGLE. They'll observe the tsunami and then monitor the succession, from a safe distance of course."

"The pilot's one of our best," Nikko interjected. "She'll get that EAGLE off the beach before the tsunami and then back in place for your studies. Just let me know what else you'll need, and where."

"Thank you. And, once the tsunami subsides, the *Calypso* will position off the coast to resume our research."

"Excellent." David turned back to Rajiv. "Any issues with my predictions?"

Rajiv was still reviewing the data sent by David. "Huh? Oh, no, this is… Well, this is fantastic! I'll, uh, not insult you by asking your confidence in these numbers." He looked up and smiled. "Yes, this is good news; this won't slow us down much at all!"

David lifted his chin with pride. "Yes, exactly. Let's be clear. Tomorrow's going to be a very interesting day all around Eden. But we chose our surface settlement site well!"

Elke cleared her throat to regain control of the room.

"Thank you David. Questions?"

When she was met with silence, Elke continued. "We have an expedition in the western foothills of the Garcia Mountains. They're looking for whatever killed two surveyors yesterday. According to their last update, they expect to catch up with whatever killed them sometime tomorrow. David, can they safely proceed? Or do we need to recall them?"

David grimaced slightly. "Ah yes, I…I'd heard about the survey team; I'm sorry. But, to answer your question, the Garcias are on the same tectonic plate as we are. It's about the most stable place on the planet. They'll feel some activity, maybe an intense tremor or two, but they should be okay. Now, if they cross the Garcias, if they're in or near the rainforest, they'll need to stay at higher altitudes. We're predicting a significant tsunami, something on the order of about 100 m, so, in an abundance of caution, I'd advise them to stay above, say, 200 m elevation."

Elke's brows furrowed at the word "tsunami." "What about the city? Will this tsunami reach the city?"

"Wu City is the most stable place on the planet. Elevation is 350 m and shielded by the mountains. When we were planning the base station, given the, uh, extreme seismic activity of the planet, we modeled potential disasters. You'd need a much larger tsunami to reach Wu City. We've seen no evidence that there's ever been a tsunami remotely large enough to reach the settlement."

Rajiv spoke up. "And, in that incredibly unlikely event, the domes are designed to protect the city. Sounds like we'll feel some shakes. But nothing significant."

Elke looked around the room. "Anything else? No? Very good. David, thank you. I'd like to meet daily at this time until we're through the alignment."

# ▪DAY 2: 15:42
## SECURITY FOOTAGE

Bhavia sighed and leaned back in his chair. He'd been sitting there, reviewing drone recordings, for hours.

He rubbed his eyes, then stood and walked to his window. His quarters were on one of the upper floors, facing north. He used to enjoy his view of the desert expanse, bordered to the right by the Garcia Mountains. Then another dome was built to the north, filling his field of view. He was sure there must be folks that would appreciate such a view, but he was not one of them. Not that he could bring it up around Nur. Nur was justifiably proud of her work as lead foreman and proudly enjoyed looking at the dome.

Bhavia sighed again and closed his eyes, reviewing the long day. He had left the park, found some lunch at a favorite café, and came back to find he had the place to himself. He sat by his workstation and began experimenting, trying to find the best way to review the recordings. They were usually a few hours long, so reviewing all of them in real time would take days. His first thought was to speed them up, so he pulled up the recording of the victim's final survey assignment and tried different playback speeds.

The recording started when their Falcon landed and they deployed their drone. As the drone ascended to its patrol altitude, its field of view expanded. Bhavia could see them exiting their Falcon and waving as it lifted off and flew away.

He experimented until he found the fastest playback speed he could absorb, then paused and did some arithmetic. He was looking at fewer days, but still…

*Damn it, I just don't have that kind of time.*

He needed a way to narrow down which recordings to review first. Each recording had a set of properties: times, dates, name of the survey team, durations, locations, etc. Narrowing it down to surveys in or near the Garcia Mountains helped, but there were still too many.

Clearly, he should start with the victims.

*Most recent first, then work back from there…*

Bhavia resumed the playback, watched them climb the formation, periodically pulling their survey equipment from the kits on the suspensor pallet to do their work. Then, as the team approached the clearing where they'd meet their fate, the recording stopped.

At no point could he see anything in their kits that might be connected to the shards.

On the other hand, the kit sizes did offer him an upper limit on the potential size of the, whatever it was, so he opened his iterative program and added that constraint.

*Damn it, still too many results. But it helps.*

Bhavia blinked. He remembered that they'd deactivated their patrol drone. That gave him an idea.

He spent a few minutes tinkering with his wrist computer. He couldn't find a way to filter for which recordings had an interruption. So, Bhavia created a bot to run through each recording at a much higher speed than he could possibly absorb and flag the ones that included such an interruption. He turned the bot loose to sort through the recordings and started reviewing the victims' previous outing.

A ding went off behind him. The bot had compiled the first results. *Finally!* Bhavia went back to his chair.

"All right, what did you find for me?"

Once again, as the drone ascended, its field of view expanded. In this particular recording, Bhavia could see they were in a rover rather than a Falcon. He did a quick check and saw they weren't traveling as far; so, apparently, they drove themselves in a rover rather than schedule a Falcon. This difference encouraged him. He might get better visibility on the open rover than the enclosed Falcon.

Bhavia watched them set up their suspensor pallet and transfer their kits to it from the rover. He still didn't see even a glimpse of whatever the shards were from. The team made their way to the formation, stopping periodically to take readings.

They reached a clearing, and then the recording stopped. When it restarted, there was a gap of forty-seven minutes.

*Interesting…*

They hadn't moved very far from where they'd deactivated their drone. Bhavia paused the recording and zoomed in. He could see quite a few prints in the sandy areas of the clearing. Some of them were from bare feet, suggesting they'd taken off their environmental suits while the drone was off.

*What the hell were they up to? A fuck break? Are the shards from some sort of sex toy?*

They continued their work, then turned around to return to the rover. Nothing interesting happened until they reached the rover and transferred their kits back to it.

Bhavia rewound and played that again, then once more. He got the impression the kits were heavier when the team put them back than when the team unloaded them. Just a vague impression, nothing he could document or measure. He jumped back and forth from when they transferred the kits to the pallet, then back to the rover.

*It sure seems like they are struggling, like they're working a little harder transferring them back.*

Bhavia made a mental note of this, then checked on his bot. It was still running through the recordings, but it had identified dozens of videos with interruptions. So far, they had one thing in common.

Every recording with an interruption involved the same survey teams, three pairs of them.

"Interesting!"

Bhavia let the bot continue as he pulled up the victims' previous outing.

# ▪DAY 2: 16:12
## QUAKE

It was getting late. Ronnie checked the vitals once more. Nutritional supplements had run out, and one of the support staff had less than an hour left in his pack. *Sloppy.* He should have let her know the moment his pack crossed that threshold. Ronnie made a mental note to pull him aside when they got back to the EAGLE.

"Edana, how are we doing? Does it look like we're nearing another clearing?"

Edana brought up a topological map and shared it with Ronnie. "We're… here…and it looks like the pack went through another clearing…here. I'm guessing you're monitoring our packs. I know I have just a bit over an hour left and I'm pretty good on air. I think we'll make it to this next clearing no problem, but I don't think we can count on getting to another."

"I agree." Ronnie opened a channel to their EAGLE pilot. "Jenny, are you there?"

After a moment, she heard "yes, Ronnie. Go ahead."

Ronnie shared the map and highlighted the clearing. "Have you moved to a location near here? Can you arrange a Falcon pick-up from this location?"

It took a few moments for Jenny to respond. "Yes, I've already repositioned the EAGLE; Don's back with his Falcon. He'll be in that clearing by the time you get there."

"Very good. Thanks."

Ronnie raised her hand to activate her intercom and address the whole group when she froze. She felt something. She heard some small rocks falling. She brought up a link to the planetology lab and saw a seismograph. *Definitely a tremor!*

She and Badru took point, walking with the trackers. She looked forward along the trail and felt queasy as she realized the ground ahead of her was moving. It was subtle, but it was definitely moving up and down. It was like watching a small wave approach. As the tremor approached, rocks began to shift and fall.

"Brace yourself, people!"

Ronnie spread her feet and clenched her fists as the ground roiled beneath her feet. She could hear exclamations from her team, everything from chuckles to cries of shock and fear.

Then it was over.

"What the hell was *that*?!?!"

It took her a moment to recognize Nijaz' voice.

"That was a quake! There's a subduction zone off the coast; it's a place where one plate is being pushed under the other."

"Well, don't let it happen again!"

Ronnie laughed, rather loudly. The joke caught her off guard. "I'll, uh, take that under advisement."

The team continued walking quietly. Everyone was tired and looking forward to a meal and some sleep.

Ronnie heard Deirdre exclaim, "hey!" She stopped and turned. Deirdre slowly approached an opening in the rocks.

"What do you see?"

Deirdre pointed but didn't answer Ronnie. "Marta, do you see this? Do you see these bones?"

Ronnie asked Badru to stay on point and walked back. As she approached Deirdre, she felt a little odd.

Deirdre scanned the rocks. "Do you feel that? That's electromagnetic interference. There's definitely something in here, something related to kraken…"

A chill ran down Ronnie's spine. Even after all these years, the kraken still filled her nightmares.

"Be careful!" she hissed.

Marta stood quickly while Deirdre continued scanning. "It's not like the kraken you faced on the orbiting platform, Ronnie! Yes, it's hitting us with a little electromagnetic interference, but this one hasn't encountered earthly nervous systems before, so it doesn't know how to fine tune to affect us. Besides, I think it's one of the smaller 'sit and wait' predators related to the kraken. There's quite a large group, actually, that hunt this way, with a number of species found through these mountains. We've found two species that range through the passes, but I've never seen either of them this far away. Might be a new species."

"Sit and wait?" Ronnie spoke through a clenched jaw. Marta's words had done little to soothe her.

"Yes, we suspect it's an ambush predator. Think of a spider on its web. Not hard given how well they can match the color and texture of…"

Abruptly, Deirdre stood and pointed. "*There* you are!"

She pointed at some rocks. Ronnie stared at where she was pointing, but saw nothing, until…

"What the fuck is *that*?!"

Suddenly Ronnie could make out the rounded body, the beak, the sensory cluster, the claws. It was small, as Deirdre said, about the size of a house cat. Similar to, but not the same as, those monsters.

"Amazing camouflage!" Deirdre and Marta stepped closer to investigate, oblivious to Ronnie's rising panic. "Damned hard to see, but you can always tell when they're nearby. You can feel the electromagnetic impulses, and you can see the debris from their prey."

Deirdre leaned towards it, then stood straight and turned towards Marta. "This is the larger of the two species we've seen in this area. Apparently, they range further from the mountains than we realized! I'll note the location for our records."

Ronnie glared, horrified by this little version of the horrors that had killed so many of her friends.

"We need to go. *Now.*"

She walked past Badru, her eyes glazed over. "Trackers, get us to the next clearing!"

Elke ducked to enter her conference room. John, Nikko, and Dieter were already there. Guido and George were present virtually.

"Ronnie, are you there?"

Ronnie appeared virtually, looking a bit stiff as she took her seat. She smiled broadly as she replied, "yes, I'm here! A little winded, but here!"

"Yes, I'll bet. We'll keep this as brief as we can. Updates, please."

Ronnie sent a projection to Elke's conference table of the formation, with their day's hike highlighted.

"As you can see, we followed the trail for some 40 km, a pretty good distance given the terrain. People are pretty tired; I'm sure they'll eat heartily and sleep well. Nikko, I'm impressed your people kept up! Our pilot, Jenny, is recharging our packs and she'll be adding additional nutritional supplements. We exhausted our original supply early."

She pointed at the projection. "Once our trackers found the trail, it was easy to follow. The formation has a number of these clearings interconnected by game trails that follow the features of the formation." She glanced around the room. "If David were here, I'd love to understand the geological processes that created these structures, but I'll find him or one of the other planetologists after the alignment is complete. For what it's worth, we have a number of tremors today. No injuries, but they sure got our attention!

Anyway, the pack's trail follows these game trails, which is understandable given the severity of the terrain bounding the trails. We didn't lose them often. Biggest challenges were these clearings. Not sure what they were doing in the clearings, but they spent a lot of time in each of them, so it took a bit of time for the trackers to sort through it all and figure out which way they went.

So far, they're generally moving southeast rather than randomly wandering, but we can't risk making any assumptions. The good news about the time they spend in these clearings is that the trackers are confident we're gaining on them."

"Won't you lose them tonight?" Elke asked.

"No, I don't believe so. The trackers are thinking they're diurnal. They said they can tell the pack spent the night in one of the clearings we reached this morning because of their activity level and the quantity of their droppings. We think they probably settled down for the night by now. And, frankly, I'd rather not find them in the dark. We were hoping we could dispatch the drones to visually inspect clearings while we rested, but they're getting low and need to be recharged. Once they're fully charged, Nijaz and Pascal will send them out to patrol." She laughed and added, "they promise they won't oversleep! Does anyone have any questions or issues with our plans?" Hearing none, she continued.

"You can also see we're getting close to the mountains." As she spoke, the projection shifted and expanded. "Deirdre and Marta are fairly confident the pack is heading for this pass into the range."

The projection shifted again. The team's path remained highlighted, but another, longer path was highlighted as an arc starting at a northwestern pass, then parallel to the team's path, then continuing southeast towards the pass Ronnie had just highlighted.

"We still have no idea why they're in the formation, by the way. According to Deirdre and Marta, they probably came through this pass, ranged down here through these clearings, and are now, as I said, heading towards this other pass. It's clearly not a shorter route. Based on our surveys of that valley, the terrain isn't any more challenging than the path they've taken. So are they avoiding something we don't know about in that part of the valley? Are they looking for something along this path? It's a sparse environment, not much to sustain a pack of creatures this big. We've not seen anything we think would interest them. No idea what drew them down from the mountains or motivated their attack on our survey team. Lots of theories, none of them terribly convincing. We'll see what we learn tomorrow."

The room was silent as everyone in the room contemplated the projection. After a few moments, Elke stood and addressed her. "Ronnie, thank you. Please pass along our appreciation to your team. Go get some food and rest, and we'll talk tomorrow. "

# ▪DAY 2: 23:20
## A GLIMPSE

Bhavia rubbed his eyes. It was getting late, and he was very, *very* tired of watching drone footage. He wasn't very good company either; Nur went to bed more than an hour ago, pausing to kiss his forehead as she passed. Bhavia paused the recording for a moment, smiled, then, with a heavy sigh, resumed the playback as Nur shuffled away.

He'd been working for hours. He took a quick break around dinner time, then sent a quick note asking Guido to cover for him at the Governor's next staff meeting when Ronnie reported on the tracking team's progress. Bhavia wasn't looking forward to explaining why, but Guido, thankfully, didn't ask. He simply acknowledged the request and then, later, sent a copy of the meeting recording.

Bhavia rubbed the back of his neck and cracked it, grimacing at the pain. Hours. He had spent hours on drone recordings, hours of reviewing footage. He learned all recordings with interruptions involved the same three survey teams and only involved surveys of the formations in the western foothills of the Garcia Mountains. They never shut off their drones when working anywhere else, only those mountains. Every so often, he'd see something useful. A partial outline through the kits on their suspensor pallets had helped him fine tune the iterative modeling of what the shards might be from.

He'd almost given up an hour ago, aching for sleep. But he decided to review one more, then another. But Bhavia couldn't bear the thought of watching another recording tonight! It was late and he needed some sleep. He stood and stretched and was about to shut down the footage when he paused.

*Wait, what the…*

Finally, a glimpse of a container. A cylindrical container with clear walls. It was just a quick glimpse, but enough.

He snipped that image and fed it into his modeling tool. The tool rapidly narrowed down the possibilities, and now, Bhavia had an image.

The next step was clear. He needed to verify it wasn't a normal piece of surveying equipment. He knew nothing of survey work, but he'd done some quick searches of the equipment used. Bhavia hadn't seen anything remotely resembling this container.

*Well, there's no substitute for diligence…But not tonight, fuck it. I'm going to bed.*

He'd ask Nur about it in the morning. He was tempted to ask her now, but she wouldn't be able to do anything with the information until morning anyway. And Bhavia was pretty sure of the response he'd get for waking her up.

Besides, Bhavia was already convinced the survey teams were using those containers to smuggle something. There was nobody outside to smuggle anything to, so they must be smuggling something into the colony. He had no idea what, but he would find out.

*Soon…*

# ▪ DAY 3: 05:00
## SECOND DAY OF TRACKING

Jenny brewed some coffee as she puttered around the kitchenette table. Most of her charges diligently cleaned up after themselves last night, but a few, thoroughly spent, missed a thing or two. Jenny didn't mind picking up after them. Now, as the scent of freshly brewed coffee permeated the kitchenette and wafted through the EAGLE, she could hear the teams stirring. Some of them rose in response to alarms, but not all. Others seemed to respond to the smell of coffee and the thickly sliced bacon nearing perfect crispness.

Ronnie walked into the kitchenette, selected a mug, and muttered gratitude as she poured herself some coffee. She held the mug with two hands, her face brightening as she took her first sips and more of the team trickled in.

"Thank you Jenny for the coffee, the dinner, and the life support packs!"

Jenny smiled and whipped her hair away from the popping grease. "My pleasure! The least I could do. I'll be napping and enjoying the view while you're all out there trudging through the wilderness. Eggs?"

"Three. Over medium, please."

Ronnie watched a sleepy crowd pour themselves coffee, make tea, or ponder this morning's selection of fruit juices. Pablo stepped up and started taking egg orders as well. Some loaded their plates with scrambled eggs; a few filled bowls with oatmeal. Jenny produced with a smile a plate carrying Ronnie's finished order. Ronnie accepted her eggs, added some bacon and oatmeal, then sat down to eat. She took a bite, closed her eyes, and uttered, "Jenny, you're a magician!"

She spoke through thick mouthfuls of food as the others took their seats.

"Pascal? Nijaz? How'd the drones do last night?"

Nijaz put his spoon down and checked his wrist computer, then brought up a topological display over the kitchenette table. He centered the display, leaving the edges of the table visible while everyone continued eating.

"Well, let's see! Pretty well…I think. You can see the highlighted trail, generally heading east towards the mountains. No surprise there."

Pascal, tracing the track with his finger, added, "see this clearing? There's a lot of activity within this clearing. There's also another inbound track similar to what we've been following, but only one outbound track. Not sure what that means, could be…"

Nijaz, staring at his wrist computer, interrupted him. "I'll tell you what it means! Look at this!"

With a flurried motion, the topological display was replaced with a view of the clearing from one of the drones.

As the team leaned in to look closer, Deirdre gasped. "Those bodies! I think that's our pack!"

Finn shook his head. "I don't know. The drones are showing another set of tracks just like the ones we've been following coming into the clearing. I think we're seeing the aftermath of two packs running into each other. With all due respect to your drones, guys, I don't think we'll know for sure until we examine the site ourselves. I want to work through which inbound track matches the creatures we've been tracking, and whether they're the ones that left that clearing alive!"

Bhavia sat patiently at the worktable in his quarters. He was alone; Nur was at work. He'd sent Guido a request for a quick meeting. He knew Guido was busy, but Guido was also punctual. Bhavia was confident that it would be brief.

Guido appeared across the table from him.

"Good morning."

Guido smiled. "Good morning, Bhavia. I understand you had a few tremors this morning. What's that like? I've only lived on stable planets and orbiting platforms. I've never experienced a quake."

Bhavia hummed and tilted his head slightly as he looked past the projection of his boss, then looked back. "It's hard to describe. I was sitting at the park when it hit. I haven't been here that long, and I'm told we get tremors all the time, but this was the first one big enough for me to notice. I was expecting to be shaken, right? Side to side? But it was more of a rolling motion. I talked with Nur, and she said that, if we weren't in one of the domes, we would have seen a motion like a wave in the ground. Nur said it was like being on the water when a wave rolls by. And being in a dome was like being on a big boat. You don't see the roll. You just feel the whole thing rise a little, tilt up, then down again."

Guido nodded thoughtfully. "I've been here since the second year. Had my first opportunity to get on a boat a few years later. Strange experience. Water, all the way to the horizon. I mean, of course, it's an ocean, but I've never stood on a planet's surface without seeing the edge of a dome, you know? Sure, if you're outside, in an environmental suit, you can see whatever barren or primordial landscape that planet has extending to the horizon, but a blue ocean? A blue sky? And feeling the boat move with the water, rolling as waves went by? It made me sick! Zero-g doesn't get me, but being on a boat? Ugh, I'm nauseous just remembering!"

They looked at each other for a moment, then Guido clapped his hands together matter-of-factly. "I'm sure you didn't ask for this time to discuss quakes and boats. What can I do for you?"

Bhavia thought Guido was a good boss, no nonsense.

"I know everyone's top priority is tracking down whatever attacked our survey team. And there's not much I can directly contribute to that effort."

Guido nodded. "Understood. Go on."

"The deactivated drone bugged me. Why would they do that? Made no sense. And the discarded shards caught my eye as well. So, I've been doing some digging."

Guido leaned forward with interest. He was getting to know Bhavia, and Bhavia was living up to his reputation of good instincts and tenacity.

"So, I've been following two threads." Bhavia explained how he worked through what the shards were from and how he narrowed down which recordings to watch. Bhavia brought up a projection of one of the containers.

"I spoke with Nur this morning and she assured me there's nothing like this in the normal kit for a survey team. Then I met with Dieter. First, he told me this looks similar to the specimen containers they produce for the xenobiology expeditions. Second, he checked and there's no log of anyone fabricating this. Finally, he did a little digging of his own and found that one of his fabrication engineers has a materials discrepancy, enough to suggest the engineer made seven to eight such containers."

"You suspect smuggling?"

"Exactly. And, since I can't imagine who they might be smuggling out to, I figured they must be smuggling something in. All of the drone recordings with voluntary deactivation are from the same three survey teams, and only when they were sent to the formation near where the team was attacked. There's not much out there, so I think the target was a life form. Some Eden life form is being smuggled into the city."

Guido sighed. "Right on cue."

The PIP did their best to screen migrants, but, invariably, as colonial populations grew, so did crime. Security teams for new colonies rarely dealt with anything other than escorting drunk patrons back to their quarters. Then, as the population grew, petty crimes increased, eventually becoming violent. He made a mental note to speak with Elke about increasing their police force. And he'd need talented investigators like Bhavia.

"Next steps?"

"Next? Round up the surviving survey teams and find out what the hell they've been smuggling."

# •DAY 3: 11:45
## INTERROGATION

Bhavia groaned. It was unfortunate that the colonial brig only had two cells and two interview rooms.

"Well, it's all a matter of perspective, I guess," he muttered.

The colonial jail certainly had space for more cells. Overall, it was probably a good thing that they hadn't felt the need to build that space out any further. But, right now, it was inconvenient not having more options for isolating people of interest. As he brought in the surveyors, he didn't want them to compare notes.

Bhavia decided the best strategy would be to simply bring them in together. He considered going to them for "an informal chat" rather than bringing them in, but he wanted to move fast and thought a cell would be intimidating. So, he sent Harry and Bob to get them. Now, the four surviving surveyors sat in pairs across from each other. Harry sat at a desk at the end of the hall, inhibiting conversations between them. Bhavia figured they'd also be a bit shaken by the deaths of their friends.

He remotely observed for a while. One was angry. Two were sullen. The fourth was twitchy.

He'd start with "Twitchy."

Harry moved Twitchy to an interview room, where Bhavia watched him marinate in his anxiety. When he thought Twitchy was ready, Bhavia walked silently into the room and stood next to the subject as he wordlessly brought up the projection of the container. Bhavia knew his height and build made him physically intimidating. The man's subtle attempt to lean away from Bhavia confirmed it.

Bhavia stared at Twitchy. Twitchy stared at the container.

"We know. I just need you to fill in a few details."

The guy wouldn't take his eyes off the container.

"We know what you were smuggling. I'd like to know if that was the only thing you were smuggling."

A lie, of course. Bhavia didn't have a clue what they were smuggling. But he was decent at poker, and the nervous wreck before him looked ready to believe anything.

It worked. Twitchy collapsed. He didn't hold back.

"No! Just the pineapples! I swear! Nothing else! I swear!"

*Pineapples? On Eden? Where the hell were they finding pineapples?*

"Okay, good. If it was just the pineapples, we can work with you. See if we can't minimize the penalties."

Twitchy blanched at the word "penalties."

"Penalties? For what? They're harmless! They're just pretty! A novelty! Folks like having a bit of Eden in their homes. What's the harm in that?"

"Where did you find them?"

"Growing out of the rocks. Just takes a little tug to pull them out. Then, we bring them in and plant them in a pot. A lot of them die, so we hang on to them for a few days, make sure they'll survive, then sell them. Hey, there's plenty of them out there. It's not like anyone's going to miss a few."

Bhavia needed to think. He walked around the room slowly. He came back to the table, turned the chair around, straddled it, and leaned on the chair's back.

"So, nothing but these pineapples?"

The guy nodded, his face downcast. Bhavia kept staring at him.

"So, you put them in these containers, then bring them back? Who do you deliver them to?"

Twitchy stayed silent. Bhavia slapped the table in a show of force.

"Hey! I'm willing to give you a break for just being stupid. But my patience is limited! WHO DO YOU GIVE THEM TO?"

Twitchy flinched, then looked up. He looked away and slumped down in his chair. "Pete. Guy named Pete. He approached me and my partner. Gave us the containers, showed us how to use them. Buys the pineapples. Sells them, I guess. You know! You've seen 'em! They're all over the place. Everybody's got one!"

Bhavia stared at him; a chill ran down his spine and his hands felt cold.

*All over the place?!*

"Pete who?"

# ▪ DAY 3: 12:06
## NEW ARRIVAL

Lara Waltz had little trouble following her wrist computer's directions through the passageways of the orbiting platform's topmost ring.

A recent immigrant, it was her first time navigating the shuttle bay ring of Eden's orbiting platform, but the layout was pretty much the same as any other colony's orbiting platform. Rotating the drum to simulate gravity made the inner surface of the drum "down." As a result, only the end rings had an exposed side that could support hanger bays. Since the first, or bottom, ring faced the planet, providing spectacular views for the poshest pubs and restaurants and most senior government offices, only the last (or top) ring could be used to serve shuttle tugs and landing craft.

Lara arrived with the most recent inbound deep space vessel. She'd grown up under a dome on a lifeless rock, then emigrated to a colony orbiting a primordial world to earn an undergraduate degree as a mining engineer. After a few years supporting mining operations for that colony, she'd heard of the discovery of Eden. She immediately applied to one of Eden's programs to earn a graduate degree and her pilot's certification.

Now, she was on her way to one of the mining operations in the asteroid belt as part of her graduate studies. To get there, she'd take the next shuttle tug to an interplanetary craft station, where she'd meet Reiner Marina. He was a geophysicist already heading to that asteroid to support their search for more precious metal deposits. He was also a master pilot, and this journey would be the first step in her certification.

She found the right bay. The shuttle tug, built on the same platform as EAGLEs and landing craft, was a large, boxy, dull gray utilitarian vehicle festooned with sensors, hooks and ties, maneuvering thrusters, and robotic arms. Clearly not suitable for use anywhere but space. It was surrounded by support staff preparing it for launch. After a moment, she realized which one was loading luggage.

"Excuse me! I'm Lara Waltz, and I'm on this shuttle. Can I leave my suspensor pallet with you?"

The loader looked past her at the luggage on her pallet, then checked the passenger list on his wrist computer. He lifted an eyebrow when he found her name.

"Ah, you're new. Welcome to Eden! Sure, you can leave that with me, no problem. We'll be on time, so don't go far!"

"I won't. There's a break room next door, right? I'll grab some tea and be right back."

He laughed and said, "make sure they put it in a bulb, not a cup. And I hope zero-g doesn't make you nauseous!"

The shuttle tug did indeed leave on time. As they left the shuttle bay and the simulated gravity of the drum's rotation, Lara felt her body lighten. She also heard sounds of distress from fellow passengers apparently less comfortable in zero-g than herself. She took a sip from her tea bulb as she pondered why people chose careers that subjected them to such discomforts.

As the shuttle turned, Lara focused on the restraint of her harness against the inertial movement of her body relative to her seat. She leaned a bit to the right to see past the rows between her and the pilot's cockpit to catch a glimpse of her new home. Eden was a jewel of green and blue and she didn't think she'd ever see enough of it.

The shuttle tug continued to turn until headed directly for the station. Really, it was just an automated, zero-g, pressurized hub facilitating movement of people and cargo between shuttle tugs and interplanetary craft. She could see a number of them docked and wondered which would be taking her to the mine. It didn't matter, really; they were all pretty much the same.

Lara admired the skill of their pilot as he smoothly maneuvered their shuttle tug into docking position. She knew one of the station's tubes was about to snap in place over their airlock but she never felt anything. But she did hear that wonderful "ping" indicating it was safe for passengers to undo their harnesses.

Lara knew the folks stressed by zero-g would soon be struggling to get through the tube and didn't want to wait behind them. She launched her now empty tea bulb towards the nearest trash receptacle, smiling with satisfaction as it went through the center of the opening. Then, she reached out for the back of her seat and propelled herself to the stairwell of the lower deck. She floated gracefully over the ladder she'd climbed before launch, found and unlashed her suspensor pallet, and pulled it towards the airlock. Activating the suspensors wasn't necessary, but even in zero-g, her luggage had mass to maneuver through the tube.

# DAY 3: 13:30
## NAVIGATING THE CRUISER

Reiner was busy prepping the ship when his wrist computer alerted him that Lara's shuttle tug had arrived. He set aside the project of the moment and floated through the airlock and tube to the station. As he entered the hub, Reiner could see people exiting a tube on the far side. One of them should be Lara. He tapped his computer to bring up a picture of her again. He also figured she'd be one of the few that wouldn't have a clue where they were going.

*Wait, is that her? Tall, slender, blond, dark skin, hovering and…looks lost. Yeah that's her.*

Reiner chuckled to himself. He crouched and launched himself across the sphere in her direction, calling her name as he approached. Lara looked up and saw him approaching.

"Reiner?"

He reoriented himself to aim his feet at the wall, legs bending to absorb his momentum as the magnets in his boots secured him to the station wall.

"Yes, and you must be Lara."

"I am indeed! Pleasure to finally meet you!"

"Same. Our cruiser is…" Reiner looked across the sphere and pointed to the proper tube. "That one. You have all your gear?"

Lara glanced at her suspensor pallet and replied, "everything I'll need, thanks!"

He nodded, then looked at the tube from which she'd emerged.

"We had some supplies on your shuttle. I'm sure they'll find us eventually. Ready to board? Feel comfortable making your way across?"

Lara laughed, nodded, crouched, and expertly launched herself, towing her luggage across the sphere towards the proper tunnel. Reiner watched her cross the space, relieved that she was zero-g proficient. He paused for a moment to make sure the way was clear, then launched himself to follow her.

He found her waiting for him to lead the way through the tunnel. Lara followed Reiner into the ship's airlock at the aft end of the craft. He secured the airlock, then said, "welcome aboard the *Rock Hound*. You've been aboard an interplanetary craft before, haven't you?"

She nodded.

"Great. But, as captain, I'm required to give you the grand tour and safety briefing, ok? Won't take long; it's a standard configuration."

She smiled and nodded again. "Lead on, captain!"

He laughed. "Ok. Pay attention. You'll have to brief me later, as part of your pilot's training. Meantime, put your environmental suit in that locker and bring your luggage with you. We'll leave it by your bunk."

As she closed the locker, she looked at her left ankle and swore. Her heel seam was giving way again. Environmental suits came in standard sizes, but undergarments had to be precisely tailored for waste reclamation. Precision was even more important for interplanetary travelers relying on an intravenous port for integration with high-g life support systems.

A good quality undergarment was expensive. Like most recent graduates, the best she could afford was a retailored used undergarment. She was really looking forward to indulging in a new, custom tailored unit when she earned her pilot's license

Once their suits were secured, Reiner cleared his throat and began.

"All decks connect through that hatchway." He pointed to the clear, wide tube at the center of the circular deck. "These hatches are opened through this panel, and close automatically behind you. Please remember that, while you can hold a hatch open when necessary, in the event of a pressure differential, they *will* shut to isolate hull breaches!"

She nodded. Hull breaches were rare, but they did happen, and she'd heard her share of stories of people losing fingers.

"There are emergency suits in lockers next to every hatch. They won't fit as well as your personal suit, but they'll keep you alive in a pinch and their reclamation systems will integrate with your undergarment." He moved towards the hatch.

"Always check this light, which will be green when there's equal pressure on both sides of the hatch. It'll be yellow if there's a pressure differential that's reconciling, and it'll turn green when the differential is resolved. If it's red, there's a pressure differential that's not reconciling or getting worse. It won't open unless it's green."

Reiner pressed a button and the hatch hissed open. He reached in, taking hold of the triangular ladder at the center of the tube to pull himself in. Lara could see conduits running inside the ladder and along the walls of the tube.

"This was the airlock, obviously." He pointed at the other hatches at this level as he said, "this deck also has lab space, life support, and environmental suit maintenance, accessible through these hatches."

"Engines are below us," he pointed aft. "And the next level has our high-g chambers."

He pulled himself along the ladder as she reached in to follow. He paused at the next level. Three hatches led to three wedges, each holding two white containers that Lara always thought looked uncomfortably like coffins. They connected to equipment mounted on the curved walls of each wedge.

"As you can see, we're a light cruiser, designed for up to six, but there will only be the two of us on this run. You'll like these chambers; they're equipped with the latest control panels. Makes it a lot easier to manage the process."

She grimaced. "I don't like high-g chambers. I hate breathing that shit!"

He laughed and nodded. "Everybody hates high-g chambers, and everybody hates breathing 'that shit'. But breathing 'that shit' lets us tolerate heavy acceleration and I'd rather breathe liquid for a few hours then spend a few more weeks to months in transit. Hey, could be worse! While you were crossing, they developed a new, less viscous liquid. Still carries plenty of oxygen, but breathing it's a lot easier."

She sighed. "All that's great, but the drowning sensation is still awful. Does it ever get better?"

He shrugged. "No, not really. I wish it did."

Reiner pulled himself through to the next level. "Galley over there, bunks over here. Bunks have integrated zero-g sleeping bags. This would be a good place to leave your luggage."

He opened a hatch, and Lara pushed her pallet towards the bunks, figuring she'd come back later to stow her things. He continued forward. She followed him into a conical space with six seats equipped with control panels.

"And here's the cockpit. That completes our tour. We'll be ready to depart as soon as our supplies are delivered. While we're waiting, if you'd be so kind as to take the pilot's chair, we'll go through pre-launch checks. You want your pilot's license? Well, you're about to have your first launch experience. Don't dent my ship!"

# ▪ DAY 3: 13:55
## THE KILLING GROUNDS

Elke entered her conference room and found John, Nikko, and Guido settling into their seats. George was present virtually from the *Calypso*. Dieter was expected any moment. Bhavia hadn't responded yet.

"Ronnie, what do you have?"

A detailed projection of the clearing appeared on the table.

"We let the drones track the pack through the night. Apparently, our pack came across another pack's trail and followed them to this clearing. You can see the result. Deirdre, Marta, what's your analysis?"

Deirdre and Marta were examining bodies strewn across the clearing. Deirdre said, "looks like our pack followed and then attacked another pack of the same species. Gives us an opportunity to collect some information about the creatures we're following."

"Including how well they fight," Pablo interrupted. "We should bear that in mind. This looks like a coordinated attack. That makes them, potentially, far more dangerous."

Deirdre concurred, then continued. "As we thought, they're from the bilaterally symmetric super-kingdom. It's a little challenging to reconstruct from what's left, but this head has what's left of a vertically oriented mouth. You can see the damage done to the face and…" She turned the head. "You can see two arcs of three punctures on the backs of the heads very much like the wounds inflicted on the surveyors. You can see that the bodies have been torn open, again, very much like the wounds suffered by our surveyors. Looks like seven dead individuals."

"Is there any way to know whether any of the dead animals are from the attacking pack?" Guido asked.

Ronnie responded. "We can't tell which individuals are from which pack. On the other hand, the trackers are pretty sure that tracks leaving this clearing are from the pack we've been following."

"How would they know that?"

Finn spoke up. "First, we can tell that the pack we've been following had more individuals. Hard to be sure, but we think about a dozen individuals. The pack they engaged here was smaller, maybe four to five individuals, so we believe our pack probably prevailed. We also see some signs that are distinctive, maybe an individual crippled from a major wound. That individual was with our pack and appears to be with the group that left the clearing. Now, there's seven bodies here. These seven could include the four or five individuals that were attacked and maybe a casualty or two from our pack. Or maybe there are more casualties from our pack and a survivor or two joined our pack. No way to know for sure."

The room was silent as Deirdre and Marta continued to make their examinations of the bodies. "Definitely a new species," Marta said. "I'm guessing a new order, but we'll see. Powerfully built creatures. This forelimb is interesting."

She held one up, turning it and manipulating the digits as she continued. "The paw is elongated with seven digits. The center three are thick and strong, ending with these talons. Along each side there are two long, thin fingers that are opposable, like our thumbs. An interesting balance of strength and delicacy; I'd really be interested to see how precisely they can use these side digits. The hide is covered with skin flaps similar to what we've seen in other species from this group. They're attached with a thin stalk and end in a fringed diamond shape; something roughly analogous to a bird's feather. Most of the flaps are this brown color but there's a more colorful fringe about the neck."

She paused, then continued. "Note that, behind the vertical beak, there's a throat mill like what we've seen in related species. Presumably, they use their beak to bite off chunks of food that are ground in this mill before passing to the gut." She paused again, turning to look around the clearing. "All of these individuals have had their faces destroyed in the same way, so there's not much we can learn from them in that regard. On the other hand, it's pretty clear that the way they killed each other, and probably the way they killed our surveyors, was by using the three powerful digits of each forepaw to hold their victim's head and then use their beak to…bite away their face."

George nodded, an almost pleased look on his face. "Very good analysis, Marta. Supports the notion that our survey team was lost to some kind of territorial dispute rather than an attempt at predation. Do you two see any-thing suggesting their normal diet?"

Deirdre crouched by one of the eviscerated bodies and reached in. She spent a few moments rummaging through what was left of their digestive tract, then used a knife to open the throat mill.

"Everything after the throat mill is too thoroughly ground to be identified, but I'll take some samples we can analyze in the field lab when we get back to the EAGLE. Here, though, in and before the throat mill, I can see some larger pieces. There's some thin green tissue suggesting a leaf, but it's kind of leathery, and some thick, yellowish green tissue. We'll bring some of that back too."

"What else do we need to know here?" Ronnie interrupted before an inquisitive George could ask another question. "The drones are following the outbound trail. I'd really like to catch up with our pack today."

Deirdre sighed. "I could spend days examining these bodies. But I under-stand. George, Marta and I will come back to this site in a day or two. Marta, let's take as many images as we can. Ok?"

"Alright," Ronnie nodded. "Pascal and Nijaz, find a place for our Falcon to pick us up while the drones follow the trail. Let me know when you think they've found the pack. Deirdre and Marta, you have until then to examine the site."

# DAY 3: 14:28
## HIDDEN STASH

After they completed their pre-flight checks, Reiner decided to put Lara through some simulated disasters while they waited for their supplies. He was pleased to see her manage them all calmly.

Reiner wasn't the only master pilot in the system, but he enjoyed teaching while others viewed it as a burden. In the twelve years since he'd reached Eden, Reiner had trained most of the system's aspiring pilots. They were running through another simulation when his wrist computer informed him their supplies had finally arrived.

"Lara, you're doing great. Why don't you take a break and settle in while I go accept our stuff. We're going to be spending a lot of time together!"

"Sounds good. I'll take a quick breather and then I'll help you stow everything away."

He nodded, then opened the hatch to head towards the airlock.

Lara released the pilot's harness and floated away from the seat a few centimeters as she stretched. She went through the hatch, pulled herself through the tube, and went through another hatch into the sleeping area. She found a compartment to stow her suspensor pallet, then opened her luggage and started finding places for her personal effects.

Lara paused, bit her lip, and glanced at the hatch.

She wasn't sure how Reiner would feel about her bringing her pineapple along. She heard about them when she first arrived and couldn't resist getting one. But Lara knew she'd be heading to a mining operation soon, so she asked for the smallest one they could find. She finally settled on one that was only 30 cm tall, about as big as her head. It was still beautiful, and she enjoyed feeding it table scraps, though she did so sparingly to keep it from growing too fast.

Lara pondered whether to mention the pineapple to Reiner before departure. She decided it was easier to seek forgiveness than permission, so she'd kept it hidden in her luggage. She tucked it into one of the compartments near her bunk, thinking she'd bring it out once they climbed out of their awful high-g chambers. It probably wouldn't be good for it to be in the dark too long, and she wasn't sure how well it would tolerate high-g forces while she was in the chamber, but she couldn't think of a way to protect it. It wouldn't survive being in the chamber with her while she was breathing liquid. She shrugged, resigning herself to the high probability she'd find the poor thing dead from lack of light or crushed by their initial acceleration.

But, hey, it was only a plant. She wouldn't be at the mine forever, and she could always get another one when she returned.

*And who knows, it might survive!*

# ▪ DAY 3: 15:17
## AWAKE

*Pop!*

It felt a "pop." Strange.

It hadn't felt anything in a long time. A very, very long time.

It felt a pulling sensation, then a "pop."

It was groggy. Very, very groggy.

It had been asleep for so long. So very, very long.

Slowly, it began to remember.

It remembered its emergence.

It gradually became aware, for the first time.

It made its way into the light. Seeing, stretching, then feeling urgent needs.

It fed. It fed insatiably.

Then, it became aware of the others around it, and new, insatiable urges.

Feeding, yes, but now, mating. Mating as insatiably as it was feeding, indiscriminately, in pairs and clusters.

A brief, intense, sensual riot.

Then, it began to feel groggy.

It needed to find a safe, quiet place.

It flew, and flew, and flew.

It flew further than it had ever been.

It knew it needed to find a perfect place, a place with high, safe perches.

It found one, then settled in, and fell asleep again, dreaming strange, strange dreams.

Then its dreams faded, and it faded, faded into a dreamless quiescence.

For a very long time, it did nothing, nothing but reach for the sun, and, occasionally, feed.

Then, the "pop."

It did not move. It could not move.

But it began to dream again.

And the dreams were different.

Things were changing. Internally, there were things to do.

Deep, deep inside itself, it still held all the sex cells collected from all the mating during that torrid phase of its youth.

It sifted through them, dreaming, somehow, of the feeding, of all those years of feeding while it was quiescent. The kinds of things it fed upon. The types. Their sizes. Their activity. Their composition.

Their resistance.

As it dreamt these things, without waking, without conscious thoughts, its body conducted evaluations, weighed options, chose strategies.

It was time. Time to choose from those cells, time to choose which ones to combine with its own.

These were not conscious thoughts. These were biochemical processes. Processes running deep inside its body. Processes driven by the tidal sensations, influenced by hormonal patterns , stress levels, consistency of feeding. All resulting in a blend of hormones circulating through its tissues, designating some gametes rather than others.

Choices were made as it continued to dream.

# ∎DAY 3: 15:35
## OBSERVING THE PACK

Elke returned to her conference room to find John chatting with George's projection. John was fascinated by xenobiology and never missed an opportunity to talk with George about his latest findings.

"So, you've found the Eden equivalent of the Krebs cycle?"

George's eyes lit up. "No, now we've found all five of them! Biology, ultimately, is chemistry, right? Any life form anywhere is going to need to process sugars to release energy, right? You'd expect Eden life to use something very much like the Krebs cycle, so that's not a surprise. What's really interesting, even though it's not entirely surprising, is that each of the five super-kingdoms has its own version of the Krebs cycle…"

They both looked up as Elke was followed by Nikko, Dieter, and Guido. As they took their seats, John asked, "did something happen?"

Elke smiled. "Well, John, you need to pay more attention to your messages. Ronnie reported they may have found the pack!"

John blushed slightly. "Oh! Great! Sorry…I wasn't opening messages that weren't marked urgent. George was catching me up on their latest research!"

Elke kept smiling as Rajiv and Bhavia entered. "I'm glad you were enjoying yourselves."

As the stragglers sat, Elke looked up. "Ronnie, what have you found?"

Ronnie's voice barely betrayed any exertion as she narrated from the trail.

"Our drones followed the trail from the clearing where they engaged that smaller pack to the clearing up ahead."

The map display zoomed in on a highlighted clearing ahead of the team.

"Our Falcon carried us here, and we've positioned a drone above them. High above them, actually; we didn't want to spook them. Right now, all we can see is the movement of large creatures. We're about to zoom in and thought we should share the imagery with you."

Elke looked around the room, then said, "proceed!"

They could see on the map where the team reached a slightly widened part of the trail not too far from the clearing. The secmeds took defensive positions around the group. The map expanded and the resolution of the highlighted area improved to reveal a clearing very similar to the one where they'd found the surveyor's bodies.

As everyone in the conference room leaned in and the resolution cleared, they could see ten large creatures. Their vertically oriented mouths ended in bright red beaks with yellow markings. Their bodies were covered with brown, frilled, diamond-shaped appendages like they'd found on the bodies of the other pack, with brightly colored frills about their necks that periodically flared out. Their powerfully built hind legs had two articulations compared to human single knees, enabling an odd sitting position; their round, flat feet pressed against each other with seven stubby, clawed, flared toes and their short, stout tail extending horizontally.

Most sat in groups of two or three. The animals held the strong middle digits of their forepaws up while using the delicate, opposable digits on either side of their forepaws to examine each other's bodies. Occasionally, the creatures would use the delicate digits to pull something out and put it in their mouths or hold it while pressing their beaks into their partner's skin and gently biting it away.

Other individuals worked their way around the periphery of the clearing, occasionally standing to reach up the rock faces, stretching out their forepaws against the rocks. Elke and the others watched one use the strong middle digits of its forepaws to pull something from the wall. It sat, holding the object between the forepaws, and used its beak to bite the top from it. They saw a small bulge progress from the beak to the throat mill, then watched the muscular contractions of the mill grind the bulge before swallowing.

As they observed, another creature from the pack searched the scrub growing in the corner. It found a long branch, grasped it with its forepaws, and used its beak to sever the branch from its roots. The animal sat back on its haunches and used the delicate digits to pull the green growths from the branch; its beak severed twigs from the branch until it had a long, stout length with a forked end. It waddled awkwardly, holding the branch to a rock face, then reached up and used the branch to pry an object from the wall. As the object came loose and fell, it dropped the branch and caught the object. The creature then sat, holding the object, and began to eat said object as its compatriot was doing.

"This is amazing," George whispered. "Grooming behavior. Tool use! We haven't seen anything like this among any other Eden species!"

"This is comparable to primate behavior on Earth!" Deirdre added in amazement.

As they continued watching, Elke asked, "what does this tell us about the pack?"

"Well," George mused, "it tells us that these creatures are, probably, about as intelligent as an Earth ape. Maybe more, maybe less, time will tell. They cooperate with each other, which strongly suggests some ability to communicate. Some ability to…remember past events and plan for their future." He paused again, then added, "I'm not sure what else you might be asking."

Elke leaned back in her chair. "*I'm* not sure what I'm asking. Now that we've found them, we need to decide what actions, if any, we must take. We planned this expedition with the expectation of protecting our people from a threat. Then we decided the attack might have been more of a territorial dispute than deliberate predation. Now, we're seeing primate level intelligence. How does that inform our decision making?"

The creatures continued to groom each other and search the rock walls. After a few minutes, Bhavia swore and stood.

"There! Right there. Can you zoom in on what they're eating?"

Elke and the others startled slightly at Bhavia's sudden emotion. Elke and George exchanged a look. Elke stood, held her hands together over one of the feeding creatures, and pulled her hands apart. As she did so, the image enlarged until they could see that the object the creature was holding. It was about the size of a human torso, with green fronds on either side, and a yellowish, green scaly exterior.

Bhavia sank into his chair. "I don't fucking believe it…That right there, that's why they attacked the survey team. It's a pineapple."

Both the team and the conference room were silent, tensely waiting for an explanation.

"Would you care to elaborate?" Elke asked, almost sounding impatient.

"The dead surveyors…it turns out they were smugglers. I discovered this while examining the unidentified shards from the attack site. The shards were from an unsanctioned container used to transport a…well *that* thing there. I pulled in the two surviving survey teams, and we had a chat."

Bhavia looked somberly from Nikko to Rajiv to Dieter. "Nikko, there's a guy on your team, one of the gondola operators, named Pete, who apparently was friends with one of the dead surveyors. They had a few drinks, and the surveyor told Pete about these pretty plants growing out of the walls of these clearings. Called them 'pineapples' because they look a bit like Earth's pineapples. I haven't seen one personally, but that beastie's snack sure fits the description.

Anyway, Pete came up with the idea to sell them. Dieter, they found one of your people that made sample containers for the xenobiology teams; Pete convinced him to make a few extra. Rajiv, we apparently don't have any screening process for returning work crews. They realized that, if they just put pineapples into these containers and tucked them inside their kits, nobody would notice. They did some experimenting and figured out how to keep them alive. Apparently they're popular, because the smugglers sold enough of them to bring in two other survey teams. I don't know how many of these things are growing in colonists' homes, but it's more than a few."

John shook his head. "A pineapple! An Eden plant!"

Nikko had a horrified, quizzical look. "I've seen these things! I…I've seen them around the settlement! I don't know much about plants, so I never paid any attention. I just assumed it was something from Earth!"

Guido leaned forward and said, "good work, Bhavia."

Elke nodded, frowning. "Yes, excellent work. Thank you."

George almost seemed sad rather than upset. "I certainly haven't seen one of these things, but then again I've been aboard the *Calypso* for quite a while!" After a moment, he continued, "so you're suggesting that the pack came across the survey team harvesting some pineapples? That they saw this as a threat to their resources and attacked the surveyors to keep the team from taking the pineapples?"

Bhavia shrugged. "Seems that way to me. We've had people work throughout these formations without any incidents. It's only when a pack found them taking pineapples that we had an attack. I'm guessing that, when you analyze the gut samples from that other pack they killed, you'll find the animals were eating pineapples."

George leaned back, fingers meshed behind his head, looking upward. "It makes sense…" He sat back up, absentmindedly tapping the table as he made his points.

"Okay, let's posit that these creatures are territorial, and they defend these clearings. We don't know how common these pineapple things are, but the overall ecological productivity of the formations west of the mountains is fairly low. There's not much to eat, and these pack creatures are fairly large. They need more food than they're going to find in these formations. So, I'm guessing these creatures spend most of their time in the mountains, feeding on more abundant food sources, but come down into these clearings to supplement their diets with these pineapples. Maybe they find the pineapples really tasty, or they offer some nutritional value that's in short supply in the mountains? I don't know; we'll need to figure that out. Either way, though, it would help us understand why they'd defend pineapple bearing territories. And it would explain why they didn't feed on the surveyors. They're herbivores, so they're not interested in eating them, just stopping them from taking the pineapples, just like they stop other packs. Yes, that follows."

George paused, then continued. "This observation also suggests that we may not need to take any action against these creatures. They only attacked the surveyors when the surveyors interfered with their food supply. And when they did, the team wasn't in their environmental suits, so I don't think they'll attack other survey teams. I can't say that for sure, of course, and I'd recommend we escort survey teams to this area with armed secmeds. But I doubt we'll have any more incidents."

Elke looked around the room, eyebrows raised. "People? Thoughts?"

Guido shrugged. "If these were humans, then that's how I'd expect them to behave. But they're not human. We can't really *know* what they'll do."

Bhavia held up a hand. "I agree with Guido. But…should we kill this particular pack anyway? They have attacked and killed humans. It may not matter that they weren't in their environmental suits."

Elke saw George and Deirdre exchange a panicked look. Before George could interject, she asked "do we have enough secmeds to escort survey teams for a while?"

"That depends on how frequently Rajiv needs to survey those rocks," Bhavia replied.

Rajiv sighed. "Well, we could think about this another way. The reason we've been surveying those rocks is that we're planning more agricultural domes, and we're trying to balance proximity to the settlement versus blasting zones. We haven't started considering environmental impacts. But, if we blast and build there, we'll be removing those clearings.

Unfortunately, once we decide to build a surface settlement, well, we can't build anything without impacting something. The domes we've built displaced a lot of desert creatures. But we're really doing our best to minimize that effect."

He waved his hand towards the projection of the clearing.

"We presumed these formations were as biologically sparse as the surrounding desert. Now, we're discovering there are unique life forms in what seems to be a more bounded environment. Of course, we have contingency plans, other options to place the agricultural domes if removing these formations would prove infeasible. We have plenty of room to the north, west, and south. If we stop surveying that area, then there's no need to guard survey teams."

George said, "I applaud that direction."

Elke looked around the room. "Anyone else?"

No one spoke but everyone nodded in solidarity.

"Well, I applaud that as well." Elke straightened in her chair.

"Ronnie, thank you, and thank you to the team. No need for further action on your part. Make your way to a clearing so a Falcon can get you to your EAGLE."

"Thank you, Governor!"

Elke turned to Nikki and asked, "what's next? Do we get them home, or do they have another assignment? I'd sure like to get them a night or two in their own beds. They've earned it!"

Nikko nodded and turned to Dieter while Elke turned to Bhavia. "How do we find out where these pineapples are?"

Bhavia drummed his fingers on the table angrily. "I need to find this 'Pete' character. He's the source of…"

"What's that?" Guido stood abruptly, pointing at the display.

As they watched, a creature like the ones in the clearing rapidly approached the trail.

Elke stood in sudden alarm.

"Ronnie! Ronnie, one of the things is closing in on your position. From the north!"

Ronnie unslung her rifle and faced north.

"Pablo! Badru! Get ready! Sasha, lead the party back, away from the pack! Activate your camouflage! NOW!"

As Sasha led the team along the trail, Ronnie, Badru, and Pablo followed, facing north to keep watch.

"See anything?"

"Not yet!"

Once the team's camouflage activated, they could no longer be seen. Instead, the map marked each team member's position with a dot color coded to their role. Elke and her staff watched the creature continue southward.

"It's still heading your way. Looks to be about…100 m from you. It seems to be patrolling the clearing rather than tracking you. Keep backing away and let's see what happens when it crosses your trail."

"Very good, We'll look for a defensible position. Be advised," Ronnie spoke with urgency, "we've activated our camouflage, which should help, but it's draining our packs."

"Ronnie, we can't know how it will react to finding you. If it senses you, it might not care. Or it might attack in defense of its territory. We just can't know!"

"Understood."

"Your Falcon is already on its way to ferry you to the EAGLE." Elke looked at Nikko. "Please see whether we can send another Falcon rather than rely on this one to return for a second trip."

Elke held her hands over the display and brought them together slightly in order to expand their field of view.

"Looks like the nearest extraction point is the last clearing you passed through. I was hoping there might be something closer, but that's your best option."

Ronnie paused. "Agreed…We'll remain still until it crosses the trail. I don't want any noise or motion giving away our position."

The tension in the room continued to rise as the creature approached the path.

"I can see it! Everyone, be *still*!"

The creature nimbly made its way over the rough terrain, pausing periodically to raise its head and scan the area. As it reached the trail, it paused and lowered its head to the dirt. It turned one way, then the other, taking a few steps along the trail, raising and lowering its head. It sat down, looking towards the clearing and the rest of the pack.

After a few moments, it stomped towards the clearing at an aggressive pace.

"Ronnie? It's moving away from you, but I don't like it. I'd feel better if you and the team made your way back to that first clearing ASAP."

"Acknowledged! Sasha, lead the way. As quickly as you can!"

Elke turned to Nikko. "I want that Falcon waiting for them when they get there!"

The creature reached the clearing and raised different combinations around its neck. After a few moments, it turned back towards the trail, followed by six of the other pack members.

"Ronnie! There are seven, I repeat, seven pack members heading your way!"

"How far away is our Falcon?!"

Elke glanced at Nikko, who tapped his wrist computer before saying, "it'll get to the clearing before you do!"

After a moment, an exhausted sounding Ronnie yelled, "Sasha deactivate your camouflage and go as fast as you can. When you get there, put the team on the Falcon and get them in the air. We'll hold a perimeter until it returns."

"I have a second Falcon en route!" Nikko reassured her. "Should get there minutes after the first one!"

"Acknowledged!"

Elke looked at the team and then the pack making its way along the trail.

"Ronnie, I think you'll get to the clearing before the pack, but I'm not sure you'll be able to load both Falcons before they get there."

Ronnie, clearly out of breath, said, "we'll take up a defensive position and do our best."

As Elke, Nikko, and the others watched, a Falcon entered the image and descended to the clearing. A few moments later, everyone except the secmeds boarded. The Falcon lifted off and left the image.

The four secmeds moved to the center of the clearing. Two faced the trail. The other two scanned the rest of the clearing.

The pack neared the clearing, then stopped. The lead creature turned and flashed the feathery appendages around its neck as the other creatures watched. Occasionally, one of the others raised its appendages as well. After a few minutes, two of the creatures began moving right and two more left as the remaining three approached the secmeds' position from the trail.

"Amazing!" George couldn't help himself. "That's simply amazing!"

John leaned forward to look past George. "But, Elke, we have to warn them!"

Elke, as calmly as she could, said, "Ronnie, they've split up. There are two animals flanking you from the north, two more from the south, and three about to enter the clearing the same way you did."

Ronnie swore quietly as she scanned the area, then pointed up a gentle slope.

"We need to climb up here and get away from the trail. If we're quiet and still, they should pass us by. But have your weapons ready!"

The secmeds scrambled onto the rocks, taking turns monitoring the trail and the map to see how close the creatures were. After about 100 m, the climb became more challenging.

"Here's where we make our stand. Everyone, be as still as you can!"

As they all watched, the first of the creatures came into their field of view. Two more flanked it as the thing periodically lowered its head to inspect the trail. As the first approached, they could see two more entering the clearing from the north, following another trail that would intersect the one they'd climbed away from a few meters to the west. Ronnie, consulting their map, saw that two more entered to the south, behind the rock formation they'd climbed.

The team was now surrounded.

Intellectually, Ronnie knew the creatures could not hear her headset radio, but she still winced when the incoming Falcon pilot hailed her to let her know he was approaching.

Quietly, she responded. "The creatures are about to pass us. We're not in a position to board. Recommend you hover nearby and be ready, on my signal, to descend near our position."

"Copy."

As they watched with bated breath, the lead creature approached from their right to reach where they'd left the trail. It lowered its head to the ground, then moved to its left and right, inspecting the sides of the trail and nearby terrain.

The team held their breath.

The creature paused. The extensions on its neck flashed with new colors. The rest of the pack froze, as if waiting for instructions.

Ronnie moved her finger onto the trigger of her weapon.

Finally, the leader of the pack turned away and continued along the trail, passing them by. As they watched, the seven creatures rendezvoused a few meters to their left, then continued west. When the creatures left their field of vision, Ronnie switched back to the map on her heads-up display. She watched the creatures leave the clearing, then make their way along the trail to the next one.

"Falcon! Falcon, we're ready for pickup!"

# DAY 3: 22:40
## PETE MEETS PRAKASH

Pete sat at the end of the bar, fascinated by the crowd. People tweaked their bets as the pineapple's three tendrils drew struggling crickets to their doom; those who lost exchanged insults with each other. Fernando tried to keep up with drink orders as his daughter prepared to drop the next round of crickets on to the pineapple's scarlet fronds.

The place was not nearly at capacity, but the restaurant definitely had a bigger crowd than Pete had ever seen before. He got the feeling most of the bar denizens were looking for someplace to celebrate peak alignment, but failed to make a reservation at any of the big parties and so wound up here. Pete shook his head. He didn't understand why anyone would get excited about the alignment.

*Some people will find any excuse to party!*

Well, whatever brought them here, they were enjoying the pineapple. Pete was very pleased with its popularity. He started wondering whether he could sell Fernando another pineapple before disappearing.

He sipped his drink and checked his wrist computer.

*Ugh, that fucker's late. Again!*

He needed to talk to Prakash about replacing the containers lost when those damn fools got themselves killed. He also needed to talk about replacing the dead team too, just for appearances. Not that he really cared; he'd made his money and he'd be leaving soon aboard the *Mother Lode*. But Prakash didn't need to know that.

Pete lifted his glass to take another sip when he spotted Prakash exiting the transportation hub of the base station. Must have gone home after his shift.

"Finally!" Pete threw back the rest of his drink, grimaced, and raised his hand for another. Prakash was a bore to talk to; this wouldn't be a fun meeting.

As he walked in, Pete stood and raised his eyebrows, then pointed to a quiet table in the corner. He went to the table as Prakash stopped at the bar to order a drink. Pete's face darkened with a scowl. Prakash was behaving oddly, even for Prakash, and that was saying something. He kept pausing, looking over his shoulder.

*Damn idiot, gonna get us caught looking that guilty.*

The crowd erupted. He checked his wrist computer. Yep, alignment was peaking. *Lousy timing.* It took an extra long time for Prakash to get the bartender's attention. Eventually, he placed his order, got his drink, and walked over, glancing right and left.

"Do you think you could behave more suspiciously? Maybe carry a sign?"

Prakash snorted. "Easy for you to say. Aren't you worried?"

"About what?"

Prakash stared at him. "Don't you know? Our…'friends' were rounded up."

Pete stared back, then looked down and swore.

*So that's why I couldn't find them?! Damn it, those assholes getting caught, it was going SO well! Just a few more days! I just needed a few more days!*

Pete had arrived at Eden a few years before. He needed to make a quick exit from one of the older colonies. A deal went south and some of his partners weren't very happy about it. Fortunately, a colony ship was prepared to leave for Eden, just in time for him to disappear.

Through the crossing, bored silly, he became increasingly excited about the prospects of Eden, about the chance to walk the surface of a green planet, to breathe real air. But, as their ship neared Eden, they heard about the kraken. They were informed they'd be living under domes. That all citizens were required to develop and regularly demonstrate weapons proficiency in case another predator threatened the colony.

Pete had *no* interest in being a soldier or training like one, and if he was going to live under a dome, he might as well be enjoying the amenities of a more established colony! He most definitely did *not* sign up for battling alien monsters!

Not much he could do about it, though. He arrived, and, per his PIP agreement, he enrolled in the local DSSA to earn his "useful" degree. The degree turned out to be more useful than he envisioned. It got him a job in gondola operations that would keep him fed until he became eligible for another PIP migration. More importantly, he earned a little extra through his access to the unofficial storage spaces of the gondolas.

Pete had never dabbled in contraband before, so it was an eye-opening experience. There was a guy in another operational role on the orbiting platform that was particularly talented when it came to moonshine. And Pete discovered he was particularly talented at finding customers. They made a tidy profit together. That got Pete thinking; his job gave him plenty of time to think.

He wanted something more exotic!

Fortunately, the support personnel talked about their jobs. A lot. Most of the line jobs weren't particularly demanding, so everyone moved around to avoid boredom. That meant people expected to talk about what *they* did all day in exchange for hearing about what *he* did all day. That included a couple of surveyors. After a few drinks, they told Pete about seeing a particularly interesting plant that reminded one of the surveyors of something very few outer colonists had ever seen.

He called them "pineapples."

Meanwhile, another operator told Pete about the specimen containers they used. He'd damaged one and took it to the fabrication department for repair. The fabricator, Prakash, offered to repair it. But, to the guy's outrage, Prakash wanted compensation for not reporting the damage.

That's when things clicked for Pete. A beautiful ornamental plant would entice new colonists eager to decorate their homes with a touch of Eden. A corrupt fabricator could make the specimen containers to smuggle them in. It was perfect!

It wouldn't be easy, of course. And he had to be careful. As the things proliferated, Pete figured the wrong people would eventually get wind of it and shut him down.

He needed to start slowly and carefully, and he needed an exit strategy.

It wasn't hard to find the next emigration opportunity: the *Mother Lode*. He applied, creatively, for another PIP migration and was approved. That gave him a timeline, a few months for the ship to arrive, unload the next round of colonists, and get reconfigured with outbound freight and space for aspiring young pippers like himself. Pete figured he had about a year, if he played his cards right, to build a nice cache before boarding. That bank, invested before leaving, would compound nicely during a roughly fifteen year crossing. He'd never have to work again!

He had approached Prakash carefully. This was the first questionable step he'd taken. After all, if Prakash reported him, the whole thing would be over before it began. Prakash, fortunately, had expensive tastes, weak ethics, and even worse, no strategic thinking. He agreed to make a few extra containers and looked forward to taking over the operation after Pete left.

It took a little time to find empty spaces to experiment with the pineapples. They lost a bunch figuring out how to keep them alive. Then he had to find places to stash the dead ones. One of the operations people warned him they monitored refuse for Eden proteins to guard against kraken infections, so he couldn't just discard them. When he ran out of room for the dead ones and started having to smuggle them back out, he almost gave up.

Then, a breakthrough. After seemingly endless experiments with lighting, soil conditions, watering, and so forth, it turned out they really weren't that picky. All the plants needed were a little soil around their twin roots, a little light, and some food. That was the big surprise; they needed *food*. He remembered staring at one that wasn't dying, trying to figure out why, and seeing a fly light on the red petals. Once he started feeding them, he found he didn't need to water them at all!

*These things are even cooler than I hoped,* Pete remembered thinking. They were going to make him rich, so rich before he left! They started slowly. He managed to find the right kind of initial customers, people he could trust to limit his exposure. They told a few friends who bought pineapples, and then those friends told a few friends. The business grew, steadily and relentlessly. Now that his emigration was finally looming, he'd become bolder. He sold less discriminately. He knew the things were popping up all over the colony, but he didn't care. He was about to leave, after all!

*Now those two idiots got themselves killed?!* Pete heard they'd stripped.

*Why the hell would they do that? Weren't they worried about these kraken things everybody kept talking about?*

*Whatever...Doesn't matter.*

And it didn't matter that security picked up the other survey teams.

Pete worked with Prakash, and Prakash worked with the two dead idiots. The dead idiots worked with the other survey teams. He'd never met them. They knew his first name, probably, but would they be able to help identify him?

*Probably not...I wasn't that indiscriminate. But...*

Pete glared at his present company. Prakash was another matter. But, since Prakash was eager to buy his interest in the operation, he figured Prakash would keep his mouth shut.

Yes, things were blowing up sooner than expected, but, in just a few days, the *Mother Lode* would be leaving for a fourteen year long crossing. If he played his cards right, Pete would be on a deep space transport, accelerating beyond communication range, before anybody figured out who he was. And then he'd have a couple of years to figure out what to do when they decelerated enough to restore communications.

*As if anyone will still care after fourteen years!*

# ▪DAY 3: 23:57

## HUNGER

*Darkness…*

*Movement…*

Slowly, so slowly, it became aware of surrounding movement.

Stretching, it experienced something new, an urgency. A hunger.

It was *hungry*!

It reached forward, claws outstretched, until it met resistance. It pressed its talons into the resistance and pulled. It pulled and it shredded and it tore into the resistance. It pulled itself through the openings created by its claws, pressing the claws of its hindlimbs into the tissues surrounding it, seeking purchase to push forward as its forelimbs tore and pulled.

Slowly, then faster, then faster still, it extended its forelimbs, shredding its way through layer after layer of tissue, pulling and pushing, until, finally, there was no resistance. Instead, there was light. Light, and air.

It pulled and it pressed and it pushed, extending its beak out of the body of its parent. It unfolded its sensory cluster, eyes exposed to light for the very first time, gradually, slowly, making sense of what it saw. Its other sensors began to function. It could smell the body of its parent, it could sense the electromagnetic signatures of its siblings as they emerged. It could hear the soft rustling of their bodies as they emerged, as they spread their winged mid limbs.

It sensed that some of its siblings were special, more special than the others. It loved those siblings, more than it loved itself. It would die for those siblings. Nothing was more important than those siblings.

As it stretched, as it used its forelimbs to clean itself, its hunger returned. As its hunger returned, it knew what it needed to do first. It stretched, arched its back, and, from deep within itself, a long, sharp tool emerged from between its hindlimbs. It stretched out its wings, then stretched out the digits of its forelimbs and hindlimbs, deeply grasping the flesh of its parent.

Suddenly, instinctively, it thrust the tool from between its hindlimbs into the flesh of its parent, pressing itself into the flesh. It felt an exquisite pleasure from deep within itself as something warm pulsed and pumped out of its body, through the tool, and into the flesh of its parent.

As it recovered, as it retraced the tool from its parent's body back into its own body, it could see the others doing the same. Without understanding why, it grasped its parent's body and squeezed, kneading the flesh, working the venom through the meat. It did not know why it kneaded the flesh, nor did it know how it knew the flesh was ready.

But it did know that it was *hungry*.

It jabbed its beak into the flesh near where it had thrust its tool. It extended its tongues through the tip of its beak into the liquifying flesh, tasting the viscous, indescribably delicious liquid, mixing it, smoothing its texture as it sucked, satisfying its hunger.

As it fed, it began to grow.

# PART 2:
# EMERGENCE

# ▪ DAY 4: 01:37
## TSUNAMI

Katy's eyes snapped open. She couldn't see very much. It was still quite dark. For a moment, she struggled to interpret what little she could see.

*That glow…what was that glow?*

It came back to her slowly. She wasn't in her quarters. She was on a sleeping pad aboard an EAGLE. Her EAGLE was in a clearing on a beach east of the rainforest near a river delta. She was surrounded by sleeping pads. Sleeping pads that were occupied by slumbering xenobiologists on a beach in the middle of the night.

But why was she awake?

Katy glanced at her wrist computer and winced at the time. *Much, much too early.*

She'd set an alarm. There was going to be a quake. And a tsunami.

She needed to be ready. They all need to be ready.

But the models projected the quake would happen between 03:00 to 04:00; the alarm wasn't supposed to go off for another hour or so.

*Sigh.*

She must just be anxious. *No matter.*

Katy rolled over onto her left side and closed her eyes. She smiled as she thought about her husband and their little girl. Sighing again, she drifted back to sleep.

The EAGLE shook briefly. Violently, but briefly.

She sat up. This time, she wasn't the only one to wake. She could hear others stirring, grumbling, muttering. She slid her feet into her shoes and started to stand.

The EAGLE shook again. She lost her balance and flopped back onto her sleeping pad, *hard*. The EAGLE kept shaking.

"Lights! 50%!!"

The lights came on. Katy stood, cautiously, and held onto what she could when she could as she made her way to the cockpit.

"Anyone not on board?!"

The EAGLE stopped shaking.

She froze, mid step, and breathed a deep sigh of relief. Perhaps it was over.

She reached the cockpit, took her seat, and started the EAGLE's engines. *Just in case…*

Her wrist computer vibrated. She tapped it, and a series of figures corresponding to the members of the expedition appeared. Two were highlighted. Two xenobiologists were not on board.

*God damn it. They'd better be close by!*

She thought she'd been sufficiently clear about not leaving the EAGLE after midnight.

*And why the hell are they out there without a secmed? Probably because they knew a secmed wouldn't have let them go! Idiots better at least be armed…*

As she focused on her instruments, she tapped one of the figures. The display disappeared.

"Yes?"

She continued to focus on the EAGLE's instrumentation and control panel. "You two ok?"

"Yes…yes. A bit shaken, that's all. Knocked us off our feet. But it seems to be over now. We're running a transect to see…"

The EAGLE shook violently! Katy held onto the arms of the pilot's seat. She could hear exclamations behind her. Something crashed to the floor.

"Get back here. NOW. Abandon your transect and get back here RIGHT NOW. I think I need to lift off!"

"But the quake isn't due for hours!"

She grunted. "Eden's on her own schedule. For the last time, get back here. I'm not putting everybody else at risk waiting for you. NOW!!"

The shaking continued. She tapped her wrist computer to open a channel to the planetology lab and check the latest modeling results. She stared at the display.

She spoke urgently to her wayward scientists.

"This is it! *This* is the quake! The epicenter is only 200 km offshore! The tsunami will be here in fifteen minutes. You have twelve minutes to get your asses back before I have to take off! MOVE IT!"

The shaking stopped.

"Did you hear me? I'm not risking everyone else because you went for an unauthorized stroll! MOVE!!!"

"We're moving!"

Katy continued her pre-flight routine. She was relieved to see the diving skiff was still aboard. She'd insisted, before lights out, that the skiff be secured as she was worried someone would try to redeploy it.

*Kids. It's like dealing with kids…*

Without looking up, she yelled, "everybody! Prepare yourself for emergency liftoff!"

"Can we launch some drones?" She heard one of the operational people shout. "They'll want some video of the tsunami coming in!"

Katy paused. He was right; they'd want the video. She glanced at the model to see how close the tsunami was getting, and then how close the wayward xenobiologists were.

"In nine minutes, I'm lifting off. You tell me!"

She heard feet running for the lift. She continued to prepare for take-off. She heard more movement behind her as people put things away and strapped themselves into their seats.

The door opened below. *Must be the scientists…*

"Lights! 100%!"

The ship brightened. The EAGLE started shaking again, not as intensely, and not as long. But it was unnerving nonetheless.

"Anyone not ready for liftoff?" Katy really hoped no one responded; they were lifting off whether her team was ready or not.

She checked her manifest one final time. Everyone was aboard.

Katy looked nervously through the cockpit panels. The alignment peaked a few hours before, but the four moons were still close enough for their reflected light to thoroughly illuminate the beach.

The tide had been exceptionally high, pulled by the moons. There'd only been 100 m or so of beach between her EAGLE and the water. Now, the water was receding, quickly.

*That's too quick…Oh god…*

"The door needs to close NOW!"

A voice responded, "GO!"

Katy lifted the door on the model on her instrument panel. She heard the door closing, then saw the status light.

"If you're not strapped in, hold on to something!"

She felt the engines rumble as the EAGLE lifted vertically. Katy wiped the nervous sweat from her forehead and glanced out the panel again. She let out an audible gasp. As the water receded, she could see, in the distance, a black wall of water rushing towards them. Statistics flashed through her mind.

*800 km/hr. Tsunamis move at 800 km/hr.*

She tried to estimate the height of the tsunami, but she didn't dare lose focus on flying her EAGLE.

The wall of water continued rushing towards them.

*Are we high enough? Are we high enough??*

She thought they were high enough.

Drowned out by the roar of the engines, Katy watched the roaring water rush underneath her ship. They made it above the wave.

She exhaled rather loudly. She hadn't realized she was holding her breath.

Keeping the EAGLE faced towards the incoming tsunami, Katy flew backward, over the trees, taking care to rise as they flew to ensure she cleared their tallest branches.

"Did you launch the drones?"

"Yes! We're getting amazing images!"

She eased to a hover. She didn't think the tsunami would reach this far, nor reach this high, but she remained on alert, ready to move as needed.

The wall of water rushed up the beach. The others unbuckled, moving forward to watch the tsunami as it crashed through the coastal rainforest. It was breathtaking.

The hand of God was wiping the beach clean.

As they watched in awe, the water continued to rise, then gradually receded, taking with it everything it could, trading stranded sea life for trees.

They continued to hover; then, with a deep sigh, Katy moved the EAGLE gently forward to light on the beach. Katy wiped the water from her lips, a mixture of sweat and tears. Her instruments told her they were precisely where they were before take-off.

But it might as well have been another world.

# ▪ DAY 4: 06:00
## DANGER

The alarm went off.

He shot out his arm to tap it before it woke her up. Then he remembered she wasn't there.

He sighed. She had a twelve hour shift at the hospital today, so she would have left by now. Between her schedule and his piloting schedule, they didn't see enough of each other.

He stared upwards in the dark for a moment, then threw the covers aside and swung his feet over the side of the bed. He sat up, slowly rubbing his face. When he couldn't ignore his bladder any longer, he reached for his wrist computer, put it on, stood and said "lights! 25%."

He stiffly shuffled to the lavatory. As he relieved himself, he thought about his day. He washed his hands, then padded towards the kitchen to start breakfast.

*Coffee first…*

"Lights! 75%!"

He was on autopilot.

*Fill the kettle, set it to boil, spoon the coffee, open a cupboard for a mug.*

He paused, just about to place his mug on the counter. He glanced around their quarters. Something wasn't quite right.

"Lights! 100%!"

He shrugged. *Too bright for this early.* "Lights, 50%…"

That was better. He looked to the corner.

"Ah, damn it!"

Her pineapple was sagging, like it had somehow deflated. The petals of the blossom and the leaves were drooping, and nothing was as brightly col- ored as it had been last night.

*Weird…*

His shoulders sagged. She was *not* going to be happy. She loved that stupid thing! At least it wasn't his fault. Not that he knew of, anyway. She hadn't asked him to do anything to take care of it. At least, not that he could remember.

The kettle was ready. He poured the boiling water through the ground coffee, watching it drip through.

*Eggs.* He would love some eggs. He glanced at his wrist computer. He had time. He started thinking through the steps for preparing some eggs and bacon and…

He slouched further. *Too much work.* He'd just have cereal: a nice, boring, tasteless, whole grain, high fiber cereal. That was the smart thing to do, the healthy thing. After all, she wanted him to take better care of himself.

He reached back into the cupboard for a bowl, then the drawer for a spoon, then padded into the pantry to consider his options. He made his decisions and sat at the counter to enjoy his breakfast. As he chewed, he glanced at the pineapple in the corner again. He froze mid spoonful.

*Is it…moving?*

# ■ DAY 4: 06:10
## POST ALIGNMENT DIVE

Deirdre looked east as the last glories of dawn faded against the azure sky. It looked so beautiful, so serene. Such a contrast from the tsunami devastation surrounding her on the beach.

She could see the *Calypso* anchored offshore. Out there, George was preparing for a dive to observe how the tsunami impacted the photic zone. She knew he was also hoping to discover new species of squirts as they emerged from the deep. Meanwhile, her team gathered on the beach and prepared to enter the shallows. They wouldn't go deep enough to need secmeds, but they launched drones to patrol at one, two, and three kilometers each.

As the water rose about their legs, the gentle rolling of the surf began to slow their strides. As the water reached their waists, their environmental suits added air for buoyancy, and they attached swim fins to their boots. Then, checking to ensure everyone was ready, Deirdre leaned forward, lowered her face into the water, and let the sea take her weight as her team followed suit. As they continued forward, they saw rock outcroppings encrusted with life, as any rocky reef on the planet. On Eden, as on Earth, life flourished where light penetrated. Every stable surface was a riot of color and texture as the Eden equivalents of Earth's sponges, polyps, and the like filtered nutrients from the surrounding water and gathered solar energy through phytochemicals.

Entering the deeper water, the shapes attached to the rocks became more elaborate. They knew, from previous expeditions, that these were colonies of smaller organisms built on the shells of their predecessors, competing for stability and light. But they could also see that many of them were broken by the passage of the tsunami. Closer inspection of the larger colonies revealed where they had once broken and resumed growth after previous catastrophic events.

The free-swimming life forms seemed none the worse for wear. The tsunami abandoned life forms all across the beach, some from much deeper water than this. But Deirdre would never have guessed that swimming through here. She wondered whether these creatures had been carried by the tsunami and then returned, or had found shelter among the rocks.

As they passed 27 m, a drone picked up something large. It was in very deep water, more than a kilometer away. It appeared to be swimming parallel to the shore rather than heading towards them. Consulting her heads-up display, Deirdre said, "I think we should consider turning back. We could go another, oh, 20 m, but I'm feeling conservative. Thoughts?"

"Disappointing that we haven't seen any squirts," one diver lamented. "Perhaps George and his team will have better luck. Otherwise, I think we've seen what we've come to see. The tsunami clearly tore up the more elaborate structures and you can see where they have, and haven't, recovered."

In the absence of objections, Deirdre turned back and motioned the others to follow. As they swam up the slope, a debate ensued.

"I'm telling you," one diver said, "this is why we haven't found anything equivalent to hard corals. Coral reefs on Earth took a decade to recover from a tsunami. Tsunamis happen too often here to support the evolution of a coral equivalent!"

"That's assuming Eden corals would be as slow growing as Earth corals," another diver countered. "Coral reefs on Earth are or at least were among the most stable environments on the planet. Immense water volume stabilized temperature and water chemistry. Absolutely essential marine ecosystems that, after centuries of environmental effort, are finally recovering! There's no reason something roughly equivalent couldn't evolve here with a growth rate enabling recovery!"

"Then why haven't we found any?"

"We've only explored, what, 20% of the planet's equatorial photic zone? Who's to say there aren't coral reef like structures out there?"

"I've heard you two go on and on about this so many times I swear I could repeat it word for word," Deirdre groaned. "Could we, please, talk about something else, or not at all? Look at the pretty fish!"

"It's *not* a fish…"

"I know that…" she muttered.

After a few silent, sullen minutes, one of their patrol drones alerted. The large subject from the deep was cruising towards them now, fast enough to trigger an alarm from their drone.

"We've been in these waters more times than I can count," Deirdre said to reassure her team, and herself. "We've never seen anything remotely threatening this close to shore. But…it might be something hoping to capitalize on the tsunami. Maybe there's easier pickings after the disruption? Maybe less cover? In any case, we don't have time to get out before it gets here. If we go back to deeper water and activate camouflage, it'll likely pass us by, but we'll need to follow a decompression schedule before surfacing. We have enough breathing gas. Does anyone have a better idea?"

The divers looked around at each other, but no one offered a suggestion.

"Alright, then, let's head back to 18 m and wait for it to pass."

They turned and swam back down the slope as the outermost drone passed monitoring responsibility to the midrange drone.

"Do we have any reason to consider this thing a threat?"

"Do we have any reason to *not* consider it a threat?"

"Fair point."

"Didn't the initial dive teams lose someone to a deep sea creature?"

"Hey!" Deirdre snapped. "Less talking, more swimming."

They continued down the slope to a particularly large outcropping at about 17 m depth.

"Let's stop here."

"Will we be able to see it pass?"

"It'll be hazy, but it should be visible, given the clarity of the water. That also means it'll be able to see us, so we'd better activate our camouflage."

"We'll be using energy…"

"Can't be helped."

Their bright yellow environmental suits suddenly matched the life encrusted rocks around them as they carefully pressed themselves downward, trusting their environmental suits to protect them from anything with spines that might be beneath them.

"Try not to move; it may be able to sense movement. It shouldn't smell us given the suits. Be quiet, and let's hope it doesn't pick up our electromagnetic signatures!"

They waited.

To their left, in the gloom, something gradually approached. It was *large*, big enough to swallow any of them whole. As it approached, they saw a massive silver body, a stout beak, three pairs of fins, and a broad, sweeping tail.

"I bet that's like the thing that attacked Sri's boat the first year we were here!"

"SHHHH!"

It slowed and its sensory cluster extended, six eyes scanning about as it moved forward. Its beak opened slowly; its tongues extended, tasting the water.

The divers remained motionless as the underwater giant searched the area.

Finally, it withdrew its tongues, slowly closed its beak, and withdrew its sensory cluster. With a few broad strokes of its tail, the Eden leviathan propelled itself forward at its previous, cruising pace. Deirdre and the others lost sight of it, but they remained motionless until their outermost drone reported it out of range.

"I told you to be *quiet*!"

"I know! I know…Sorry. But I was on that boat, and I swear that's an even *bigger* version of whatever took a bite out of the hull!"

"All the more reason to not draw attention to ourselves! No more commentary, we're heading back up, and now we have to see how much extra decompression time we need because *you* slowed it down!"

■ ■ ■

Once the rest of the team arrived and began donning their environmental suits, George finished donning his. He grabbed his fins and stepped through the airlock to the aft deck dive platform. From there, he could see an EAGLE serving as a mobile base on the shore. He heard they had an exciting flight when the quake and tsunami hit a few hours earlier than predicted. By now, he presumed, Deirdre and her team were in the water.

He was struck, as he often was, by his good fortune. For xenobiologists and biologists, nothing compared to Eden. The best biologists in known space were either here, on their way here, aspiring to be here, or were being trained here.

George turned to see Bernard working with their operations lead to configure their patrol drones.

"Drones ready?"

Bernard nodded, then said, "standard protocol. They'll circle us at one, two, and three klicks in case anything threatening appears. Not that I'm expecting anything. We've been running observation drones under the boat through the night, and they haven't picked up anything big."

"Good to hear!" George turned to see their secmed, Diego, at the edge of the dive platform in his armored environmental suits. He wouldn't enter the water until the operations lead was ready to hand Diego his weapons.

Underwater weaponry was a challenge. Few weapons performed well. A spear gun delivered explosive charges, but the charges themselves were limited by water resistance and only effective for a few meters. He also carried a bang stick for closer quarters, and a knife as a last resort.

"Alright people!" Diego shouted. "The depth here is 65 m, so, per your dive plan, swim towards shore as you descend. The depth will be decreasing as you swim. Your environmental suits will monitor and guide your descent, adjusting your breathing mix until you reach the substrate at about 40 m depth. You'll then continue towards shore. Drones will be circling you watching for anything large"

"We're here to observe in general," George said. "But I'm particularly interested in the squirts." He heard some chuckling. "Should be an amazing day!"

With that, George walked to the edge of the dive platform. He held a rail while attaching his fins; then, looking towards the horizon, he took a long stride from the platform and fell into the sea. He bobbed at the surface as the rest of the team made their entries. He put his visor into the water to see what could be seen beneath the surface. Small, silvery creatures darted about just under the surface. George knew the visibility was excellent, but, given the depth, he couldn't see the bottom yet.

As they reached 20 m, they spread out and swam steadily towards shore. George was torn between wanting to hover and wait to see if the squirts came by and racing towards shore to see whether they'd already missed them. In theory, that shouldn't be possible; the observation drones have been watching for hours. The biodiversity here, on the equator, was simply stunning. The drones and his environmental suit cameras recorded everything; a soft "ping" sounded every time something new was seen.

"Something coming!" Diego's voice was calm but clipped; the "something" had his attention.

"There's something, well, a lot of somethings, coming up from the deep. They're big."

George stopped swimming, hovering about 20 m above the bottom. "How big?"

"Human sized. Ranging upwards of 50 kilos. Wait, some are larger than that."

"Do we need to go to the surface?"

"Not clear. Whatever they are, they're on the bottom. Nothing's more than a meter above the substrate. I don't like it…" Diego sounded concerned now. "There's too many to defend against if they come up. I have a drone heading closer to get some images."

As they hovered at 5 m, their dive instruments displayed a countdown; they all stared at the images on their visors shared by Diego.

Squirts. Big squirts, bigger than any they'd seen before. An army of squirts heading their way.

The large vertebrates of Eden belonged to the two dominant super-kingdoms. The squirts, only observed during alignments, did not. Instead, they belonged to a super-kingdom otherwise only known for plant equivalents and small invertebrates. They were a mystery. Dozens of species emerged from the depths during alignments to breed on beaches all over the world.

To date, all recorded squirt species bore complex, beautiful color patterns for no discernable reasons. Squirts were also blind, just as Earth's cicadas are deaf to their own din. Their jawless mouths were round, reminiscent of an Earth's lamprey, with a snout resembling a puppy.

Their bodies were thick, and they had, depending on the species, up to six paddle-like limbs with which they pulled themselves along sandy and rocky beaches in a bizarre, serpentine motion. A long, thin, fleshy fin ran along their dorsal surface and along the top and bottom of their long, thick tail. The squirts had flaps of tissue along their side forming tubes through which they pumped water for gas exchange. On land, they drew air through those tubes, period-ically immersing themselves to keep the tubes wet. Their snouts were richly equipped with chemoreceptors and designed to detect vibrations. The squirts also had organs sensitive to the magnetic fields generated by potential prey.

The squirt's appearance during alignments was a lively debate topic. Some mated on the beach, leaving eggs behind. Others, apparently mating before leaving the water, emerged to leave eggs or live young. Either way, the squirts spent a few hours to a few days on the beach, then returned, fol-lowed by their young. There was no way to know whether they were driven out of the water to evade some awful predator; but, once on the shore, they and their young were a buffet for the hordes that came to capitalize on their presence. They were a scientific marvel, but choosing safety over science was still George's priority.

With a heavy sigh, George said, "I think we need to exit. As much as I want to watch them, the drones will relay and record. If they're anything like their smaller cousins, those rasping mouths could do some damage."

Diego agreed. He also pointed out that they hadn't been that deep for too long, so a speedy exit was a higher priority than completing their safety stops. They surfaced, taking turns detaching and handing up their fins, then climbed one by one up the ladders back onto the *Calypso*. Disappointed and wet, they gathered to watch the drone feed.

"Hey! Did you see that?" George leaned forward, clipping and replaying a bit of video for the others.

A squirt buried its snout into the sand; apparently it found something to eat.

"Can we zoom in on that?"

The drone feed focused on the creature, then zoomed in. Through the cloud of fine sand, they noticed its rasping mouth tear into something that was slowly moving away. Blood seeped into the water around them, and eventually obscured the squirt from their cameras.

"Fascinating! Any idea what it's feeding on?"

"Not a clue. Not something we've seen before, but something to look into!"

# DAY 4: 06:35
## DANGER

Fernando whistled as he cleaned the bar. He'd arrived about forty-five minutes earlier, opened the place, and set up the coffee machine for the morning rush.

Folks streamed out of the transportation hub, and many stopped by for a quick cup of coffee or tea. More than a few stayed for breakfast. Now, things would be slow. He still had a few stragglers, many of them regulars. At the moment, though, the place was basically empty.

Fernando finished cleaning up, then decided he should feed his pineapple.

He hadn't really looked at it yet this morning; he'd been too busy with the morning crowd. He went into the back and selected an older chicken breast that really wasn't fit to serve anymore. Such waste used to bother him; now he could still get some value from it. He put it on a plate, grabbed a knife, and walked out to the end of the bar.

As he approached the pineapple, he slowed, then stopped. He put the chicken breast and knife down on the counter.

*What the…what's wrong with it?*

It was drooping. The leaves were wilting and a bit yellow. The petals weren't as brightly colored.

Fernando sliced off a piece of chicken and put it on one of the petals. Nothing. He slouched and swore.

"Great. Just fucking great!"

What did he do wrong? He'd done exactly as he was told! And customers loved the damn thing!

He'd ask Pete what to do. Pete should revive it. Or he had better replace it! *And before the dinner rush too!*

# ▪ DAY 4: 06:51
## FOOD

The parent was dry.

They'd been feeding since their emergence, taking turns finding spots still firm with underlying flesh. It was *so* good. But as they explored the shriveled body of the parent, they couldn't find any remaining tissue. Yet they remained hungry.

They needed sustenance. They needed to grow, to fill, to release. They needed it desperately.

They explored their strange surroundings. There was no prey, nothing to sustain them, nothing to fill them.

Their sense of urgency grew.

They felt the movement of air. They followed that air to a series of wide, thin gaps in the firm material that bound the space. They explored the gaps, pulling on the material, picking at every irregularity they could find.

Then, a noise. A strange noise, a shift in a magnetic field, and movement.

Food was coming.

■ ■ ■

She sighed and mumbled, "I'm awake." But the alarm continued to grow louder.

"I'm awake, ok? Stop!"

She tried to speak loud enough to get the alarm's attention without waking her husband. She sat up and swung her legs over the side of the bed to satisfy the alarm. If the motion sensors didn't detect her movement, the alarm would resume. And she really didn't want to wake him.

Well, maybe she did want to wake him, a little. She was experiencing some early morning resentment that he didn't have to wake up quite yet. But she quickly regretted her petulance as she reminded herself how much later his shifts ran compared to hers. How he never complained about cleaning up the kitchen after she went to sleep. How careful he was to not wake her when he came to bed.

She, sighing again, looked over her shoulder to see him sleeping soundly. Standing, she pulled on her robe and inserted her feet into her slippers. She stepped through the portal into their living room.

"Lights, 50%."

As the room gradually brightened, she heard a strange sound. Cocking her head, she looked about the room. Seeing nothing, she shook her head and made her way towards the kitchen.

She wandered sleepily as she reached for their coffee pot. She wasn't interested in a fancy breakfast; however, being a nurse and him a pilot, they both appreciated fine coffee. She made enough for two. He'd be up in an hour or so, and it was the least she could do, given the pile of dishes she'd left for him in the sink.

She yawned loudly and waited. Then, when it was ready, she poured herself a cup and meandered into the living room. She sipped carefully, enjoying the flavor and the warmth as she stared into space and thought about her day.

She found herself staring at their pineapple. There was something different about it this morning. She set her mug down next to the carafe and walked over to the corner.

"Lights, 75%."

She needed more light, but couldn't handle full strength quite yet.

It did not look well. Its leaves were sagging instead of spreading to take in the increasing light. The petals encircling the top were wilted. And it looked faded, even in the slightly subdued lighting. The whole thing looked wilted, shrunken in fact.

This made her sad. They'd really enjoyed it. The flower was so pretty! It had grown so much! Initially, they fed it sparingly. But it never turned down food, and it just kept looking happier the more they fed it. Their guests always got a kick out of seeing it snap a tendril from the center of the blossom to snatch anything they put on one of its petals. Great way to get rid of table scraps too; they'd never cared for leftovers anyway.

Then one of their friends suggested putting it by the air duct. Apparently, it could catch anything and everything that came out of the ducts. They never saw another bug! She'd lost count of how many friends she referred to that Pete guy who sold the plants. He really should have offered her a commission!

At least he repotted it for free as it grew. It was huge now. They set it on the floor rather than a table. Had to weigh as much as she did!

*But, now what?*

If the thing was dying, how would they get rid of it? Maybe Pete would dispose of it for them?

*After all, I'll definitely buy another one from him. Least he could do, right? Better offer me a discount.*

Walking around the kitchen counter towards it, she noticed a hole in the side, a large, ragged hole.

*Weird…*

She heard something. It was a fluttering sound, like there was a piece of paper or cloth near the air vent. She looked at the vent, wondering what could be making that noise. She heard the noise again, but this time it didn't stop. In fact, it was getting louder.

She paused and began to turn towards the sound when she felt the impact.

Something hit her upper back hard, knocking the breath out of her. She lost her balance and fell forward. As she hit the floor, the fluttering sound intensified, then stopped. Strong fingers gripped her shoulders and sharp claws pressed into her skin. Then, suddenly, something hot and sharp stabbed her in the lower back! It was an awful, stabbing pain followed by an unbelievably intense burning.

She screamed and shuddered as the heat intensified and spread. She struggled to get up. She tried to reach and get whatever was on her back off of her, but it was increasingly difficult to move. After a moment, she couldn't move at all. She couldn't move anything but her eyes. The left side of her face pressed into the floor, tears dripping from her eyes.

Something was *crawling* on her back.

That awful, horrific, burning sensation spread through her body: through her core, through her limbs, to her fingers and toes. Everything was on fire!

# DAY 4: 08:12
## HUNTING FOR PETE

Bhavia sat brooding over a mug of coffee in the brig office.

He needed to find and confiscate the pineapples, quickly. But he hit a roadblock. Of the four surveyors stewing in the brig, only Twitchy was cooperating, and he said they had no idea where the pineapples were. They smuggled them in and gave them to that guy named "Pete." Pete was the one selling them and the only man within the whole operation who knew the customers.

Bhavia *had* to find Pete.

Unfortunately, that wasn't going to be straightforward. Bhavia reviewed projections of every gondola operator with the surveyors. Again, only Twitchy responded, and he claimed to not recognize any of them.

Bhavia drummed his fingers on his coffee mug. He had observed each surveyor carefully; he knew how to read people. Either Twitchy was lying, or Pete lied about being a gondola operator. Hell, maybe "Pete" wasn't even his real name! Twitchy, at least, seemed to be trying to help himself by cooperating fully. Still, the four prisoners protested their punishment. "They're just plants!" they complained.

"Are you a trained xenobiologist? Do you know what exactly these plants are? Do you know if they're carrying any little critters that might escape? Might be dangerous? No, of course not. You've exposed all of us to risks. And for what? Money?" Bhavia shook his head at their apparent greed and stupidity.

Bhavia set down his coffee mug angrily and groaned.

*What now?*

His eyes snapped open.

*The containers!*

Bhavia had worked with Dieter to figure out which fabricator had a materials discrepancy, and got a name: Prakash. If Prakash made the containers, it stood to reason he would know Pete. Bhavia accessed the dome's security systems from his wrist computer. As the Security Chief, he could see where individuals registered within the dome by tracing their wrist computers.

*There you are…*

Prakash was currently in his quarters in the residential dome.

Bhavia sent a message to Harry and Bob: fetch Prakash and bring him to the brig. Satisfied, Bhavia resumed drinking his coffee, and waited.

■ ■ ■

Harry and Bob dragged Prakash into the cell with Twitchy. The other three surveyors watched anxiously from the second cell. Prakash didn't look at Twitchy, nor did Twitchy say anything to Prakash. Their body language suggested to Bhavia that they didn't actually know each other.

Bhavia, initially worried Prakash would be uncooperative, could now see the sorry fool wouldn't hold out long. He walked into the cell.

"Prakash! Thanks for meeting me," Bhavia said sarcastically. Prakash glared at him, but didn't respond.

"Oh, and thanks for being so easy to find!" His smiling face rapidly changed to a serious one. "You do realize that you and Pete are in a world of trouble?" Prakash's face twitched at Pete's mention, and Bhavia noticed.

"I didn't do anything!" Prakash snapped at Bhavia, but his brow was already sweating. "I don't know why I'm here!"

Bhavia shook his head slowly, then brought up a projection of one of the containers. "Do you deny making this?"

Prakash started to stammer, but Bhavia cut him off.

"Dieter and I have already reviewed your materials consumption logs, so let me save you from embarrassing yourself. You made these containers, which that sorry lot used to smuggle in a dangerous life form!" Bhavia waved his hand at Twitchy, who flinched as if struck. Prakash stared at the projection open mouthed, trying to formulate some last second excuse. Bhavia leaned in.

"I don't care about you, and I don't care about these containers. I care about finding Pete, and finding these…'pineapples.'"

Prakash sagged further as he mentioned the name for a second time.

"The penalties you'll face will be a lot lighter if you help me find Pete!"

Prakash tilted his head to the side, thought for a moment, then nodded sullenly.

"Emil Pederson. Gondola operator. He was the one to approach me about making extra containers. The whole scheme was his idea."

Bhavia inhaled sharply through his nose. *So "Pete" is short for "Pederson"?*

He tapped his wrist computer, then shook his head.

"There's no gondola operator named Emil Pederson, Prakash."

Prakash went pale. "What do you mean? He…he's a gondola operator, look it up! I, I'm not lying, I swear, that's his name!"

"What do you think I just did!" Bhavia snapped. "Besides, I already reviewed every profile of that department this morning. There's no one by that name working in Gondola Operations. So don't bullshit me, *I need Pete's real name!*"

Prakash picked at his hands. His eyes went glassy, and he started tapping his foot nervously. Whether he was in shock, or trying desperately to come up with an excuse, Bhavia couldn't quite tell. Suddenly, his face lit up.

"Ah wait, wait! Maybe not now, but there was! I…I bet he quit! He…he had an exit plan. He told me!"

Prakash leaned forward so hard his chair screeched backwards on the cell floor.

"Check the manifest of a ship called the *Mother Lode*. I'll bet you he's already on it!"

Mike walked from his livestock pens to his neighbor's residence, and no one responded. He looked out across their fields. He turned to look past their residence towards the central tower supporting the dome. There was no sign of them anywhere.

*Where the heck are my neighbors?*

Earlier that morning, Mike walked out to his pens and found his livestock shriveled and decaying. It was like his animals had been deflated, all of the air, meat, and guts sucked out of every cow, goat, and pig. He checked on his neighbor's animals; they had suffered the same fate. His wife ran to the veterinarian's office while he roamed about looking for help, or answers.

*Could they be in the tower? Don't see why, the tower's convenience stores aren't open yet. They might have gone to the transportation hub...but would they have taken all the kids?*

He paused, looking up through the dome at the blue sky. He missed the larger, agricultural domes of his home world. Eden's agricultural domes could only support four farms, so there were only four residences encircling the dome's central tower. They had to contend with a fairly limited social life when they didn't have the energy to take the shuttle to the primary dome.

*But that blue sky! So much prettier than home. And, at night? Those stars...*

He tapped at his wrist computer. "Emma? Emma, did you reach the vet?"

"No response. Left a message, for what that's worth. Called her primary dome office, too. Nobody's there. Guess they're both out. We're probably not the first to report this. She's probably out at one of the other agricultural domes."

He sighed. *Doesn't really matter, does it?* Not like a vet could fix his animals. And, whatever kind of sickness it was, it was affecting his neighbor's livestock too. A timely response wasn't going to keep the disease from spreading. It was probably already happening under the other agricultural domes.

Mike decided to continue on to see the next residence to see if they'd heard anything. After a bit, he reached their pens. The chickens were the same as his own, and the goats. Mike trudged on frustrated, but paused at the pig pen. One of them was alive!

Or so he thought. Mike walked closer to the boar; he leaned over the side of the pen, getting within a meter of it. The pig was buried in mud in the corner of the pen, under the trough. Just the top of its head, nostrils, eyes, and ears, was exposed. He stared at it, then waved at it. First, he waved a hand, then both arms rapidly. The pig gave no reaction beyond following him with its eyes. He could tell, from the nostrils, that it was breathing steadily but slowly.

*Weird. Just weird.*

He couldn't imagine how it managed to bury itself like that, and it wasn't like a pig to not react. He straightened and looked about until he found a table scrap dropped during the last feeding. He picked it up, then tossed it half a meter in front of the boar.

There was no reaction.

Shaking his head, Mike walked to his neighbor's residence, then tapped the portal. It wasn't sealed, and he heard something inside. Hesitantly, he entered the residence.

It struck him that all the residences in all the agricultural domes were the same, albeit decorated differently. The Hackneys had a family photo above their living room table, just like his family did. If he merely swapped the faces, it *could* be his family portrait. It was almost like stepping into a pocket of another reality, where his family was someone else's…

He walked through the family room to the kitchen and froze.

On the floor were three shriveled bodies, barely recognizable as human. Their only identifying markers were shredded clothing. A chill ran up his spine as he stared at them. He leaned forward, horrified, fascinated. His mind struggled to understand the scene before him. His eyes darted from the family portrait to the gruesome picture, trying to figure out which family members he was staring at. With a start, he realized it didn't matter.

He heard something again, a grunt, followed by a whimper. Softly, gently, he stepped through the kitchen, navigating around the bodies, towards the back door. He stepped carefully, avoiding the blood spatters. As he reached the back portal, he looked outside at the garden.

There were two things, strange things, digging in the soil, uprooting his neighbor's flowerbed. They were about the size of a small dog, with leathery wings and powerful legs. They had beaks and weird eyestalks growing out of their bodies just behind the beaks. On the lawn, near where they were digging, lay his neighbor's daughter, a teenager. She'd been dragged there from the house. The kid wasn't moving, except for her eyes, which suddenly reminded him of the pig. Her clothes were torn and bloody. There were, on her chest, small puncture wounds that had recently stopped bleeding. There was a bloody slash, a couple centimeters long, to the left of her navel; it too looked like it had bled freely before closing.

Mike steadied himself against the portal frame; he felt like he was going to faint. He looked back at the flowerbed. He noticed, a couple of meters to the side, freshly disturbed soil surrounded by uprooted plants.

In that soil, there was a face. A *human* face. It was a child's face, staring upward, with just the eyes, nose, and mouth exposed.

*Like the pig!*

He turned back to the teenager and saw the kid's eyes were turned towards him.

She moaned slowly, softly, painfully.

It was the most horrifying thing he'd ever seen.

Mike took a frantic step back into the kitchen and rushed towards the butcher block on the counter. With a trembling hand, he pulled out the largest knife in the set. He turned back, a tight grip on that knife, and braced himself. He had to try to help, to try to chase those things away. He took a deep breath in, ready to start screaming at them when he heard a rustling sound.

*Impact!*

Mike fell forward, sharp claws digging into the meat of his shoulders. It knocked the breath out of him; the knife hit the floor, sliding beyond his reach. As he hit the ground, he felt a sudden stabbing pain in his lower back, followed by an awful burning that spread through his abdomen. He was imobile, locked in place with pain. All that he had left were his eyes.

His eyes looked to his arm, motionless, numb, inches from his face. His wrist computer lit up.

Emma was calling.

# ■DAY 4: 09:17
## TAKI

*Busy, busy, busy day!*

Taki didn't like busy days. He was a quiet, contemplative soul. He liked peace and quiet. He liked routine. He liked to set his own (leisurely) pace at work.

That was one of the reasons he chose botany. And for the lab work! Botanists don't have to chase their subjects. And, being a lab rat himself, Taki didn't want to go gallivanting around the planet. He could sit in his lab, study his specimens, and take a break whenever he felt like it. And if such a break involved a glass of wine or perhaps a fine cheese? Who's to judge?

Not today, though.

He might be a lab rat, but that didn't insulate Taki from the activity frenzy inspired by the alignment. All sorts of things were happening out in the field, with specimens and samples piling up by the landing field. It made sense to process those materials in a lab outside the dome, but trudging out there was such a bother. Fortunately, there were more than enough images and measurements to occupy his time without having to leave his teaching lab.

Except that he'd been in the lab all night, and now Taki really needed something to eat. Something *good*, not what could be scrounged from a nearby breakroom. Taki much preferred his own kitchen to any of the fine restaurants he'd discovered near his apartment under the residential dome. There were some fine restaurants here at the base station, but they were a fair trek. Along with being a homebody, Taki did not care much for exercise or exertion in any form.

*Ah! Fernando's! The place just outside! A decent option…*

**…**

Taki walked along the bar towards the tables and scanned the room, looking for the owner. It was a bit late for breakfast but far too early for lunch, so Taki thought he'd be treated well.

He spotted Fernando coming out of the kitchen. His mind was already made up as to what to order. As he approached, Taki could see the man was somewhat stressed. He pulled a stool well back from the countertop. He really needed to do something about his thickening middle…

As the stool scraped the floor, the owner looked up. Taki smiled, cleared his throat, and was about to sit down and place his order when the man interrupted.

"Hey! You're a botanist, aren't you?"

Hesitantly, Taki replied. "…yes?"

"Oh, that's great! Need you to look at my pineapple!"

The man turned and beckconned as Taki asked, "pineapple?"

The man turned, looked at him quizzically, and said, "yeah, pineapple. Y'know, a pineapple! Everyone's got one. Don't you have one?"

"No, no I don't." Taki slid off the stool to follow. The man kept talking as he led Taki to the front of his place.

"Yeah, a pineapple. Thing's amazing! You can feed it table scraps or live critters. The crowds love that thing! They buy food to feed it, and drinks to secure a place in line. And they bet which food it'll snag first!"

Taki followed him to an olive green thing in a pot. It *wasn't* a pineapple, but he could see why folks might call it one. It was a round shape like a pineapple, with a thick, spiny, olive green rind. But it has a pale red blossom and sagging green leaves.

"I haven't had it very long. You drop the food here on the petals, and the tendrils come out to pull the food in the mouth. Except it doesn't react to food anymore! And the flower's faded and wilted and…"

Taki stared at the thing, largely ignoring Fernando.

" I need it eating! Lots of people come around to see it, and they won't be happy, let me tell ya, if they come around later and the thing won't eat! Can you help me? Can you tell me what to do?"

Taki blinked twice. "Where…where did you get this?"

"From Pete. The gondola guy. He sells them."

Taki's eyes locked on the thing.

"Do you…do you mind if I take it? I'd like to examine it, figure out what's going on. I'll, uh, bring it back. But I can't do anything for it here!"

The guy thought for a moment. He didn't want his prized attraction disappearing; but then again, if it wasn't eating, it wasn't much of a draw.

"Sure, go ahead. Just remember where you got it!"

Taki nodded, then crouched and gently grabbed the pot. He grimaced as he stood from the weight, and turned to leave.

"Wait! Did you want to order something?"

Taki paused, turned halfway, and said, "sorry, I can't stop now. I'll, uh, be back!"

# ▪DAY 4: 11:47
## A LUNCH DATE

It got progressively harder to focus on his work as the morning wore on. He kept glancing at his wrist computer. It was getting close to lunch time, but not fast enough!

Last night was amazing! He'd met some friends at one of the new, fashionable restaurants under the residential dome during one of the alignment parties. Not that he gave a crap about the alignment, but he took any excuse to party. And *what* a party!

The bar set up a big screen with a countdown to the alignment. Next to it, a projection of Eden displayed every quake by making the affected part of the projection shake. They even rigged the dance floor to shake to simulate the tremors as they happened! It was a blast!

He enjoyed a fine bourbon distilled right here on Eden, from corn grown under one of the newer agricultural domes. It was just as good as the insanely expensive imports and so, so much better than the algal substitutes they usually settled for.

He and his buddies were waiting for a table and sharing a laugh when he saw her walk in.

Well, she didn't walk in alone, but he hardly noticed her friends. There was something inexplicably special about her that immediately caught his eye. His friends could tell; he stopped talking and set down his nearly empty glass. They followed his line of sight and began to tease him until he raised a finger, looked each of them in the eye, and said, "wish me luck!"

They watched him saunter over with envy. Some of them were married, others were in relationships of varying degrees of solidity. And he had a reputation.

She was clearly a recent arrival. He could tell by the way she looked around, the way she dressed, all slightly out of step with current fashion.

The intoxicated group of gentlemen watched him approach her, saw him extend a hand, saw her smile back at him and laugh gently at something he said. After a few minutes, she spoke to her friends. Some of the other girls smiled and nodded, some shook their heads, but all waved farewell as he led her out of the restaurant.

They walked down the row of shops and pubs and restaurants along their left, with the railing to their right and the dome beyond. He took her to his favorite pub for such occasions: a broad, impressive bar with a dance floor and tables nestled in quiet little nooks. It was popular with the sunset and stargazer crowds and, albeit for a higher price, offered a fair bit of privacy.

He splurged on real, imported wine and a light dinner as they sat together looking through the dome at the stars of Eden. Stars were new to her. Her home world had a swirling, stormy, primordial atmosphere that obscured the night sky.

As they sat and spoke, they touched occasionally. A finger laid on a hand, a hand grazed a forearm. Their touch lingered; their eyes met. Then briefly, lightly, they kissed.

After dinner, holding hands, he led her to a quieter part of the rooftop for an even better view of the stars. They relished being alone; there was no one else around. He pointed to the heavens, naming stars and constellations. They paused, arms reaching around each other's waist, then looked into each other's eyes and kissed more passionately.

He sighed. He wasn't getting any work done. He looked at his computer again.

*No messages…But that was a good thing, right? Lunch is still on?*

He'd ordered some really tasty treats and arranged their delivery. If he left in about four minutes, he should arrive at her quarters at about the same time as the food. He shook his head. No point in waiting; he wasn't getting anything done anyway.

■ ■ ■

Sure enough, as he reached her door, the delivery bot was a moment behind him, ready for his grand entrance. He reached for the bell, then remembered she'd given him an access code. He smiled broadly.

He tapped his wrist computer, and her portal became translucent. He stepped through, pushing the treats into the dim lighting. He tapped the portal control and it turned opaque again.

He paused, deciding what to do next. Turn up the lights? Call out her name? Just explore the room and find her?

He took a few tentative steps into the room, then paused as he heard a fluttering sound. Slowly, carefully, he moved forward, his eyes adjusting to the dim lighting.

Something was moving.

He paused, crouched a bit, alarmed by movement on the floor a few meters in front of him. He fought a strong urge to leave. The hairs stood up on the back of his neck. Something about this was wrong.

"Lights, 50%!"

She was lying on the floor, naked. She was on her belly with her head turned towards him. Her eyes pleaded for help; a spilled glass of something light and clear lay beside her. White wine perhaps?

She wasn't moving.

He let out an audible gasp.

There were *things* on her.

One was between her legs. Her beautiful, shapely, smooth legs were *deflated*. Her two legs looked like baggy skin draped over bone.

The thing was about the size of a cat. It had broad, leathery wings, and its forelimbs ended in strong, clawed digits. It was massaging her right buttock with those claws. It reminded him of the way cats sometimes worked their forepaws on a surface. Somebody told him, once, that cats did that to comfort themselves, a motion from when they were nursing kittens.

Six long fingers extended over its beak, hovering with weird alien eyes. It stared at her butt as its long, thin, sharply pointed beak sucked her slowly diminishing ass. Its throat pulsed. Her ass *shrank* as he watched.

Another was on her back. It gripped her shoulders tightly with its clawed digits, and a sharp, curved *thing* came out from between its hind legs, a drop of clear fluid at its tip. One of its six fingered eyes turned to him as the others stared at the side of her face. Her eyes left his and turned towards the eyes of the thing on her back. Her gaze widened with terror as its grip tightened even more. Its wings stretched out as it suddenly stabbed her with its extension, pressing itself into her, wiggling its hips as it pressed harder and harder into her flesh. Tears flowed but she said nothing and made no sound.

The monster pulled itself out of her, blood dripping from its retracting organ. More of the clear liquid dripped from it as its *thing* retracted back into its body. It began to massage her shoulder, then jabbed its beak in and began sucking.

Conflicted, horrified, he started to back away.

He told himself there was nothing he could do. She was gone. There was no saving her now; the things had her. Even if he could, somehow, drive them away, she was as good as dead. No, nothing could be done.

He stared into her pleading eyes as he backed away, mouthing apologies as he slowly shook his head and backed away.

Suddenly, he heard the fluttering again and was struck from behind. He felt sharp claws tear into the meat of his back as he fell forward. He grunted as he hit the floor; he painfully tried to pull his arms under himself to push up to and run away. Then he felt a horrendous stabbing pain in his lower back, followed by an intense burning sensation.

He scrunched his eyes as he screamed in pain. Whatever it was stabbed deeper and deeper into him, through his back, into his abdomen. The burning intensified and spread.

He tried to get his arms under himself, but realized he could not move.

He opened his eyes, looking into hers.

He could not speak. He could not move. He couldn't do anything but stare into her eyes as he felt it pull itself out of his back, felt it turn and walk across his buttock, felt its claws pierce his skin, heard a tearing sound as it ripped his trousers, felt another stabbing and burning sensation in his calf, felt the claws massaging his leg, felt something else stab him there, felt the strangest, most awful pulling sensation from deep inside his burning leg.

# ▪ DAY 4: 12:34
## BOTANY

Taki was exhausted. His initial excitement had waned. Although he saw new life forms regularly, he was still a recent enough arrival to Eden to not be jaded by such novelty. Finding a fresh life form within the colony was unprecedented, to be sure. But his preliminary examination strongly suggested it wasn't a particularly interesting life form.

And he had missed breakfast.

Taki left *Fernando's* with his prize, but found himself wondering where to take it. He put it down for a moment and pondered. The best labs were the ones adjoining the landing pads, but he knew they were swamped with alignment related specimens and samples coming in from the field. Besides, he really didn't want to don an environmental suit, and there wasn't any point to isolating the thing. It was already inside.

After waffling a few minutes, Taki decided to just take it to his office. At least there he had *some* equipment. His office wasn't as good as the landing pad labs, sure, not even as good as an EAGLE's mobile lab, but it would do. And this pineapple thing was *heavy*! It had to be 15 or 20 kilos, easy!

And he *had* missed breakfast.

He reached the base station and took an elevator to the DSSA's botany floor. On reaching his office, he put the pineapple on a worktable and rolled his now very tired shoulders. He examined the lifeform a little more closely.

Fernando said it had wilted. Having never seen it before, Taki didn't have a reference against which to compare. He did his best to imagine the thing before him a bit more…vibrant? Colorful? Robust?

Taki realized he'd never actually seen an Earth pineapple. He was familiar with them, of course, a Bromeliad native to South and Central America. He pulled up an image of one, and he could see the superficial resemblance. The differences were obvious to the trained eye, but he could see how a lay person might look at the thing and call it a "pineapple".

He pinched and rubbed his chin with a thumb and curved forefinger, pondering what he should do next. He didn't have much in the way of imaging equipment to see internal structures, and he didn't want to slice into it, at least not yet. He did have photographic equipment that would allow him to capture and enlarge images of external structures. And he could see that it was clearly part of the trilateral super-kingdom.

That annoyed him.

Not that the pineapple was part of that super-kingdom, but that the zoologists called it the "trilaterally symmetric" super-kingdom. Eden's five life lineages were all well represented in her oceans and among the tiny things flourishing across her lands. But most of the larger plant equivalents and most of the larger animal equivalents identified to date were from two of the five super-kingdoms. So everyone (even the botanists!) had taken to referring to those super-kingdoms as the "bilaterally symmetrical" and "trilaterally symmetrical" super-kingdoms in honor of the distinguishing features of their animal equivalents, even though these labels meant nothing for their microorganism and plant equivalents.

*Typical zoological chauvinism!*

Because humans focused on animals, of course, especially large animals. They ignored the plants, ignored the invertebrates, and ignored the microorganisms. It had always been so. Everybody walked right by the bugs and the plants to look at the big animals.

*So annoying!*

Taki groaned. This wasn't helping.

He rolled his sore shoulder again. The burning pain from the pineapple's weight had faded to a deep ache. Shrugging off the pain, Taki resumed staring at the pineapple.

It was unlikely anyone else on Eden had ever seen a real pineapple, and again, nobody paid that much attention to plants. *That* was probably why nobody noticed these Eden pineapples proliferate around the settlement. Taki had to sheepishly admit that he hadn't noticed them either. And, he *should* have! But he didn't really get out much. Taki spent most of his time working in his lab with specimens collected by other people.

Taki realized his mind was wandering again. He really needed to eat something, and some caffeine. He really needed some caffeine.

In any case, the pineapple was clearly from the trilateral super-kingdom. He could see that right away. It had four big, broad leaves and a big, red blossom with a hard, yellowish-green rind. And, according to its owner, this was a wilted version.

*Well, if this was wilted, then a happy pineapple must be something to see!*

Also, according to Fernando, it was a carnivorous plant, like a Venus fly-trap or sundew. That, at least, was interesting. They hadn't found many carnivorous plants on Eden thus far.

*Grrrrrrgh…*

His stomach rumbled, reminding him once more that he'd missed breakfast. With a sigh, Taki decided to settle for something from the nearest break room.

■ ■ ■

Taki pinched his nose, deep in thought.

When he got to the breakroom, he was surprised to find another pineapple just sitting there, among the snack displays, like it was no big deal! He couldn't remember the last time he'd gone to a breakroom; but, if it had been there for long, *surely* he would have noticed.

He looked at it, shrugged, scrounged something semi-edible, and contemplated the thing while he chewed. There was nobody else in the breakroom; so, without anyone to ask for permission, he decided to just confiscate the thing. Now it sat next to the one from *Fernando's* place.

As each moment passed, Taki regretted that he hadn't gone to one of the landing field labs. Sure, it would have cost him an hour or two, but now he was burning far more time without proper equipment. A genetic analysis would have told him in minutes what he spent hours trying to figure out through visual inspection of the pineapple's external structures.

Well, now he had two. Maybe he should inspect the other breakrooms, see if there were more. At this point, there was no getting around the need for proper lab equipment. But the thought of taking one or both of the things to a xenobiology lab was even less appealing from here than from *Fernando's*.

*Later, maybe.*

So far, Taki had managed to convince himself it was *not* related to any of the plant equivalents encountered thus far. That was interesting, but not terribly helpful. Fernando's pineapple continued to wilt, and this new one looked about as bad.

Taki stared at the two pineapples.

He raised his hands, slapped them down on his thighs, and stood. He was *not* going to the labs. That's what grad students are for! He went to one of the teaching labs to fetch sampling equipment. He'd take samples and leave them on the desk of one of his students with a note.

Taki knelt, rummaging through the supply cabinet for a sampling kit. Nobody would see his note until morning, but that didn't really matter.

Suddenly, he stopped, stood, turned, and groaned.

*Of course…Every desk in the teaching lab has a genetic analyzer!*

Taki sighed and shook his head with embarrassment. He really wasn't at his best!

Teaching equipment had limitations, but it was good enough for what Taki had in mind. He took the sampling kit and returned to the pineapples. He left a sample on his student's desk; sometime tomorrow, he'd get a detailed analysis. In the meantime, he also took a sample back to the teaching lab and fed it to one of the analyzers.

Taki listened to the analyzer hum for a moment, then looked down at his wrist computer. He had time for a nap, and he really needed one. He set an alarm for 17:00, padded back to his office, leaned back in his chair, raised his feet to his desk, and closed his eyes.

# ▪DAY 4: 13:51
## CAPTURE

Pete celebrated, albeit quietly, with a double shot of whiskey.

He sat at a bar in the first residential ring of the *Mother Lode*. He turned, leaning his back against the bar, and looked through one of the floor panels. The rotation of the ring, in addition to providing the comforting feeling of gravity, periodically filled that panel with a view of Eden. He toasted that view and bid the colony farewell.

Pete sighed deeply. The small fortune he had amassed selling pineapples was now invested in a series of diversified accounts, ready to become a *large* fortune by the time they reached their destination. He snorted, realizing he wasn't even sure where they were going! He remembered looking it up before signing on; but really, he didn't care. He couldn't imagine any destination he wasn't willing to commit to, as long as it got him away from weapons proficiency drills and gave his investments time to grow.

*Fuck it, I'll never have to work again, ha!*

He continued to stare through the panel as the ring turned. Eden gave way to space, then a view of the orbiting platform, the space elevator trailing down to Wu City on the surface. It wouldn't be long now. Soon, they'd be underway. The chimes would sound, the drum's rotation would slow to a stop, and they'd all suffer through a few hours of zero-g while the ring was reconfigured for departure. The bar, in sections, would transfer to what was now a wall but would become the floor as the ship's acceleration shifted their sense of "down." He knew, from previous crossings, that there'd be a few people sneaking off to join the "zero-g club." He made eye contact with a few prospective partners and felt confident at least one would be willing when the time came.

Pete returned his gaze to the panel as Eden came back into view, and was surprised to see a landing craft rising towards the ship.

*Interesting…*

He'd never seen that before. As far as he knew, all 200 pippers were aboard. Not that pippers flew aboard landing craft. They, like he, usually endured a long ride up the stalk, then a zero-g crossing aboard a shuttle. He hadn't heard about any missing crew members, either.

As the ring turned and Eden returned to the view, Pete could see the landing craft much closer, apparently heading to one of the shuttle bays.

Something about this seemed off, and he started getting nervous.

■ ■ ■

The security chief of the *Mother Lode* stared at her bridge console. They were about to run another simulation prepared by Eden's Deep Space Service Academy. Eden was a young colony with a modest academy, but the first two simulations were impressively sophisticated. The simulation had just finished loading when an alert caught her attention.

"Captain!"

The captain, displeased by the interruption, sighed deeply and responded. "Yes? What is it now?"

"Landing craft arrived, shuttle bay 3."

"Wonderful. Have you found this Emil Pederson yet?"

"He's in the bar. Two of my people will join the colonials and escort him back to the shuttle bay."

"Just make it quick. We have a few more simulations to run before departure. I would appreciate it if you minimized the impact of this stunt on our departure time!"

■ ■ ■

"You ever hear of anything like this?"

Bob shrugged as if to say no.

Harry shook his head. "I've never heard of anything like this!"

Bob shrugged again. He was enjoying the ride up. Only two people aboard a landing craft, three including the pilot? Best view he'd ever had! He couldn't wait for the descent.

Harry, checking his wrist computer, muttered, "where are these guys?"

A young man and an older woman entered the shuttle bay and introduced themselves as security officials from the *Mother Lode.*

As they walked, one of the guards asked, "you work for Guido Heideko?"

"Yes," Bob replied, "well, we work for Bhavia, who works for Guido. We're Wu City security."

She nodded. As they approached the lift to the residential ring, she said, "he must have a lot of pull to make this happen! Captain is *not* happy, and will be a lot *less* happy if we're delayed."

They stepped into the lift as Harry retorted, "trust me, we want this to go as quickly as possible!"

■ ■ ■

As they approached the bar, Harry asked, "now we haven't actually seen this guy in person. I assume you've seen the image we sent?"

"Yes, we have. There's two bar entrances; we'll take this one, and you two take the other. Sound good?"

Harry and Bob exchanged a glance, nodded, and headed towards the other entrance. The security guards waited for Harry and Bob to take their places, then entered the bar.

■ ■ ■

Pete was getting antsy. He really couldn't explain why, not rationally; but something had him on edge even if he couldn't explain why.

He drained his glass and stood. There really wasn't anywhere to go! It was a deep space vessel, after all: just a command ring, two residential rings, and then ring after ring of processing pods. There was a plenum space above the ceiling, he supposed; but Pete wasn't sure how to get up there. And, even if he did, how long could he evade a search?

He glanced about, then froze. A man and a woman were scanning the crowd by the entrance. Pete hadn't seen the woman before, but he remembered the man oversaw boarding from the shuttle. He was definitely security.

*God damn it, did those bitches sell me out already?!*

Pete edged back, doing his best to be nonchalant. He shook his head at a flashing memory of Prakash, who looked so obviously guilty the last time they met. Trying to play it cool, he did his best impression of a guy who just realized he needed to be somewhere, and made his way towards the other entrance.

*So far, so good…*

Pete stepped through the portal and found two men waiting for him.

One, smiling, said, "Pete! At last we meet!"

# DAY 4: 14:02
## ON THE BEACH

George was delighted!

He crouched next to the biggest squirt he'd ever seen. It was bigger than him, a swirl of reds and yellows and blacks, its body glistening in the afternoon sun. There were more squirts along the beach, as far as he could see, a riot of bright colors and slow, clumsy movement.

A variety of species appeared, many never before seen. Big ones, small ones, some had four pairs of flippers, others had five pairs. Some were coupling, one of each pair possessing some sort of intromittent organ to pass sex cells to its partner. Others appeared to have come up the beach already impregnated, their bodies filled with, what? Eggs? Young? Time would tell.

George watched his team walk carefully among them, taking pictures. Some of the smaller ones could be taken as samples. For the larger ones, they used ticks deployed and retrieved from a pouch carried at their waist. The ticks distributed themselves across the subject's body, taking minute tissue samples for DNA analyses. The ticks also scanned the creature's internal structures, and returned for redeployment on the next subject.

The data they collected would keep them busy for a very, very long time!

"George?"

He stood and looked about, then checked his display. The message came from a coastal outpost a few hundred kilometers to the southeast.

"Yes?"

"George, it's dusk here, and we're not seeing the usual suspects."

"What do you mean?"

"It's winter here, right? So the sun set a while ago. And, as the diurnal community dissipated, we should have seen the crepuscular community emerge, then the nocturnal community. But we're not. That's a lot of different species that have, effectively, disappeared. We've never seen anything like it."

George scanned the area around him, and was surprised to realize how quiet it was. He'd been so focused on the emergence of the squirts that he missed the disappearance of everything else!

George set his environmental suit to broadcast to all stations.

"This is George Sied. Everyone, we're now on a party line, so please keep your responses crisp. Please take a moment to assess your area. Are you seeing any difference in the communities around you?"

The messages started coming in. All stations reported a significant reduction in the number and variety of animal equivalents in their area. George spoke again, saying, "ok, everyone stop. I want drones running transects, quantifying any differences in the life forms present in your areas."

# ▪ DAY 4: 14:43
## INTO THE VENTS

The creatures were hungry. All of the prey were consumed. There was nothing left to eat.

The feeding had been glorious! The prey were large, easily subdued, and so, so tasty. Just one thrust was enough to take one down. Some fought a little more than others, but others offered no resistance at all.

The food was deliciously alive, and the prey that could still move a little made delightful noises as they were consumed.

They were still experimenting, learning the best way to feed. With a bit of care, if they started with the extremities, they could take their time and feed and feed and feed. Sensing, enjoying, the prey lasted a good, long time.

Eventually, though, their digestive venom began to liquify core organ systems. Once that process began, the prey began to die. It was time to finish quickly, draining the last bit of sustenance before the prey's tissues lost their flavor.

The biggest challenge was the prey's sensory cluster. A thick layer of bone and tissue encasing a rich, tasty treat. It was rich in blood and fats and proteins, just the things their bodies needed most to prepare for a release.

They were preparing to inject a host with spores.

The creatures wanted, *needed*, a release. But they were not ready. They needed more prey, needed more sustenance, and then they needed to find hosts.

But there were no more prey here.

They were ravenous.

They needed to find more prey.

They could sense more prey nearby, but the sensation was vague. They could feel their electromagnetic signatures. They could *smell* them, but they couldn't see them.

How frustrating! Some of them were *so close* to a release!

With increasing desperation, they searched and searched, seeking some way out. But there was no way out. However, there was a movement of air.

Different parts of the enclosure had different textures and were made of different materials. The creatures pushed and pulled and probed and clawed to no avail. But there was one part of the enclosure that had gaps, and through those gaps, they could sense an escape.

They focused on those gaps. They clustered around those gaps, eyestalks and forepaws exploring, searching for a weakness in the materials. The moving air bore the scent of prey, driving them nearly to madness as their hunger intensified.

They gripped the material, digits pressed through the gaps, grasping the material, squeezing, pushing, pulling.

The material moved ever so slightly, but not enough.

They explored, touched, tapped, pulled, pushed, twisted, turned, until...

*Squeak!*

They all stopped and pulled back, their eyestalks aimed at the thing that moved.

It *turned*.

The creature reached out, concentrating on the vulnerable part. The rest quivered with excitement as it slowly turned the piece until it *fell out*!

The creature rasped the material nearby and pulled, and it gave a little bit more. The others began exploring the corners of the strange opening for other segments that turned.

The parts began to turn and turn and turn.

# DAY 4: 15:30
## CHECKMATE

Harry and Bob found Bhavia sitting at his desk in the brig. As he spoke, his voice filled with disdain.

"So, this is the infamous Pete? Or should I say Emil Pederson?"

Slowly, Pete raised his eyes to meet Bhavia, then lowered them.

Bhavia couldn't resist a small smile of satisfaction as he slowly nodded. He stood and stepped around the desk, then folded his arms as he stood in front of Pete. He turned his head slightly but kept his eyes on the scoundrel. "Harry, cut him loose!"

As Harry approached, he leaned forward.

"Here's what's going to happen, Emil Pederson. You are going to tell me where every damn pineapple is. And I don't care how long it takes you to answer me."

He jabbed Pete in the chest with his right forefinger. Pete's eyes came up to meet his again.

"Here's what's *not* going to happen. You are *not* going to insult my intelligence by pretending you don't know what I'm talking about. You can see that all your little friends are here, and they've been very, *very* helpful. And, you are *not* going to waste my time or test my patience by trying to impress me or buy me!"

He stepped back, then sat on the edge of his desk as he refolded his arms. "Start talking!"

Pete paused, then glanced around the brig. None of his co-conspirators met his eyes. Twitchy and Prakash blushed.

Pete nodded. The game was up.

"What can you offer?"

Bhavia cocked his head, then laughed gently.

"What can *I* offer? What can I *offer*? There's no bargaining here! *You* are in a great deal of trouble. You've endangered the colony…"

Pete scoffed. "Endangered what? They're just plants. Harmless!"

Bhavia stood up sharply and grabbed Pete by his collar. "How the *hell* do you know they're harmless? Do you have a degree in xenobiology? Did you do an extensive analysis of the soil they came in? Can you *guarantee* there's no kraken spores on them? Nothing nasty living in the soil?"

Pete glared, gritting his teeth. Of course he knew about the kraken, but they never bothered him. Trumped up stories, he figured. Not terrible enough to get in the way of his business.

"No sir," he sneered. "But we've been selling them for weeks and nobody's complained."

Bhavia scowled, frustrated at Pete's lack of concern.

"Ok, so you've been lucky. Good for you. But your luck's run out. I want to know where you keep your inventory, and I want to know who you've sold to."

Pete shrugged. "I, uh, don't keep records. I can tell you where my inventory is, and I can offer you a few names, but I can't remember everybody."

Pete relaxed into his chair, seemingly unphased by the whole ordeal. Besides, he figured the less he talked, the better off he was. Bhavia sighed loudly. The two, stubborn men were at a standstill.

"We'll start with your inventory," Bhavia growled. "Then we'll work on your memory."

# ▪ DAY 4: 16:06
## A NEW PREDATOR APPEARS

Deirdre crouched by a large squirt and opened her sampling kit, allowing the ticks that had been gathering information to run back inside their pouch. She stood and stretched and glanced across the beach. Given the number of researchers on the beach and the diversity of squirts, they'd directed one of their bots to analyze drone footage, optimize sampling order, and guide each of them to whichever subject should be next.

Earlier, she'd asked the drone for a count of the creatures; she couldn't get her mind around the numbers. Over 100,000 individuals of nearly 200 species of squirts lay on this beach alone. Some lay quietly, their side breathing tubes opening and closing; others writhed together in mating frenzies. Some left egg masses on the sand; others excavated pits and buried their eggs. Some of the species, according to the ticks, were carrying live young that would presumably be birthed any time.

Deirdre turned slowly until one of the squirts highlighted on her heads-up display.

Gingerly, she made her way towards it, stepping between the bodies on the sand. They really didn't seem at all disturbed by the presence of the science team. She reached her next subject, crouched to release the ticks, and opened the pouch to watch them pour out over the creature's body.

She turned to the west, looking up the beach. Movement caught her eye. She relayed a request to one of the drones to fly over; a few moments later, she could see, on her heads-up display, the drone's point of view.

There was a fair-sized creature, about the size of a large dog, from the bilaterally symmetric super-kingdom, lying on its side. It was a scavenger species she'd seen feeding on some of the tsunami-abandoned carcasses. Seeing the thing on its side was unusual.

What was even more unusual was the thing apparently feeding on it.

It was from the trilateral super-kingdom. Its beak, long and thin, was inserted into the body like some kind of nightmare mosquito. Its forepaws pressed against the prey's body on either side of the beak, steadily kneading. Its midlimbs were wings folded against its body.

She instructed the drone to keep recording and pinged George.

"George, can you see this?"

After a few moments, he responded, "yes…interesting! That's new…we haven't seen anything quite like that before! Are there more of them?"

Deirdre scanned the area, then noticed another feeding on one of the squirts high on the beach. She relayed that image to George, then continued scanning.

"I see, uh, four of them at the moment. I'm sure there weren't any until recently. I'm going to ask the team at the EAGLE to launch another drone to look for more of them."

"Good idea. Please keep me posted. I'll ping the other research teams and see if they noticed anything like them."

She continued to scan while her ticks worked, then retrieved them for her next subject. Eventually, as she walked, she heard George's voice again.

"Ok Deirdre, so I've polled our other teams and they're all reporting them, some in significant numbers. They're aggressive and we have reports of attempted attacks. They can't get through our environmental suits, but at least one team reports the attacks frequent enough to force them to retreat to their EAGLE."

Deirdre was stunned. She turned to face inland and could now see more of the predators than she could count feeding. They were all feeding on squirts.

"George, there are quite a few out here. We need to know what they are, but they're too big to take a live sample. If we have a secmed nearby, can we kill one for study?"

# ▪DAY 4: 17:15
## INVENTORY

Bhavia, pacing, glanced at his wrist computer. It was getting late, and he had things to do.

Pete held out for a while and tried to negotiate a way back to the *Mother Lode*. Bhavia finally reached out, through Guido, to the ship's security chief, who made it clear to Pete that he was no longer welcome on board that ship. Once Pete realized he was staying on Eden, he did his best to wring concessions in exchange for information. That wasted even more time.

Finally, he gave up and told them where to retrieve his inventory. Bhavia sent Harry and Bob with a suspensor pallet, and now he was waiting for them to return. In fact, he was becoming concerned. The alcove Pete found near gondola operations wasn't *that* far, so Harry and Bob should have returned by now.

With a sigh, he raised his wrist computer to call them, just as he heard noise through the brig portal.

Bhavia stopped and watched as Harry backed through the portal pulling a suspensor pallet filled with pineapples of various sizes. Harry glanced over his shoulder, nodded at Bhavia, and grunted, "sorry for the wait!" He then walked through the portal and came back with another pallet filled with pineapples, followed by Bob pushing yet another pallet.

Bob stopped and explained. "We had to find a couple more pallets!"

Harry looked around the brig. "We need to return the pallets we borrowed. Where do you want the pineapples?"

Bhavia stared, then shook his head and pointed to the open space beyond the cells. "Put them there!" He watched as they pushed the pallets and then began unloading them. "How many did you find?"

Bob looked up. "Eleven."

Bhavia whistled. Some were relatively small, about the size of a human head. Others were bigger, much bigger. A few were as big as barrels. Pete gaped at them.

"What the *hell* did you do to my inventory?!?"

Bhavia looked at him, baffled by his response.

"What are you talking about?"

"They're all *wilted*! What did you do to them?"

"What do you care?"

"They're valuable!"

Bhavia laughed.

"No they're not. Not anymore. Now they're contraband, and I'm going to call the xenobiology team to come take them for analysis." Bhavia looked sternly at him. "And *you*, my friend, are going to tell me who you've sold them to!"

# ▪ DAY 4: 18:04
## THE RESULTS

Taki nearly fell out of his chair when his wrist computer buzzed. He regained his balance, shifted his feet from his desk to the floor, blinked a few times, then remembered where he was, and why. He groaned slightly, realizing with some embarrassment he had snoozed his 17:00 alarm.

Coffee first? Or the results?

*Coffee for sure.*

He made his way through deserted hallways to the nearest breakroom to fetch a cup.

It had only been a few hours since Taki had been in search of a belated breakfast. He was embarrassed to see his plate and utensils were still where he'd left them, too tired to clean up after himself. He took a moment to take care of his mess now.

As much as he preferred real coffee, he prioritized speed. Taki settled for the self-serve dispenser, yawning as it progressed through its sequence. When his coffee was ready, he picked up his cup, sipped tentatively, sighed, and walked over to the counter.

He picked out a pastry and nibbled on it as he carried his coffee back to the lab. Bleary eyed, pastry finished, coffee nearly consumed, Taki placed his cup on a counter and walked over to the sequencer.

He looked at the display. He blinked slowly, then rapidly; the last bite of pastry fell from his agape mouth. He rubbed his eyes furiously.

*It can't be…*

Focused now, he abandoned his coffee cup and practically ran back to the breakroom to fetch a knife.

# DAY 4: 19:37
## SLUMBER

It took Lara a moment to remember where she was. Only a moment, though, because there was no mistaking the inside of a high-g chamber.

The display mounted inside the chamber's lid informed her they were now accelerating at a modest 1-g. While she slept, they'd peaked a bit above 23-g. They continued accelerating for another couple of days, then re-oriented the ship and decelerated all the way to their destination. Given the relative positions of Eden and the asteroid, they'd saved themselves weeks of travel time. And, though she felt comfortable in zero-g, she enjoyed the simulated gravity of their deceleration.

Truth be told, she would have gladly spent the extra weeks to avoid using the chamber. Chatting with Reiner, she'd referred to it as an "oubliette," then had to explain the reference. Oubliettes were medieval torture devices, essentially an extremely confined space limiting one's movement, only accessed through a trapdoor. He laughed. After that conversation, they continued to refer to them as "oubliettes" in casual conversation. Sadly, keeping to their schedule required using the oubliette, so she cringed, stepped into the chamber, and surrendered to the liquid sleep.

Lara leaned back into the cushioned lining as the interfaces connected with her environmental suit undergarment. She gripped the hand controls and, with her right forefinger, pressed the "start" button. The lid swung closed, positioning the display panel before her eyes. Her legs and arms were held firmly in place by the lid's padding, triggering her claustrophobia. Lara could feel the liquid filling the chamber as she closed her eyes. She focused on her breathing, and resisted the urge to scream.

The fluid rose past her knees, fingers, hips, elbows, and chest. As the liquid reached her chin, she began to panic. It took all of her willpower to not press the "abort" button as she held her breath and the liquid rose past her tightly closed eyes.

Lara held her breath as long as she could. Logically, she knew she would be fine. Intellectually, she understood all she had to do was breathe deeply and her body would instinctively remember the womb. That she could, once again, breathe liquid.

But in the moment? Lara knew she was about to drown.

When her body's demand for oxygen overrode all else, in full blown panic, Lara breathed in the liquid as her body spasmed against the restraints.

Then, it was over. Lara breathed deeply. The liquid moved in and out of her lungs smoothly, bearing more than enough oxygen to satisfy her body's needs. It was, as Reiner said, a less viscous fluid than the last time she'd endured this. She opened her eyes to look at her vitals on the panel as the last bubbles escaped her lungs and were removed by the chamber.

Slowly, she calmed. As she calmed, the chamber deflated the padding restraining her arms. Lara used her left fingers to scroll through the panel's interfaces. Suspended in the liquid, she could not feel the ship accelerating at all, but she could see the gauges telling her that they were already accelerating beyond what her body could otherwise have endured.

She finally relaxed, and closing her eyes, she slept deeply.

And now, it was over. Lara was awake. She was still breathing the liquid though. She scrolled through the interfaces on the panel. All seemed well.

She knew she needed to exit the chamber. She also knew exiting was almost as awful as entering. But there was no alternative; she had to press the "end" button.

Lara closed her eyes, braced herself, then with her right thumb, hit the button.

The liquid drained quickly as the chamber reclaimed the fluid. She felt the level dropping, exposing the crown of her head, then her face. She began to cough and choke violently. As the last of the liquid drained, the door of the chamber opened and she fell to her hands and knees, retching as her body cleared the liquid from her lungs. After what felt like an eternity but was only a few miserable minutes, she collected herself and slowly stood. Gravity felt good!

Lara could see that the other chamber was already empty. Hopefully, Reiner was making coffee. She walked to the hatch, hit the button, and began to climb. As her head cleared the next level, she looked around.

Lara saw Reiner through the transparent central core. He was in the kitchen, standing by the coffee maker. She was *so* hungry. The chamber provided nutritional supplements through her environmental suit; but getting nutrients through an intravenous port was no substitute for real food! She hit the button and stepped through into the kitchen.

Reiner turned his head slightly. "Good morning! That wasn't so bad, was it?"

Lara grunted. "Yes, yes it was. Just awful!"

He laughed. "Yeah, I know. I hate it, too. Part of the package. The glorious experience of interplanetary travel." He shrugged. "Coffee's almost ready!"

"Thank you!" As the coffee dripped, tantalizing odors wafted her way. She breathed deeply. She smelled coffee, and other things cooking. "You're really making me appreciate breathing air versus liquid!"

"You're quite welcome. Your turn to cook tomorrow."

He opened the refrigerator drawer, bent to look, and grimaced. "No dairy."

"I drink mine black."

Reiner grunted. "I'd rather not. Not the first time I found the larder lacking. And I know there's nothing dairy in the supplies we put away before we chambered. No worries, I packed some condensed milk in my kit. I'll be right back."

He turned and walked towards the clear hatch and wall separating their sleeping area from the kitchenette. He hit the button, opened the hatch, walked through the core, and let the hatch close as he headed to the storage cupboards next to his bunk. As he did so, Lara rummaged to find a mug, poured herself a cup, and sat at the table facing the wall, idly watching Reiner.

She scanned the quarters. One of the storage areas by her bunk was open. That was strange. She tried to remember what she put in that cupboard.

*How'd that happen? Did that happen on take off? Or while I was asleep?*

Reiner walked back towards the hatch when something flew down and hit him in the back. Lara jumped to her feet, spilling her coffee as she watched Reiner's arms flail about, trying to reach whatever was on his back.

Reiner began to scream.

Lara ran over to the hatch to help.

Another shape hit Reiner's shoulder and he spun around.

Lara saw two somethings crawling on him.

He was still flailing, and his movements made them hard to see. They were about the size of rats. They dug into his back and shoulders, blood welling where their claws pierced his skin. Reiner reached for the hatch control.

In a complete panic, Lara screamed gutterally and hit the lock button.

Reiner was losing the struggle, desperate to shake the monsters loose. His arm was now blocking the bunkroom hatch from closing. And he could see the kitchenette hatch was locked.

"Lara? Lara, let me in! You have to let me in, help get these things off me!"

Lara backed away slowly, shaking her head in shame and horror, tears in her eyes.

"I...I can't! I can't let those things in!"

His mouth opened, a silent cry as his eyes closed tightly. Struggling to stay on his feet, he stood shakily by the bunkroom hatch, leaning through the door, his hand on the core ladder, blood droplets splattering on the metallic floor.

"PLEASE! PLEASE LARA, LET ME THROUGH! LET ME THROUGH! YOU'VE GOT TO LET ME THROUGH!! HELP ME!! PLEASE, GODDAMMIT, HELP ME!!! LAAAARRRAAA!!"

Lara fell to the ground shaking; she clutched the table leg of the kitchenette. She kept shaking her head in fear and shame, tears streaming down her cheeks, silently mouthing "no, no, I can't, I'm sorry..."

Reiner ducked as another of the strange creatures flew by his head into the central core.

Lara gaped, transfixed by the horror. A terrible thought snapped her back. She hopped up on her knees and started fumbling with her wrist computer, desperate to lock down all the central core hatches. She knew what that would mean for Reiner, with his arm blocking the hatch, but she *had* to find a way to isolate the things. The hatches were only designed to isolate parts of the ship in the event of a hull breach. If there had been a pressure differential, the hatch would have closed, even if it meant severing his arm. But, without a pressure differential, his arm prevented the hatch from closing.

Reiner yelled and fell, writhing in pain. Lara could see one of the creatures tighten its grip as something long, sharp, and curved protruded from its body. It thrust itself into Reiner's abdomen. His eyes went wide, his mouth agape in a silent scream, unable to resist as it pressed its wriggling hips against his body. After moments that felt like an eternity, Reiner went limp as it slowly withdrew its shaft, covered with Reiner's blood, a clear liquid dripping from the tip. Its eyes held Reiner's as its grip slowly loosened and its organ retracted into its body.

The monster turned, eyestalks wavering. Then it ripped away the material of his undergarment until it tore a hole that exposed the flesh of his calf. It widened the tear, then gripped his leg tightly as the curved lance re-emerged from its body. Suddenly, it thrust the lance into Reiner's calf, eliciting another scream. The monster swayed slightly as it filled Reiner's calf with venom. Then it lifted its hips again and she watched the lance retract into its body.

The creature began to massage Reiner's calf with its forelimbs, kneading the muscle as he moaned. After a moment, holding his leg, it stabbed the muscle with its beak, eliciting another shriek from him. It resumed massaging the muscle. As she stared, as Reiner cried, the muscle shrank.

Lara tore her eyes away to see that the one by his shoulder had moved to his arm, its throat pulsing as it inserted its beak deeper into the shrinking meat of his bicep.

*It's eating him, it's eating him alive, it's eating him alive…*

Lara watched wide-eyed as the two nightmares fed on him, as Reiner moaned, his eyes pleading for help. There was nothing she could do. Movement in her peripheral area drew her attention. Lara let out a shaky cry.

There were more of them, in the tube, walking along the ladder, searching, hunting, moving to other decks.

One of the nightmares stopped; its eyestalks turned towards her.

It flew straight into the wall of the tube, like a fly looking for entry. It tried to grasp the wall, looking for a way to get through to her.

The others came back through the tube. They'd been unable to find a way out of the tube, so they returned and landed on Reiner's body.

One grabbed his buttock, stabbing his ass with its member, then massaging it as it inserted its beak to feed. Another attacked his shoulder. The last one, the one that tried to get through to Lara, gave up and attached itself to Reiner's other leg.

Reiner shriveled as she watched, moaned as she stared, until finally, he went silent. His eyes continued to tear up and to dart about, until they too were silent and dead. As his face shriveled, his right eye bulged from its socket. It was too much.

Lara's head hit the kitchenette as she passed out.

# DAY 4: 21:32
## TAKI CALLS GEORGE

All available aerial drones were now fully committed. George absentmindedly drummed his fingers on the lab table. There was no point in asking for more to be fabricated; Dieter just couldn't turn them around fast enough. This phenomena would be over before Dieter could produce more drones. Nikko freed up drones as quickly as he could, but George completely understood the importance of monitoring facility recovery efforts. That left only the drones still patrolling around his research teams. Could he, in good conscience, reallocate any more from security monitoring?

George leaned forward, elbows on table, rubbing his temples. More and more of these "things" were appearing along all the coasts. There appeared to be a number of species and, as far as he could discern through drone footage, they all appeared to be related species, members of the trilaterally symmetric super-kingdom. They probably were not all in the same genus. George theorized they were all in the same family, like dogs, coyotes, and wolves.

He needed some specimens; there was only so much he could get from imagery.

But, as aggressive as they were, they were also difficult to approach. Every time one of the researchers or secmeds tried to get close, the creatures either bolted or attacked. In fact, a few of his research teams were being attacked so heavily they had to abandon their research. At least he could reallocate their patrol drones.

A secmed, one of their better marksmen, managed to shoot one, and should have it to a mobile lab in another hour or so.

What bothered George the most was he had no idea where they were coming from, or where else they were appearing beyond coastal environments.

None of the scientists on the teams did. He thought it highly probable their emergence was triggered by the quadrilunar alignment; that their sudden appearance had to do with feeding on the squirts. It was also possible that the disappearance of so many creatures normally present was due to evading these predators. The few individuals that were foolish or desperate enough to linger were being fed upon.

George leaned back. It was fascinating to see this horde of predators appear out of nowhere to capitalize on multitudes of potential prey hauling themselves onto the beaches from some mysterious marine depth. He could only assume the squirts were driven to their emergence by some relentless marine predator, only to become sustenance for another persistent marauder. Sheer numbers worked in the squirts' favor, though. Many were lost to predation, but it barely made a dent in their total number.

George checked the status of the creature shot by the secmed. It was still a long way from the lab. He might as well grab something to eat.

His wrist computer buzzed with a ping from one of the botanists at the settlement. George tapped the computer, and a rather disheveled Taki appeared before him.

"Taki! Are you alright?"

Taki blinked, then responded. "Oh, I must look a mess. Didn't get much sleep last night."

"As long as you're ok. What's going on?"

After a pause, Taki said, "George, I think you need to come back to the settlement. We might have a problem."

George stared at Taki, then asked, "are you serious? What could possibly be urgent enough to bring me back now?"

Taki tapped his wrist computer and an image of the pineapple in his lab appeared. As the pineapple slowly turned, George saw a breakroom knife stuck in the pineapple beside a rather sloppy incision.

"I stopped at a place near the base station for breakfast yesterday, George, and the owner asked me to look at his pineapple. Have you seen one of these?"

George sighed. "No, I haven't seen one myself, but I've heard about them. Have you heard about the surveyors killed a few days ago? Apparently, they were smuggling these plants in. And, apparently, there's a species that preys on them and viewed the surveyors as competition. They killed the surveyors to protect their pineapple supply. Anyway, the dead team were smuggling them in and selling them as novelties. We're tracking them down now so we can get them out of the settlement."

Taki nodded furiously with bloodshot eyes. "I'd heard about the surveyors, but not the pineapple connection. Interesting."

His expression shifted to one of concern.

"George, I took a tissue sample and ran a DNA test against this thing. The results surprised me, so I took a knife to it to verify what the DNA test was telling me. George…"

Taki's voice dropped to nearly a whisper. "George, it's from the trilateral super-kingdom. It's *not* a plant…"

# ∎DAY 5: 02:31
## REVELATION

Elke walked slowly but with purpose down the hall to her conference room. She saw John yawning as he entered the room. She followed him, then took her seat at the head of the table. George and a younger man she didn't recognize stood at the base of the triangular table. Behind them, the transparent wall facing east offered a stunning view of the Garcia Mountains, starkly beautiful in the aggregate moonlight of the fading alignment.

Greetings were exchanged as Nikko, Bhavia, Rajiv, and Dieter trickled in. After another moment, Guido appeared virtually. She cleared her throat and folded her hands on the table.

"Okay, George, what's going on? Why are you here, rather than at your field site? Why the urgent meeting request?"

George and his guest did not sit. They did not look good. After a moment, Elke realized by their facial expressions that they were more than stressed.

They were terrified.

"Governor, I didn't make the request lightly. We have a problem."

He gestured to the younger man accompanying him.

"This is Taki. He's one of our best botanists. Taki, please explain what you've found."

Taki was clearly more than a little nervous. He blushed. He'd never addressed colonial leadership before. He cleared his throat before speaking.

"Uh…uh, hi, um yes, I, uh, stopped for breakfast at a restaurant near the base station transportation hub. Nice place…I go there a lot, um…Convenient, and the food's good." He blushed again, his face now a bright red. "Anyway, yes, um, so I stopped and while I was there, the owner, who remembered I'm a botanist, asked me to look at his pineapple."

The room was silent. A projection of the restaurant's pineapple appeared on the conference room table.

"George uh, he told me you're aware of pineapples and that they have something to do with the attack on the survey team? I, uh, don't know much about that. But the owner, Fernando, nice guy, really nice guy, uh, well he let me take this one and I've been examining it."

He paused and looked anxiously around the room.

Elke nodded encouragingly. "Thank you, Taki. Please tell us what you've learned."

Taki blushed again. "Uh, it's not a plant."

The room was silent. Taki, clearly taken aback by the lack of response, repeated himself: "it's *not* a plant…"

John raised a finger as the rest of the senior staff exchanged confused looks. "Well, obviously, we understand that it's from Eden. We understand that Eden's life forms are alien and they're not really animals or plants like we're used to. Is that what you mean?"

Taki, wide-eyed and disheveled, shook his head vigorously.

"No. I mean, that's all true, and it's great to know senior staff understands all that. But, no, that's not what I meant." He paused, searching for the right words, then started speaking rapidly.

"Okay, okay, so, as you seem to know, Eden has five super-kingdoms, all as alien to each other as they are to us, because, we believe, unlike Earth, life happened multiple, distinct times on Eden. So, we have five distinct evolutionary trees, and, in each evolutionary tree, we see rough equivalents to Earth's major life groupings. Because each lineage has rough analogs to Earth's bacteria and animals and plants, right, and each lineage's bacteria, animals, and plants have rough equivalents to Earth's algae and vascular plants and insects and fish and so on, right?

And we see, for example, among Eden's distinct plant equivalents, we see phytochemicals, mostly green, like Earth's chlorophyll, but different, right? Because that's the most efficient color for photosynthesis, so green predominates, and we see all sorts of green things growing all over the planet, and so we think these things are like Earth plants, right? Like this pineapple… uh, well it's not *really* a…well this pineapple-looking *thing*, right? Looks like one, with a thick rind and broad green leaves and this blossom on top. But, it's not a plant! Not even by Eden standards! It…" Taki realized he was babbling and froze.

Elke looked about the room, noting expressions ranging from bemusement to annoyance. She smiled slightly at the nervous wreck. "We understand. If it's not a plant, then what is it?"

Taki's eyes widened further. "It's from the trilateral super-kingdom. From one of the animal-like groups in that kingdom. It's related to…" Taki looked at George nervously, like a kid afraid of being punished. George turned to face the senior staff. He looked pained.

"It's related to the kraken."

The room was silent as everyone's gaze shifted to stare at the pineapple. Elke's smile disappeared. She spoke slowly.

"I'm going to need you to explain that *again*. That thing is like the *kraken*? How can that be? It's growing in soil, it has leaves, green leaves, and even flower petals!"

"Yes! Yes! That's what makes this all so cool!" Taki raved. "Time and again, we find Eden creatures that break the rules! Well, not really. They don't break the rules, because Earth rules don't apply here! That's what makes xenobiology so exciting; we're discovering, as we go, what has to be the same and what can be different! It's in our nature to form conceptual frameworks, paradigms, that allow you to make sense of the world, but, then, *then*, when you find something that breaks your paradigm, that breaks your conceptual framework, why then, that's what leads to true discovery! Newton, Darwin, Lavoisier, Einstein, all of them observed something in the world around them that just…broke their paradigms! We've been looking at Eden's life forms through this, this lens, through these blinders, if you will, about plants and animals being a fundamental divide on Earth, but not on Eden!"

George put his hand on Taki's shoulder to stop his monologue. "Taki, you've done great. Let me take it from here."

He stood as Taki sat down hurriedly.

"Let's step back, because what we're about to tell you will sound crazy if we don't put it in context."

He paused to collect himself, then continued.

"Remember that Eden has enormous biodiversity. Every year, as our colony grows, so does our xenobiology team. But, even so, even after fifteen years, we've barely scratched the surface. There are just *so* many life forms. There are major groups that we haven't seen, and many of the ones we *have* encountered, well, we simply haven't had the time to examine them in detail, delve into their internal structures, anything."

He shrugged, hands outstretched.

"I'm not complaining! It's a scientist's dream! But, when I tell you that one of our best botanists looked at this pineapple thing and couldn't immediately categorize it as a plant or animal equivalent, you have to understand two things. One is that he's never seen one before, and the other is that, as Taki said, Eden doesn't follow earthly rules about animals and plants."

He began to pace.

"On Earth, vascular plants are completely different from their animal counterparts. No nervous system. Circulation depends on tubes called xylem and phloem. Rigidity from the cellulose of their cell walls, including, for woody plants, the cambium layer. Here? Not only does Eden have these five life lineages, within each lineage, there are completely different internal structures among their plant equivalents. We *have* found, in the trilateral super-kingdom, a group of plant equivalents with internal structures including a rudimentary skeleton; though they have nothing like limbs or skulls or anything of that kind. They have a nerve net without a brain, not unlike an earthly starfish. They have a circulatory system rather than xylem and phloem. So, when Taki first saw this pineapple, as he began to examine it, he thought it was from that group. But it's much, much more!"

The image of the pineapple was replaced with a stylized kraken. As he spoke, the image changed.

"Now, the kraken has some specializations from our typical trilaterally symmetric beastie. The forelegs, for example, have evolved into these claws. Let's generalize them."

The claws transformed into forelimbs much like the hindlimbs, ending in six digits.

"And let's put the tails into soil and add some bristles, not unlike an Earth plant's root hairs, to increase surface area for absorbing water and nutrients. Let's modify the sensory cluster, losing the eyes, and adding the forelimbs, extending the eighteen digits into these red petals. Let's shrink the beak and tuck it down, hidden by the petals. Let's extend these wings and the hindlimbs, broadening them into leaves. Now let's do the same for the two dorsal limbs that were sex organs for the kraken, add phytochemicals, make them green, and voila! We have a pineapple."

He turned from the image and could see nods around the room. An image of a pineapple appeared next to the highly modified kraken.

"You can see that, unlike the rudimentary skeleton Taki expected, let alone anything like the internal structures of any Earth vascular plant, there's a skeletal structure aligned with what we just discussed. Now we'll add internal organs and, once again, very similar to what we see within kraken and any of their kin."

The image stopped changing. Now, the two images were virtually indistinguishable.

"We're here, folks, because we've just dissected two of these pineapples. They're haploid, like the kraken. And they have wombs, like the kraken. And, in those wombs, I found diploid young in very early stages of development. We found tidal sensors during the dissection; a lot of Eden life forms that synchronize their life cycles to lunar alignments have them. We think the quadrilunar alignment triggered the development of the diploid young… Whatever, the point *is*, these pineapples are now gestating diploid young that may be hatching soon, or even as we speak, around the colony, and we have absolutely no idea what these diploid young will turn out to be."

The room was silent until John, staring at the pineapple, swore.

George nodded. "You see it now, right? You see how much trouble we're in?"

The room filled with nervous murmurs until Elke cleared her throat and turned to Bhavia.

"Do we have *any* idea how many of these things have been smuggled into the colony?"

Bhavia shook his head slowly.

"No, not a clue. And I can't say how many domes might have them, or whether any have made their way to the orbiting platform."

Guido leaned forward. "I thought you'd taken the ringleader into custody?"

"Yes, Emil Pederson, or 'Pete' as he went by. One of your gondola operators, Nikko, or he was before trying to slip away. He's in the brig with the guy from your team Dieter, who made the specimen containers, as well as the four surviving surveyors."

Bhavia splayed a hand and sighed. "Pete's trying to be clever. He gave up his inventory of unsold pineapples and we confiscated them. But he claims he hasn't kept records of what he sold. I'm thinking he's holding out, hoping we'll let him go back aboard the *Mother Lode*. I'm letting him simmer overnight in a cell to see if that helps his memory."

"They're everywhere!" Taki exclaimed. "Have you noticed them in break rooms? I found one near my lab! It was in the middle of the food displays, so

I think somebody put it there to control bugs. The restaurant owner told me people are buying them to control bugs. Said something about them attracts bugs and they catch them and eat them. Said he bought his as a novelty, that his customers loved watching him feed his table scraps, crickets, mice, all sorts of stuff!"

John leaned back, clapped his hands, swore, and then turned to Elke. "We saw one! When I met you in that break room, remember? They had one of the damned things on the counter, by the serving trays! I never gave it a second thought!" He turned back to Taki. "But you say it's carnivorous? Like a Venus fly trap?"

As Taki nodded, John turned to George and continued. "How is that possible? They didn't start out as parasitic worms, dammit, not like the kraken! This 'Pete' and his guys were sneaking them in from outside! How the hell is it digesting table scraps and mice?"

Bhavia snapped his fingers. "Pete said it took them a while to figure out they need to be fed! Said he saw a fly land on one, watched it eat the fly. That's when they started feeding them. He said they still lose a lot of them, but the ones that take food thrive!"

George sat down in his chair for a few moments, fingers meshed on top of his head, then placed his palms on the table as he leaned forward.

"Speculation, okay? But rooted in ongoing research, intense research, as you might imagine, since the kraken. Organisms from Eden should be no more able to digest earthly tissues than we could stomach Eden tissues. But, as we observed, Eden's five distinct organochemical suites led to the evolution of a digestive plasticity we never imagined. You're right, John. With the kraken, we had infestation by spores, and we theorized that the spores, somehow, tailored the worms they spawned in their host to whatever biochemistry they encountered. But understanding 'why' still leaves you with the question of 'how', right? How would it tailor digestion to an alien biochemistry? Or, if it isn't tailoring, then how does it take sustenance from alien biochemistry?"

George shrugged. "It's like Taki said. We have these conceptual frameworks, these fundamental assumptions about how things work, these lenses through which we interpret the world around us, and it's only when we find something that breaks our conceptual frameworks that we realize they even exist. Like Einstein realizing the speed of light was a constant regardless of your frame of reference. That observation broke everything, and our understanding of the universe changed!

On Earth, plants build organic chemicals from inorganic sources, powered by the sun. They do this through chloroplasts, organelles, cellular structures that have their own DNA, which we believe means they're symbionts. Tiny, simple cells that were incorporated early in the history of Earth life by plant cells, allowing plants to evolve into everything from grass to trees. Then, because everything on Earth shares the same biochemistry, the animals that eat the plants, and then eat each other, don't need to break their food down to their inorganic components. They only need to break complex sugars into simple sugars, proteins into amino acids, and so forth. So, they have enzymes in their digestive systems to partially break down their food into usable components in an endless cycle. And, of course, organic material that is not consumed and digested is left to decompose. That decomposition is the process by which bacteria break organic chemicals into inorganics, completing the cycle. You can see, then, that we came to Eden with a conceptual framework that only plants can convert inorganics to organics and only bacteria can convert organics back to inorganics. Animals, feeding on plants or each other, apply enzymes to break their food down to simpler, reusable organics.

What we've recently found was that the kraken, and their close relatives, have organelles, organelles unlike anything on Earth, in their digestive tissues. Their digestive systems subject their food to harsher acids than ours, breaking complex organic material down, to a degree, without enzymes. Then, as their digestive systems absorb this organic material, a set of organelles, like the decay bacteria, break them down into inorganics, then reconstruct them into the basic building blocks of the kraken's organic chemistry. It's less efficient, sure, but it means they can digest anything. *Anything*. And, it's really quite fascinating, especially because the DNA in these organelles doesn't come from the kraken's organochemical suite! That suggests these organelles might be found in other super-kingdoms!"

Elke held up a hand. George paused.

"George, that's all interesting. But I need you to explain what we should do with this information."

He blinked, blushed, then looked around the room.

"Right, sorry, so here's the bottom line. This Pete and his compatriots smuggled in these pineapples, believing them to be harmless plants. But they're not plants, they're haploid, like the kraken, and they're about to give birth to diploid young like the kraken eventually did. We don't know how many there will be, we don't know how big they'll be, we don't know anything about them, except that they'll have the digestive plasticity of kraken and we've already trained them to be nourished by earthly organic material. So, whatever they're going to be, they're not going to just starve, right? That's always been one of our presumed safeguards should something from Eden get loose, right? Anything from Eden should just die from starvation. But not these things! And, I suspect, based on their relatives, that they'll be predatory, but what will they prey upon? Vermin? Pets? Livestock? Us? We've no way to know!"

Elke rubbed her temple; a throbbing headache was starting to set in. "And that's why you called us all into this meeting in the middle of the night."

It was a statement, not a question. George and Taki exchanged a quick look, then nodded. The room was heavy with silence. Elke leaned back, swore, then looked around the room.

"First thing we need is more information. Bhavia, you said you have more pineapples in the brig?"

Bhavia, expressionless, nodded.

"I want you to take whomever George tells you to take to the brig. I want the pineapples you confiscated brought to the lab for dissection. Got it?"

Bhavia nodded, then looked at George and Taki. They exchanged a look, then Taki said, "I'll go, George. I'm, uh, already familiar with the pineapples."

"Second thing," Elke continued, "we need to find and remove every pineapple we can. I want every pineapple here under the main dome brought to George and Taki's lab."

She turned to Nikko and said, "wake up your people. I want every break room, every public space searched for pineapples, and I want them *all* taken to the lab."

George raised a hand. "We should really take everything to one of the landing pad labs. Taki's lab is just a teaching lab. We're going to need better equipment."

Elke sighed. "I really want you two nearby. Nikko?"

Nikko stopped tapping at his wrist computer and said, "George, get me a list of what you'll need, and I'll have it brought from one of the landing pad labs to Taki's lab. Good enough?"

George nodded and moved towards Nikko to discuss said list as Elke continued. "Thank you, Nikko. I know we're asking a lot in the middle of the night. You're going to have to wake up a lot of people, but I think it's justified."

She paused before she began to pace. She needed to walk off the rising nerves, and her headache. It was starting to come back. That pulsing, throbbing headache those monsters created, the panic, the dead friends…

Elke noticed her hand was shaking. She stopped and tapped it on the table. "Okay, between the brig pineapples and the ones we confiscate from base station public spaces, you should have enough research subjects. We still need to clear the rest of the colony of these things. Nikko, we're going to need a plan, a methodology. We need to inspect and clear every public space. We need to do wellness checks for every residence. We need to find and destroy every pineapple."

She turned to Bhavia. "I want this 'Pete' interrogated. I authorize the use of any method necessary, you *have* to get him to talk. I want to know how far these things have spread. I'm guessing they've made it to the residential dome. What about the agricultural domes? Any of the mining outposts or research or infrastructure domes? Or the orbiting platform?"

She turned back to Nikko. "I'd like you and Guido to prepare a plan for a thorough search of the orbiting platform. We'll press Pete, but I'm not willing to take his word for it."

Nikko looked at Guido, turned back, and nodded.

Elke sighed, then looked about the room.

"We can't know when these things will start hatching, or whether any of them have already hatched. We don't know what these things will look like, how big they'll get. Suggestions?"

George raised a finger. "The pineapple Taki found in the breakroom was about 17 kilos, and the one from the restaurant was closer to 25 kilos. The wombs we examined had a *lot* of diploid young. We know unborn kraken eat each other, but we can't say for sure whether the pineapples will follow the same pattern. I'm thinking we're dealing with a large number of smaller critters from each parent. And, if they follow the pattern of the kraken diploid phase, siblings will start working together."

He shrugged, then added, "I'm sorry. I hate to be vague, but we just don't have enough information yet. For now, the best I can offer is a scientific wild ass guess. What I can say with some confidence, though, is that we have a serious problem."

# DAY 5: 02:46
## THE BRIG

Pete swore.

It hadn't been a great night for any of them. The two cells were not designed for long term residency, with only two bunks and a lavatory per cell. Bhavia wanted to isolate Twitchy from the other surveyors, so he was in a cell with Pete and Prakash. Unsurprisingly, nobody wanted to share any of the little bunks, so that left at least one of them pacing at any given time. At the moment, that was Pete.

It didn't help that the lights dimmed but never went out. It was a little too well-lit for him to sleep anyway. Pete knew the others were trying to ignore the light and sleep. He didn't care. It was *their* fault he was in here.

*Couldn't keep their fuckin' mouths shut!*

He'd been so close, *so close*, to getting away. Pete squeezed the bars and bowed his head in frustration, muttering to himself. Prakash, irritable from lack of sleep, sat up in a huff.

"Shut up! I'm trying to sleep."

Pete would not cooperate. He kept moving around and tapping on the bars, almost happy to irritate Prakash.

"Jesus, Pete, Would you please shut up?" Prakash swore loudly. "We can't do anything about the lights, so could you please just be quiet?!?!" The other inmates started to stir and turn on Prakash for talking loudly.

Pete whispered angrily, so as not to turn the crew against him too. "Fine! Fine…ok?"

He swore again, but quietly this time. Suddenly, something moved, something in the corner just beyond the cell. Pete squinted, staring at the confiscated pineapples.

"Lights, 25%."

The lights brightened as the others grumbled and swore.

"Pete, what the fuck?"

He pointed.

"Did you hear that??"

"Pete, would you PLEASE…"

"No! Did you *hear* that? There's something over there, behind those things…"

Prakash sat up and looked across at Pete, who was looking through the bars. He stood, walked over to the bars, looking in the direction Pete was pointing.

There was movement by the pineapples sitting in the corner.

Prakash said, "lights, 50%!"

The lights continued to brighten. Prakash saw that one of the pineapples looked like it had collapsed. Another was moving, strangely, and there was a ragged tear on its side. Something was crawling out of the hole.

"How many are there?" Pete's voice started to quiver.

The others were standing by the bars now, blinking hard as the lights brightened.

They could barely process what they were seeing. Small, alien horrors crawled out of one of the deflated pineapples. Tiny, clawed, winged monsters wriggled and yawned with tri-part beaks as they emerged. Snakelike tongues flickered in the air. Some had their beaks jabbed into the pineapples, like they were sucking something out of them. A limb with six long, thin fingers hovered above their bodies. As the light gradually brightened, the prisoners realized the long thin fingers were *eyes*.

"What the fuck?"

The trapped prisoners stared through the bars. The pineapples shriveled as the creatures jabbed them with their beaks. One of the things, perched on a shriveled pineapple, turned towards them. Its eyestalks, one by one, turned their way.

It stopped moving. Its eyestalks wavered as it watched them. Another turned, and its eyestalks turned towards them as well. The first one's wings began to unfurl as its legs tensed.

A cold chill seized Pete. He slowly backed away from the bars, shaking his head, softly whimpering, "no…no…no…"

As he backed away, the backs of his calves hit one of the bunks. He lost his balance and landed with his rump on the mattress.

The first creature launched itself towards them. The only sound was the barely detectable movement of its wings as it flew across the space.

The other prisoners backed away from the bars.

The thing reached the bars, grasped them as it lighted, briefly thwarted until it made its way through. It stretched its wings again and then, with limbs splayed, hit one of the surveyors in the chest, knocking him off balance.

As he fell beside a bunk, the monster dug its claws into the meat of his left shoulder. It locked eyes as the surveyor desperately floundered on his back, trying to get away. A long, thin dagger emerged from between its hind legs. It raised its hips, stabbed him, then pressed its hips into him. Its eyestalks stared at his face as he screamed.

Pete backed further away on the cot, pressing himself against the wall of the cell. He heard the rustling of more wings and saw a swarm coming through the bars.

He stared helplessly as the others, screaming and yelling, ran to the far sides of the cells. They desperately tried to find a way out as the creatures flew to them and dragged them down to feast.

Twitchy lay at Pete's feet. He was staring into the eyes of his tormentor as it withdrew its organ. Pete couldn't look away as the thing slowly moved to Twitchy's arm and tore through his sleeve. Twitchy grunted as it stabbed his bicep with its organ, then began to gently massage his arm, wrist to shoulder. After a few moments, it paused and jabbed his arm with its beak. Twitchy cried out as it resumed the massage, his arm shriveling as it sucked the life out of him.

Prakash and the surveyors were now all on the floor, staring at the ceiling, moaning in agony as the things worked their bodies. Pete watched the victims exclaim with each sting and shrivel up as the creatures massaged their musculature and sucked them dry.

The first to be attacked arched his neck, letting out a long, woeful cry as a nightmare came over and grasped his head. As it cradled his head, as he stared up into its eyes, Pete saw the muscles of its forelimbs flexing. The man stared up, his mouth widening into a soundless scream.

Suddenly, Pete heard an awful, crunching sound that crescendoed as the man's head imploded.

The creature gazed into his lifeless eyes, then jabbed its beak through his ruined forehead into what was left of his braincase. It began to sip. Pete sobbed quietly, sitting on the cot, too terrified to move.

As each of the prisoners died, one nightmare perched on what was left of Prakash pulled its beak from Prakash's body. Its eyestalks moved independently, scanning the room.

One of the eyes locked on Pete.

Pete muttered softly, "…no, no, not me, no…"

Its other eyes moved towards him, locking on.

He stayed still, absolutely still.

Another eyestalk turned, then another.

All six eyes looked at him.

The wings unfurled.

# ▪ DAY 5: 04:10
## SOMETHING IN THE DARK

Dad's eyes snapped open. He lay there, on his right side, in the dark, suddenly wide awake. He could hear his wife breathing softly on her side of the bed. Everything seemed in order. He sighed, looked at the time, then flipped his pillow to the cool side and returned to sleep.

▪ ▪ ▪

The hungry creature pressed its body forward and extended its eyes through slots in the air vent. It had a strange feeling! It held its beak downward and extended its eyes as far as it could, trying to see whether there were any screws within reach.

There *were*!

It pulled back, and, as it did so, the others were pushed back, making too much noise. It reached through the air vent, one slot at a time, feeling for the screws. It sensed prey on the other side of the vent. It couldn't see them; there was something on the other side of the vent blocking its view. But it could smell them, and it could feel their electromagnetic presence.

It was hungry, so, so hungry! And it was getting close to a release, a glorious, glorious release!

Slowly, steadily, straining, it managed to get one screw to move, then turn, and then fall out.

It felt around for the next one.

▪ ▪ ▪

Dad's eyes snapped open. He *definitely* heard something this time, some kind of rustling sound. And it sure wasn't one of the kids.

He swung his legs over the side of the bed and sat up, staring into the darkness. He turned his head slowly.

*There it is again!*

It sounded like it was coming from outside their bedroom. He realized it was coming from the common area, by their entertainment system. *What the hell was that?*

He reached for his wrist computer and put it on, then put on his robe as he stood. He padded slowly out. He tapped his wrist computer to make sure all the bedroom doors were closed, then whispered "lights, 25%."

As the lights came on, he walked slowly towards the intermittent sound. The rustling was accompanied by the sound of something small and metallic falling to the floor. He cocked his head and rubbed the back of his neck; it was too early to be dealing with…well whatever it is. And why did he hear thin metal bending?

He realized it was coming from behind the sofa. He stood beside the sofa, looking into the dark space behind it. The sofa itself cast a shadow in the dim lighting, preventing him from seeing the true source of the noise.

"Lights! 50%!"

As the lights brightened, he saw movement. He bent over, his left hand on the back of the sofa as he shifted his center of gravity forward. His robe fell open slightly.

The father realized with a cold start that the vent cover was bending outward and *something* was on the other side of the vent, pushing against the cover, trying to bust into the room!

He straightened and ran his right hand through his hair as he looked about the room, trying to figure out what he could do. Inspired, he quickly pushed the sofa as hard as he could against the wall and held it there. That might buy him a little time. He muttered quietly, "shit, shit, shit, shit, shit…"

The noise stopped.

"Daddy?"

As he kept pressing the sofa against the wall, Dad turned to see his adolescent son standing bleary eyed by his now open bedroom door.

"Dad, what are you doing?"

Suddenly, the sofa started to move, as whatever it was resumed working on the vent cover. As calmly as he could muster, Dad said, "Juaquin, go to the weapons cabinet and get Daddy his scattergun, right now!" He braced his forearm against the sofa so he could tap his wrist computer and unlock the cabinet for his son.

He heard a clatter from behind the sofa. He froze, not sure what that meant. One of the cushions fell over. Something was tearing its way through the back of the sofa.

"Joaquin! NOW! Daddy needs his scattergun NOW!"

"Why Daddy? What's going on?"

"NOW, dammit, bring it NOW!"

One of the cushions fell forward and he saw sharp claws cutting through an opening, urgently tearing at the edges.

"Daddy, what is that?!"

Realizing the sofa was not an effective barrier, he abandoned it. His robe flew wide open, but he didn't care. He stepped back towards his son, grabbed for the scattergun, and spun back around.

As he hit the safety, something launched itself out of the hole in the sofa and onto him. The small attacker hit him hard, causing him to lose his balance and his grip on the scattergun.

"DAD?!? Dad, what the…"

Flat on his back, struggling against the strong claws digging into his chest, Dad tore his eyes from the thing and turned his head to see his son falling down with two more monsters on him.

He turned back to look into the six wavering eyes of the thing perched on his chest. He brought up his hands to fight it as he saw something emerge from the base of its tail, between its hind legs. He gasped in pain as it stabbed him in the belly, pressing its hips into him. He screamed in agony as burning fire spread through his abdomen. The vermin kept pressing into him, its hips wiggling.

He had to fight, despite the pain. He balled up his fists and swung at the creature, but his blows had little effect. He lost control of his arms and they fell uselessly to his side as he heard his son scream.

He felt the thing pull itself out of him, then its claws loosened their grip. It turned to walk along his leg, just as he watched another nightmare walk along his boy's arm.

Dad could hear more of them now, fluttering around the room. He felt two more monsters land on his arm and his leg. He whimpered as he felt the one on his leg stab his calf, then again as the one on his arm stabbed his bicep.

He tried to raise his arms again, but he could barely lift his shoulder now. He felt them knead his arm and leg, then stab him again. But this time, instead of the burning, he felt an odd, nauseating, *pulling* sensation, unlike anything he'd ever felt before.

He could still move his eyes, but he couldn't move his head. He could hear them scurrying towards the hallway, but he couldn't guess how many there were.

He couldn't speak.

All he could do was lie there while they slowly mutilated him, knowing he was helpless to warn his wife and other children.

■ ■ ■

The food was *so* delicious.

It grasped the end of the prey's limb, squeezing gently but firmly. The creature drank the thick, viscous, liquified muscle oozing slowly as it worked its way up the extremity. The creature could taste the fresh, warm juices with its tongues, smoothing out the lumps to make it all easier to sip, especially the bone tissue. The bone tissue liquified very, very slowly.

*Glorious.*

But now the limb was nearly drained. It worked the limb again, trying to wring out every last morsel, staring into the prey's eyes as the prey stared back. The prey had stopped seeping moisture from its eyes a while ago, but it could still sense the prey's fear and pain.

*Delicious.*

Satisfied that the limb held no more sustenance, it withdrew its tongues and then its beak. It looked across the body of the prey. It had already drained one of the other limbs, and the final two limbs were being enjoyed by its siblings. As it watched, one of them finished its limb as well. They raised their eyestalks to look into each other's eyes. The creature could tell its sibling's need for additional nourishment was greater than its own.

It was nearly ready for a release, but its sibling was not.

It stepped away from the prey as its sibling moved to the prey's torso, stabbing the prey's abdomen with fresh venom. The prey's eyes bulged. Its sibling inserted its beak into the prey's body to feed. This would, finally, end the prey's life. The meat would liquify, then the organs. Its sibling would feed as carefully and gradually as it could to extend the experience as long as possible. But ultimately there was no avoiding the expiration of the prey.

As its sibling fed, the creature contemplated the prey's sensory cluster. The prey's eyes followed as its sibling fed, its beak buried in the prey's torso. It knew there were nutrients behind those eyes; but the treat was encased in thick, heavy bone that resisted their venom. It moved towards the prey as its sibling fed, sensing that the prey's life was ebbing. It reached forward and grasped the prey's sensory cluster with its forepaws, one on each side, and squeezed. The creature tried to crack the bone as the prey's eyes widened and shifted to its own. The thick, protective shell did not budge; the delicious meal was still out of reach.

But it had an idea!

It moved just a little further forward, still grasping the prey's head. There *must* be a pathway through those eyes, to bypass that bone. It pulled hard on the prey's head as it stabbed its beak down through the eye. The prey made a wonderful, piercing noise! Then, it extended its tongues through its beak, into the space behind the eye, and tasted the yumminess. The beating of the prey's heart had indeed pushed some venom into the prey's head. It swirled its tongues ecstatically to accelerate the liquification, and began to sip as the prey moaned. As it sipped, as its sibling fed, it could feel the prey start to die.

The creature continued to feed as it looked about the space.

Across the space, its siblings enjoyed themselves, feeding on more captured prey, working their bodies to harvest every drop of nourishment. One sibling grasped the head of another dying prey, stabbing the victim's eye to get at the nutrients in the head. It could feel the dimming electromagnetic signals from the prey as they suffered.

It enjoyed their misery.

Finally, it was no longer hungry. It was satisfied, its belly was full, and its body processed what it had consumed. It felt a different pressure now, a pressure coming from deep in its body. It was time to satisfy a different urge. The creature extended electromagnetic senses until it felt the presence of another prey, one whose signal was not dimming.

*That way!*

It unfurled its wings and flew a short distance, then lighted and walked slowly through a narrow portal into a darkened space. It paused, reaching out with its senses. Every time it fed, it monitored its prey, learned their signals, read their feelings, and got better at finding them.

This one was feeling *fear*, yummy, delicious *fear*.

It moved slowly towards it, eyestalks splayed in the darkness. It listened for any sound. It felt for vibrations. It yearned to follow a scent.

*THERE!*

Something small was hiding in the corner of the space. The creature shifted direction, moving towards it. Suddenly, the prey reared up, made an awful noise, and began to accelerate across the space. The creature unfurled its wings and leapt towards its quarry. Claws splayed, the creature impaled the prey on impact, bringing it down as it screamed. As the prey hit the ground, the creature flexed the joints of its limbs to absorb the force; its tails and wings spread to keep its balance.

It allowed the prey to roll so that it could look into the prey's eyes.

It moved to the prey's torso, forelimb and hindlimb claws grasping the meat as it struggled. The creature kept its wings partially unfurled and tails extended for balance. It stared into the prey's eyes as they seeped moisture, the mouth emitting sharp, shrill noises. The creature tightened its grip, then thrust itself into the prey as the prey's body arched. Its whole body throbbed with pleasure as it pressed itself deeper into the victim. From deep, deep inside itself, a squeezing sensation welled up as warm liquid pulsed out of its member, venom and spores together, subduing the prey as the victim was impregnated.

Gradually, the sensation eased. The pleasure waned in favor of a glorious warmth. The prey ceased to struggle, its mouth slowing before going slack. Liquid dribbled from the prey's lips and moisture seeped from its eyes. The creature withdrew itself from the prey's body. Then, eyestalks splayed, it searched for a place to hide the prey so that it would not be vulnerable to predation while the spores grew.

# ▪ DAY 5: 04:23
## SURVIVOR

"Why are we here again?"

Harry and Bob, bleary eyed, stood in the hallway outside the brig with suspension pallets. Bhavia's call had woken them from a sound sleep. He impressed upon them a sense of urgency. So they dressed in their respective quarters, met at the transportation hub of the residential dome, and made their way very quickly to fetch a set of pallets, only to stand in the hallway and wait for someone named "Taki."

Bob snorted, then responded, "you tell me. I just work here!"

"Well then, why are we in the hallway instead of inside, where we could at least sit down and maybe get some sleep?"

"You heard Bhavia! We're not supposed to go in until this guy shows up. I don't know why, I just know how he gets when we don't do exactly as we're told, ok? Especially when he's stressed. You heard him, he's *stressed*!"

"But it's the middle of the night!"

"I know, I know…wait, is that the guy? Gotta be, this time of night!"

A disheveled young man approached them, pushing his own suspensor pallet filled with equipment. As he approached, Bob asked, "you Taki?"

The man nodded panting; he wasn't the fittest man. "Yes…yes, you must be Harry and Bob. Sorry to keep you waiting; I didn't think you'd get here that fast."

"Bhavia says 'jump', we jump."

Taki chuckled nervously, wiping sweat from his chin. "Are uh…you two armed?"

Bob nodded and Harry pointed to his sidearm. "Why do we need to be armed, going into the brig?" Harry asked suspiciously.

Taki looked at the door for a moment, then back at them. "Do you know about the pineapples?"

Bob and Harry looked at each other, then back at Taki. "Pineapples?"

"Pineapples. My understanding is that you guys rounded up Pete and his friends, then brought his pineapples here, right? So they're still in there, and something might be hatching out of them. My job is to confiscate and evaluate any pineapples, and your job is to shoot anything that's been released, if anything's hatched that is. Got it?"

"What the hell do you think is going to hatch out of a *plant*?"

"I haven't a clue, really. Might not have happened, might be something harmless, might be something really nasty. I haven't a clue."

Bob and Harry looked at each other again, then Harry turned to Taki. "Alright, how do you want to do this?"

"Well, judging from the last pineapples I dissected, I'm pretty sure nothing's hatched yet. But we have to be certain. So, I'm going to set up these barriers to block the corridor on either side of the door. Then we'll open the door, turn up the lights, and take the pineapples to my lab so I can remove the wombs."

"*Wombs*? In *plants*?"

Taki looked Bob in the eyes and nodded unblinkingly. "Yes, wombs."

Harry shrugged, then said, "give me one of the barriers and we'll set it up while you set up the other."

Once the barriers were in place, Harry and Bob stood by the door, weapons drawn. "Okay," Harry said nervously. "I'm accessing the cameras in there, not that I expect to see much until we…hey, the lights are already partially on. That's weird. Still pretty hard to make out, so I'm turning them up."

He stared at his wrist computer and swore. Bob and Taki looked at theirs as well. The smugglers weren't in their cots. And there were things on the floor. It wasn't clear what the things were, but there was something wrong about them.

Slowly, Harry said, "I have a bad feeling about this."

"I don't like this," Bob whispered. "Not one bit."

Harry sighed. "Okay, here's what we do. Taki, stay behind us." He turned to Bob, "stand ready. You see anything move that *isn't* human, put it down, and we'll reclose the door and get more people down here."

"Why don't we get more people here before we open the door?"

"Because it's the goddamn middle of the night! Besides, nothing's moving in there, so there's probably nothing to be concerned about. I think we can handle it, don't you?"

Bob stared at him, then turned to Taki, who tapped his left hand with his right forefinger nervously.

"Alright, go!"

Harry tapped his wrist computer and the portal transitioned open. They looked through the door. Nothing was moving. Harry, sidearm ready, stepped cautiously through the door, looking left and right. He stepped again, making his way to the nearest cell. He glanced down, then realized what he was seeing.

"Those are *bodies*! They're dead. They're…I don't know, they're…*empty*. Just skin…man, I've never seen anything like it!"

Taki stepped through, followed by Bob. Taki asked, "where are the pineapples?"

Bob pointed. "We put them over there."

Taki stepped slowly over towards the pineapples, then said, "they're shrunken, too. Torn open and shriveled. Any sign of anything that might have come out of them?"

Bob and Harry were slowly exploring the space. Bob found an air vent torn open.

"I think whatever hatched out of those pineapples got out through here!"

After a moment, Harry shouted. "Hey! We got a survivor!"

# DAY 5: 05:40
## THE WEIGHT OF RESPONSIBILITY

Elke stood by the windows. Dawn was breaking behind the Garcia Mountains, dark against the glow, the desert in their shadow as the sky erupted in brilliant colors. She held a cup of coffee; its rising steam danced in the angled light. She was tired, and she knew her team was tired.

Fifteen years ago, they'd been caught unprepared by the kraken. Painful lessons had been learned. Steps were taken. Plans were prepared. Drills were conducted. Fifteen years passed with mostly minor incidents, a scare here or an injury there.

Every death mattered, but Eden's per capita accidental death rate was lower than most. Every effort should be, and was, made to prevent and learn from these deaths. But deaths are an unavoidable fact of life, and every colony suffers losses. She shook her head.

The colony paid a very dear price for their naivete and overconfidence, *her* naivete and *her* overconfidence, in those first few weeks. And for fifteen years, she committed to not repeat those mistakes.

*But now, this.*

Despite all their preparations, all their planning, simple greed exposed them to a threat greater even than the kraken. For all she knew, the colony was already lost!

Elke knew she'd be forced to choose lesser evils, to make choices that would haunt her the rest of her life, as some choices she made fifteen years earlier haunted her still. But the colony *must* survive. Thousands of colonists' lives depended on her, and thousands more were aboard inbound ships. Eden's promises manifested a higher than typical cadence of inbound colony ships. Ships she could not contact. Ships that could not change course even if she could reach them.

And, for thousands of those colonists, kraken were nothing more than a history lesson, someone else's history. With each inbound cohort more skeptics flooded in, dubious about the tales of monsters that nearly wiped out their nascent colony.

She shook her head, filled with doubt. Doubt she must not reveal to her team. They needed, and deserved, strong leadership, and dammit, they'd get it.

Elke heard John entering the room behind her. A few moments later, she felt his hand on her shoulder as he leaned in and asked softly, "finished flogging yourself yet?"

She blushed, then let her chin fall to her chest. He knew her so well!

"God only knows how many are already dead!" she whispered.

He nodded.

"And it's your responsibility, I know. But there's a difference between being responsible and being at fault." He paused, then continued. "I've heard you, countless times, coach someone after an incident, remind them that all of this is new. That we can't foresee every possibility. That every best practice, every standard that keeps us safe was learned by critically reviewing what did and didn't work in the past."

"People have died, John." The pain in her voice was apparent. "More people are dying, right now, and all I can do is stand here and look out the window. I feel so useless! I should have…"

"Should have what?" He interrupted her. "What exactly, without clairvoyance, could you possibly have done? Imagine you're the coach here, Elke. What would you say right now?"

She nodded, sighing deeply.

"I know, I know."

"I'm not saying anything to you that you haven't said to me when I've needed it."

"And I appreciate it. And I also need to be able to say this shit to somebody."

He laughed ruefully, looking out the window, thinking of the times he needed to say shit to somebody. She'd been his somebody every time he needed one.

"I know you do."

She looked out the window, scanning the horizon. Without conscious thought, she straightened, took a deep breath, rolled back her shoulders,

242

lifted her chin, and turned back to take her seat. After a moment, John followed and took his seat.

Elke swept her eyes across her team. "What did you find?"

The others returned to their seats as John leaned back in his chair, his arm outstretched as he absentmindedly tapped the table.

"We have five dead bodies and one survivor," John began. "The bodies are not readily identifiable, but Bhavia has identified the survivor as Pete. It seems safe to assume the dead are Prashant and the four surveyors. We are running DNA checks to be sure. The, uh, bodies, are the damnedest thing I've ever seen. They're drained, shriveled. There's no muscle, no fat, no organs. There's skin and some residual bone tissue from the body's larger bones. The skin is punctured in multiple places. Big and small holes, as well as little perforations that look like claw marks to me."

He shook his head as he leaned forward.

"I've never seen anything like it. I did a little research, and the nearest thing I could find is what's left after a spider feeds on a small vertebrate, like a mouse."

John paused and looked down at the table. "You know…I've been a doctor for a very long time. I've, uh, I've seen some things, nasty things. Mostly accidents, especially sudden decompressions. It, uh, comes with the job, right?"

He paused again, glanced towards the ceiling, then around the room, then at Elke, then looked down again.

"I've never seen *anything* like this! The worst part, though? The worst are the heads. They, uh, they seemed to want to get at the brain tissue. Three of the skulls were fractured. And the fourth, it looks like whatever we're dealing with went through the eye socket."

The room was deathly silent as John spoke. For the senior members who survived the kraken, this was a waking nightmare, a horrible reality repeating itself. For the others, this gruesome terror made everything they'd ever heard about the kraken too real. The stories were true, and now the monsters were coming for them, too.

"Anyway," John continued, "we're analyzing the skin tissue. So far, we've found some Eden proteins with the same organochemical suite as the trilateral super-kingdom, which is consistent with what you've said about the pineapples. So, while I can't say for sure, I think that whatever did this to them came out of the pineapples. I hope to have more information later in the morning."

Elke nodded, then asked, "and your survivor?"

"Pete. They found him under one of the cots. He's alive, but he's in agony. He can move his eyes, but is otherwise immobile. As you walk around the room, he follows you with his eyes. And he can hear. If you ask him simple yes or no questions, he can use eye movements to respond. Beyond basic diagnostic questions, I'm not sure what to ask. Otherwise, he's in a great deal of pain. There's involuntary movement, spasms. I've pumped him full of everything I can think of, and nothing takes the edge off, at least not yet."

"Good!"

John raised his eyebrows in shock as he turned to Bhavia, whose anger and frustration was glaringly clear.

"Those bastards put us all at risk. Smuggled in who knows how many of these things! So no," Bhavia turned to John and glared back. "I don't feel sorry for the idiot. None of you should. It's fucking poetic justice!"

Many in the room lowered their eyes following Bhavia's outburst, some in sympathy, others with embarrassment at his callousness. Elke wasn't sure how many of them knew Nur was missing. She responded softly yet firmly. "I understand, Bhavia. I'm sure a lot of us feel the same way. Right now, though, right now we need to understand what we're dealing with. We need an actionable plan. Justice will have to wait."

Bhavia stood in a huff and walked away from the table to a window. Elke caught a glimpse of tears on his face just before he turned away. With his loved one missing, she did not hold his disrespect against him. Elke turned to John. "Please go on."

John's eyes lingered on Bhavia for a minute, then he turned back. "We found a wound in his abdomen similar to what we found in the others. We found a number of Eden proteins in his blood, suggesting an immobilizing venom of some sort. It's probable that the wound might have been caused by whatever came out of the pineapples. And it's sealed, like the last part of the injection had an adhesive quality that closed the wound. We also found these…"

He tapped his wrist computer and an image of Pete, lying on his back in a hospital bed, appeared over the table. John tapped his wrist computer again and the image became translucent, except for a number of red threads.

"Pete's body is filled with worms, just like a kraken infestation; but the nanobots we developed to clear kraken worms are not effective. There's something different about these parasite. We've only had him in treatment for a little over an hour, and the worms have demonstrated a rapid growth rate.

They're in every part of his body. If you look closely, you can see some of them moving under his skin. They're not feeding selectively like kraken worms; it's like they're not concerned with how long he lasts. And I can't remove them the old-fashioned way, he wouldn't survive it.

On the other hand, I'm quite sure, based on our experience with the kraken, that they'll mature fairly soon and emerge, killing him in the process. The poor bastard's in agony. He's fully conscious, terrified because he understands what's happening to him, and there's not a blessed thing I can do for him."

John hung his head. "I believe we should put him in a coma. Of course, he'll still die when the things hatch out of him, but at least he won't be able to feel the pain."

The room was silent for a few moments.

George cleared his throat. "John, uh, we've found some species related to kraken that do this. Remember the kraken life cycle, alternating generations? The haploid worms emerge from the host, metamorphosize, eat, grow, then eventually, mate. They're hermaphrodites, so any two can impregnate each other. Then the diploid young eat their way out of their parents' bodies and feed voraciously until they are able to release vast numbers of spores. These spores, when they land on a host, become worms and start the cycle all over again."

He leaned forward. "We've found some related species that don't release spores the way kraken do. Rather, in the haploid phase, there were dorsal limbs modified to be sex organs, since they're trilaterally symmetrical. In the diploid phase, one of the dorsal limbs is further modified. It's analogous to the ovipositor of a bee or wasp. It can inject venom, and it can insert spores directly into a host's body."

He raised his left hand to emphasize his point. "Now, I'm guessing here, because we haven't seen one of these things yet, but I would assume, after feeding on the pineapples and the other prisoners, one of these things injected Pete with a venom cocktail to immobilize him and then injected him with spores. We should compare what you're finding in Pete's body to the venoms we've found in these species."

John sighed, then asked, "what about the bodies? Any idea what happened there?"

"I think you said it perfectly. They look like what's left after a spider feeds. From the remains, I'd guess that if they don't inject a host with spores, they're capable of injecting a venom that liquifies their prey's tissues, allowing them to feed by sucking out the predigested flesh. We'll know more after you finish your tests, but I suspect you'll find traces of venom in them as well. I think that's how whatever's hatching out of the pineapples, the diploid young, are feeding."

George sat back in a slump; John ran a nervous hand through his hair. The room was heavy with dread. Elke looked again at Bhavia, who still hadn't returned to the table, then asked Nikko, "can you give us an update?"

Nikko leaned forward, resting his elbows on the table. "Every pineapple in the room was in the same condition as the bodies. I, uh, don't know what word to use. Drained? Shriveled? You can tell they used to be pineapples, but…"

"My team is conducting necropsies," George interrupted to make a point. "What's interesting is that only one has a gaping hole reminiscent of an exit wound. So, it would appear the one with a hole produced diploid young that fed on it first and subsequently ate the other pineapples that never hatched. The internal organs of those unhatched pineapples were liquified and extracted, so we can't tell for sure. The young hatching from the same pineapple are strongly related to each other and would likely work together, but they are not related to the other pineapples, so they would see them as competitors. The first ones to hatch probably fed on the other pineapples before attacking the prisoners."

"Yes, we didn't find any of the things in the room," Nikko continued. "We did find the air duct cover removed, so we believe they escaped through the air ducts."

The word choice visibly caught Elke off guard. "Explain 'removed', please."

"We found scratches, presumably claw marks, around one of the air duct covers. We found the screws from that air duct cover in place on the floor, with lots of scratches around the holes. The air duct cover was bent out of shape, suggesting they pulled at it as they removed the screws."

The senior staff looked around at each other incredulously.

"Are you…are you saying these…" Dieter stammered in disbelief. "Are you suggesting these…these *creatures* figured out how to *remove screws*…and then the air duct cover?"

Nikko nodded grimly. "Yes, that's exactly what I'm saying."

Elke turned to George. "Is this possible?"

"Certainly is." George saw the discomfort his answer caused. "Remember, the kraken were, unfortunately, good problem solvers. They were about as intelligent as Earth cephalopods, ah, octopus and squid. If you put a treat, say a crab, in a jar and present it to an octopus, it will quickly figure out how to unscrew the lid and take the crab. As these things seem to be related to kraken, I wouldn't be at all surprised to find these things are just as smart."

Elke leaned back, shaking her head. "So, to be *clear*, we have some unknown number of pineapples distributed throughout the settlement, and possibly the orbiting platform. We've trained each one of these things to thrive on earthly biochemistry, and we've probably been feeding them generously, because that's what people do with pets. Furthermore, each of these things is somewhere in the process of producing God only knows how many diploid young that, when they hatch, can overpower and feed on their owners, then escape through the air ducts to attack other colonists. And we could, for all we know, already be overrun by the damn things?! Is that right??"

In the absence of any correction from her staff, Elke heaved a big, exasperated sigh. "What, if anything, can we deduce about our unwanted guests?"

George looked at Taki, then back at Elke. "Not much. We know they're small enough to fit through the air ducts, right? So no bigger than a cat or small dog. As I said, the diploid young we found were in early development, so that doesn't give us much insight. I was hoping to learn more by dissecting pineapples from the brig."

"You'll have more specimens soon," Nikko said. "My people are checking breakrooms now. They'll bring any pineapples they find here."

Elke turned sharply to Nikko. "Are they armed?"

"Absolutely!"

"Good, good…well done." Elke paused; her hand was starting to shake again. She steadied her breathing. "George, Taki, we need to understand everything we can about this new threat. Keep us posted." Elke looked about the room. "Anything else?"

Rajiv raised a finger. "Remember that the air duct system is compartmentalized, but not like the orbiting platform. On most worlds, domes are pressurized against either no atmosphere or a toxic atmosphere. But not here on Eden. Our biggest concern here is spores from things like kraken. We breathe Eden air after we filter it. As long as we keep positive pressure, we're not worried about leaks, so we didn't design our duct systems for isolation. But we did, as part of our post kraken planning, put fine mesh barriers at major junctions that should limit these creature's movements."

John snorted. "Are they held in place with screws?"

"…yes." Rajiv grumbled, insulted by the insinuation. "But lots of screws given their size. And, unlike the duct covers in the rooms, they're too rigid to bend. Should at least slow them down. But how long they'll be contained, how long it might take for them to make their way from one air duct system to the next?" He shrugged. "I'm actually more concerned with whether they can escape the duct systems. I have some of my people reviewing schematics."

"Okay people," Elke resumed control of the room. "Since the kraken, we've planned and drilled to respond to threats. A lot of lives depend on us acting swiftly and effectively." She paused, then looked at each member of her staff as she gave orders.

"Guido, alert everyone. Get them up. Get them armed. Nikko, open the armories. Guido, activate our militia. Have your squad leaders gather their teams. I want them going door to door doing wellness checks. It's what, now, almost 06:00? Target to begin sweeps at 06:30. And Nikko, monitor all transportation sites, any point of exit or entry. Rajiv, find and provide any schematics to Dieter as he prepares the duct crawlers. George, Taki, continue your work, and coordinate with John in the event of more casualties."

Nikko tapped at his wrist computer as he spoke. "Not much transportation activity yet. People are just waking up. Usually peaks around 07:00, so 06:30 doesn't give us much time. But I wouldn't wait any longer. And I'm shutting down interdome transportation. We'll have some frustrated passengers, so I'll send some folks to the transportation hubs to send people home."

Guido turned to George. "We have quite a few secmeds deployed with your research teams. Have your teams retreated to their mobile bases?"

"Yes. Research sites have been inundated with predators…" George suddenly snapped his fingers. "I wonder! I wonder if the things that have been attacking the squirts and my research teams are the same things we're dealing with here! They're from the kraken group, too! I'll see if any of my teams have completed a genetic…"

"George!" Guido interrupted him. "George, we need more secmeds. If your teams have withdrawn from their fieldwork, I need to reassign those secmeds to lead squads!"

George opened his mouth to object, but thought otherwise. "Ok…ok. Taki, follow up with the field teams, see if anyone's done a genetic analysis we can cross reference with the dissected pineapples. I'll work with Guido to reassign some secmeds back here, ok? Nikko, we'll need some Falcons shuttled out to the research sites."

"How do we protect the field teams?" Elke asked. "Are they at serious risk?"

George paused. "I don't think so. It's only the field teams at coastal research sites. The teams at inland sites are not seeing any of these beasties and they're continuing their work. There won't be any pineapples at outposts."

Elke nodded, then asked, "what are we arming our people with?"

George and Guido exchanged a glance, then George responded. "Excellent question. Well, we know they're relatively small. Siblings will work together, led by the strongest one: the 'alpha'. And, if they are the same as the things on the beaches, they can fly. I'd recommend flamethrowers and scatterguns."

"Fine then," Elke nodded. "Dieter, I need duct crawlers. Get what you have to Nikko and redirect your fabricators to crank out more. Nikko, I want a set deployed from the brig. See if they can find any sign of the diploid young to follow."

Taki piped up. "We, uh, I mean, sorry to interrupt, but we did find something in the brig. A strange substance, mostly white. We weren't quite sure what it was."

George asked, "do you have any pictures?"

Taki quickly produced a picture. A projection of chalky lumps appeared on the conference room table.

George nodded knowingly. "Ah yes, so you may recall kraken droppings include uric acid. It's nitrogen waste, like our urine, but more concentrated to save water. There's not much fecal matter, which makes sense considering that they seem to use their venom to predigest their prey before feeding. So, yes, I'm sure this is the sign we'll find from our unwelcome guests."

Elke paused, then turned to Dieter. "I want something that secures air ducts and I want it immediately. I don't care what it is. Glue them. Tape them. Weld them. I don't care! Figure out something the little bastards can't get through and get the teams prepped to secure air ducts as they go."

Dieter nodded, pursing his lips, already thinking about solutions.

"John…" Elke's voice caught in her throat. John looked at her knowingly, lovingly. Elke reached to take his hand, but stopped at the last moment. Now wasn't an appropriate time.

"John, I don't know what to ask of you, other than to mobilize your team and be ready. I have a feeling you're going to be very, very busy very, very soon."

"I know."

# ▪DAY 5: 06:44
## WELLNESS CHECKS

*Jeez, what a morning.*

An hour ago, Ronnie was twiddling her thumbs aboard an EAGLE. The field research team she was babysitting had been recalled the evening before. Apparently, new predators descended on their research subjects and harassed them to the point of abandoning their field work. At first it was a welcome break; then she got bored as the xenobiologists crowded around the main lab table monitoring drone reports.

Boredom didn't last long. She was summoned by Falcon back to the primary dome and assigned a team for wellness checks.

Ronnie felt a bit of déjà vu crossing the Garcia Mountains by Falcon. It had only been a few days since a Falcon plucked her from the megafauna team to lead the hunt for the pack of predators that killed that survey team. From the outside, the settlements didn't look any different. But, as she and the other secmeds aboard the Falcon listened to the briefing, she realized everything under those domes had changed.

And that triggered an ominous feeling in the pit of her stomach.

*At least it wasn't kraken.*

They landed, armed themselves, and made their way from the dome entry to the armories. She arrived at her assignment to find a member of the ops team completing a weapons check. Anyone that brought a weapon was issued ammunition. Everyone else was issued whatever they were rated to use, from scatterguns to flamethrowers.

Ronnie wasn't sure what to do about the people that didn't show up. At least one resident was required to attend from every residence on the floor, two if one of them demonstrated sufficient proficiency to earn a spot on her squad. By her count, nobody showed from five residences, and that left her two short for her squad. Ronnie began to fear the worst.

But she couldn't wait any longer. She sent a brusque note to the delinquents reminding them of their duty and attached a link to help them locate her squad as they conducted wellness checks. She raised a hand to get her squad's attention.

"Okay, people, here's what I know. We are hunting for Edenic creatures loose in the dome. They're small, roaming in packs, and dangerous. They have already killed some colonists. Nobody's seen one, at least not yet. Leadership thinks they're hatching out of these pineapple things, so we're to incinerate any that we see. These creatures can also get into the air ducts, so we must weld any air duct covers in place. As for the things, kill them on sight."

She observed her squad. Some began whispering to each other as soon as she'd mentioned pineapples.

"What?"

One raised a hand and said, "some of us have pineapples. Should we be worried?"

A chill ran down Ronnie's spine.

"How many of you have a pineapple in your quarters? Raise your hands, now."

Four hands went up.

Ronnie tapped her thigh with her hand rapidly; she didn't have time to strategize. "Okay, here's what we're going to do. We're going to go to your residences first, then the residences of our missing personnel. We'll sweep the rest of the floor afterwards. Understood?"

There was some murmuring and some nodding. She pointed to one of the pineapple owners.

"I know you! You're Sandy, right? An EAGLE pilot?

Sandy nodded.

"Let's go to your place first."

■ ■ ■

As they entered Sandy's residence, things went relatively smoothly. Ronnie stood in the corridor as Sandy did her best to explain to her partner and kids why the rest of the squad was pulling their beloved pineapple into the hallway to incinerate it. As Sandy spoke to them, Ronnie could hear someone from the squad torch the pineapple. Then, after a few minutes, they heard the fire suppression system put out the blaze. Finally, they welded the air duct covers in place and moved on to the residences of the other squad members that had pineapples. Their pineapples were also destroyed without incident.

Now it was time to find the residences of the delinquents. As they reached the first door, Ronnie pressed the bell. There was no answer. Ronnie pressed again, waited, then signaled to the squad. She overrode the lock. The door cleared, revealing a dark, silent room.

"Hello? Anyone home?"

Silence.

Flamethrower ready, she stepped through, and said, "lights! Full!"

The room brightened as the rest of the squad followed her into the family room. On the counter by the kitchen was the deflated husk of a pineapple with a gaping hole in its side.

As the squad distributed themselves about the room, one asked, "how many?"

"Two adults, three kids," Ronnie answered soberly.

She walked to the master bedroom and stepped through. "Lights! Full!"

She froze.

"In here!"

The squad members stepped into the room, looking at the bed. There were two shriveled shapes on the bed, barely recognizable as having once been human. The remains reminded Ronnie of deflated balloons. The lumpy remnants of the larger bones were draped by wrinkled, empty skin, and hair. One was partially covered by a shredded nightgown.

Softly, she commanded, "check the other rooms."

She could hear her squad walking into the other rooms as she looked about. She saw an air duct cover on the floor, and what appeared to be droppings by the air duct. She heard voices from the other room.

"This one's gone."

"This one, too."

"And this one."

She walked from room to room, seeing what she could only assume had once been three beautiful children. Though, at this point, she couldn't even guess what sex they'd been. One was still on its bed. Beside it lay the skeleton of a dog. The other two children were on the floor, in the far corners of their rooms. They must have tried to get away from their attackers.

The squad was silent as they put the duct covers back and welded them in place. Ronnie notified health services of the remains, but she didn't think they would retrieve them for a while. It felt disrespectful to leave the bodies like this, but she had to resume their search. As they moved on to the next delinquent squad member's residence, Sandy walked up to Ronnie.

"That could have been us!" Sandy's voice was thick with emotion. "When the alarm sounded this morning, Jim and I thought it was another drill. I joked that I wouldn't try so hard in the next marksmanship competition, so I wouldn't have to report in. If we'd gone back and found my family like… like *that*?" She shuddered.

Ronnie didn't know what to say, so she remained silent. When they reached the next residence, she stood by the door, as her squad arranged themselves around the opening. She waited for a "ready" signal, then simply said, "opening the door."

She overrode the lock and the portal opened. Once again, it was completely dark inside.

"Hello? Hello, is anyone home?"

From the shadows, Ronnie heard a strange rustling sound she couldn't place.

Flamethrower ready, she stepped through and yelled. "Lights! Full!"

As the lights brightened, the rustling sound intensified. Then, suddenly, motion as a swarm of winged things flew out of one of the bedrooms. Ronnie jumped back through the door into the corridor, raised her flamethrower and screamed.

"FIRE!"

She aimed the flamethrower through the doorway and held down on the trigger. Something flew right through the flames, igniting as it hit her; it knocked her off her feet, causing her finger to slip off the trigger. It writhed on the floor as it burned, then was still. More things followed. Three of them were hit by her squad's scattergun blasts, and the rest flew over them, down the corridor, and disappeared around a bend.

Ronnie stared at the smoldering nightmare at her feet, then the three others as their movements slowed and stopped. From behind her, she heard a voice.

"Holy shit! Now what?"

She shakily got back to her feet. She felt like she was going to throw up.

"Someone report in that several now identified creatures escaped and in which direction they fled. Another squad will likely encounter them. The rest of you go inside, count the bodies, and weld the duct covers in place."

## UNDERSTANDING THE ENEMY

Elke sat by herself in a daze.

Her conference room had been transformed into a command center. Members of her staff wandered between discussions at the main table and workstations facilitating virtual conferences with non-present individuals. The snack bar was now a fully stocked kitchenette. One corner held cots.

Nearby, George, Taki, and those few xenobiologists not in the field dissected wombs and performed necropsies of pineapples that had already hatched. They had a growing collection of carcasses, some partially burned, others shot. George and Taki confirmed from dissections of pineapples that their unwanted guests had wings.

A few colonists had made their way to the primary dome despite the early alarm. They were found and escorted to secure break rooms for the time being. Transportation between the domes was shut down.

Residential dome well checks were underway, but the number of known colonist casualties was sobering. Families whose pineapples had already hatched were found dead; a number of other families were attacked when the creatures came through their air ducts. The good news was the duct covers were now sealed, but the number of predators trapped in the air ducts and roaming freely under the dome was anyone's guess. Meanwhile, Rajiv and Nikko's people were poring over construction blueprints to determine whether the trapped diploid young might find a way out of the ductwork. Dieter's team refitted duct crawlers with torches and ramped up crawler fabrication.

All contact was lost with six agricultural domes. The others had not reported problems, at least not yet. Infrastructural and industrial domes were not reporting any sign of pineapples or diploid young. Nikko's team was busy calculating how long the infrastructure systems could be left unattended. Searches aboard the orbiting platform were underway. No evidence had been found thus far that any pineapples had made their way up the stalk.

*How could such a beautiful world harbor such horrors?*

She leaned back and tapped her wrist computer.

"George? It's 09:30. Can you give us an update?"

"On our way."

She sipped her drink, grimaced, stood, and walked stiffly towards her seat at the conference table. After a few minutes, George and Taki walked into the room and took their seats. The rest of the present senior staff trickled towards the table as Elke acknowledged George and Taki's return. "What have you learned?"

George generated an image that appeared above the table. The projection was about the size of a small dog; its similarity to the kraken was obvious. Everyone leaned in to get a better look.

"This is what we're dealing with. Similar body design as the diploid generation of the kraken. If their feed conversion rate matches the kraken, we can expect them to grow quickly. We have the same trilateral symmetry: left, right, and top, with a three-part beak with nine tongues. The beak is thinner than the kraken, which we'll talk about in a moment. You can see the six eyestalks derived from one of the dorsal limbs. The other dorsal limbs in the diploid generation of the kraken were vestigial, but not in our friend here. I'll get back to that, too, in a moment."

He sighed heavily. "I'm sorry; I'm exhausted. I know you all are, too, but I'm getting a little old for this. It's…taxing."

He leaned forward and continued. "Note the forelimbs end in six clawed digits arranged in two opposing sets. They're quite strong and dexterous, which helps our friend solve little problems like unscrewing an air duct cover. The mid limbs are wings, and our field teams report they fly very well. They're fast and agile, and they've been observed hovering like earthly hummingbirds. The hindlimbs are similar to the forelimbs, less dexterous but stronger, so it can rear up and stand on its hind legs. Excellent eyesight, with independently moving eyestalks. Remarkable brain development to manage and integrate all sensory information. They have excellent chemoreception, uh, sense of smell; they also have excellent hearing. They have lines of mucous-filled sensor pits along the sides of their bodies for sensing motion, reminiscent of an Earth fish. They can sense electromagnetic fields, but unlike the kraken, we see no indication it can use this organ to suppress brain functions. So that's one bit of good news."

He paused. "On the other hand, given they have the same body design as the kraken, they will be challenging to kill. The primary brain is at the base of the limb supporting the sensory cluster, so it's inside the body cavity with the rest of the internal organs and protected by the three spinal columns and rib cage. The ones we've gotten from wellness teams were killed with either a scattergun or a flamethrower. As you might imagine, we prefer the ones shot by a scattergun, leaves us more to work with."

George replaced the projection of the pineapple diploid with a detailed projection of the alignment. "Pineapples appear to be just one species in a group that spend their haploid generation photosynthesizing. They are car-nivorous plants, it turns out, supplementing whatever they draw from air and soil by capturing small prey. Then, during alignments, particularly the rare quadrilunar alignment, they release diploid young that feed voraciously and then inject hosts with spores."

George collapsed into his chair; the presentation seemed to wind him. Elke reminisced on the energetic, younger man who tackled the kraken threat. Now, the wiser, older scientist put his head in his hands in distress.

"We missed this. We missed this entirely. We're so indoctrinated in the earthly animal/plant distinction that we never questioned our presumptions. Beyond genetic tests to verify these organisms were in the trilaterally sym-metric super-kingdom, we didn't even look at internal structures. That would have immediately revealed what they are! Our Earth-oriented conceptual framework blinded us to this possibility!"

He recovered himself and shifted forward in his seat. "We see something analogous among the kraken and related species here on Eden. Bear with me, it's important to understand for a number of reasons. I'll try to make it as simple as I can.

Remember that the haploid phase are hermaphrodites. Any two individ-uals can mate, every individual providing sperm to its partner with which to fertilize eggs. Second, because they're haploid, all of their sex cells should be identical. Diploids have two copies of each chromosome, so, when diploid creatures like ourselves produce sex cells, we need to go through a process that selects one from each pair. Then fertilization recombines one chromo-some for each pair from each parent to produce a diploid offspring. So all of the sex cells produced by haploid kraken and kin should be identical, right? Since their sperm equivalents of an individual are identical, then full siblings would be identical, and the only variability among the offspring of a given pineapple would be from promiscuity. But! And this is *very* important, that is *not* what we see!"

He straightened in his chair. "We see far more variability, because, while every haploid individual produces a set of identical eggs, they do *not* produce identical sperm! They produce sperm with random subsets of their genetic code! So, when it comes time to fertilize eggs, to produce diploid young, each individual sifts through sperm cells containing randomly chopped up genome subsets from multiple partners. They 'choose', through a mechanism we haven't figured out yet, which genetic sequences to use based on the life experience of the parent. We see this to a limited degree on Earth, with hormonal expressions guided by…"

"George!" Elke's curt response caught him off guard; she was normally more patient with him. "Now is *not* the time. Please summarize."

George blushed and nodded. "Of course, of course. I'm sorry. Yes, yes, I'm tired. Well, like I said, there's two important things to take away from all this. The offspring of a given pineapple, a 'cohort', are not identical but are so related to each other as to form highly cooperative teams geared towards the cohort's reproductive success. The second is that their reproductive processes are highly adaptive, allowing each generation to engineer their diploid offspring based on their experiences."

John leaned back and whistled. "So, as we've been feeding the pineapples, we've helped them design diploid young perfectly adapted to prey on us!"

George nodded vigorously.

"Exactly! You see it now, right? Infection by a kraken spore gives rise to a haploid generation able to digest our tissues. But the pineapples! By feeding them, we taught them to engineer a diploid generation that's not only able to digest our tissues, but is able to produce effective venoms. I would have bet my reputation it would be impossible. But, no! We fed them for weeks, let them analyze our biochemistry, and now their offspring has a venom tuned to our physiology!"

The room was silent. A simulation of an eaten body appeared above the table. The room remained silent, with clear expressions of revulsion. George knew the imagery was disturbing and unpleasant. By using a simulated attack with a stylized prey, he spared them from viewing an actual feeding involving a human body.

"Defending ourselves requires understanding how they attack. Grasping their prey, they 'sting' with this ovipositor modified from one of the dorsal limbs, the one that would be the female organ in the haploid phase. It's long, curved, and sharp. There are a number of glands that provide it with venom to immobilize a victim. Prey are also injected with a venom to liquify tissue, whereas hosts are injected with spores.

The actual feeding process is gruesome. The immobilized victim's body shrivels as they feed; they massage the victim's body part to work the venom into the victim's tissues, even liquifying bone. As the venom reaches major organs, the victim begins to die; then the creatures accelerate their feeding. They also shift their attention to the head, crushing the skull or finding an 'opening' like the eye or ear to get through the bone to brain tissue."

The image stopped moving and became transparent.

"They periodically select a victim to serve as a host for the haploid generation. Among the related species we've found, they usually take some action to secure the host-prey, placing them in a burrow or other shelter to give the spores time to develop. As we get the diploid young under control, we'll need to turn our attention to finding these hosts and containing whatever hatches out of them.

Fifteen years ago, we struggled to deal with, what, twenty or so kraken? Each womb we dissected had somewhere between ten to forty diploid young. Here, under the primary dome, we found around twenty pineapples in public spaces, with half of them already hatched? That's what, 100 to 400 of these things loose under the primary dome? And what about the residential dome? Bhavia's people found well over 100 pineapples, most of them hatched. We have no idea how many are trapped in the air ducts, and we have no idea how many are roaming the public spaces, not to mention the agricultural domes we've lost contact with."

He paused again, then added, urgently, "we must find and destroy every one of these things. Now that we've modified them, trained them to be able to consume earthly tissues, they cannot be allowed to breed with anything on Eden. They cannot be allowed to escape!"

Elke lifted her cup twice to her lips, but forgot to take a sip. Her pounding headache made it hard to think. The growing murmur among her senior staff wasn't helping. She grabbed her cup hard, to keep her hand from shaking again.

"People! Let's just…work the problems. First, let's deal with the ductwork. Dieter, how are we doing with duct crawlers?"

"As we discussed earlier, we built some right after the kraken incident. Most are functional. But they were designed to find and destroy young kraken tiny enough to squeeze through the vents, not something as big as these. So, we're prioritizing upgrading torches on the functional crawlers over repairing or building more. We should have the first set ready to deploy within the hour."

"Very good. Nikko, Rajiv, how long will it take to clear the ducts?"

Nikko raised an eyebrow as he turned to Rajiv. Rajiv took the initiative, and a projection of Wu City appeared on the table with the primary dome at the center. Rajiv raised his hands to enhance the details of the image, including unfinished projects. The central tower's transportation hub was surrounded by a ring of public spaces, parks, playgrounds, and sporting venues. The tall, ring-shaped residential building, graduated to accommodate the curvature of the dome. Then, more public spaces ran along the dome stem wall. Rajiv adjusted the projection until about three quarters of the residential ring transitioned to a wireframe and disappeared. The remaining arc transitioned from an idealized model to the physical reality of the existing structure, including blemishes, window variability according to the tastes of the families behind them, and construction projects at either end. He repeated his hand motion to zoom in again until the building filled the table.

"This is the current residential structure, home to about 18,000 of our fellow colonists. Think of it as a ring of adjacent, interconnected buildings, with each floor's corridors lining up as a set of concentric rings, one radial corridor, and one set of lifts per building to facilitate traffic between the rings. There are a series of apartments along each corridor as well as commercial spaces for retail operations and professional services. As you might imagine, windowed spaces along the interior and especially the exterior of each floor are highly desirable."

He paused to highlight the corridors, stairwells, lifts, and duct work. "Note that most of the structure's roof is open space with restaurants, pubs, and other commercial activities. You can see at regular intervals for each building in the arc there's a structure to support environmental management, including the duct work within that building. Since the entire structure is under the dome and we manage dome integrity through positive pressure, none of these ducts are designed for pressure management through isolation. Instead, in light of the kraken incident, we decided to isolate each building's duct work through the heavy-duty mesh mentioned earlier."

He tapped his wrist computer again, and the image was replaced by a design document for an individual building, highlighting the corridors, lifts, and duct work.

"I've provided these diagrams to Dieter and Nikko for programming the duct crawlers. The rooftop venting is our best access point. I recommend that we start at one end, deploy a set of crawlers to a set of buildings, allow them to do their work, then redeploy them to a subsequent building. We've run a few simulations with different numbers of crawlers per building, and we think we can start with five buildings at a time, then increase that as Dieter's team continues to make more of the crawlers available."

Guido leaned in. "Given that some of them are flying freely around the dome, I will provide armed squads to protect your teams as they work." Guido looked to Bhavia to add something, but the security chief sat silently and sullenly. Nur was still missing.

"We're also going to want to inform each building's residents as we progress," Rajiv added. "They're, uh, going to hear some strange sounds from their air ducts, and they will smell cooked meat as the crawlers eliminate our unwanted guests. The environmental systems will vent that smell, but our colonists are going to get a whiff, can't be helped."

Elke meshed her fingers and asked, "what about the ones that are loose under the dome?"

Her senior staff whispered for a while amongst themselves at a loss before Bhavia, surprisingly, spoke up. "Can we bait them?"

Elke turned to him and said, encouragingly, "say more."

"Well, the problem is they can fly, right? If we put out bait, we could kill them as they landed to take the bait."

Elke turned to Nikko, who was shaking his head slowly.

"In principle, it's a good idea. In practice? What do we use for bait? There's no livestock under the residential dome except some of the larger pets. Big dogs, say. It'd be a challenge to get livestock from one of the agricultural domes to the residential dome."

"Still, it has promise. Does anyone have a better idea?"

"Flechettes," Dieter chimed in. "The challenge, as we see it, is that unlike the kraken, these things can fly and they're trapped within a three-dimensional space much greater than the orbiting platform. And we don't want to make a bunch of holes in the dome if we fire something and miss! So, I suggest flechettes: a large number of small, sharp projectiles. If we equip drones with a means to fire flechettes, we can do enough damage to their wings and knock them out of the air without compromising the dome."

Elke nodded enthusiastically. "Great idea! Tell me more. How will this work?"

Dieter sighed. "By early afternoon, we'll have enough duct crawlers to clear the residential dome's duct work, so we can redirect some of our fabrication capacity to outfitting drones with flechettes. I'll, uh, need some drones, of course. I understand the field teams are relying on them."

Elke turned to George. He raised his hands before she could speak. "Absolutely! We'll relinquish drones!"

Elke smiled lightly, then turned back to Dieter. "Work with Rajiv and Nikko on deployment plans. Work through how quickly you can refit and deploy drones. George will send you all the drones you can use as soon as you can use them, but let's not repurpose them until we're ready to refit them. George, can we send a xenobiologist or two with the residential team? I think it would be useful."

George nodded. "The grad students I have working here in the lab know everything we know about our guests."

Elke thought a moment before speaking. "What I'm hearing…is we have the beginnings of a plan to clear the residential dome." Elke smiled lightly again and tapped her cup nervously. "What about the primary dome? And the agricultural dome? Any update on the orbiting platform?"

"We think we caught a break here!" Taki piped up, happy to deliver some good news. "Remember how our dissections showed the pineapples have tidal sensors? That their young started developing when the tidal forces of the aligning moons tripped those sensors? Well, the orbiting platform is a zero-g environment, therefore no pineapple that made its way up the stalk should hatch."

Guido leaned back. "Ah! That makes sense! We've found and destroyed eleven unhatched pineapples in public spaces, and seven more among residences." He smiled ruefully as he continued. "I thought we were just lucky, which is always hard to reconcile with my naturally pessimistic outlook! We'll remain diligent, though. Cross your fingers."

"Thank you, Guido, we will." Rajiv returned to his feet. The primary dome appeared on the table. He held his hands over the projection and spread them, zooming into the base station and surrounding buildings.

"Beyond the base station, we have smaller structures supporting various commercial and public activities. None of these structures were deemed large enough to bother sealing their duct work. They may well have diploid young sheltering in them, but we'll deal with them the same way we deal with the creatures freely roaming the residential dome."

The base station depiction was replaced with a schematic revealing internal structures. "Unlike the residential buildings, the base station was built as an integrated structure. However, like the residential structure, the air ducts are designed in sections segregated by mesh barriers and the environmental management is handled through equipment here, on the roof, near the space elevator airlock. As duct crawlers become available, we can deploy them there. That will clear the building, and then we can use the same drone strategy as the residential dome."

"How about the agricultural domes?" Elke asked.

"No need to deal with duct crawlers, just drones."

Elke paused, then grimaced. "I hate to say this, but there isn't much in the way of shelter under the agricultural domes other than the transportation hub. If any of those domes had pineapples, then the farmers are either in their hub and able to wait. Or they're gone. Be prepared."

# ■DAY 5: 11:07
## ALONE

Lara came to on the floor, a large lump pulsing on the backside of her head. She sat up, put her back to a cabinet, and stared numbly at Reiner's remains.

As his body shriveled and shrank, as the predators kneaded his body like a lump of dough, the parts of him blocking the hatch were pulled out of the way. Still hungry, the creatures rummaged through everything. They also flew through the central core, up towards the cockpit, down towards the labs and airlock; but mostly, they perched on the ladder and stared at Lara through the transparent hatch.

Lara stared back. She counted them, then recounted. She was sure there were five of them.

She kept hoping that, at some point, they'd all move into the bunk room. Then she could close the hatch and trap them there. But they kept going through the hatch. They kept exploring the core.

Occasionally, Lara felt a thrill of excitement and hope when she couldn't see any in the core. Then she'd count and come up short, just before seeing one fly up or down, past her level.

Still, she hoped. She planned. She rehearsed in her mind jumping up and hitting the hatch control to trap them in the bunk. All Lara needed was an opportunity, a moment when all of them were in the bunk room.

If only she could get to the cockpit! From there, she could seal the hatch from the cockpit. She could also override the controls and open the hatch to the airlock, then the airlock itself to flush them out. The ship would lose a lot of air, and the sudden decompression would shake the ship violently. Perhaps even tear it apart given their velocity. The ship's safety systems might attempt to thwart her, but she'd rather die suddenly as the ship came apart than be slowly consumed by those flying bastards. Like Reiner…

There was one final option. Lara could, instead, go to the chambers. She could get into a chamber, and, from there, she could control the ship: stop accelerating, reorient, then decelerate, *sharply*. The deceleration would have to generate enough Gs to kill the monsters, at least as many Gs as she could endure within the chamber.

But she had *no* idea where the ship was, *no* idea how fast they were traveling. They'd accelerated at high-g while she was in the chamber, then slowed to a steady 1-g since she came out. How long had it been? How fast were they going? How far had they traveled? Hell, for all she knew, they would hit something any second.

Well, the odds were poor. Last Lara remembered, they were in a broad arc towards the asteroids, out of the ecliptic plane, planning to adjust course towards their target. They *should* still be in the clear, but way past the asteroids, towards the outer planets of the system, possibly at an angle to the ecliptic. There shouldn't be anything to hit. At some point, the ship would run out of fuel. She would run out of food; she would even run out of breathable air, especially with those things breathing it too!

Lara's breath caught in her throat. She was out of options.

She *had* to get to a chamber.

# DAY 5: 11:10
## DETERRED

There was no more prey.

The diploids were hungry and there was no more prey.

A cohort of fourteen young flew to the upper reaches of the agricultural dome and lighted among the arch supports at the top of the central structure. From there, they had a commanding view of the four farms, the residences, and, through the dome, the desert stretching eastward towards the mountains and the sea beyond.

From deep within themselves, they felt a calling, a need to fly eastward, over those mountains. An instinct said there would be abundant prey beyond those mountains. But they had flown around the dome repeatedly, searching for a way through the transparent barrier.

There was no more prey in this place, and there was no way to escape this place.

The alpha weighed options. The last prey they'd found was in the structure upon which they now perched. As they had circled, they picked up a faint electromagnetic signal. They'd missed it before. All of the other prey was found at ground level, in or around the smaller structures. This one was much higher up, and the central structure interfered with their ability to sense the signal.

They hovered outside the structure, as near to the signal as they could get, probing and testing the structure until, eventually, they'd found a weakness. They found something they could open, then poured in. The prey sensed them and tried to escape, but the cohort flew through the structure until they cornered it. The prey didn't last long with all of them feeding; it barely offered enough nourishment to make up for the energy they spent hunting it.

The alpha hadn't felt another signal since.

There were two other diploid cohorts in the area. Attacking them as prey was dangerous. Earlier, the alpha observed one cohort try to prey on another group. The larger cohort prevailed, but at great cost, losing four individuals. Perhaps that cohort was now weak enough to attack? But how many siblings would it lose? Would they gain enough nourishment to justify the loss of individuals? What benefit was such nourishment if there were no hosts to be impregnated? They could try to find hosts impregnated by the other cohorts, but the other cohorts would protect them for sure.

Perhaps there would be more prey further in? Perhaps, against all reason, they should go into the structure, and work their way down?

What other option did they have?

# DAY 5: 11:28
## REMEMBERING

Ronnie and her squad rested in a break room near the armory. They'd completed wellness checks for their section. They returned to the armory, restocked their ammunition, then walked into the break room.

Ronnie poured herself some black coffee and selected some protein bars. Wearily, she took a seat by a window and stared out through the dome to the desert beyond. Her squad followed behind her. They made their selections without a sound, without commentary, without enthusiasm. They moved randomly throughout the breakroom, settling at various tables sporadically. They were clearly avoiding the incinerated husk of the pineapple that had, until a few hours ago, shielded the break room's snacks from vermin.

Ronnie understood. They'd seen things that morning, things they'd never forget, things that changed them. She looked down at her mug, then closed her eyes tightly as her mind replayed the morning's events interspersed with memories.

Nobody on her squad remembered the kraken. That wasn't surprising, given the number of colonists lost to the kraken in those first weeks, how many of the survivors left at their first opportunity, and how the remaining were quickly outnumbered by wave after wave of new colonists. Kraken survivors were a shrinking minority.

Sure, the newcomers heard about the kraken. Given the distances traveled, they'd all left their homes before the first colonists reached Eden. That's when they heard the first reports of what the colony had been through. Eden became the only colony to establish weapons proficiency requirements. Some excelled enough to be assigned to squads like hers. Incidents occurred, but it was nothing compared to the kraken. People on expeditions or people building the surface settlement were occasionally startled by Eden wildlife. Very few people were attacked, although their environmental suits limited their injuries to bruises or, on rare occasions, a broken bone.

Ronnie could feel their eyes. She opened hers and glanced around the room self-consciously. She saw other eyes abruptly avert; others briefly held her gaze before looking down. She turned to look out at the dessert again.

She was aware of her reputation. She'd heard that, for some of them, she was a legend.

Ronnie shook her head.

She'd fought the kraken. She'd lost friends to kraken, seen her friends attacked and killed by kraken. She'd watched people be eaten alive by kraken. She leaned back in her chair.

*The estuary…*

There was an expedition a couple of years after the kraken, when the colony was beginning to feel confident again. She and a team were called to an estuary. They came across a kill, a large herbivore, taken down by a pack of diploid hunters. The team split up. She took half the xenobiologists to continue exploring the estuary while Sven, another secmed, took the other half to track the pack.

What Sven's group didn't know was that the pack was tracking *them*.

Ronnie did her best. She ran back, but not fast enough. They took Sven down. They crippled him through his environmental suit, then tore at the suit until it gave way. Then they tore at Sven.

She could see there was no hope, no way to save her friend.

From that distance, the best she could hope to do was take out a few sensory clusters. There was no way to kill that many things from a distance, not with a rifle. Taking out a few sensory clusters wouldn't stop what they were doing to Sven.

She made the call. He couldn't be saved. She alone bore the responsibility for the rest of the team.

She made the call.

She took the shot.

Given the distance, it was a hell of a shot.

She granted Sven mercy, and deprived the pack of their play. Then she led the rest of the expedition to safety.

*That* was how Ronnie became a legend.

A lot of their standards and best practices came from Ronnie's experience: what worked, what didn't. She knew it would take time for her team to process what they'd seen this morning. She understood what they were going through. She'd been there.

They left her alone. So, she stared out the window. She didn't see the desert, or the mountains, or the sun, or the clouds.

She only saw smoldering pineapples, shriveled children still in their clothes, and the flying shadows of the escaped creatures.

Ronnie sighed and leaned back in her chair. She looked up when a figure entered the break room, leading a squad like her own.

Neal was his name. Tall, athletic. She had received a directive that he and his squad would meet hers there. His squad, also quiet, browsed the food selections, then sought seats. Some sat alone, some in groups, and some offered curt nods at tables with members of her squad.

None sat near the pineapple.

Neal walked towards Ronnie. She stood at nearly his height, looking him in the eye as he approached. He held out a hand. She shook it and gestured towards the table.

Neal spoke first. "I was told to join you here as soon as we finished our wellness checks."

She nodded, then asked, "how did it go?"

He raised his eyebrows, then looked down as he slowly shook his head. "About the same as yours, I'd guess. I've never seen anything like it. Whole families just…like rags. Like wrung out rags."

She looked away, then nodded.

"I've heard about you." He leaned forward. "I heard you were here for the kraken."

Ronnie didn't react.

"Was it like this?"

She curled her lip as his question irritated her. She didn't need to dredge up memories from the past; she needed to *focus*.

"It was different. It was awful. But this? This is worse."

They sat quietly for a moment, then she said, "an engineering team is going to deploy duct crawlers. We're supposed to meet them at the transportation hub, then escort them to the roof of the residential building."

"Did any of the flying things get past you?"

She nodded. "A few. We didn't know what we were dealing with." She looked him in the eye. "We got smarter."

"Us, too." Neal smiled. He liked her tenacity. "We managed to take a few down, send 'em to the labs. But, the first couple times? They got past us. They're going to be waiting for us out there."

"Yep. A lot of 'em. I've no idea how many of the things are out there. Nobody does."

"I guess we're going to find out!"

# ▪DAY 5: 13:16
## AT THE TRANSPORTATION HUB

Ronnie, Neal, and their combined squads arrived at a residential structure entryway. At the end of the broad avenue stood the central tower. Its transportation hub was their objective. They were to meet a team of engineers and operational support personnel at the transportation hub and escort them back to the residential building, along with duct crawlers, drones, and related equipment.

On a normal day, colonists would walk along those grand streets, nearly a kilometer of small shops, public venues like parks and fields, and beautiful landscaping. On a normal day, the average pedestrian could traipse through trees, shrubs and grasses, all basking in the glory of Eden's sun through the transparent panels of the dome. Individuals not able to enjoy the walk, whether burdened by packages or years, were carried by autonomous vehicles. Most of the vehicles were open, allowing occupants to enjoy their journey.

Now, nothing moved along that open avenue.

Neal turned to Ronnie and said, "a vehicle or two would be really nice right now."

She nodded with a small smile, and, without turning, addressed a member of her squad.

"ETA?"

After a pause and some consultation, he said, "three minutes."

Ronnie's smile broadened as she turned to Neal and said, "You'll have one in three minutes."

Neal shook his head, smiling. Her cleverness intrigued him. "Something with an enclosed cabin?"

"You'll see."

"Comfortable seating? Ample leg room? Good lumbar support?"

Ronnie laughed, her first real laugh in days. She then explained to Neal that a member of her squad was part of a construction team and suggested they request use of the large autonomous transport vehicles to ferry materials.

Four large transports, driving along the roadway at the base of the residential building's inner wall, pulled up to the portal. The front half of each was a passenger cabin, the back half was an open cargo bay.

Ronnie gestured towards them. "Ample room for our squads and equipment."

Neal grunted. "Well, the interior's rather spartan, but it'll have to do!"

"I'm sorry?" Ronnie chortled. "Were you expecting first class?"

Neal shrugged and muttered something about deserving fine treatment. Once again, Ronnie laughed.

"Okay, people," Ronnie addressed both her squad and Neal's. "We're taking a ride. We don't know how many of our unwanted guests are outside. They could be on the other side of the dome or be perched on the roof directly above us. So keep your eyes open and your weapons handy!"

She turned and nodded towards Neal. He tapped the portal control to open it. Ronnie, holding the wand of her flamethrower, ran out to stand in front of the vehicles. She scanned the vicinity, then began directing traffic. Neal closed the residential portal after the last squad member boarded, then joined Ronnie on the lead transport. Their adrenalin levels were too high to sit down.

Tensions eased as they approached the central tower, until one of Neal's people pointed through the window and yelled, "look at the top of the tower!" Everyone aboard turned to look. Ronnie, like Neal, crouched to look up. She could see movement.

"Ooooooooh, fuck!"

She turned to look at the people aboard the transport; she activated the speakers in the other vehicles.

"Everyone, we have unwanted guests atop the central tower. Remember a typical clutch is somewhere between fifteen and twenty individuals, and that clutches don't cooperate with each other."

She looked towards the hub's doors. There must be at least a dozen of them, designed to accommodate the needs of the dome's eventual total population. She pointed to squad members on the transport as she spoke.

"We'll use the first two doors on the right. You two take point and provide primary security. Remember, small bursts. They're hard to kill! You two secure the rear, then join them at the door. The rest of us will run past and get into the hub. We'll lock the doors behind us."

She paused, then added, "There shouldn't be any of these things inside the hub, but don't take any chances. When you open the door, have your weapons ready. All you should find waiting for us are engineers with crawlers and drones. Got it?"

She hesitated, making eye contact with each of them, then declared, "GO!"

The first two reached the doorway, followed by another duo. They opened the door and found no one immediately inside. They turned back and signaled Ronnie watching through the vehicle window.

Ronnie nodded and gritted her teeth. "Everyone, when I say 'go', run through and into the hub. Last ones out secure their transport."

She paused, and threw up a silent prayer for good measure. She checked on Neal. He gave her a serious nod.

"GO!"

Neal ran out towards the hub, then stood in the doorway, waving his arm as the squads ran past him. Ronnie, last to leave, secured the vehicle door. As she ran towards the hub, she heard that distinctive rustling sound.

"GO GO GO!"

They cleared the door and closed it behind them. A cohort of the creatures hovered outside the hub's portal. A few lighted on the vehicles.

Neal turned to Ronnie. "Might be interesting getting back to the transports."

# ▪ DAY 5: 13:31
## BACK IN THE CHAMBER

Lara was on her feet.

She'd watched the things for hours as the ship hurtled further and further into the void, further and further from the Eden system.

She'd played with the idea of closing one hatch, then opening another hatch on another level, thinking she could attract them out of the core and trap them there. But, even with her face pressed against the transparent core wall, Lara couldn't see the whole core. She couldn't *know* whether there were any more in the core. The only way to be certain was to see all five of them in the bunkroom.

She decided her only option was to get to a high-g chamber. If she could get to a chamber, she could pilot the ship almost as well as from the cockpit. She could decelerate aggressively, maybe enough Gs to crush the things. But, Lara still had the same problem of getting to it safely.

But, she had an idea.

If this worked, she was going to need fuel. She wouldn't have time to set up additional nutritional supplements for the chamber. Lara watched the things watch her as she went to the refrigerator, grabbed what she could, and shoveled it into her mouth until she couldn't eat any more.

The things in the bunkroom continued to stare at her as she walked towards the kitchenette's comms panel. Standing by the panel, she braced herself to sprint towards the hatch controls. She'd been watching them search the bunkroom. They seemed intelligent, curious. She thought they might react to hearing her voice.

Lara tapped the comms console, selected the bunkroom, and started yelling into the console, mostly obscenities. As she yelled, she could see the things turning towards the bunkroom comms panel! They began moving towards it.

One of the things from the central core flew through the hatch into the bunkroom!

*Another!*

*One more…*

*Just one more…*

*There!*

All five of them were in the bunkroom!

She sprinted to the hatch control, smacking it repeatedly with the palm of her hand. The hatch closed, then sealed. She stared at the five monsters as they turned, one by one, away from the comms console to look at her through the central core.

Lara realized she was laughing, laughing and screaming obscenities at them.

They moved towards the hatch. Some walked slowly, others flew. They began touching the hatch, probing it. Happy tears rolled down her cheeks.

*What a relief! They're trapped!*

Then Lara saw that one of them was not probing the hatch. It stared at her, at her hand, still on the hatch control. Its eyestalks shifted to the bunkroom hatch control. She watched it rear up, brace itself with one forepaw against the central core as the other began poking at the hatch control.

"No, no, no, no, no, NO!"

In a panic, she dove through the opening hatch, grabbed the central core ladder, climbed to the chamber room hatch, stepped through, and quickly closed the hatch behind her.

Lara couldn't see them anymore.

*How the hell could animals figure out the controls?!?!?!*

She tapped at the chamber's controls.

All that mattered was getting her ass inside the chamber.

As it opened, she stepped inside, and as the chamber closed, she connected her undergarment's reclamation interfaces to those of the chamber. The reclamation systems would keep her from dehydrating, but without jerryrigging extra nutritional supplements, there was a limit to how long she could stay in the chamber.

But what if that thing figured out the hatch controls, if it would be waiting for her outside the chamber. What if it was already in the room, trying to figure out the chamber controls?

Lara swore, then resumed connecting to the control interface.

As the fluid level rose, instead of her usual anxiety and revulsion, Lara felt relief and a sense of victory.

# ▪DAY 5: 13:43
## WAITING IN THE HUB

As Neal gawked at the creatures, Ronnie turned towards the transportation hub, the heart of the residential dome.

Like most Wu City citizens, she traversed this space regularly. An original colonist, she remembered her excitement when the dome was completed and she first saw this space. But she'd long since stopped noticing it.

It was a beautiful space. The broad, round floor bore an artist's conception of a completely built out surface settlement. The vaulted ceiling encompassed a detailed working model of the Eden system. Eden and her sister planets slowly orbited a glowing sun illuminating the space. The surrounding wall would, one day, be an alternation of small shops and passageways to shuttle stations for connections to other domes not yet built. For now, the only working shuttle headed to the primary dome.

In front of that portal, under the artistic rendering of a gas giant, a cluster of people waited by suspensor pallets loaded with equipment.

"You must be Ronnie?"

One of the engineers raised a hand in greeting as Neal and the rest of their combined squad shifted their attention away from the creatures exploring their vehicles.

Following a brief round of introductions and a high-level description of the suspensor pallet payloads, conversation turned to the practical challenge of getting personnel and equipment aboard the vehicles and to the residential buildings. Neal and Ronnie returned to the doorway closest to the vehicles. The creatures, having apparently satisfied themselves that the vehicles harbored no potential prey, now wandered the area. One explored the cargo bay of one vehicle; another alighted on the roof of a vehicle's passenger compartment. The rest were casually exploring the surrounding landscaping.

Ronnie turned to Neal. "If we go out there with flamethrowers or scatter-guns, we're likely to damage the vehicles."

"Yeah, and some of them will take off, then come back to harass us."

From behind them, a voice said, "might be a nice time to test the flechettes."

Ronnie and Neal exchanged a look, then turned. "Say more."

One of the engineers answered. "We refit the drones to fire flechettes." He explained what they were, then continued, "we're anxious to learn how well they work so we can refine the design. The flechettes were designed to not damage the dome, so they shouldn't damage the vehicles, either. If we can launch one from over there," He pointed at the doors furthest from the parked vehicles. "It'll be our first field test!"

Ronnie turned to Neal, who shrugged and said, "worth a try!"

The engineers scrambled to unpack a drone and launch it from the far door. They secured the door and rejoined the group gathered around the first two doors. They all watched the creatures, one by one, pause and turn as the drone rose to a 5 m height and then slowly moved towards them.

The one perched on the passenger compartment spread its wings, then flew to meet the drone as it approached. Its wings beat slowly, back and forth, as it hovered in front of the drone. its tails moved slowly to counterbalance the wingbeats. Its hindlimbs dangled; its eyestalks wavered. Its forepaw digits randomly twitched as if it were debating whether to reach out and touch the drone.

One of the xenobiologists spoke as the other creatures, one by one, rose to surround the drone.

"That first one is almost certainly the alpha. We expect the movement of the drones to get their attention as potential prey, but we expect them to be confused by the drone's electromagnetic signature. It'll feel all wrong to them."

The drone remained motionless in the sky as the creatures encircled it. The alpha moved up, then over the drone, hovering precisely as its eyes, still moving independently, scanned the dorsal surface of the drone. After a moment, it reached out with one forelimb; it slowly lowered itself to make contact. It pressed the paw against the drone, its digits splayed, then swiftly moved up a meter, hovering there, as if to ponder its next move.

A large array of small tubes slowly extended from the surface of the drone. One aimed at each creature. Each puffed a small cloud of flechettes.

As the crowd watched, the flechettes knocked back the flock of creatures. The seventeen little monsters fell *hard*. All were bloodied. Four were obviously dead, five were moving but unable to get on their feet. Another five were able to hold themselves up. The final three attempted to spread their wings, but the now useless leathery membrane between the long, thin fingers of each wing was shredded.

Ronnie heard whoops behind her as she said, "Neal, you and I will put ourselves between the ones that can stand and the vehicles, then take them out with flamethrowers. I want the rest of you to set your rifles to single shots and put the bastards out of their misery."

# DAY 5: 14:30
## HOPE

"The flechettes worked beautifully!"

Elke and her staff surrounded the table as they listened to Ronnie's report. Her squad loaded the vehicles without incident and were making their way towards the residential structure.

George asked, "Ronnie, the ones you shot. How did you dispatch them?"

Ronnie barked a rueful laugh.

"That's the question, isn't it? I remember the kraken. All the vital organs, even the brain, are in that rib cage! From a distance, best you can try to do is shoot the sensory cluster, but that just takes out their vision and hearing. The least damaged ones we hit with flamethrowers. The rest, we shot off their sensory clusters. Then, you position the gun to fire through the base of the dorsal limb that supports the sensory cluster, through the rib cage, directly into the brain. Best way to put them down."

Elke slapped the table and stood.

*The flechettes worked!*

It was the first good news in a while, and they needed some good news. Her team was tired. Stressed. They remained in dire peril from an existential threat.

*But the flechettes worked!*

Dieter leaned in.

"Okay, this was our first test, and it went well. The kill rate was higher than we'd hoped, which is great. Now, something I've been talking with George about…I hadn't realized how fast these things can heal. We might only be grounding them for, what, ten, twelve hours?"

George shrugged, adding, "you all remember how fast the kraken healed. We've seen phenomenal growth and repair rates across the species in this group. Until we have more data, let's assume shredded wings will heal to the point of at least some ability to fly within twelve hours."

"Right. So, we can use drones to wound them, even kill some of them. But we still rely on humans to accompany the drones and destroy any survivors. Yes, it's better to fight them on the ground than in the air, but it puts our people at risk. And, given how smart the little bastards are, we don't want any survivors getting away. They won't fall for the same trick twice. Having more than two drones work together would improve our odds. Working in sets of, say, four or five, could eliminate whole cohorts and would address the risk of any getting away."

He turned to George and asked, "is there anything distinctive about the diploid young we can use for targeting?"

"I'm not completely sure what you're asking. You mean, like a scent? Or body heat?"

""Can't use body heat," Dieter shook his head. "Not unless it's a unique signature. How similar is their body temperature to humans?"

"Oh, within a few degrees. They are endothermic."

George paused, then snapped his fingers and grinned.

"Wait a minute, we programmed drones to find kraken electromagnetic signatures. We can do that again! You can track them that way!"

Now Dieter was grinning.

"In that case, I suggest we stop refitting drones to fire clouds of flechettes. Give me a couple of hours, and we'll make smart ammunition. The drones will fire rounds that can hone in on the diploids' electromagnetic signatures and fire flechettes directly into their rib cages on impact. That'll shred their internal organs!"

Elke nodded vigorously. This was the kind of solution they needed!

"Dieter, I need you to make these smart rounds as fast as humanly possible. Anything you need, ask. Keep us posted on progress."

Dieter nodded, stood, and walked to one of the consoles to work with his team.

# ▪DAY 5: 15:23
## CRAWLER DEPLOYMENT

Unloading went smoothly. Ronnie and Neal met by the elevators with another squad led by Sasha and Omar. It took a few rides to get everyone and everything to the rooftop room enclosing the elevator bank.

The secmeds stepped aside to plan while the engineers and support team prepared the drones and crawlers. They looked through the doors. A few meters away was a set of shaded picnic tables, presumably for enjoying the view through the dome. Beyond that, they could see the first hutch enclosing HVAC equipment servicing that unit's air ducts.

"These doors are a chokepoint," Neal commented. "We have no idea what's waiting for us out there."

Ronnie nodded and said, "I'll take point. I'll take three of my best and run to the picnic tables over there." She pointed at Sasha and Omar, then continued, "You two cover us, then we'll pivot and cover the group as you send them out. Then you two and Neal, bring up the rear. We'll keep the engineers, xenobiologists, and ops people in the middle as we go from one air duct hutch to the next."

Sasha looked over towards where the engineers were setting up the drones and asked, "should we really take all of them with us?"

"What's our alternative?" Neal asked. "Leave them here? Don't forget, some of our guests got past us during the wellness checks. They're somewhere in the building."

"We could send a couple of our people to escort them to one of the breakrooms."

"Yeah," Ronnie shrugged. "But then what if one of the machines breaks? We need them with us. It's six people. We can do it."

Sasha hesitated, then nodded.

When the drones and crawlers were ready, Ronnie led the way to the picnic area. She scanned the rooftop, then looked up and saw nothing but the dome, its supporting arches, and beyond it, a beautiful blue sky.

She turned back and beckoned them to join her. The combined squads, with four hovering drones, encircled the xenobiologists, engineers, and support staff, as well as the two suspensor pallets loaded with crawlers. As the entourage made their way to her position, she found herself considering how ungainly a group they were.

It was already midafternoon, leaving them maybe three hours of daylight to clear all the ducts. She didn't want to be out here after dark. As the group reached her, she turned to lead them towards the first hutch. Sasha and Omar took the sides and Neal brought up the rear.

"How do we want to do this?" Ronnie asked. "I think we should encircle the hutch, let the ops people open the ductwork."

She heard Omar ask, "what if one of our guests is near the hutch? We don't want to open the duct to deploy the crawlers if it means letting one out!"

"Just hit any you see with the flamethrower."

"That's what I'm thinking."

She turned to one of the ops folk and asked, "what happens if I use a flamethrower in the ductwork from the hutch?"

The guy paused, then answered. "As long as you're firing for short range, shouldn't be a problem. We don't want anyone's residence to catch fire. That's why the crawlers have such short-range torches."

She nodded, then said, "and if short range flamethrower bursts don't drive them back, we'll just go on to the next hutch and plan to come back."

She heard Neal, from the back, "great way to spend an afternoon, right?"

Sasha barked a short laugh, then responded. "Great party idea!"

That got a few nervous chuckles.

They walked by a small rooftop restaurant, its tables surrounded by empty chairs, some of which were on their sides. But there were no abandoned plates or cups on any of the tables. No signs that anything bad had happened there. As they reached the first hutch, they encircled it as one of the operators opened the hutch door, looked in, and swore. Ronnie and Neal looked over his shoulder.

The equipment mounted atop the ductwork was a shambles, and there was a hole in the roof of the hutch.

Ronnie swore. "Is there any point deploying a crawler in there?"

One of the xenobiologists answered, "yes, it's possible there was more than one cohort in there, and, if so, then one or more cohorts may have not found this exit yet. So, it's worth deployment, but we'll need to secure this hutch so the crawlers can eliminate them rather than just drive them out."

"Do it then."

It took longer than Ronnie anticipated, but she thought they'd get better with practice. The second duct system was uncompromised. They were able to deploy crawlers and secure the ductwork without incident. They did get a little faster.

The third one was more complicated. As they opened the hutch door, they could hear movement in the duct work. Ronnie, her flamethrower already set on the shortest possible range, set a few bursts into the ductwork. They could hear more movement.

She looked at the lead operator and asked, "what do you think? Deploy, or come back?"

He shook his head slowly, looked at her, and said, "you think I know something you don't?" He looked back at the duct, then added, "my gut says we should deploy. Just keep your flamethrowers handy!"

They worked without further incident. As they secured the duct work, one of the engineers, apparently reacting to something on his wrist computer, yelled, "the crawlers in that first hutch found a cohort. Good call!" After a moment, he continued, "they've cornered a group of thirteen. They've destroyed four so far. Shouldn't have any trouble eliminating the rest of them."

"Great!" Ronnie cheered. Let me know when you're satisfied the rest of the ductwork is clear. We need to redeploy them soon."

They went by another restaurant on their way to the next hutch. Ronnie pondered if this one offered an early breakfast, perhaps for patrons that enjoyed watching the sun rise while sipping coffee. But now, amongst the overturned furniture and interrupted meals, were a number of shriveled corpses. A horde of flies buzzed about the bodies and abandoned food.

The squads, numb by now, stoically assessed the horror, hoping to find a survivor. But the operators, engineers, and xenobiologists, all of whom had not yet encountered victims of the diploid young, were deeply shaken. The secmeds exchanged a look. Omar shrugged, then left the remnants of the restaurant to help the scientists deal with their shock.

After the group wrapped up at the fifth hutch, one of the drones suddenly shot up 10 m to hover above them. Neal pointed at four members of his squad, gestured towards their charges, and said, "take them to that structure over there and guard them. Leave the gear, we'll come back to it!"

As they complied, Ronnie heard the fluttering of leathery wings. The four secmeds and the remaining squad members positioned themselves in a 3 meter-wide circle, facing outward, as the four drones leveled out to hover above them. A relatively large diploid flew up over the edge of the building from the dome wall, then hovered above the first drone. As they watched, more flew up and arranged themselves around the drones. There were easily twenty of them.

The drones maintained altitude as the diploids encircled them, some flying higher than others. Ronnie wordlessly gestured to pull back into a tighter circle; they needed to get out of the drones' line of fire. Suddenly, the drones fired. The cohort fell roughly onto the rooftop, a sickening crunch as some of the finger bones supporting their wings snapped on impact. The secmeds stepped forward with their flamethrowers and doused the least damaged individuals. The rest of the squad used their rifles to methodically dispatch each individual with a shot to the brain.

Ronnie looked at the dead creatures, then exchanged a weary smile with Neal.

Something moved in her peripheral vision.

Ronnie turned abruptly to her left and noticed two more creatures perched on a rooftop structure about 15 m after the next air duct hutch. She guessed they were from a different cohort. There was something undeniably different about them. They kept their distance, but Ronnie could see their eyestalks wavering as they continued to watch the drones.

"Oh, shit!"

Neal followed her gaze. His shoulders slumped.

"What do you think it means?"

"It may mean that cohort won't fall for the same trick. I don't know."

She turned to the xenobiologists and asked, "any indication that cohorts share information?"

"You mean with other cohorts? No indication, not yet, but who knows?"

"I guess we're gonna find out!"

# ▪DAY 5: 16:08
## DECELERATION

The chamber's command interface was frustrating. Once the chamber filled and she got through the drowning sensation, Lara began working with the command interface, such as it was. It wasn't remotely adequate.

The ship had not been designed with an infestation of horrific aliens in mind. The designers intended pilots to do most of their work from the cockpit and provided a console with all the tools required to do that work. Once a course was plotted and laid in, if it involved otherwise intolerable forces, the pilot would move to a chamber and execute from there.

She didn't have that luxury. There was no way to reach the cockpit.

Lara's only option was to go directly to a chamber, where the command interface was limited, to say nothing of how the damn fluid hampered her ability to interact with said interface. But, again, she normally wouldn't need to do this much from within the chamber.

Part of her mind appreciated how interesting the problem was.

They had accelerated aggressively while enchambered, then continued to accelerate at 1-g. Their flight plan called for a course adjustment followed by a gentle deceleration to the mining colony. That course adjustment never happened. The deceleration never happened. Now, they were headed into the void of space at a very high velocity and accelerating.

In the cockpit, Lara would have the tools required to plot a return course, balance their remaining fuel and life support capacity. She didn't have those tools here. It was possible that, even if they had sufficient resources, the chamber's command interface didn't have the utilities necessary to plot a feasible course.

But she had no choice. She had to take her best guess.

Lara looked at her current velocity and acceleration and did the math as best she could. She did her best to remember the theoretical limits of what she could tolerate within the chamber. She reoriented the ship and fired the engines, decelerating as hard as she thought she could stand.

Even within the chamber, it was brutal.

Her only consolation was thinking about the little bastards that killed Reiner. They should be puddles by now.

As they decelerated, she eased off. She couldn't bring the ship to a dead stop, not if she wanted to drain the fluid from the chamber. Instead, she brought the ship to 0.5-g, figuring she was, at least now, accelerating in the right general direction.

Now, all Lara needed to do was drain and exit the chamber, head to the cockpit, and work through her options. If she couldn't make it back to Eden, perhaps she could, at least, get within range of a feasible rescue. But, in addition to how unpleasant it would be to cough all this fluid out of her lungs, she also couldn't be completely sure those things wouldn't be waiting for her.

*Shouldn't be...I hope not.*

Nothing should be able to survive the g-forces she'd subjected them to. The ship should be safe now. The alternative was to stay enchambered, but that wasn't an option. She'd starve.

Lara sighed, then hit the button on the control interface. She felt the fluid level drop as the chamber reclaimed it. The door opened and she fell to her knees, coughing and retching. Eventually, she regained her composure, then stood.

As she looked about the room, Lara froze briefly and shuddered. The monsters had, indeed, figured out the hatch controls. There they were, all five of them, crushed beyond recognition, on the floor. Right in front of her.

She stared at them. Then, slowly, she smiled, then screamed a guttural scream of victory.

But there was nobody to hear.

Saddened, Lara disconnected her undergarment from the chamber, walked towards the hatch, and started climbing towards the cockpit.

# ▪DAY 5: 17:32
## RETREAT

The crawlers were doing an excellent job, with nearly 200 confirmed kills in the ductwork. The team had gotten pretty efficient at reclaiming crawlers and redeploying them. There were only three more hutches to deal with. Ronnie began to believe they would finish before dark!

And that was a good thing. Along the way, they found a number of shriveled bodies, individuals who had gone out for a morning walk or perhaps a run. The corpses of a couple draped off a picnic table, their coffee cups still steaming. They even found the remnants of a dog, given the presence of a collar and leash.

The flies were telltale. The incessant buzzing of the flies warned them of bodies. Sasha expressed amazement at the number of flies, and one of the xenobiologists explained that the colony had, unfortunately, a healthy fly population. They just weren't aware of it because the flies and other vermin spent most of their time in the interstitial spaces of the colonial infrastructure. But the flies, smelling the bodies, came out. The remains would need to be dealt once the diploids were eliminated.

Ronnie and the squads had two more encounters with diploid cohorts. The first went smoothly. The diploids surrounded the drones and stayed within range. Once the drones hit them with flechettes, they fell to the roof and were readily dispatched.

The second was a different story. It was a larger cohort, with nearly thirty individuals. Most hovered within range of the drones, but the alpha and a few others held back. The drones, tuned to optimize their targeting, waited until some of the closer individuals lost interest, then fired. The squad dealt with the wounded, but the ones that held back flew away. They counted twenty-three dead diploids and estimated half a dozen got away.

This led to some discussion between the two xenobiologists. One thought the survivors would not come back, and the other speculated they might try to join another cohort. This debate turned into detailed discussion of the genetics of the diploids, a conversation beyond what the others could follow.

They approached the next hutch when Ronnie heard that familiar sound of leathery wings. But this time, she heard it coming from multiple directions. This was different.

The drones shot up to 10 m and spaced themselves as the squad tightened their circle, weapons ready.

"Keep your eyes open! They may be trying something new!"

Suddenly, two streams of diploids came at them from opposite directions. They flew low near to the rooftop avoiding the drones.

Ronnie and Omar turned towards one inbound stream of creatures, Sasha and Neal the other.

The first diploids, hit by flamethrowers, fell and skidded into the squad, forcing them to scatter to avoid the burning bodies as they came to a stop. But the creatures kept coming, flying over their burning siblings, taking advantage of the momentary confusion. Ronnie saw one spread its wings as it tilted its body upwards, forelimbs and hindlimbs raised to attack a member of her squad who lost his balance. It knocked the man down, claws digging into his flesh as it followed him to the ground; its dagger-like ovipositor thrust into the man's belly. He shifted from shouting deep voiced obscenities to a high-pitched shriek as it pressed itself into him, then went silent as the venom took effect. As soon as he stopped shrieking, it pulled itself out of him, then leapt at another secmed, taking her down too.

Ronnie froze, horrified. Half her squad was down. Neal was down. Sasha was down. She saw Omar drop his flamethrower and take up a rifle, stepping forward to engage. He shot the sensory clusters off of several. She followed suit and exchanged her flamethrower for a dropped rifle.

One of them hit Omar from behind. He fell forward and hit his face hard as the monster quickly impaled him near his spine.

The drones hovered uselessly above them, unable to fire at the diploids without hitting humans. The diploids ignored the drones.

The xenobiologists were down. One of the engineers was down. Both operators were down. All but seven of her squad were down.

Ronnie dropped the rifle and picked her flamethrower back up.

She screamed at an engineer. "YOU! PICK UP A RIFLE!"

She stepped back, then screamed. "ON ME! NOW! FORM A CIRCLE!"

As the survivors ran over, a diploid took down another squad member, stabbing him in the ass as he shrieked. They stood in a tight circle facing outward. As diploids flew towards them, they fired outward. The diploids banked to fly away.

One of the squad members realized she'd hit a fallen comrade and started to run forward to aid the dying secmed. Ronnie turned and grabbed her shoulder.

"There's no time, LEAVE THEM!"

She scanned and saw an elevator bank about 10 m away.

"The elevators! MOVE! Stay in formation!"

The group moved too slowly and awkwardly, walking backwards. They tripped over the bodies of dead friends and dead diploids. Another diploid flew towards them, then turned away as they fired at it.

They kept moving.

As they reached the doors, Ronnie stepped forward with her flame-thrower, spraying blindly.

"GET INSIDE! NOW!"

She heard them go through the doors, then ceased fire, sprinted, and closed the door behind her. They all stared through the doors.

There was nothing they could do.

The diploids were no longer interested in them. The diploid were only interested in the bodies of their friends.

# ▪DAY 5: 17:47
## CALLING THE SHOT

"Governor?"

Elke stood by the window when she heard that voice. She recognized it as Ronnie's, but, in the fifteen years she'd known Ronnie, Ronnie never sounded like that. She and the rest of her staff exchanged glances and slowly walked towards the table.

Elke said, "Ronnie?"

A long pause haunted the room.

"They're down, they're all down. The diploids figured it out. They attacked from the sides, ignored the drones, kept us in the line of fire so the drones wouldn't shoot. The first ones were a sacrifice. The damn things flew in hard, took our fire, then slammed into us, burning alive, just to make us break formation. The rest of them followed and took everyone down."

Elke fell down into her chair and raised a shaking hand to her temple. She looked visibly disturbed. John moved closer to her out of concern. Protocols be damned.

"How...how many Ronnie?"

Ronnie spoke with grief and frustration; Elke had never heard her speak like this before.

"The secmeds, Neal, Sasha, Omar, are down, almost the whole squad. I have six with me, and one engineer. Everyone else is down."

Ronnie spoke again, her voice more strident.

"Governor! They're not dead! Do you read me? They're not dead, dammit! They're wounded, and those monsters are feeding on them! We need to get them! How fast can you get me reinforcements?!"

Elke gritted her teeth, turned to Nikko and asked, "can you get a feed from one of the drones?"

Nikko stared at her, then nodded.

After a moment, an image appeared on the table. Gasps erupted from members of her staff. At least four diploids lay burning. More, apparently brought down by gunfire, were completely still. And all around, human bodies strewn across the rooftop.

Elke knew that everyone in the room was, like her, recognizing faces. People she knew, people she cared about, were lying on that rooftop, helpless as the things fed on them.

Sasha stared silently upwards, eyes brimming with tears, her clothing torn to expose her right leg and left arm. One creature was kneading the meat of her upper arm, its beak inserted into her bicep. Another was feeding on her thigh.

Omar was on his belly, his head turned to the side. A monster sucked on his right calf, another on his left thigh, a third on his upper arm.

Neal was nearly gone. The venom didn't work as well on him, which seemed to intensify their interest. His eyes moved, his lips trembled as he weakly moaned. There were four of them feeding on him; each of his limbs was nearly gone. As Elke and her staff watched, one by one, as they each finished a limb, the creatures moved to his torso and started kneading his chest and abdomen before stabbing him with their beaks. A fifth creature, possibly the alpha, walked over and used its forepaws to cradle his head, looking down into his eyes. His lips moved, although it was unclear what he was struggling to say. The alpha waited, for what they did not know. Suddenly, its grip tightened, its claws dug into the flesh of his head as it stabbed its beak through his left eye in a swift motion. Neal screamed, then went silent. It continued to hold his head as it wiggled its beak gently, pushing further through his eye socket, deep into his brain. The others continued feeding on his shriveling torso.

After a moment, Elke turned to George and whispered. "Why aren't they feeding on those two?"

George, horrified, stammered. "I, uh, I, I can't be completely sure, b-but I'd guess they've, uh…*injected*…those two with spores."

She nodded, then turned to John and asked, "am I right, John, that even if we could somehow get those people to you, you couldn't save them?"

John sighed, tears in his eyes. "We can't counter the venom. The ones they're feeding on, well, their tissues are liquifying. They'll be dead very soon.

And if those two are going to be hosts? We can't save them either. They'll die, miserably, but it'll take a lot longer."

Elke nodded again, then turned to Nikko and Dieter. Her voice was eerily calm as she said, "I want you to override the safety protocols on the drones and shoot every last one of those fucking things right now."

They stared at her.

Nikko sputtered. "They'll hit the people, too!"

She turned back to the horrific imagery on the table.

Softly, she asked, "wouldn't you rather be shot?"

# ■ DAY 5: 23:43
## BACK ON TRACK

Lara, strapped in the pilot's couch, stared at the command console. She had worked through scenarios, and none of them were good. The ship was a very, very long way away from Eden or any of the asteroid mining projects. Far enough that she needed to consider fuel and oxygen reserves in her calculations.

She expected fuel to be a constraint. And, sadly, with Reiner gone, she had plenty of food. It was the breathing gas that surprised her. Apparently, the little bastards burned oxygen at a fairly high rate. Lara almost hadn't bothered checking, presuming that without Reiner she should have plenty. But her attention to detail served her well.

Her preferred option, of course, was to avoid the chamber. But her calculations quickly showed that it was unavoidable. Even with the most efficient course she could plot, with the highest acceleration she could endure, with the current fuel and oxygen constraints, Lara would never make it anywhere civilized in a normal human lifetime.

So, back in the chamber she would go.

Going back in the chamber opened possibilities. The breathing fluid in the chamber pulled oxygen from a separate source, and, with a bit of creative plumbing, she could tap into the oxygen reserved for Reiner. And, between her chamber and Reiner's, she had plenty of nutritional supplementation.

This, of course, left fuel as Lara's primary constraint. She needed to chart an acceleration schedule that would get her home but would not exhaust her fuel. She came up with such a course, then groaned.

She was going to be in that chamber for a very, very long time.

The logical thing to do was program the chamber to knock her out, then revive her as she eventually approached Eden. The problem was being the sole occupant of the ship. Protocol required at least two people aboard when chambers were used, especially if she was going to sleep through the trip. It was one thing when she used the chamber earlier. She had no choice. Lara needed to get the ship under control and crush the damn things that killed Reiner. But this would be a second run in the chamber, and she wouldn't be awake.

The good news, such as it was, was that Lara would probably set a record for enchambered sleep.

*Not exactly one of my top aspirations…*

Lara ran through it a few more times to convince herself it was the only way.

*Ugh, alright, let's just get this over with.*

Lara recorded and sent a message to Eden with her predicament and course. Worst case scenario, if something did go wrong in the chamber, this ensured someone would find her and revive her. She did another quick calculation to figure out how long it would take that message to get to Eden. Lara deeply regretted vessels like this didn't have subspace messaging; then again, this ship really wasn't designed to be this far out. Thankfully, the message would get there before she did.

Lara had a lot to do. She laid in the course and primed the command so she could execute it from the chamber. She had a quick bite of real food, then loaded up her chamber's nutritional supplementation.

Now, all Lara had to do was find some tools, get creative with the plumbing to draw oxygen from Reiner's chamber, endure yet another "drowning," and take a very, very, very long nap.

# PART 3:
# RESURGENCE

# ■ DAY 6: 06:12
## DEPARTURE

Deirdre was bored. She felt guilty about it, but there was no denying that she was bored!

She felt guilty because she knew how lucky she was to be away from the settlement. She didn't know all of the details about the infestation, but she knew enough. She knew people were in peril, and she was here, safely on the beach, sipping her coffee. They'd sent most of their drones back to the settlement for the campaign against the pineapple diploid. It was the right thing to do, no question, but it meant taking turns using their remaining drones in lieu of fieldwork, and that meant a lot of boredom.

She meandered through the kitchenette of their EAGLE mobile base. It was safe, but also cramped. It really wasn't designed to be more than a resource for field personnel that spent most of their time in the field. But when the creatures preying on the squirts arrived, Deirdre and the rest of the scientists were forced to retreat to the EAGLE. Given the number of xenobiologists and support personnel, it was crowded.

So now the enemy was boredom and the natural tension of cramped quarters. But the alternative was unacceptable. Not that the creatures could compromise an environmental suit, or rather, they *shouldn't* be able to compromise an environmental suit. But aggressive creatures could do a lot of damage to the wearer even if they couldn't rip through it. The operations folks stepped up with a methodology to fairly allocate drone time, but that still left inquisitive people with little to do, and card games only went so far.

So, Deirdre slept in a bit, ate a leisurely breakfast, and then went to work analyzing yesterday's data collection. She finished her work over an hour ago. Deirdre sighed and tapped her mug anxiously.

"Is death by boredom possible? I'd rather face the predators…" she muttered under her breath.

"Deirdre!"

She looked up and saw one of the other xenobiologists, Oyana, standing by a lab table interacting with the projection relayed by the drone. Deirdre carried her mug to the table.

"Good morning! What's up?"

"They're leaving!"

Deirdre faced the projection. It took her a moment to process what she was seeing. A light rain obscured the drone's perspective. Rain was common on this side of the mountains; they'd learned long ago to integrate multiple drones' perspectives to improve projection quality. But, given the settlement's needs, they only had the one drone.

Oyana fiddled with the controls, and the view of the beach became clearer. The squirts were making their way down the sand, back to the water.

"When did *that* start?"

Oyana shrugged. "Unfortunately, I really can't say. The drone was being used elsewhere and my turn just started. I'd say about 10% of them have already left."

Their dialogue attracted attention from the other bored scientists, who gathered and hovered like flies to a carcass. Too focused to notice, Deirdre sipped on her coffee excitedly and addressed the computer. "Monitor the departure rate of the squirts. Compare with last known population density. Extrapolate, presuming a consistent rate, an estimate of when they began departing and when they will finish exiting the beach."

A computerized voice responded. "Given population density yesterday at 15:42 and presuming a consistent departure rate, estimated departure began 05:24 and will conclude 18:14. The quality of the extrapolation will improve as time passes and more data is gathered. Would you like revisions to these estimates?"

Deirdre hesitated, then said, "please provide hourly revision updates, starting at the top of the hour."

"Acknowledged."

One of the grad students pointed at the display and said, "I don't see any of the predators!"

They all leaned in, scanning the projection.

Deirdre made an adjustment. "Please add monitoring for the winged trilaterally symmetric predators that have been preying on the squirts."

"Would you like to specify species?"

"Please track individual species, but for the purposes of this exercise, do not distinguish between species."

"Acknowledged. Since monitoring began, no predators have been observed. An update will be provided if one is detected."

Deirdre looked at the display and mused. "No more predators…I wonder what that means?"

# ▪ DAY 6: 06:35
## HELL

Mike had no idea what time it was.

He knew it was morning. He could tell that much. He'd given up trying to understand what was happening to him. He didn't care anymore. He just wanted the pain to end.

It was awful. The pain was constant, just unrelenting.

*Please, God, please, if you're there, please let it end…*

He wondered what became of his wife, Emma, his children. He couldn't imagine a benign reason why they hadn't found him. He feared the worst. Were they dead? Or, worse, were they too lying somewhere, unable to move?

Mike regained some limited ability to move his eyes; he could even turn his head, ever so slightly, to the left and right. Yesterday, when he regained control of his eyelids, he'd gratefully closed his eyes once the sun was directly overhead. Such a small thing was such a tremendous relief; the sun was too bright while directly overhead. The other domes could filter the midday light and temper the blaze; but here, in an agricultural dome, they needed all that light for the crops. His limited range of motion offered him little choice but to simply close his eyes and wait for the afternoon to wane.

He had some difficulty swallowing. Mike never liked lying on his back; but he couldn't move, so he had no choice. He'd suffered through panicked, gagging sessions that he struggled to regain calm, to force himself to swallow.

Beyond that, there was only pain.

A burning sensation throughout his body contrasted oddly with the cool, damp soil covering all of him, save his face. If he turned his head as far as he could, all the way to the left, Mike could see his neighbor's adolescent daughter buried in the flower bed. Only her emaciated face was exposed. He had to assume that he was similarly entombed.

He wished he could scare off the flies. They would not leave him alone, probably because there was no livestock left to torment. He could close his eyes, at least, but he could feel them on his lips, in his nostrils. At least no ants had found him. Yet.

His neighbor stared blankly upward. It seemed like she had regained less motor control than he did. There was no way to know. She wasn't looking his way. She made no sounds beyond the odd, soft moan. Nor did he. Despite his best efforts, his most ardent concentration, he could not muster anything beyond a groan.

Mike had never given his eyelids much thought, but he realized he was blessed to have recovered control of them. She did not. Her eyes were moist as she stared upward, into the sun, the odd fly walking across her face, stopping to take moisture from her eyes. Their disgusting mouthparts leisurely dabbed against the surface of her eye, the white sclera, even the cornea and the pupil itself. Mike couldn't imagine how that felt, what that looked like from her perspective as they defiled her eyes. But there wasn't a thing he could do for her.

He knew there was another child. Before he had been attacked, when he went to investigate the noise in the garden, he saw nightmares taking two of his neighbors' children. There was no sign of the parents. One child was already buried. But they had a number of children close in age, and he couldn't tell which one it was, even whether it was a son or daughter.

Their older daughter, the girl he could now see, had been lying, naked and motionless, on the ground. The things ripped out his neighbor's flowerbed and dug a shallow hole near the buried child. Eventually, they had dragged him out of the house too, laying him on his side. They resumed their digging. They dragged the neighbors' daughter to the hole, laid her in the hole on her back, then covered her with soil. They fussed as they worked, manipulated her limbs, pulled soil out from under her here, and pushed some soil back until they were satisfied. Then, he watched them rip out more flowers and dig another oubliette. And he knew this grave was for him. They ripped his clothing from him, dragged him to the hole, and covered him slowly and carefully.

Then they'd left.

He'd been lying there ever since.

*Emily was her name. Sweet kid, only, what? Twelve years old or thereabout? Fit, athletic. She would have become a very pretty young woman. Favored her mother.*

Not anymore. Now her face was just papery skin over bone, the structures of her skull clearly visible. It made Mike wonder what *he* looked like. It made him think of his children again.

The stabbing pain eventually eased. But the burning sensation that started in his gut intensified and spread throughout his body. That pain was so intense, Mike feared he would lose his mind. Then he hoped he'd lose his mind. He burned, then he ached, an intense aching, followed by an odd, incessant, tearing sensation. It was as if little knives or teeth were cutting away tiny slivers of him, but from *inside* somehow, rather than through his skin. It started in his fingers and toes, then progressed gradually inward, through his calves and forearms, his knees and elbows, towards his torso. He could no longer feel his arms and legs, and now he felt the tiny cuts in his core.

As Mike lay there, he swore he felt little things moving. For all he knew, there *were* tiny things on or in his skin, tiny things from the soil. At least they'd be earthly things. Maybe some ants finally found him. *Oh, God, that would be awful!*

He was a farmer, so he knew all the tiny things that lived in the soil of his fields. Some were pests, things constantly evolving to evade any and all efforts to eradicate or at least control them. It was a never-ending arms race. But, for him, the ants were the worst. As valuable as he knew ants were for maintaining healthy soil, there was just something about having ants crawl on him, feast on him, tear away little parts of him that terrified Mike more than he could explain.

His skin crawled, burned, ached, tore, minute after minute, hour after hour, day and night.

But then, this morning, he felt something new.

There was a small, sharp pain on his chest. It was like getting an injection, except it didn't stop. It just continued, then steadily grew. Then another shot of pain, and another, and another cropped up across his torso, chest, and belly, until he lost count. Until it became a constant experience.

Mike couldn't aim his eyes down towards his body. Even if he could, he felt sure that since he was covered with soil, he wouldn't be able to see anything anyway. He turned as best he could and looked over at the girl. She continued to stare upwards expressionlessly, but in the soil covering her chest,

Mike saw tiny movements. Little disturbances at first, then, through the soil, a long, thin protrusion shot up. It was slender, a wormlike tendril, covered with little, tiny hairs, unfurling in the morning air.

Soon, from the base of the little tendrils, sticking through the soil, Mike saw a shell. A fingerlike shell grew through the soil, with two antenna-like stalks sticking out of it, waving in the air. More of them popped out through the soil, presumably from her body, as she moaned.

Mike couldn't see his own chest or belly, but he could feel more of the sharp, tearing pains. The pain started small; now it was growing, and his skin was ripping.

Mike stared helplessly up at the sky and prayed for deliverance. Not rescue, not anymore. Deliverance, now, would be death.

*Please God, just let it end…*

# ▪ DAY 6: 06:46
## BUDDING

Elke never tired of the stark beauty of the sun rising behind the mountains. All too soon, the sun would claw its way above the peaks, and there'd be a changing of the guard from nocturnal to diurnal life. She missed this vision most mornings; she rarely woke until the sun was already peeking over the mountains. When she did wake early enough, she chastised herself for ever missing it. Each sunrise was a rebirth, a fresh start filled with possibilities.

This vision always filled her with hope and restored her soul. But this morning, she struggled.

She saw the mountains as a metaphor for herself and her staff. The mountains were guardians standing up to an onslaught, protecting Wu City from Eden's challenges just as the mountains held back the harshness of the desert sun.

*No, the mountains were Eden herself. Mountains for whom this is just another day. Mountains that have seen countless mornings, just like this one, oblivious to the aspirations and suffering of the colonists, intruders undeserving of such a morning. Mountains that no more cared for unwelcome guests than the planet itself.*

Did Eden have suspicions about them? Some insight into their reputation as a species? Elke softly swore, then shook her head. Momentarily embarrassed, she turned to see whether she might have been overheard or observed. But everyone was either focused on a console, busy in the kitchenette, or napping on a cot. Elke was relieved.

She shuddered. This wasn't healthy. This wasn't helping.

"Elke?"

She turned from the windows, then realized John's voice wasn't in the room. "Yes, John?"

"It's Pete. He's budding."

She looked at her wrist computer.

"John? Is that possible? It can't have been that long."

"I know. But they're erupting. I'll route a projection to the room and join you."

"Okay. I'll find George."

She hurried over to the table and called for George. She looked around quickly for her drink; this was the second time she'd misplaced it within the hour.

John entered the room as the team gathered around the conference room table. A projection appeared of an isolation chamber containing a hospital bed. A few people gasped at the sight of a naked, emaciated figure, barely recognizable as an adult male. Now, he was just a thin, baggy layer of papery skin draped over bone.

From his neck down to groin, brown protrusions had emerged in various stages. Some even grew as they watched. From each bud, two long, sparsely haired threads waved very slowly in the air.

John began speaking as George entered the room, followed by Taki and a few other xenobiologists.

"Pete is in a medically induced coma and in an isolation chamber. The kraken parasite removal therapies were ineffective against these parasites. When we found him, the infestation had already progressed so far that any attempt at conventional surgical removal would have killed him. His life signs are extremely weak and he's down to a bit over 30 kilos. There's not much left of him. We decided that our need to understand what's happening to him was more important than his modesty, and, frankly, he's beyond caring."

John paused.

"We know he was impregnated in the brig two days ago, between 22:00 that night and 04:00 the following morning. That's less than thirty-six hours between impregnation and emergence. We've never seen a kraken infestation progress that rapidly."

George leaned in for a closer look. "For kraken, an infected host remains mobile. It takes time for that one spore to multiply in the host's body, and it creates the opportunity to pass worms to other hosts, as Esteban did fifteen years ago. This improves the odds that at least one will survive to reproduce.

So, the worms feed selectively, keeping the host alive and mobile as long as possible. But for these pineapple hosts? Injecting them with multiple spores ensures impregnation with multiple worms. Rather than being concerned with whether the prospective host will successfully be infected, these creatures can be confident of infection. So, once impregnated, they want the next generation to emerge as quickly as possible."

He leaned back, then continued. "In the wild, when the diploids inject their usual victims, the venom immobilizes them and anesthetizes them. They're alive, but they're not feeling any pain. We believe this is to their advantage; anesthetized hosts are less stressed, and therefore more nutritious for their parasites. Their ability to develop a venom that can immobilize human prey is amazing, and, unfortunately, it's not surprising that it isn't a perfect adaptation. Human prey, unfortunately, is not anesthetized."

"Thank you, George," John responded. "Yes, as you and I have discussed, the host immobilization without analgesics is, presumably, an incomplete adaptation to Earth organisms as hosts. We will, I fear, soon have more than enough hosts to study in order to determine consistency."

John held up his hands, then spread them apart, enlarging the image to focus on a set of the protrusions erupting from Pete's chest.

"We noticed the first chrysalis a few minutes ago, seventeen minutes to be exact. As of right now, we have more than fifty 'buds', our current nickname for the next stage of the pineapple's infestation. And you can see more just starting to tear through his skin. No way to know how many more will emerge, but the protrusion rate has slowed significantly. Note that they're all emerging from his upper torso, nowhere else. It's not clear to us why. George, any theories?"

George answered. "Related species sequester their hosts, presumably to prevent predators from taking advantage of an immobilized host as an easy meal. If you look at the chrysalis, you'll see those feathery threads. I think you'll find those are the haploid's two tails, and the little hairs are increasing surface area for gas exchange. Imagine the host has been buried under a thin layer of soil or leaf litter. As the creature metamorphoses within the chrysalis and the host's body fails, their ability to get oxygen from the host's bloodstream degrades. At some point, they rely on the tails to facilitate gas exchange above the soil. Later, when they settle as pineapples, those structures will become their roots."

George pointed at one of the things and turned towards John. "Any imagery of the insertion?"

John nodded and muttered something inaudible. The body became transparent. From each chrysalis, a root extended into the body.

"You can see, here, the alien tissue highlighted in red, that these eruptions are quite different from what we saw with kraken. Kraken worms made their way to the skin, leaving the body weakened but alive. They erupted through the skin within their chrysalis, then relied on fat reserves as they metamorphosed into little kraken. When they emerged, they fed on their chrysalis shells, then the host's body, then each other until the strongest got away. Here, the chrysalis forms and continues to feed on the host's body. We can't be completely sure about the feeding, but, since these things started erupting, we found digestive juices in Pete's body. We think the worms have shifted from the feeding methods of the kraken worms to the liquification feeding strategy of the diploids, and are absorbing predigested fluids."

John paused, then continued. "I can only imagine what he'd be going through if he was not comatose. We don't think he'll last much longer."

The room was silent. Everyone continued to stare blankly or with visible expressions of either pity or revulsion. Bhavia was the only one who refused to look. Whether it was out of guilt or spite, John and Elke couldn't tell. As the senior officers watched, some of the larger buds moved slightly as their occupants shifted position. Other buds continued to grow as they erupted from his body.

With a sad, strained voice, John spoke to the sea of traumatized faces. "I know this is awful, but we need to understand this process. We believe the buds will hatch after they retract their feeding structures, which we believe they'll do as he dies."

John hung his head. "Pete is going to die miserably, and our only debate has been whether to allow the buds to progress or to euthanize him. But we needed to understand what we're dealing with. Right now, there's probably a substantial number of our fellow colonists out there serving as hosts for these things. But they're enduring everything Pete is going through without the relief of an induced coma. They're enduring the closest thing to pure hell that I can imagine."

A few turned away as Pete's torso slowly deflated. John looked around the room, then turned to Elke.

"We need to make an awful decision. We cannot know when the hidden hosts will erupt, or when they'll hatch, or when they'll die. But we *do* know that they *will* die "

He paused, looking around the room, and saw quiet, sad acceptance of the veracity of his assertion. Then he nodded towards Pete.

"The kindest thing we can do for the hosts is find them as quickly as possible and kill them as humanely as possible. End their suffering, hopefully before we face another infestation."

He turned towards Elke again and she met his gaze as he concluded, "I know you want to give people a rest, but we can't. We can't let the hosts suffer, and we can't let these buds hatch."

The room was silent as Elke shifted her gaze to the image of Pete.

Without taking her eyes from Pete, in the weariest voice John had ever heard from her, Elke relented. "You're right, John. Sadly, you're right."

She straightened, rolled her shoulders back, and looked John squarely in the eyes. With a tone faking confidence, she said, "get me options. I need humane options to euthanize the hosts as they're found."

John held her eyes a moment, nodded, and went to work with his team.

Elke turned to George. "I need your best guidance, based on your knowledge of related species and observations from the beaches. Work with Dieter and help us find hosts before they hatch."

Next, she turned to Nikko. "I need you to work with Bhavia, Guido, and Rajiv. I want a search strategy for every dome. We need to find and eliminate hosts. And we must ensure parasites are destroyed as their hosts are euthanized. I'm open to suggestions, but I think that means immediate incineration. Do not anticipate preserving any bodies for burial or study."

She paused, then concluded. "We don't have much time. Once we clear the residential dome, I need to address our surviving secmeds and their squads."

# ■ DAY 6: 07:43
## CONTINUING THE RESEARCH

"George?"

The beach team stood encircling the lab table aboard the EAGLE. Deirdre tried to raise George at the surface settlement. She was about to try again when he appeared virtually at the head of the table. He looked like he'd been up all night.

With a weary smile, he asked, "yes, Deirdre?"

She hesitated, briefly questioning her decision to interrupt him. But she weighed the potential significance of their discovery, and chose to continue.

Deirdre gave him a high-level summary of their observations and the results of their subsequent research. The squirts were returning to the water, their breeding behaviors presumably complete. Unfortunately, the xenobiologists' ability to observe these behaviors had been constrained by the harassment of the predators feeding on the squirts and the need to reallocate drones back to the surface settlement. But they had observed a range of behaviors.

Some squirt species mated, including ritualized behaviors by which prospective partners evaluated each other's suitability. Some were observed spawning on the beach, leaving masses behind that, presumably, contained something analogous to eggs. Some squirts did not return to the water. In fact, they were not moving at all. Overall, they'd demonstrated limited ability to move out of the water, but some of the smaller species were partially buried, suggesting they'd been impregnated with spores.

George nodded along. While it paled in comparison to the horrors endured by the settlement, he knew they'd missed an important research opportunity. The next quadrilunar alignment would be almost forty years from now. If he were fortunate enough to still be alive, he'd be well past 150 and beyond any possibility of participating in field work. He sighed and decided to count his blessings rather than dwell on missed opportunities. He also realized he'd lost track of what the team was telling him.

"Deirdre, I'm sorry. My mind wandered off. Can you say that again?"

She smiled, then continued. "We haven't seen any of the diploids since sunrise. A number of their bodies are on the beach, but not enough. So, we think some have left. There may also have been a predator taking some of them, but we haven't observed this. Most of the dead ones have been scavenged, but not all, at least not yet, and they show no signs of trauma. It looks like they simply died."

After a moment, George asked, "are any of the dead diploids the same species we've been dealing with here at the settlement?"

He was overwhelmed by the possible irony that the damn things were dying of their own accord.

That would be consistent with the kraken; their diploid generation was short lived. On the other hand, the diploid kraken generation fed until they were able to release spores into the air and then died. This pineapple diploid generation kept feeding and injecting spores into hosts, so there'd been no reason to expect them to have a short life span. There was just so much they didn't know about this group of creatures!

Squad members had been killed. Drones had been diverted from this exceedingly rare research opportunity to hunt and kill diploids. For all of this to have potentially been unnecessary was almost too much to bear.

He realized Deirdre had stopped talking and looked concerned.

"I'm sorry; mind wandering again. What was that?"

"No worries George…As to whether any of the dead diploids are the same species, we can't confirm that unless we go out and take samples. And that, really, is why we wanted to talk with you. Now that the predators have left, we think it's safe to resume our field work. The life forms that are usually present have returned, and we expect they'll find and feed on egg masses and impregnated hosts. We should be safe."

George nodded, but he still worried. In theory, it should be safe. On the other hand, they had safety protocols for a reason. Field scientists were supposed to be escorted by secmeds and drones, and those secmeds and most of their drones were currently at the settlement.

George raised a finger, tapped his wrist computer, and turned to talk to someone else in the room. After a few minutes' conversation, he turned back.

"There's agreement in the room with regard to the importance of this research opportunity. There are things we hope to learn relevant to our situation here at the settlement. But we can't send back any secmeds or drones, not yet. So, first, deploy aquatic drones from *Calypso* to monitor the squirts as they leave the beach. You still have a full complement of those, thank goodness. No divers, not unless you clear it with me. On the beach, go out in groups. You stay together, you stay on the beach near the EAGLE, and make sure your trackers are fully armed. They can focus on safety rather than tracking. Understood?"

As she nodded, he continued. "One more thing. We need to know everything we can about impregnated hosts. Keep me informed about what you find."

# DAY 6: 08:10
## SMALL VICTORIES

The sun was now well above the mountains, warming the arid desert plains. Beyond the mountains, rain fell. Elke didn't need to check any meteorological display. She could see the upper edge of the rain clouds between the peaks.

She shook her head and sighed. *Water.* She'd much rather be worrying about water. Or about expanding the residential structure. Or adding agricultural domes. Or other infrastructure expansions in anticipation of inbound ships already in flight, each carrying a thousand new colonists. *Anything, please, ANYTHING other than weighing the relative value of lives. Which aggie dome to clear first? How to find and eliminate hosts before they hatch? Eliminate? Euthanize? Kill?*

Who was she to decide who lives and dies?

With a brusque shake of her head, she straightened and looked out the window.

Who was she? She was the Governor. If the colony were to survive, somebody had to take on the responsibility. Someone had to make the best possible, or perhaps the least awful, choices, and live with the mistakes. Her people needed and deserved proper leadership. Her hand started to shake again.

*Am I still capable of that?*

She turned around and walked towards the table.

"Status?"

Nikko looked up from his station and said, "Dieter came up with a drone formation to maximize detection precision despite interference. That let us drive the last cohort out of the building into a waiting cloud of drones. Ronnie and her squad are buttoning up the last hutch."

"Ronnie?" Elke interrupted.

Nikko nodded and smiled. "Yes, Ronnie. She volunteered. Insisted, in fact. Said she wanted to finish what she started, and already had enough volunteers for a full squad. I talked to Bhavia about it. He said focusing on the job would…well it's just what she needs right now. And we are running out of time. So he conceded. You?"

After a moment, Elke shook her head slowly. Part of her understood; part of her knew even Ronnie had limits. And nobody really healed completely from something like this. But, right now, ending this threat to the colony was all that mattered. They needed a victory. And Elke suspected Ronnie needed it more than her.

"The crawlers have a cohort of diploids cornered in the ductwork," Nikko continued. "When they're eliminated, the residential dome will be clear!"

Elke heard a couple of half-hearted cheers. She looked around the room, making eye contact, weighing what needed to be said.

"We've achieved an important milestone but paid a very dear price to reach it. Guido, Bhavia, we owe your secmeds and their squads an enormous debt. Their long hours, hard work, and sacrifice will long be remembered."

She paused. Her eyes showed sincerity, but her voice was dull, quiet, tired, so tired.

"Dieter, the drones performed beyond expectations. Well done. Nikko, as always, without your team, nothing happens. Thank you. But the job's not done yet. We need to clear the other domes. We need to find the hosts before they hatch. We have a lot to do and not nearly enough time!"

She turned to Dieter and asked, "how are we doing for more drones?"

"We have a set nearly ready, within the hour. The next lot is due six hours after that."

He paused, then said, "you know, the drones from the residential domes could be reallocated. We'll want to refresh ammunition. I can have a team go to the residential dome. They'll call in the drones, reload them, and take them wherever you want them. Give me, oh, an hour to have the team prep and get to the residential dome transportation hub."

Elke nodded, then paused to reflect.

"Nikko, work with Dieter. Let's get the new drones deployed here. They can start by clearing the open spaces. Then I want the residential drones reallocated to the agricultural domes. I don't have any thoughts on prioritizing the ones we've lost contact with, so, flip a coin or something."

Nikko nodded and beckoned Dieter to step away from the table with him.

"Bhavia and Guido, we need a plan to clear the base station. Rajiv, this'll be harder than the residential building, won't it? More interference?"

Rajiv, yawning, nodded. "Yes, the residential building is an arc, and the base station is more of a massive cube. Well, the upper levels are smaller, so there's a bit of a pyramid shape, but it doesn't taper that much." He yawned again, then said, "sorry, been up for a while. What matters is that there's a lot more building infrastructure between where the drones can fly and the interior of the building, so I don't know how well they'll sense any diploids within the base station."

Dieter held up a finger to pause his conversation with Nikko. "I'm confident they'll pick up the diploids, but the interference will weaken the signal and make the sensing less precise. They'll be able to tell you there are diploids in the building, but the further in they go, the broader the potential range of location will be. Does that make sense?"

Rajiv shrugged. Elke looked at Bhavia, who nodded, then said, "it helped to have a fairly precise location for the little bastards in the residential structure. It would still be useful to know which end of the base station they're in. We'll just have to plan accordingly. It'd help to have a floor plan of the building available to the squads."

Rajiv nodded and said, "on its way!"

Elke turned to Bhavia and asked, "do you have enough people to clear the base station without the residential dome squads? I need them searching for hosts."

Bhavia thought for a moment, exchanged a look with Guido, and replied, "we'll make it work."

Elke sighed, then looked around. Nikko, after finishing his conversation with Dieter, deep in calculations and last minute details. Elke walked over, got his attention, and led him to John and Rajiv.

"I'm thinking about whether we can lift the lockdown in the residential dome. Thoughts?"

The three men grimaced at the weight of her question. "As long as we're clear that they can't leave the dome," Rajiv responded, "I think it's okay. But we need to keep interdome transportation locked down."

John shook his head. "Elke, we've lost a lot of people. A *lot* of people. Right now, survivors are focused on their own survival; they aren't thinking about anyone else yet. When they do, when they realize how many friends they've lost? It's going to be traumatic. And, of course, there are the hosts. If they hatch, you'll have to lock down again. Elke, if you don't have a compelling need to lift the lockdown, don't."

# ■DAY 6: 08:57
## COST OF WINNING WAR

Residential dome secmeds and their squads assembled in the transportation hub. It was a somber gathering. It was one thing to track progress as the last of the diploids were found and dispatched. Everyone knew there had been losses. But this was the first time since this nightmare began that the secmeds were in the same space at the same time. They could not help but notice how many were missing.

Conferencing equipment was set up at the center of the hub's broad space. The operations team that, presumably, set up the equipment waited near the entry with suspensor pallets of additional equipment. Ronnie wondered whether they knew any more than she did why they were assembled here. She spotted Badru, and in a rush of relief, went to stand by a friend.

At precisely 09:00, the conferencing equipment activated, and the senior staff appeared in the middle of the room. Governor Lubandi's projection stood, cleared her throat, and the room went silent.

"Hello. I know this is unexpected, bear with me. I know many of you remember, as I do, the kraken. We'd just reached Eden. We were overwhelmed by the beauty of our new home. We were confronted by an existential threat that should not have been possible. We responded, we adapted, we survived, but our naivete cost precious lives.

Many of you have conducted after action analyses with me. You know that I always point out two things. First, the importance of harsh lessons. Every rule, every best practice that we rely on is the fruit of mistakes. We all, when confronted by a novel threat, make the best decisions we can with limited or even erroneous information. Sometimes, we get it wrong. This is the burden of leadership. It is impossible to avoid this. All we can do is our best, and then frankly and honestly assess.

She lowered her eyes, then, scanning the room, continued.

"Second, we are sometimes forced to make harsh decisions. Impossible decisions. Life and death decisions. Sometimes, we have no choice but to risk, to even sacrifice, the lives of some to preserve the lives of others. This is also a burden of leadership, also impossible to avoid. We asked some of you to take on the awful responsibility of making decisions that might cost some of the lives entrusted to you, knowing full well how much pain can come with such decisions. Too many of you have paid the ultimate price. Each of you has the gratitude of every colonist for your willingness to accept these risks.

I know, you're tired. You're tired, and you're hurting. This war has cost you dearly. But we have cleared the residential dome. This is an important milestone, but the fight isn't over yet. There are other domes to be cleared, other lives at risk, other heroes that are preparing to apply the lessons you've learned."

She waited for the weary cheers to die down before continuing softly. "You've earned a respite, but I cannot offer you one. The job is not over, not yet. We must proceed to the next step, and it will be difficult."

She nodded towards John who stood as she took her seat.

John slowly rose from his chair, a frail shadow of what he once was. He swallowed hard before he began speaking. Ronnie thought, even as a projection, that he looked almost green, like he was going to be sick. "I know you've directly engaged with the predators. I know you've seen some awful things, the remains of their victims. Some of you have witnessed attacks and even fought off attacks. But now, I need to show you something you may not have seen."

John's image was replaced by a projection of Pete. Not in his current state, but as he was when first discovered in the brig, taken to the hospital, and placed in an isolation chamber. John began speaking, and, as he spoke, the image progressed. Pete gradually shriveled until the image froze with the erupted parasites covering his torso. Many in the room had to avert their eyes. Ronnie put her hand over her mouth to stifle a gasp.

"Some of you are aware that not all diploid victims are consumed. All victims are injected with an immobilizing venom, but not all victims are consumed. Some are, instead, injected with spores. Spores that hatch into parasitic worms."

The image shrank as John reappeared. The tremble in his voice grew as he explained.

"You need to understand that although a host is immobilized, they are not anesthetized. Each host is in agony. Immobilized, conscious, and in excruciating pain. Nothing we have eases their suffering. This patient is in a medically induced coma. That cannot be done in the field, and we have a very limited capacity for this in the hospital."

John heaved a tearful sigh; his already haggard face aged with every word. "I took an oath. An oath to preserve life, to ease pain, to do no harm. Those of you that are security/medics took the same oath. But this? This is beyond anything we've encountered. Because we cannot help these hosts. They will die soon, in excruciating pain. There's nothing we can do to save them; there's nothing we can do to ease their suffering.

And, as they die, they will hatch. Something…something we haven't seen before, will hatch out of them. George, our chief xenobiologist, doesn't know what will hatch out of them; but he told us that, among similar species, the hatchlings are also predators."

Elke appeared beside John as he lowered his head. Ronnie caught how tenderly she laid her hand on his upper arm as they exchanged places.

"You've earned a respite, but we cannot offer you one," Elke lamented. "Instead, we need you to press on and serve this community, and that includes handling this…terrible situation with the hidden hosts."

She paused to beckon the operations team to come forward. The operations team pushed the suspensor pallets towards the center of the room. The operations team began distributing kits from the pallets.

"We must find the hosts. We must find them, and we must prevent them from hatching. John and his team have prepared ampules containing a lethal dose of an anesthetic cocktail. It will not ease the suffering of the hosts, but it will not add to it, either. It will end their lives as humanely as we can. And, once the host has died, their remains can be incinerated to eliminate their parasites." Softly, she added, "some of the hosts will be too far gone to be injected. They will still have to be incinerated."

The room erupted with everything from horrified gasps to exclamations of outrage. The already traumatized secmeds greatly opposed the idea of "dispatching" the parasite victims. Ronnie and Badru exchanged a horrified look.

"I know this is awful!" Elke raised her voice over the angry yelling; as tired as she was, she would not tolerate disorder. "Two things. First, the hosts are in agony. Their suffering cannot be eased, and their lives cannot be saved. They are going to die no matter what we do. Second, the parasites they carry will hatch and put all surviving colonists at risk. Euthanizing the hosts is the most humane option you can offer them and absolutely essential to the colony's survival!

I know this will be horrific. And I cannot offer you any guidance. We know nothing yet about the hosts. Our xenobiologists suggest, based on similar species, that they'll be hidden somewhere, by the diploids. We're counting on you to figure this out, because your peers, here at the primary dome and under the agricultural domes, will need to do the same as soon as they've eliminated diploids."

She gave them another moment, then concluded. "We must find them, we must end their suffering, we must eliminate this threat to our colony, and we must do this as quickly as possible."

# ▪ DAY 6: 10:09

## MERCY

Ronnie opened her kit and stared at the ampules, then realized she was softly sobbing.

It was too much, just too much.

She shook her head to regain her composure. She couldn't argue with the logic, not after what she'd seen. During these last fifteen years, she'd seen things. Things beyond anything she'd ever imagined. Beautiful, unspoiled wilderness. Spectacular vistas. A world of promise and possibilities.

She'd also seen horrors. Kraken eating people alive. The predators that tore into Sven before she shot him to spoil their fun. But the image of that *thing* feeding on her squad! That *thing* holding Neal's head, driving its beak through his eye into his brain…

Was it truly more awful than what she'd seen before? Or too fresh? Did she just need time to process it? How much of herself was already lost, hurt, scarred, beyond repair? Ronnie still couldn't talk about the nightmares from the kraken. How was she expected to survive this fresh hell? Was it time to give up? To PIP out, make a fresh start on another world, an antiseptic world? Not that a lifeless world was without risk; death was death, but somehow such risks seemed far more impersonal.

She exchanged a glance with Badru, gauging his level of sanity. His dazed, glassy eyes made Ronnie worry he was already disassociating. But he motioned to move on anyway. Ronnie wiped her tears angrily, upset that she was upset. She straightened, and yelled to her squad, or those still alive after the last mission.

"We have our assignment! Let's start walking!"

With a nod to Badru, they made their way through the transportation hub doors and started walking towards the residential building. The trip was rife with déjà vu, given that just yesterday, they'd taken the same route with vehicles laden with drones and crawlers. But it was the assignment they'd drawn.

They fanned out at 2 m intervals, secmeds at the ends, scanning for hosts, not completely sure what they were looking for.

After a few false alarms, a male voice called out from her left.

"Hey! What's that?"

She turned to the voice, saw an arm raised and a finger pointing. She broke formation to run and see what had caught his eye. Something was buried in the dirt under a tree.

Ronnie walked up to a low mound of disturbed soil. At one end, a face stared up at the branches. She beckoned to Badru and the rest to approach; slowly, she started walking towards the face, the others just behind her.

There was something eerie about that face, just looking up, emotionless, not moving, not making a sound as she approached. Suddenly, without warning, the eyes snapped to the side to look at her. The hollowed face remained impassive. Ronnie inhaled sharply and bit her tongue *hard* to keep from jumping backwards with fright. She heard Badru half yell, half mumble "fucking hell" as he took two steps backwards. Perhaps he lowered his voice out of embarrassment, for reacting so negatively towards the clearly conscious victim? They didn't mean to show fear; they were just caught off guard. Ronnie now wondered if she made the poor buried soul feel worse.

The eyes followed her as she walked up and knelt. She scanned the face with her wrist computer.

*Thomas Sanghi. Twenty-eight years old. Recent arrival. Married, two young children. One of Dieter's engineers. Damn.*

Softly, Ronnie asked, "Thomas, can you speak?"

No response.

"If you can hear me, look away and then back."

After a moment, the eyes turned away, then back.

"If you're in pain, look away and back."

The eyes turned away, then back.

Ronnie nodded.

"Do you prefer Thomas? Or Tom?"

The eyes turned away then back again at "Tom."

She closed her eyes, sighed, then reopened them. She didn't want to lie, but there was no benefit to further candor. It would take away the pain. And she had to do what she had to do.

"Tom, I have a shot to give you. It'll take away the pain. Would that be ok?"

The eyes turned away, then back.

Ronnie swallowed hard and gave a false smile.

"I'm going to brush away some of the soil by your neck and then administer the shot. Ok?"

The eyes turned away, then back.

Softly, steadily, she brushed away the soil as the eyes looked up at her. Badru and the squad stood silently in a circle around them, eyes downcast.

Ronnie raised the ampule and said, "I'm going to give you the shot now."

She reached out with one hand, pressing her fingers against the carotid artery just as she pressed the ampule against the neck with her other hand.

The eyes stared at her.

The pulse was weak but steady.

Then, as she looked into those eyes, the pulse faltered, then stopped.

Tom's eyes held hers, unchanged though the life behind them was gone. Ronnie pulled back her hands as she closed her eyes tightly for a moment. She leaned forward and gently closed Tom's eyes, then slowly stood.

"Expose the body!"

The squad members brushed away the remaining soil. The body was shriveled, just like the one John showed them. She could see, from the chest, a few chrysalises had begun to emerge. They began to vibrate as their occupants lost access to oxygenated blood in their host's body, or so Ronnie suspected. From the largest of them, a feathery tail emerged and began to wave in the morning air.

"Step back!"

As the squad took up firing positions, she unsnapped her flamethrower wand from her pack, and, after a moment's hesitation, aimed it at the wriggling monsters defiling the remains of Thomas Sanghi.

She pressed the trigger and watched the orange flume consume what remained of the man. Slowly, Ronnie sprayed her flame across the shriveled legs, emaciated arms, and lastly, the torso and lifeless eyes still aimed impassively in her direction.

Badru and the rest stood silently as Ronnie released the trigger. Smoldering flesh filled their nostrils; smoke burned their eyes. Their emotions were raw. A few turned away to vomit. Badru shook his head, muttering "fuck…fuck…*fuck…*"

Ronnie shuddered, then instructed them to push back the soil and extinguish the fire.

They needed to find the rest of the hosts, and fast.

■ ■ ■

Ronnie heard the Governor's voice on her headset. "Ronnie? Please describe what you're seeing."

Ronnie sighed. "They're all shallowly buried, just their faces exposed. We have found and dealt with seven so far; this one makes our eighth host. The ones that could respond confirmed they're in great pain. We told them we were giving them a dose to address their pain." Her voice betrayed her grief and conflict. "They all went quietly. Then we dug them out to expose and incinerate the body. So far, all of the hosts had emerging or underdeveloped chrysalis. Just…awful."

As she spoke, Badru stood, looked down silently at the host a moment, then nodded. The others backed away, and he incinerated the host's body.

"I won't lie to you, Governor. This is god awful. We understand they're in hell, and this is all we have to offer them. But I don't know what we'll do if we start finding hosts that have hatched! Please tell me we're nearly done? "

Elke thanked her and broke the connection.

"What can we infer from the number of hosts they're finding?"

Dieter shrugged. "Well, we could look at how much of the dome they've searched, how many hosts have been found, and project a total host count from that. Would that be of use?"

"Possibly, if the calculation is plausible and reliable given how little we know. But Ronnie's right? What about the chances of encountering a hatched host?"

"I've reviewed the hosts found so far and the progression of their infestation," John added. "So far, none are as far along as Pete. That's a relief, but we have to assume that they're going to find hosts that have hatched. That they're going to run into whatever hatches out of the hosts."

"And we can't assume all the hosts will be sequestered this way." Dieter, Elke, and John all shuddered at the implications of George's observation. "You found Pete in the brig. I'm sure that, if there'd been a way for them to drag Pete out to soil, they would have done so. We have to presume other diploids were unable to find soil. We're going to need squads searching the buildings."

# ▪ DAY 6: 12:36
## THE END

He was burning up, from the inside out! And nauseous. Mike was terrified that he might vomit; being unable to turn, he was afraid he'd choke on it. What he would vomit was beyond him; he hadn't eaten or had a drink since before this nightmare began.

He glanced over at the girl. Whatever was happening to him had a head start with her.

She still wasn't moving, but he hadn't heard her moan for a while, and that was a change. The moaning intensified for a while, then stopped. Her face, devoid of muscle and fat, was barely recognizable. Her eyes, still open, stared emptily upward. There was something different about them. Nothing he could identify or define. Mike began to wonder if she'd died.

He willed his eyes to shift to the soil covering her and the little things that had been growing out of her. Many of the little brown casings were intact, with their two little feathers slowly waving. Others were not. Their tips and strands were gone. And something emerged.

There were little things moving around in the shallow grave. Small, about the size of a finger. They looked superficially like the creatures that buried them in the flowerbed. They had beaks, but the beaks were shorter. Their forelimbs ended in long, red, feathery fingers. Then he realized that, instead of eyestalks, they had more feathery fingers! They had four wings, four green wings, with claws at the joints, and they were walking on those claws. As they walked, the feathery fingers would occasionally snap shut, like they were capturing something he could not see. The feathery fingers vibrated briefly, as if whatever they'd closed around struggled then ceased. After a few minutes, the feathery fingers would open again.

One by one, they spread their green wings and lifted off the girl's body. Mike watched them hover, their four wings beating steadily, their feathery fingers snapping shut from time to time. Two long, feathery tails extended behind them. Then, in small groups, the baby monsters flew away.

For some reason, their departure saddened him. It made Mike think of his children, the ones that had moved on to other worlds, the ones still living at home, his wife.

*Emma…*

The pain skyrocketed; his vision blurred. He couldn't breathe; his body demanded oxygen.

He panicked.

Mike took a sudden, sharp breath, then the pain stopped again. His eyes cast about, his mind went blank as he thought about breathing.

But he couldn't.

He could no longer breathe.

Mike felt an awful, nauseating churning in his chest followed by a blinding burn in his lungs. Then, unable to breathe, the pain mercifully subsided as his field of vision narrowed until, finally, he was gone.

# ▪DAY 6: 13:32
## BLOSSOMS

"Something's happening!"

As John ran back to the conference table, a projection of Pete's isolation chamber appeared, drawing gasps from the others as they gathered. Pete's appearance was ghastly. Deflated, his thin, papery skin draped over his bones, revealing every detail of his skeleton. His face was barely recognizable. But it was his torso that demanded attention. Encrusted with chrysalises, his chest rose and fell, but inconsistently, his weakened body barely able to breathe.

Most of the chrysalises remained intact, their twin, feathery tails gently waving. Others moved without pattern. Some shook, as if their occupants were changing position. Others lost their hardened tips as something inside nibbled away.

Dieter pointed at one and asked, "what's that?"

Red, feathery fingers emerged. They formed a broad circle as a beak opened to reveal three long tongues. The hatchling continued to emerge, revealing a pair of bright, green wings bearing claws at their last joint, then a pair of bright green hindlimbs with similarly webbed, clawed digits. The finger sized body had an oval shape, skin reminiscent of the pineapples, and two long, feathery tails.

The first hatchling perched atop its chrysalis, then wrapped its red fingers around the tip of the chrysalis. Audio picked up a gentle crunching sound from within the fingers as it, apparently, fed on its shell.

As more emerged, George observed, "we're seeing the emergence of the haploid phase. They're feeding on their chrysalises. John? I'd really like to get one for more detailed analysis."

John tapped his wrist computer. A clear tube entered the projection and approached one of the creatures. The end of the tube enclosed the creature, then snapped shut, shearing off the tip of the chrysalis. The young creature ignored all of this, continuing to feed as the tube withdrew.

"We'll take a few more for you, George. And we'll leave the rest in the isolation chamber."

An alarm from the diagnostic display hummed as more of the creatures emerged.

"The host is dead." John's monotone announcement escaped the rest of the staff; they were too focused on the scene unraveling before their eyes.

One of the creatures opened its blossom, revealing the stump of its chrysalis; a small shard was pulled into the beak by its tongues. It stretched its wings and straightened its tails as the blossom stretched to form a broad circle that turned right and left.

George leaned in and squinted, then moved his hands above the thing, spreading them to enlarge the projection.

"Well, that's strange! They're blind! The first dorsal limb's fingers have no eyes. Instead, it joins the first right and left limb to form the blossom. See? Eighteen feather fingers."

John, also leaning forward, asked, "it has other sensory modalities, though…right?"

"Oh yes. Well, we'll know more after we examine them more closely, but you can see the lateral line of sensory pits for motion detection. I'd guess we'll find the fingers have chemoreceptors. Probably has electromagnetic sensors. I'm not quite sure what it's doing at the moment, though. Perhaps that movement is helping it gather information?"

The room remained quiet as more of the things emerged. The tube reappeared to collect another specimen. One of the creatures closed its fingers into a cone enclosing its beak; it spread its wings and, with a quick beat, lifted itself from the body. It rose vertically, its wings beating in a complex pattern, until it hovered half a meter above the dead host. More rose, some vertically, others moving forward or backward, until the isolation chamber was filled with flying haploids. Some hovered or moved slowly, periodically spreading their feathery fingers and then closing them.

"I think they're hunting! Or trying to…Out there, on the beach, as they emerge from squirts, there's always a thriving community of small, flying creatures to feed on. And there's a lot of carrion. The marine life left by the tsunami, the carcasses of the squirts preyed upon by the diploids, even the diploids themselves!"

Elke turned to him slowly, her eyes widening. "What do you mean, 'the diploids themselves'?"

George realized he hadn't passed along what he'd heard from Deirdre. "The field team reported that the diploids have a short lifespan. They've started dying as the squirts not impregnated with spores return to the water."

Elke paled. "You mean, after all we went through to kill the bastards, they're dying *on their own?!*"

Before George could speak, Bhavia interrupted. "Governor, every diploid we killed was actively hunting. Hunting and injecting spores. Killing the diploids saved a lot of lives!"

Elke collapsed in her chair. She hid her face with her hand; this news almost broke her. "And cost a lot of lives…so many lives."

She raised a hand, then added, "I know, I know. We can't know how much longer they would have lived under the dome, and every diploid we dispatched would have kept attacking colonists for however long it would have lived. It's just…not what I expected to hear."

Suddenly, one of the tiny creatures dropped to Pete's torso. Wings folded, it spread its feathery fingers and pressed them against a patch of flesh between chrysalises. Its claws dug into the flesh as it pressed the feathery fingers against the body, then it folded its blossom back. From the center of the blossom emerged a beak. It opened its beak and bit into the flesh, tearing out a small chunk of flesh.

As some turned away, George zoomed in again. "Interesting! Seems to prefer hunting but, in the absence of prey, will scavenge!" He leaned back, looked right and left, and said softly, "my apologies. I don't mean to be insensitive. But we need to learn *everything* we can about these creatures and what kind of threat they may represent. I suspect, like the kraken, they'll be in a race to grow, to reach breeding size. There's no prey in the isolation chamber, but it appears to be adapting quickly for survival. We should expect them to scavenge whatever remains they can find in the domes, in the absence of real prey. But, once they've exhausted that potential food supply, we have no idea what they'll do next."

He turned to John and said, "we need to transfer these creatures to suitable containment in our lab for study."

John sighed. "Of course. Do you want to just move the isolation chamber? We had the body fully instrumented. I don't think there's anything we can learn from a postmortem that we don't already know."

Elke pursed her lips. "I'm a little uncomfortable treating the man's remains so callously."

"I understand Elke. Believe me, I do. But he's beyond caring about what happens to his remains. Besides, George is right. We need to learn everything we can. Leaving his remains in the chamber will help us understand what's happening out there. I say we move the isolation chamber, as is, to the lab."

Elke grimaced, weighing the moral implications against their desperate need for information. She nodded and said, "can't argue. You're right, I think we need to learn everything we can, because I think our squads are going to start finding hatched hosts soon."

George nodded to Elke in thanks. He paused for a moment of silent prayer, then asked Nikko, "can you arrange the move?"

Nikko nodded and stepped away to coordinate the transfer.

George mused a moment, then opened a link to his lab. "Taki? Taki, Nikko is bringing an isolation chamber to the lab. It's filled with haploid young. We'll need to feed them something while we study them. I'm thinking *Drosophila*; we should have a healthy population of them."

Elke raised an eyebrow. "*Drosophila*?"

"Fruit flies," John smiled. "Used for genetic research, have been for centuries."

"Exactly!" George chimed in, staring at the isolation chamber. "We breed them for teaching genetics. We should have plenty to feed our haploids." George turned to Elke with a pained expression. "And, Elke, we're going to need more haploids to study."

Elke looked at him quizzically. Then her eyes widened as she processed the implications of George's request. But, before she could speak, John interjected.

"He's right, love." Elke jumped slightly; it was inappropriate for him to call her that, here in a meeting. But a quick look around the room revealed no scandal. She blushed. John took her hand.

"I know it's an awful ask. But we have a limited number of individuals from Pete, and they're all related. We're about to be inundated by dozens or hundreds or, God help us, thousands of these things. Studying one sample of young won't suffice. We risk missing something…and that could cost lives."

He paused, then continued. "It's hard to reconcile with my oath. But you said it yourself; we have to make some hard decisions. At least we can make a few of their deaths mean something. I'll work with Bhavia, see if we can't get another host or two back here. We'll induce comas and provide the haploids to George and his team for study."

Elke nodded, then took a deep breath. She looked at John, then George, then out the window. "Fine, do it. "

# ■DAY 6: 14:16
## HATCHED

They stood at the residential building entry that marked the end of their first assignment. Ronnie spotted a nearby set of picnic tables. It was a beautiful spot with a number of young trees promising eventual shade, a broad patch of healthy grass, and a lovely view of the central tower at the end of the broad avenue.

But none of them noticed the beauty as they silently took their seats. Nor did they pay any attention to the nutrition bars they pulled from their kits. Their minds were too traumatized from the eleven hosts they found along the way.

Ronnie knew she needed to let the leadership know they completed their patrol. Soon they'd get their next assignment. But she thought they deserved a few minutes rest. As she sat and chewed and scanned the area, she paused. Something caught her eye.

The end of her bar was a bigger bite than she normally took, but she popped it in her mouth anyway. As she chewed awkwardly, Ronnie started walking.

After a few meters, she realized it was another host. Ronnie turned and yelled before continuing; a few squad members began to follow. As she got closer, she could see the face more clearly. It was partially obscured because the dirt mound covering the body was larger, and more uneven.

As the others caught up, Ronnie observed the scene. "The soil's broken up. It's not smoothed over."

"So?"

Ronnie shook her head, then kneeled to brush away the dirt. The face remained impassive as she exposed the body; Ronnie realized this host wasn't breathing. After checking for a pulse and finding none, she exposed the torso. The chrysalises were reduced to stumps.

She stopped and backed up quickly. The others froze, alarmed as well. "Governor, we have a host that's hatched."

. . .

Elke alerted George. As they waited for him to return to the command center, she said, "get me an image."

Two images appeared over the conference table. One was the host as Ronnie had found it, and the other was a current image with the host's exposed, shriveled torso. As George walked up, he pointed at the first image.

"See? They have to expose the host's face or they'll suffocate, but they do their best to obscure the site. Once the chrysalises hatch, though, it doesn't matter anymore. They don't make any effort to smooth it over."

Ronnie grunted and observed, "honestly, there's not much left to attract anything. Speaking of which, I'm doubtful there are any remaining parasites to eliminate, but I think we should still incinerate the remains. Or does the medical group want to recover and examine them?"

John answered hesitantly. "Might be useful…Nikko, how hard would it be to retrieve those remains? I could send a couple of people to help. We can collect a few representative examples, then resume incinerations as more hosts are found."

"We're going to have to recover remains at some point. Can't leave them there, and I fear there will be too many to simply incinerate. We'll collect some hatched hosts for you."

George, scanning the projection, asked, "Ronnie, any sign of the haploids?"

She barked a laugh and responded. "I'd like to point out I have no fuckin' idea what one looks like, but I also don't see anything unusual, so no, I don't think they stuck around. Any idea how fast they can travel? Do they walk, fly, what?"

"Fly most likely. Should be finger sized. The beak will be short and surrounded by bright red feathery fingers like a pineapple's blossom. Green wings. They'll likely start hunting, presumably for small, flying, insect-like prey. In the wild, the things scavenged dead squirts. Under our domes, there will be some vermin, flies and such, but not much. They're probably wide-ranging, and we don't know what they'll do when they exhaust that limited food supply."

"Are we at risk?"

George wrung his hands. "Your guess is as good as mine. But, I'd err on the side of caution."

# ■ DAY 6: 15:14
## NEW ARRIVALS

"George?"

The xenobiology team, escorted by armed trackers and a drone, walked among the squirts a few meters from the EAGLE. The air was filled with haploids, hovering with their blossoms open, periodically snapping shut as they encountered tiny prey.

Deidre heard George's voice in her environmental suit helmet. "Yes? I'm here."

"The haploids are emerging from their squirt hosts. We have spotty coverage given the limited number of drones. But everywhere we look, there's too many to count. Millions of them hovering within a few meters of the carcasses feeding on a variety of tiny flying creatures attracted to or emerging from the dead squirts."

"That's what we're expecting based on what we're seeing in the lab. We're exhausting our *Drosophila* supplies learning what we can." He laughed, then added, "we're reserving a limited supply of the flies, of course. Won't have any for teaching genetics until our stock recovers."

"What else can you tell me?"

George leaned back. "The blossoms, as you know, are derived from the first set of limbs, including what would have been the eyestalks. They produce a number of attractants that they seem to be refining as they feed, learning what attracts fruit flies. They have stinging cells analogous to the cnidoblasts of earthly jellyfish and other coelenterates. A hooked tether injects venom and restrains prey until a tongue extends to pull the prey into the beak. We're also picking up on some electromagnetic signals that seem to attract the flies, and they're refining those signals as well. They're growing very quickly, like the kraken did. No idea how big they need to get to breed or when they'll settle as pineapples, but we're confident they need to mate before settling. We're monitoring for pheromones. As the kraken approached breeding size, they produced pheromones to attract each other for mating, so we're expecting these butterflies to do the same."

"Butterflies?!" Deirdre scoffed at the name.

George blushed. "Well, we had to nickname them *something*, Deirdre."

"Ha, alright, fine, 'butterflies'. Seems a little too tame, but sure. Matches our field observations. The air is just filled with a wide variety of small life forms. Periodic sampling shows enough new species to keep us busy for months! We're not able to track specific individual growth rates, but, informally, yeah, they're clearly growing and rapidly…" Deirdre's voice channel went dead quiet.

"Deirdre?" George started to rise in alarm. "Deidre?!"

"I'm getting an alert from one of the drones. Something large is approaching. Big enough that I think we should return to the EAGLE!"

"Do that! Can you dispatch a drone to get a look?"

The xenobiology team reboarded the EAGLE but kept their environmental suits on, at least until they knew whether it would be safe to return to the beach. George stood by the conference room table, waiting for drone imagery. John joined him, always anxious to see new Eden life forms.

Suddenly, images appeared of large flying creatures from the bilateral super-kingdom. Their backs were dark gray and their bellies white. Wings, 4 m across, carried torpedo shaped bodies ending in a long tail bearing fin like appendages. Powerful hindlimbs ending in long, clawed digits were tucked close to the body.

They swooped down, wings outstretched, to within a meter of the beach. Their vertical mouths slung open at a 45-degree angle, widening to at least a meter across. Held open, these mouths scooped countless tiny creatures from the air into a broad throat sack. With a quick beat or two of their wings, the flyers gained altitude. Their mouths closed, air forced out through a fine mesh formed by the serrated edges of their beaks. As they did this, their throat sacks constricted, forcing their catch into their throat mills for mastication.

"My God!" exclaimed George as more gathered to see the new creatures. "Feeding like baleen whales! Of course! This explosion of tiny life forms is a rich nutritional opportunity, so it's not surprising that something has adapted to capitalize on it. Such fascinating creatures!"

"Can we use this?"

George turned to Elke and responded, "no, I don't see how. It's fascinating, sure, but I don't see how…"

"Well, maybe we can," Dieter interrupted him. "We've been so focused on ways to shoot down big things like diploids that I never really thought about alternatives. Now I'm envisioning some kind of mesh trap suspended from drones. We could fly them through the dome, catching haploids as they go."

Elke nodded and slammed her hand down on the table with urgency. "See what you can come up with!"

# DAY 6: 19:10
## BUTTERFLIES

The little creature pulled itself out of its enclosure. Perched atop its chrysalis, the butterfly gripped the crumbling platform tightly with its hindlimbs as it stretched out its wings. Then, balance faltering, the creature folded them again so the tiny claws at the first joint could grasp the edge of the chrysalis. It extended its feathery forelimbs to surround its beak, opening them to form a blossom that began emitting enticing scents to attract potential prey. The butterfly opened its triformed beak, stretching and retracting its tongues in rhythmic strokes. Its sensory systems began to make sense of the world around it. The line of mucous filled pits along its flanks felt vibrations as its siblings emerged. Its electromagnetic sensors detected life signs, and its chemoreceptors detected delightful scents and flavors.

Holding its blossom open, the butterfly extended its tails for balance and began flapping its wings. The tiny creature hovered above the remains of its host. It waited. It did not feel anything approaching. It tried different potential attractants and waited to see what might bring it sustenance. It reached out with its electromagnetic senses; it sorted through the signatures of its siblings to find little things that might be prey.

There! It found something. There were tiny things flying amongst them!

The butterfly tried reading them. It tried to determine what the little bugs were attracted to and tried to influence them.

*That one!*

It increased the attractant that seemed to be working. The bug moved toward it! It could feel the vibrations of its wings, feel the patterns of its movement.

*Closer…*

The creature brushed against one of the butterfly's feathery fingers. As it did so, specialized cells in the blossom fired tiny little harpoons into its body, each carrying a tiny dose of venom. As the butterfly folded its blossom around the fly, it felt the prey's body react as the venom pulsed into its bloodstream. The creature reacted violently, but the little harpoons held fast. As the creature flailed, the butterfly fired more harpoons, injecting more venom and strengthening its hold on the creature. Its blossom tightened about the prey; the clawed tips of its feathery fingers came together. More and more of its tiny harpoons fired into the body of the prey.

The butterfly opened its beak and extended its tongues to grasp the fly, pulling it towards its beak. The butterfly's tongues coordinated their movement so that, finally, the bug was secure and the beak could bite through the exoskeleton of the prey.

The prey reacted violently but could not escape. The butterfly extended its tongues to rake the prey's internal tissues, pulling little bits into the mouth. It fed and fed, delighting in the flavors. The fly's fear was rapturous, delicious.

Finally, when the prey's shell was empty, the butterfly opened its blossom and let the husk fall away. It held its blossom open and waited to repeat the process.

It hovered. It fed. It grew.

But eventually, as the butterfly and its siblings fed, the prey were consumed and feedings became less frequent. The butterfly began to weigh its options, as it knew its siblings would. It scanned for more prey. If it could find prey too big to take alone, the butterfly knew it could work with its siblings. But it sensed nothing nearby. The butterfly sensed some of its siblings moving away, presumably seeking prey elsewhere. The boundaries of the enclosure limited how far they could go, but the butterfly couldn't sense that. Some siblings descended to the carcass of their host. As they landed, they folded their blossoms back, pressed their beaks into the body, and began to feed.

The hovering butterfly weighed a third option. Not consciously, it was not as a thought process, but as a physiological reaction to various factors. It knew from the electromagnetic signatures of its siblings that it was among the largest, having fed well while the prey lasted. It also smelled death. Some of its smaller siblings had died violently, consumed by other, larger haploids.

It *had* to grow as quickly as possible. The only thing that mattered was growth. If the biggest siblings were choosing cannibalism, it really only had two choices. Join them to outgrow them or flee.

The butterfly opened its blossom. Instinctually, the butterfly invested reserve energy to fortify its blossom. It stretched the claws of its wing knuckles and hind limbs. It began to emit attractants mimicking prey to lure in its smaller siblings. It sent out signals to influence their electromagnetic senses.

One of its siblings drew closer.

When the small haploid brushed against its blossom, the butterfly fired stinging cells into the body of its sibling to deliver venom. It folded its blossom back and reached out with its wing claws to grasp the body. As the two fell, the bigger butterfly bit deeply into its sibling's flank.

Together, they hit the floor, but the butterfly did not let go. It closed its beak, slicing through the body of its squirming sibling, then used its tongues to tear off bits of flesh.

It held its prize fast and feasted.

■ ■ ■

George stood before the isolation chamber and watched the haploids hunt fruit flies above a host's remains. Without turning, he asked, "how many haploids do we have now?"

Taki paused to consult his wrist computer, then said, "187 from three hosts, and there's one more host about to hatch. And, George? We're going through a lot of *Drosophila*."

George grunted. "We'll save some *Drosophila* breeding stock, but we must keep feeding the butterflies."

George sighed and turned, rubbing his eyes.

"We have a *lot* to learn. We're going to need to separate them into groups so that we can experiment. Work with Dieter and Nikko. Set up, oh, ten enclosures, make 'em big, about 3 m on a side. We'll put, what, twenty haploids in each? We'll need some enclosures with related individuals, some that mix individuals from different hosts. We need to be able to vary environmental conditions. Light, heat, humidity. And food supply! We need to learn how their behavior changes based on food supply."

He walked stiffly towards a table and took a seat.

"Food supply is essential! If they're anything like kraken, there's no such thing as overfeeding. No matter how much you give them, they'll just grow faster! And that's very important; I want one enclosure that provides all the food they can consume. An 'endless buffet'. I want the butterflies in that enclosure to grow as fast as possible."

Taki looked at him quizzically.

"Taki, they're in a race to grow to reach breeding size. We want one of our enclosures to reach breeding size before the ones roaming the colony do. The best way to do that is an unlimited food supply. Again, if they're like kraken, as the butterflies reach breeding size, they'll start emitting pheromones to attract each other. I want the enclosures monitored for Eden proteins. *If* we can detect and synthesize their sex pheromones, we can use them to attract the butterflies. Draw them into traps and eliminate them."

He leaned back.

"Let's get some other potential prey options in the enclosures as well. At some point, they'll lose interest in the *Drosophila*. There's likely swarms of haploids feeding happily on the little flying vermin that normally plague agricultural domes, right? What other potential prey are they likely to find? Maybe…mice? We should have a lot of lab mice, right?"

Taki's eyes brightened. "Crickets! We also breed crickets! Some of the colonists use them to feed their reptile and amphibian pets."

George nodded and rubbed his arthritic hands.

"Yes, crickets then. I want to see how the butterflies deal with prey that's not flying. And carrion, put some carrion in the enclosures so we can see how they feed on carrion." George rubbed his face again. Taki, concerned, asked, "are you alright?"

"Tired. Just tired."

"Well, get some rest. We can manage for a few hours while you get some rest!"

George nodded. "Not as young as I used to be. So, so much to do…"

George leaned forward and started to shuffle away.

"But first, we need to reach Dieter. He's building those traps to scoop haploids. We need to design traps that can be baited with pheromones when we have them! I can rest after he's contacted."

# DAY 7: 05:32
## CANNIBALS

George had a hard night. He needed rest but couldn't stay asleep. He spent the night rotating between naps on his cot and monitoring the enclosures.

George spent most of his time at Enclosure A, or the "endless buffet" as he jokingly referred to it. Like the kraken, the butterflies never slept and were never full. They just fed and grew and fed and grew. They hatched finger sized. Now, just a few hours later, they were the size of his hand. A phenomenal growth rate! If only their livestock had such a feed conversion rate. At some point, assuming they followed the same pattern as the kraken, the butterflies would be big enough to breed.

But how big? Most of the pineapples observed in the field were about the size of a human head. It was reasonable to infer that butterfly breeding size would be smaller than a human head, but how much smaller? Some of the pineapples confiscated within the colony were considerably larger than any observed in the field. Some as big as a barrel. Was this the result of overly generous feeding by their owners? How big could they grow?

Once the butterflies reached breeding size, how long did they continue mating? More mating provided more diverse genetic material and more reproductive options. So, once they start mating, how long do they continue coupling before finally settling?

George sighed deeply. Their survival required more information than the xenobiologists had time to collect. He only had educated guesses based on related species. But what if he's wrong?

The butterflies in Enclosure A were no longer interested in *Drosophila*. Crickets were the next logical step. When a butterfly detected a cricket, it hovered, turned its blossom downward, and dropped onto the cricket. The blossom would cover the cricket, injecting it with venom. The butterfly would fold back the feathery fingers of the blossom to expose the beak and tongues to feed. George ran a quick simulation of the growth rate. The butterflies would be bigger than grapefruit in just a few hours. Taki would probably need to start feeding them mice. George was confident his unlimited food strategy was working. These butterflies should be bigger than any roaming the colony. They were definitely bigger than any caught in Dieter's traps.

*So, at some point, the little bastards should start mating. And, before mating, they should start emitting sex pheromones. And getting these guys to breed before the ones roaming the colony start should give us time to synthesize the pheromones and bait traps. I think…*

George leaned back and rubbed his neck, then his hands, then his elbows. Every joint in his body ached. He needed rest, but he didn't want to miss the pheromones. On the other hand, he had assistants he could trust. He envisioned Elke admonishing him to take care of himself. With a heavy sigh, George called over a younger scientist to watch the enclosure while he went back to his cot to nap.

■ ■ ■

"George?"

A hand on his shoulder woke him from his uneasy nap. He blinked and looked up at Taki's concerned face.

"Yes? Yes, what is it? Are we getting sex pheromones?"

"I'm not sure. I want you to take a look at this."

George swung his feet over the side of the cot, put his shoes back on, and stood slowly. The cot was not good for his aging back. He staggered groggily behind Taki, gesturing to one of the grad students to bring him a cup of coffee.

Taki stopped at Enclosure B, the one with sparse food. George looked inside and was surprised to see haploids almost as big as the ones in Enclosure A.

"See this? This looks like a pheromone to me."

A model of a complex protein hovered in front of the enclosure. George looked at it a moment, barely acknowledging his cup of coffee as it was handed to him. He frowned, then brought up a model of a kraken sex pheromone for comparison.

*They are similar…*

George shook his head. Something was bugging him about the enclosure, but he wasn't awake enough to think clearly. He sipped his coffee.

He took another look at the butterflies in Enclosure B. They'd started with twenty of them. Now there were ten? Hard to count them while they were flying about. George frowned again.

"Taki, why are these haploids so big?"

Taki, momentarily flustered, pointed at the enclosure and answered, "well, they're cannibals."

"Really? You've seen them cannibalizing?"

Taki nodded.

George sipped more coffee, then leaned forward. He wasn't surprised. Kraken were cannibals. Many of the creatures in this taxonomic group were cannibals. Cannibalism combined the acquisition of resources and the elimination of competition. Still, the butterflies were delicate, adapted for hunting tiny prey. Didn't seem like they could effectively subdue each other.

Something else was troubling him. There were fewer individuals in the enclosure than they'd started with, but not that many fewer. So far, the haploids demonstrated an amazing feed conversion rate, comparable to their kraken counterparts. But still, these butterflies in the enclosure were BIG. He didn't need to model it to realize the aggregate biomass of the ten individuals in this enclosure was greater than the aggregate biomass of the original twenty.

*Where'd the additional biomass come from?*

He turned to Taki and asked, "have you been adding more haploids?"

"Yes. They're aggressively cannibalizing, so, to keep a representative population, I've been adding haploids from Dieter's traps. Every time I add some from Dieter's traps, they're quickly consumed."

"Fascinating. Taki, you realize that you've created another 'endless buffet' here, right? These individuals are almost as big…"

His voice trailed off as he leaned in to look at them more closely.

"Taki, do you see morphological changes in these cannibals?"

"Yes, yes, I do!" Taki nodded vigorously. "They're definitely larger. The blossoms are more robust, but not as wide compared to the rest of the body. The claws and beak are bigger and stronger. Behavior's different, too. The way they hunt and feed is quite different."

George stared at them and swore. He put his coffee down roughly, causing it to spill over the sides. "Taki, we need to see how they deal with larger prey items. What's available here in the teaching labs? Rats? Rabbits? What do you have?"

Taki scowled as he thought. "Well, uh, I know we have rats and rabbits. Some of the rabbits are pretty big, helps physiology students find veins. Not sure what else we have here. When we need something bigger, we uh, we usually work with the farmers."

"Got it. I want to put a rat in there. If they're able to take the rat, then put the biggest rabbit you have in there. We need to see how they hunt larger prey."

Taki stared at George a moment, then blinked rapidly and walked away. As he did so, George beckoned to one of the grad students.

"Janice, when we get our next batch of haploids, I want you to put some of them in a container. I want the air in that container monitored for Eden proteins. Once you begin monitoring, I want you to sacrifice the haploids in the container. But be careful how you kill them. Don't incinerate them, *crush* them."

She looked at him quizzically. "Why?"

He looked back at the cannibals. "We need to know whether they emit an alarm pheromone when they're violently killed."

# ■ DAY 7: 11:11
## EVOLUTION

Ivan whistled while he worked. The work was gruesome, but his job was easy.

They were walking along one of the main boulevards between the residential structure and the transportation hub. Their suspensor pallets were loaded with body bags containing the bodies of diploid victims and expired hosts. Individually, the bodies were light, but collectively, they were getting heavy. Not that he cared. The support personnel managed the pallets and medical personnel managed the remains. His job was just protection. Unnecessary protection, as it turned out, because these haploid things were harmless.

At some point, George had explained, they'd mate and then settle somewhere. George said the butterflies were like Earth's barnacles. "Barnacles," George told him, "are essentially free swimming crustaceans, like crabs! When they mature, barnacles glue their heads to something like a rock or boat or whale. For the rest of their lives, they sweep feathery legs through the water, capturing tiny sea creatures to feed on." Ivan had never given barnacles a thought but could see the analogy to the butterflies.

They were *everywhere*. Periodically, he would see one of the drones swoop through a swarm, snagging some of them. Ivan didn't care anymore; the novelty had worn off. Besides, the butterflies weren't bothering him. In fact, he appreciated them. When they started this duty, every corpse they came across was buzzing with flies. They hadn't seen any flies in a while!

Ivan chuckled softly. "Such a relief after the damn diploids. And a beautiful day, too!"

The day started with a hike to the transportation hub to meet the operations and medical people. They walked back to the residential structure along one boulevard, and now they were almost back to the hub along another.

Good thing, too. The pallets were filling up. His current entourage would take their cargo back to the primary dome for disposition. Ivan knew there should be another group waiting for him to escort them back to the residential building. At some point, they'd clear the public spaces; then it would be time to clear the building itself.

One of the medics swatted at a butterfly. Ivan didn't think much of it. *They're harmless, right? Getting big though.* The butterfly the medic swatted was as big as his hand. Another one swooped in and hit the medic on her back, making her stumble. She flailed her arms a bit, muttering expletives, then screamed.

Ivan ran over. The claws of the thing's hind legs dug into her back. The claws on its wings had torn a hole in her uniform, and the butterfly pressed its blossom against her skin. As he reached for it, the blossom folded back to reveal a cruel, sharp triform beak. The claws of its wings, reaching through the feathery petals of the blossom, tightened their grip as it opened the beak. Slowly, it bit into her back, the edges of the beak slicing through the meat of her shoulder as she screamed. The beak closed, pulled back, then swallowed. As the wound bled freely, its beak reopened, and three tongues extended out.

Ivan grabbed the thing and tore it off her, its claws ripping her skin. He threw it to the ground and stomped on it, swearing loudly. He stepped away and looked around as a medic examined the wound. He turned to scan the area. The things were too small for his rifle, so he unslung his flamethrower.

*Should we run for the hub??*

Before he could decide, more butterflies swooped in. One of the support staff was knocked off his feet as four landed on his back. They quickly ripped through his clothing, pressed their blossoms against his bare skin, then folded their blossoms back to take bites out of him as he lay howling.

"Help me!" Ivan yelled as he knelt to tear the things off the man. As he did so, two other members of his squad were knocked off their feet. As others stepped forward to pull the butterflies off their comrades, Ivan turned and fired a burst in the direction of the approaching swarm.

"Leave the pallets! Run for the hub! Help the wounded!"

He walked backward as the squad ran towards the hub. The wounded stumbled, like they'd been drugged.

*Are these things venomous?!*

They made it through the hub portals and looked through the glass to see the butterflies hovering outside. Ivan looked at one of the victims and consulted a nearby medic. The butterflies were definitely venomous. Ivan swore aloud and did a quick head count, to see how many were now poisoned. He shifted his gaze to the wounds. The bites were surrounded by broad, red, raised welts where the blossoms' fingers pressed against the skin. Ivan swore again.

"The blossoms! The butterflies must deliver venom by pressing the blossoms against our skin!"

# DAY 7: 11:35
## BAD NEWS

After listening to Ivan's report, Elke turned to Bhavia. "Have you ordered your teams to take shelter?"

Bhavia nodded without looking at her; he was busy coordinating with the squad leads on his wrist computer.

Elke lowered her head, then added, "keep me apprised."

She yelled with urgency. "George, we need you!"

After a moment she heard him. "On my way!"

"John, what do you think?"

John wrung his hands, a nervous quiver in his voice. "I just, I think, speculation, okay, until we get them in for examination, but I suspect Ivan's right. We know, from George, that there are stinging cells in the blossoms. But I thought it would take a *lot* more butterflies to deliver enough venom to affect an adult human. But he's saying one, maybe two butterflies did this? They're supposed to be harmlessly feeding on flies!"

She raised a hand to calm him. "It won't take long for George to get here; not much we can do until he does."

After a few minutes, George walked in. He could sense the tension in the room. He grimaced as Elke replayed Ivan's report for him.

"Well? What's happening?"

George sighed. He pulled at the fringes of his hair; he rubbed the back of his neck aggressively. His anxiety was overly apparent.

"I was afraid of this. We observed something in the lab that suggested this might happen, but I thought we had more time."

A projection of a haploid appeared over the table. "This is a normal haploid. It's one of twenty in an isolation chamber that provides abundant prey.

We call this Enclosure A. They're like kraken in that they never sleep, and they're never satisfied. The more you feed them, the faster they grow, and, like the kraken, they have an amazing feed conversion rate. They grow faster per gram of food consumed than anything on our farms.

We're monitoring for Eden proteins, and as soon as we see sex pheromones, we'll isolate and synthesize them. If we bait the trap with sex pheromones, we should be able to draw all the remaining haploids in and kill them. But, for this to work, we have to get those traps out before they're ready to breed."

He paused and looked about the room. Everyone seemed to understand; at least nobody objected. He rubbed the back of his neck again. Elke sighed. George was clearly struggling. The years were catching up with him and, despite her admonishments, he refused to rest. His team performed admirably but none of his protégés were really ready to step into his shoes. He had high hopes for Deirdre, though, and Elke could see why. Taki, too. He was a relatively recent arrival and George seemed genuinely surprised by Taki's potential.

"But we found something we didn't expect," George continued grimly. "While we're waiting for sex pheromones, we set up other enclosures to see how they responded to scarcity. Well, the haploids in Enclosure B were almost as big as those in Enclosure A. Turns out that when you starve haploids, they cannibalize."

He tapped his wrist computer again, and the projection shifted to one of the cannibals.

"Here's what we didn't expect. These pineapple haploids are built to feed on tiny airborne prey. They're just not built to feed on each other. But, if you starve them, they manage. And they change. Let's start with the blossom. It's much more robust, though not as broad. Each of the feathery digits is thicker, and the claw at the end is bigger. The stinging cells are bigger, the little harpoons are tougher, and they deliver a lot more venom. They press the blossom against prospective prey, deliver that venom, then fold the blossom back, like a lion's mane, to expose the beak. We think this morphological shift is triggered by the combination of food scarcity and alarm pheromones. When they can't find enough of their preferred prey and start falling behind in the race to reach breeding…"

"Alarm pheromones?" John interjected with concern.

"Yes, alarm pheromones. When haploids die violently, they emit an alarm pheromone. There are earthly parallels. Some species of bees emit alarm pheromones when they're being killed. Helps the hive swarm to defense. While monitoring for sex pheromones, we detected what we believe to be a haploid alarm pheromone."

He leaned back, fiddling with the pen in his hands. After a few awkward minutes, Elke and the senior staff exchanged worried looks. They had never seen George so exhausted. Elke was about to say something when George snapped out of it. He spoke without making eye contact, still caught in some kind of daze.

"Once they've made the morphological switch, they don't go back. They ignore the small, flying prey they were hunting in favor of larger prey. This haploid is not much bigger than my hand, but when we introduced a rat into the enclosure, it didn't hesitate. Like the kraken, they seem to like keeping their prey alive as long as possible. Same thing with a rabbit, except the rabbit was large enough it took three of them working together to bring it down. Suggests, unfortunately, what Ivan observed. If the prey's too large for one to handle, they'll work together."

He threw the pen down, leaned forward, and rubbed his eyes.

"The scoops have done a good job reducing the number of haploids flying about our domes. But, as the vermin populations decline and the haploids grow, they will face food scarcity. And the haploids getting crushed in the scoops are emitting alarm pheromones. That fact, especially in combination with food scarcity, is stimulating the remaining haploids to develop this cannibal morphology. That leaves them very limited prey options. Us."

Elke asked, "why wouldn't they all want to pursue larger prey? Why isn't this the default morphology?"

George shrugged. "Because tiny prey, if there is enough to go around, is safe and easy. Cannibals attack things that can attack them back. As long as there's an adequate supply of small prey, why take the risk?"

John, leaning in to stare at the image of the butterfly, asked, "where does that leave us?"

George shrugged again. "My recommendation? Plan A remains the same. At some point, our captive haploids will reach breeding size. We'll isolate and synthesize their sex pheromones to draw them into traps and kill them. If you're going to ask me how much longer that will take, well, I don't know. You can see how fast they're growing. Also remember that the ones out there probably won't respond to sex pheromones until they reach breeding size. We have to get ours to breeding size first with enough time to isolate and synthesize. But, once we do, once we bait and deploy traps, the traps won't attract them until they reach breeding size.

When they were harmlessly hunting flies, that wasn't a problem. Now? Now we're back on the menu. And I'm not sure what, other than us, they'll find to feed on so they can reach breeding size. That pretty much leaves us two options. Hunt them down or wait them out. We can try to hunt them down and kill them, but they fly and they're small. I don't think the weapons we deployed against the diploids will work. Flamethrowers maybe? Maybe Dieter can figure out a way to use flamethrowers on drones? Our other option? Wait them out. Hunker down, let them eat each other, and wait for the survivors to settle as pineapples. But I've no idea how long that will be. I'd guess not too long, but I can't *know*. Could be a day. Could be a month. I just…don't know."

The room was silent. Elke looked around the room.

"I'm open to ideas."

Bhavia swore and pounded his fist on the table. "We have the same problem we had with the diploids. As long as they're flying around, they're really hard to hunt. And George is right. I don't think the weapons that we used on the diploids would be effective against something this small. I like the idea of equipping the drones with flamethrowers."

"It's possible," Dieter commented. "I'll have my people start prototyping. But I think the pheromone traps are our most promising option."

Elke nodded. "Please explore a prototype. And have the traps built and ready to deploy as soon as George provides you with the sex pheromone."

Nikko cleared his throat.

"Elke, we have a lot of people that have been locked down for days now. Other than the inevitable grumbling, we're getting more and more pings from people needing supplies. Once we got the diploids under control, my people started making deliveries. But now? I can work with Bhavia to make sure my people have armed escorts, but they're exposed. And the longer this takes, the more people will run out of the basics."

Elke, eyes closed, pinched the bridge of her nose. Nobody should be running out of the basics. Since the kraken, everyone was required to stock a week's worth of emergency supplies. Must be the more recent immigrants.

"Nikko, I don't have an alternative for you. But emergency supplies only. And, when this is over, we'll need to revisit emergency supply guidelines."

# ▪ DAY 7: 12:42
## WORSE NEWS

The transportation hub was quiet. Ivan and his charges waited in the dark. Some paced, some sat on benches or the floor. A few stretched out as comfortably as they could. The injured were escorted to the primary dome for more advanced care. The suspensor pallets were still loaded with body bags.

The haploids from which they'd fled were still just outside. Ivan could see them through the transparent panels. Some hovered, some didn't. A few were exploring the area outside the hub, but most were clearly interested in the hub itself. Ivan recalled that they had electromagnetic sensory capabilities and he wondered whether they could sense the humans inside.

*Weird things. Not so clumsy on the ground.* Ivan hadn't seen many of them light, but the ones he could observe were clearly better adapted to life on the wing. Every once in a while, one of them would stop, open its blossom, and turn slowly side to side. *Like it's scanning with the damn thing.* Ivan found it disconcerting, to say the least.

"Ivan, what are they doing?"

"How would I know?"

One of them had its blossom aimed at the door. Then another. Then a third.

They just stood there, blossoms aimed.

The door crackled.

"What the hell was that?"

One of the support personnel cocked his head, then stood and walked over to the door control. He opened an access panel and looked inside, poking at something with a finger. Absent-mindedly, he began talking.

"Well, as you know, these doors are electromagnetic. Essentially a little force field. You can walk through them when they're clear. When they're translucent, you can see blobby shapes through them. They'll make a sound, an alarm, when you walk through. Or you can set them to opaque. Opaque is the most secure…"

The door crackled again. The man's voice trailed off as he leaned in, then leaned back with a quizzical look on his face. Then, his expression changed, first to one of satisfaction as he began to understand what was happening, then one of concern, then fear, as he processed what he now understood. He started backing away, talking as his pace accelerated.

"Uh, I could be wrong. I, uh, hope I'm wrong." The man gave a quick, embarrassed laugh. "But I recall that these haploid things have electromagnetic organs? I can't be sure, but I think they're figuring out how to mess with the door." He continued talking as he turned and started walking, faster and faster, towards the lift.

"Yeah, uh, I think we'd better leave. We, uh, should get the hell out of here. Get to where we have a physical barrier…"

Ivan, staring at the door, unslung his flamethrower again.

"To the lifts!"

The first to reach the lifts pressed the button. The doors parted, and they all stepped inside. As the door began to close, they heard a strange buzzing sound followed by a blip. As the doors closed, they could see a haploid flying straight towards them.

The doors closed.

Ivan tapped his wrist computer hastily.

"Governor? Governor! We have a problem! The haploids seem to have figured out how to thwart the doors!"

■ ■ ■

Elke turned to George. "How can they do that?"

George sagged. "They're clever. And they have electromagnetic sensory capabilities. As to whether they can get through the doors…"

Nikko chimed in. "The doors weren't designed with strong security in mind. The door is an electromagnetic field run by a control panel that accepts biometrics or a code. If the control panel recognizes your face or you know the code or you have rights to override, the panel generates the signal that opens the door. It's a short range signal that's consistent for all doors. So, if the butterflies have the ability to mimic the electromagnetic signal that the control panel generates when recognized, there's no reason those things couldn't open doors."

George nodded. "They are that clever. Remember they're also blind, so they depend on their other senses. If they've been observing, electromagnetically, how the door mechanism works, then, sure, they could mimic that signal."

Elke stood and put her hands on her hips. "Dammit! So much for waiting them out. Did you say that the signal is consistent for *all* doors?"

"Yes, I'm afraid it is. We depend on the device that validates your code before sending the signal. If you have the means to generate that signal, you can open any door." Nikko turned to Dieter. "Do we have any means to change that signal? To propagate a change to that signal throughout the colony?"

Dieter rhythmically tapped the table with his fingers, then shook his head.

"No. Not without physically accessing every door. The code boxes, sure. We can propagate updates to them. But the door mechanism? It's a very short-range signal. You have to be right next to the door, like the code box, to open the door. It's just not a scenario we've ever envisioned." He paused, then added, "besides, once the things get the idea, even if we could change the signal, they'd just learn the new signal."

Slowly, Elke sat down. The ramifications were enormous! The potential loss of life if those things started barging through doors! After a moment, she leaned forward.

"Ivan, now many of the things were at the door?"

"About a dozen, I'd guess."

Elke rubbed her lip, thinking. Ivan was the only one armed with a flame-thrower. And that was too many for Ivan to take on alone. Should she order Ivan to try to kill them anyway? Though his odds would be poor, it'd be pos-sible. Unlikely, but possible. And he'd certainly kill a few, at least. But the most likely outcome would be losing Ivan, a secmed, and the team he's guarding. Ivan would kill some of the haploids and that had value. But if he couldn't kill all of them, then what would prevent the surviving butterflies from passing along their "discovery"? Besides, it was only a matter of time before other haploids independently discovered the same weakness.

Elke slammed her hand on the table. She was frustrated to realize this option wasn't an option, but relieved that the potential benefit did not justify risking those lives.

"Shit…People, I need to hear ideas. What do we do? George, we can't afford to wait for the sex pheromones. We've lost a lot of people, and our survivors are on lockdown. It's only a matter of time before these things realize they can get at them. I need better options!"

She turned to Nikko and Dieter. "Imagine you're under lockdown. You depend on your door to keep the haploids out. What can you do? What could you do with whatever's on hand? I don't think a barricade's an option. They're too small. They'd get through, right?"

Nikko nodded silently. Dieter's face was grave. No one else at the table spoke. The air was thick with exhaustion.

"What else? I need options! I need options now!!"

Rajiv cleared his throat. "Cutting power wouldn't help. The doors would just open. Dieter, there's an access panel in each residence. Is there a way to override the door control? To make the door ignore the 'deactivate' signal?"

Dieter rhythmically tapped his fingers again. "Maybe. Maybe. Let me get with my people, see what we can figure out."

"Quickly, Dieter." Elke started to pace nervously. "And I need you to boil it down to simple steps anyone can follow." She paused, her eyes darting about. Her hand was openly shaking; George and John were the only ones to notice though.

"I think we've gotten all the use we're going to get from the scoops. Leave them flying, unless you can put one of the drones to better use, but I think we've pretty much caught all the haploids we're going to catch. Which, unfortunately, means they're predisposed to be looking for ways to thwart doors…" Elke pointed to one of the doors for their conference room, "including this room. I want that door secured, right now! And I want this room armed."

She wiped her brow, then said, "Bhavia, what about deploying our squads? Arm them with flamethrowers, send them out to patrol hallways, to hunt the damn things down?"

"I don't think we have much choice."

"We don't. It's not a good choice, but, unless somebody's got a better option, and I mean RIGHT NOW, it's the least bad choice we have."

She looked around the room in frustration. No one objected.

"Bhavia, make it happen."

# ▪ DAY 7: 15:00
## SEX PHEROMONES

Taki, awoken by his alarm, sat up and shuffled over to Enclosure A, hoping to finally see haploid sex.

*Still nothing?*

They were getting big. Surely, they were approaching sexual maturity soon! Taki shook his head. So many of Eden's life forms remained a mystery. As much as the colony was growing, as fast as their xenobiological staff grew too, they were still overwhelmed by Eden's biodiversity. There was just so much they didn't know yet!

Taki brought up the computer-generated model of the alarm pheromone they'd found. He turned the model slowly, reviewing its structures. He hesitated, tapped the tabletop with a finger, then brought up a model of kraken sex pheromone. He looked at the two models side by side.

Superficially, they looked similar.

He leaned forward. "Compare these two pheromones. How similar are they? Highlight common structures."

He continued to stare as the computer worked. As he watched, more and more of the two models were highlighted. After a few minutes, the computer responded. "92%"

Taki leaned back and whistled. If kraken sex pheromone and pineapple alarm pheromone shared 92% of their structure, how different could kraken and pineapple sex pheromones be?

He turned and looked through to the shared lab workspace supporting the classrooms of the teaching labs. He caught the eye of one of the lab technicians and yelled. "Please get me some kraken sex pheromone. A liter would be great, if we have it. If not, as much as you can find!"

After a couple hours of hard work, Taki and the lab tech stepped back from the new enclosure they'd set up. At one end, an emitter sat ready to release kraken sex pheromone. At the other end, a smaller enclosure held ten of the largest haploids they had. In theory, at least, those ten butterflies *should* be the closest to sexual maturity.

Taki turned to the lab tech, shrugged, then smiled awkwardly. "Here we go!"

He tapped his wrist computer. The emitter began releasing kraken sex pheromone. The sub enclosure opened.

As they watched, haploids hovered about the sub enclosure. Slowly, one by one, they stopped, turned towards the emitter, and aimed their blossoms towards it. One by one, they moved towards the emitter, flying through the enclosure.

After a few minutes, they were all hovering around the emitter.

Taki raised a clenched fist and punched the air enthusiastically. He turned to slap the technician on the shoulder, but his social awkwardness got the better of him. Instead, he offered a quiet but sincere "great job" before walking off to find George.

■ ■ ■

In the conference room, Elke returned to the table.

George, with a broad smile, presented Taki to the staff. "Taki, please explain to everyone what you just told me!"

Taki briefly explained the experiment before concluding, "so uh, while we haven't seen haploid, mating yet, they do seem strongly attracted to kraken sex pheromones. It seems sufficiently similar to pineapple sex pheromone, enough to be an effective lure for our traps!"

"Taki, George, that's great news! Dieter, how soon can you start synthesizing?"

"Send me the kraken sex pheromone model and we'll start synthesizing. The traps are ready, but it'll take some time, maybe a couple hours, to have the first ones ready to deploy."

"Understood," Elke nodded. "Dieter, get on it. Make it happen as quickly as possible." She hesitated, then asked, "how about the process for securing doors?"

"It's not. We can't find anything that doesn't require specialized tools."

Elke swore. "Keep working on it! Bhavia, how soon will you have squads hunting haploids?"

"They're starting now."

Elke stopped in her tracks and frowned. "Are we getting any reports of attacks? Any indications any of the haploids are getting into residences?"

Bhavia shrugged. "Not yet."

Elke folded her arms. "Okay people, in a few hours, we'll deploy sex pheromone traps. Eventually we'll eliminate most, if not all, of the haploids. But, in the meantime, the haploids won't be interested in anything but hunting our people."

She started pacing.

"If we do nothing, there's an excellent chance the butterflies will get into residences. On the other hand, if we deploy squads, we put those security personnel at risk. There are still a lot of haploids out there. They're fast, small, and agile, so they're hard to kill. Loss of life will be high if we go hunting rather than hunker down."

The conference room erupted with quiet murmurs as her staff and onlookers considered the two options.

Bhavia was the first to speak up. "Even if you deploy squads, at any given moment, there are a lot of hallways that aren't being patrolled. And Dieter said barricading is not really an option. We have civilians at risk no matter the resolution."

"That's true," Elke grimaced. "Instead of hunting, could you deploy your squads as quick response teams? Strategically disperse them to minimize the time to get to anywhere the haploids might attack. We will alert the colonists of the risk, and, if haploids attack, they can sound an alarm and the nearest squad assists?"

Bhavia looked upward briefly, thinking. "I could…disperse them to break rooms throughout the two domes, use the break rooms as staging grounds?"

"Good, good. That'll have to do. Hopefully, nothing will happen before the traps are ready."

# DAY 7: 16:06
## FOOD CHAIN

Hungry!

There was no more prey. Nothing flying, nothing crawling, nothing.

And they smelled death! Something was hunting them! Something out there, something outside. Here, at least, in these strange canyons, there was safety. No smell of death here.

But they needed to grow! Growth was safety! But growth required food. After decimating the tiny prey, the butterflies switched to carrion. Challenging at first, but as they fed, the butterflies grew and changed. It got easier.

Now? Now they were stronger, much stronger. But they were also hungrier, because there wasn't any more carrion.

The alpha did what it had to do. It took some of its smaller siblings. Other, larger siblings were taking smaller ones. If it stopped growing, at some point, it would be at risk, too. But now, all the smaller siblings are gone. And the ones that remained were too big and too strong, evenly matched.

So, surviving butterflies flew through these strange canyons. The canyons were made of some strange material, something that confused its senses. But, as they flew, they passed electromagnetic fields. Behind those fields, the alpha sensed prey. But how could it get to that prey?

There were side canyons that connected to other canyons. Some were pathways to the outside, but that's where the smell of death was coming from. Something was hunting them "out there." So, the butterflies flew through the canyons, more and more desperate to find food. If they didn't find prey soon, they'd have to risk it and venture towards the smell of death.

The worst part was knowing, *knowing* that there was prey nearby. The butterflies could sense the prey as they flew, lots of prey! They flew, and flew, until the hunger was overwhelming. Was there no choice but to go outside? But the smell of death was so strong outside!

There *had* to be a way to get at the prey!

The alpha slowed and then hovered by one of the strange electromagnetic fields. It felt its siblings do the same. The alpha opened its blossom and aimed it at the field. It felt the field, and probed it.

It felt something irregular. The alpha experimented, feeling the field, generating signals that harmonized with the field.

*There!*

The field changed! For an instant, just an instant, it was gone! The alpha experimented some more.

Suddenly, the field was gone, completely.

■ ■ ■

Fernando rummaged through the pantry in the kitchen. There was nothing left but canned goods. He sorted through them, putting expired items to the left and the potential makings of a tasteless dinner to the right.

*This is embarrassing, I'm the owner of a restaurant and bar!*

This lockdown shit was getting old! Their quarters were tight for a family of six under the best of circumstances. But stuck together, not able to get away from each other? He'd started making plans to upgrade to a bigger place when that pineapple thing was pulling customers into his place, but now? Would he even still *have* a business when this was over?

They came via PIP five years ago. Most of his kids now worked in this restaurant and bar, but his eldest was excited about the xenobiology program here. But none of them enjoyed the weapons training. And the proficiency testing? Drills? And now this?

Fernando shook his head. They really needed to think about whether they wanted to stay here. Their eldest could stay. He sighed. Not much he could do about it now!

Suddenly, he heard a strange sound. *Something electrical? One of the kid's toys?* Fernando paused, holding a can, his head turned slightly to listen. He could not place that sound. He put the can down and slowly stepped out of the pantry, expecting to see his wife or one of the kids with a powered object of some kind.

*Nope.* The room was empty. His wife was, presumably, still in their room, and the kids were probably in their rooms as well. It was his turn to make dinner while everyone else did their best to endure their boredom through mindless entertainment. He shook his head, then noticed that the front door was open. *Weird!*

Fernando stepped cautiously away from the pantry, fingers walking along the kitchen counter until he reached the end. He took one more step, scanning the door area to see who might have, despite all of his firm direction, deactivated that door. But there was no one there.

*Well, that was weird.* But the door needed to be closed. He'd catch all kinds of hell if anyone saw an open door! Shaking his head, Fernando continued walking towards the door, then stopped.

A big, round, bright red blossom entered the room. It turned to one side, and then the other. As it turned, Fernando could see a body behind it. There was something weirdly familiar about the creature. The creature was olive green, had a rough texture, and walked on the clawed knuckles of folded wings and powerful hind legs. It was the size of their neighbor's cat.

*My pineapple! It's my pineapple! Or at least…it looks like my pineapple. But, with wings. Bright green wings. And legs.*

Another one followed it in, then another. Fernando froze. A tingly sensation ran up his spine; he didn't like it. The first blossom turned towards him again, then stopped. It didn't move.

Fernando watched the wings unfurl.

■ ■ ■

Cautiously, the alpha stepped through the new opening that had been the magnetic field, ready to move quickly if the field returned. Once it stepped safely through, its siblings followed.

It paused, stretched out its blossom, and scanned the new space.

*There!*

There was prey directly in front of them. It was large; they'd need to work together.

The alpha called out to its siblings, gauging their readiness.

■ ■ ■

As he stared, Fernando realized the others were unfurling their wings as well.

He began to back away, his head slowly turning side to side.

"Please…no…no…please…no…"

Suddenly, the creatures shot forward. The first hit his stomach, bowling him over. As he fell backward, Fernando felt the claws tear into his chest as the blossom pressed against his face, muffling his screams. Thousands of needles pricked his skin. Then, he was overwhelmed by a growing burning sensation, like acid was thrown against him.

He struggled but quickly lost control of his muscles. Fernando lay there as the blossom peeled away from his face and folded backward. From the center of the blossom, a triform beak slowly emerged. It slowly lowered towards him. The beak hovered millimeters from his chin, then moved towards his shoulder as he felt the claws tighten their grip, tearing into his chest.

As he stared, the beak opened wide. Then, it suddenly bit down, slicing into the meat of his shoulder. His eyes widened and he tried to scream but his mouth wouldn't open. He felt the beak close and pull away, taking a mouthful of him with it. The beak raised and he could see a bulge move past the base of the blossom as it swallowed a piece of his shoulder.

The beak lowered again, hesitated, then bit down, taking another chunk of him. His eyes rolled up as his head swayed side to side before returning to stare at the beak. The claws gripping his chest tightened as it pulled back once more and swallowed again. Then the beak opened, and three long, muscular tongues reached down into him, scraping up meat from inside his shoulder. Fernando couldn't tear his eyes away as he watched this thing eat him alive.

Suddenly, he felt another bite taken from his belly and another from his thigh. His eyes rolled backward again as he lay helpless, knowing they were feeding on him. He felt their claws pierce his skin and rip his clothes as they shifted their grip. He could feel the wet, muscular tongues as they tore at him. The whole room was eerily silent, as the things quietly fed, the only sound coming from their beaks and tongues.

Fernando lay there, helplessly, unable to move.

Then, from across the room, he heard a gasp, then a shriek.

■ ■ ■

The prey was delicious, and easier to subdue than they'd feared. It hardly fought back at all!

The alpha directed the other survivors to seek more prey in this side canyon rather than share in this feast.

As it fed, the alpha felt another electromagnetic signature approach.

■ ■ ■

Fernando's wife sat up in bed, wondering what he could possibly be doing to make so much noise. It was his turn to cook, dammit. The least he could do was prepare something edible without making a fuss. Sounded like he was throwing things around the kitchen.

Then it was quiet, too quiet.

Fernando's wife threw her legs over the side of the bed, pulled on her robe, and stepped cautiously towards the door. She couldn't see anything because it was set to privacy. She tapped the control and stepped into the family room. She stared, unsure what she was seeing. Then she saw the blood.

Her eyes widened, and pointing, she screamed.

■ ■ ■

Ronnie led her squad through another creepy, abandoned hallway. She shook her head. They'd been in a breakroom, taking a much needed rest; then they received instructions to move to *another* breakroom. She could only assume this was part of some larger plan, some optimization of resources. They were supposed to be strategically located for fast response.

Bhavia explained over a conference call that the supposedly harmless haploids were not, in fact, so harmless. They'd attacked Ivan and his squad while recovering bodies (not a task she envied, but she understood the need). In any case, the haploids had grown considerably since hatching, but weren't that big yet as to be dangerous solo. But if they worked together?

So Ronnie and her crew left the breakroom, refreshed their weapons at an armory, and started walking towards their newly assigned breakroom. It really wasn't that far away, and they needed to refresh their weapons anyway. Ronnie knew the way by heart. *Left through this cross hallway, then right for another 60 m or so.*

As they made their second turn from the cross hallway to the main, she could see an open door. Ronnie raised a fist, then said over her shoulder, "probably nothing, but let's not take any chances." She unslung her flame-thrower, and as her squad did the same, walked slowly towards the door. She reached the door and gestured to a member of the squad to be ready to cover her. She stepped through and scanned the mess. Furniture was knocked over; food cans rolled on the floor. To her left, by the master bedroom door, she saw what was left of a body: a shredded, bloody robe about a skeleton. The bones were clean; the skull was crushed. The pelvis suggested it was a female. Some of the bones were out of place, as if whatever fed on her limbs pulled them from the body to pick them clean.

Ronnie beckoned and more of her team entered. She turned and saw a skeletal foot by the kitchen. She raised her hand high, then pointed down towards it. She walked over and found a male skeleton, also picked clean, its skull also crushed. She looked around the room. There were droppings that brought back memories of kraken, but no other sign of what might have done this. Turning, she saw a hallway, presumably leading to children's bedrooms. Apprehensive, she cautiously stepped into the hallway.

Ronnie turned into the first bedroom. The bed was unmade and the room a mess, but not beyond the level of disarray that seemed normal for some children. She stepped back into the hallway and made her way to the next room, where her heart sank at the sight of a smaller skeleton.

She stepped back into the hallway, then stepped into the second to last bedroom. She froze in the doorway. On the floor, four of the largest haploids she'd ever seen were feeding on what was left of a small child. The skull was exposed and crushed. The torso was ripped open, the viscera gone. The left arm and leg were skeletal, and the right limbs were not far behind. The haploids fed silently. Their hind feet sat squarely on the floor, their wing claws held fast to the body; the blossoms folded back to drape around their wings. The beaks were open, and the tongues extended, drawing strips of torn meat back into their mouths.

Ronnie hesitated, then assured herself that the child was clearly beyond saving. She raised her flamethrower and incinerated the haploids and body alike. As they burned, they briefly abandoned their prey to face her, but quickly succumbed to the fire.

As they died, Ronnie heard a commotion from the next room and ran towards it, unprepared for what she was about to see. On the floor, an adolescent writhed as a haploid ripped into his belly, tongues pulling at his viscera. His humerus was exposed at the elbow; the forearm was torn away. In the beak of another haploid, the tongues pulled the boy's hand into the mouth as the fingers dangled over the edge of the beak. A third was tearing into his thigh. On the bed, a toddler, still intact, screamed silently. A broad red circle shone on her face. A haploid folding back its blossom began to dig into the hips of the child.

Ronnie, horrified, stopped dead in her tracks. Suddenly, a boiling rage erupted within her. Screaming, she kicked the haploids feeding on the adolescent; she dropped her flamethrower, grabbed the haploid attacking the toddler and threw it against the far wall. She picked her flamethrower back up and hit the haploid she'd just thrown, then kicked the others into the corner and incinerated them too. She didn't stop screaming until the butterflies' corpses were black as tar.

She stared at the smoking carcasses of the haploids as the rest of her squad came into the room. One medic went to the toddler, making soothing noises as he began his examination. Another medic knelt by the adolescent. The boy looked up helplessly at the medic; the medic took the boy's hand as the boy slowly died. There was nothing he could do.

Ronnie, wide-eyed and pale, shook her head slowly and left the room.

# ▪ DAY 7: 23:12
## BREAKING POINT

"Elke, we're getting more reports. We have haploids under the residential dome and here under the primary dome that are opening doors and attacking occupants."

"Fuck!" Elke, at a loss, pounded her fist against the conference room wall. What more could they do? They'd given up on the quick response model; the squads just weren't fast enough. The haploids attacked a family, fed quickly, then fled. A few were destroyed, but most were gone before anyone could respond. They just didn't have enough people!

"Nikko? Nikko, I want a display on this table. Show me the primary and residential domes. Every time the haploids compromise a door, I want that door to turn red on the display so we can visualize what we're dealing with. Can you make that happen?"

"Absolutely!"

"George?"

He looked up from his console. He looked awful! "Yes?"

"How are they choosing targets? I don't understand. They attack a residence, then flee. Why is there so much distance between hits?"

George heaved a weary sigh. "I'm sorry, I have no idea. Your guess is as good as mine."

"Dammit, that's not good enough! People are dying! I can't fight these things if I don't understand what they're doing, George!"

Faces looked up. Embarrassed by her outburst, Elke briefly looked around the room, then stared down at the table. Faces returned to their tasks.

Softly, she said, "George, I'm sorry. It's not your fault."

He nodded, then leaned forward. His slumped shoulders, the gray bags under his eyes, it was like Elke suddenly saw him anew. And she realized how frail he looked.

"I wish I had answers for you. But I don't. Not for this."

Elke gripped his shoulder. "You've had a lot of answers for us, George. You've saved a lot of lives."

She walked back to the window, folded her arms, and stared out at the mountains. A steaming coffee mug appeared in front of her. She looked at it, then her eyes followed the hand up an arm to John's face.

"You're tired."

She accepted the mug, sipped, set it down, and smiled sardonically. "Understatement."

"I am, too, you know. And so is he, and so is everyone else."

She curled her lip; an unusual bitterness crept over her. "I *know*."

John pursed his lips, tilted his head, then decided to speak.

"I'm worried about him. Professional opinion? He's not up to this. He needs rest."

She looked over her shoulder at George, then met John's eyes. She rubbed the bridge of her nose in angst. "I can *see* that. But we *need* him, and a lot of lives are at stake."

John looked down, shook his head, then met her eyes.

"I'm a doctor. I look at patients one case at a time. You're the governor, and you look at the colony holistically. You're forced to decide whether to risk one set of lives to save others. I get that. Honestly, I don't know how you do it. So, I'll respect and trust your judgment." He tipped his head towards George. "But that patient is close to breaking, and I may not be able to put him back together again "

Elke crossed her arms again, nodding as she turned to look out the window. She turned to look at George, then met John's eyes before speaking. "And I, personally, am very fond of him. He's an extremely valuable asset. But you're right, I'm making decisions involving thousands of lives."

She shook her head and turned to the window again.

"I honestly don't know what's worse. Making mistakes that cost lives, or being forced to make choices that sacrifice one set of people for the 'greater good'. I know we can do the math, say I sacrificed one or ten to save a 100 or 1,000, but is any one life sacrificed less precious than any of the lives saved? And, love, I know, *I know*, that no matter what decisions I make, a lot of people have died and a lot more will die. Horribly! And there's not a fucking thing I can do about that! And, love, it stinks. It hurts!"

She wiped a tear, shook her head, and turned back to John.

"I know he's struggling." She shook her head. "And I'll bear it in mind."

John moved closer to her. Elke picked up her coffee mug and stared into it, worried that if she met his gaze, she would lose her composure.

John spoke softly. "I'm worried about you, too. I'm a student of human nature, you know. Comes with the job. And, as I've often told you, the highest performing individuals are often the most convinced they're falling short. I don't know how you do what you do, but you do it extremely well. You impress the hell out of me, and everyone else. That's why you're entrusted as governor. And, right now, you're the most valuable person in this room."

Her eyes shot back to his, then she shook her head.

He nodded, then said, "Elke, love, if you fall apart, there's nobody else ready to step up and take your place. We need you. I need you. It's just not like you to snap at someone. You need to get some rest."

She tilted her head side to side, then said, softly, simply, "noted."

# ▪DAY 7: 23:24
## NUR

Bhavia's stomach churned. John and Elke stood by the window. He couldn't hear what they were saying, but their body language was clear. Elke was understandably strained, and John was there for her.

Just as Bhavia should be "there" (wherever the hell "there" was) for Nur. *Dammit!*

Before this, Bhavia's experience with Governor Lubandi was limited and remote. He reported to Guido, and Guido was a good boss. But now that he worked directly with Lubandi? She certainly lived up to her reputation. He'd follow her to hell and back! That's exactly what they were doing, isn't it? Going to hell and back? If this wasn't hell, what was?

Bhavia shook his head in frustration. This wasn't helping.

He glanced longingly at the cots in the corner of the room. He really needed some rack time. But every time he tried to sleep, he kept remembering his last exchange with Nur. The last time Bhavia saw her, he asked her about those damn smuggling containers. Then she took his hand and tried talking about starting a family again. But he was too focused on his investigation to discuss it.

"Later. We'll talk about it later, when I get home."

But he didn't get home. Then he ignored her messages to focus on the case. He didn't notice when she stopped sending messages, not right away.

But, eventually, Bhavia realized he hadn't heard from Nur in a while. So he finally opened the messages, read them, felt like absolute shit, and replied with his apologies.

She didn't respond. He assumed he went too far, that he'd really hurt her feelings this time. So he kept trying, and kept trying. And as the death toll rose, his anxiety rose too. He started to wonder whether or not he'd ever see her again.

"Fuck!" Bhavia swore a little bit louder than he intended to, so he started to pace, walking away from the crowd that might have heard him. There wasn't anything he could do. She wasn't answering, and he couldn't leave to go look for her…

Bhavia looked around the room. Everyone was busy, focused on whatever they were doing. John was still at the window with Elke, away from his temporary work desk.

Bhavia pinched his chin, conflicted.

John's display was still up. He knew what John was working on. They were processing genetic samples to identify victims too destroyed to be recognized. He could go look. Bhavia could use his credentials to access any file, but with John's display still open, the file would be *right there*. He wouldn't have to search for it.

He could go see whether Nur was on the list. If she wasn't, then maybe she was still alive.

Maybe she just couldn't respond for some reason. Although Bhavia was at a loss coming up with a reason that would stop her from responding…

Bhavia hesitated.

He was a rule follower, a stickler for process and protocol. It came with the line of work. John's team was identifying remains, but they weren't notifying anyone, not yet. He should respect that decision, respect the process. And it would be awkward if he were caught at John's display, and *really* awkward if he were caught using his credentials at John's display.

Bhavia checked his messages one more time.

# ▪ DAY 7: 23:45
## SNAPPED

Taki started to test Dieter's latest trap design. No trap would be feasible without a device that could synthesize sex pheromones. Fortunately, developing the means to synthesize kraken sex pheromones was one of many post-kraken research programs. But that was only the first challenge.

The second challenge was designing a trap the haploids would be willing to enter to get at the source of the sex pheromones. The third challenge was creating a killing method that destroyed haploids without generating alarm pheromones. The final challenge was a way to clear the remains of destroyed haploids so the trap could be reactivated to lure more haploids to their doom.

Taki, having spent hours and hours watching haploids, helped Dieter come up with a design he was confident the haploids would enter. It was a large cylinder, 2 m wide and 2 m tall with a 1 m wide opening in the top. It was made of a heavy duty plastic mesh. A mesh would let pheromones waft through, and unlike metal, plastic shouldn't tip off the haploids' electromagnetic sensory system.

The killing method was the most challenging. If the haploids aren't killed quickly enough, they might generate alarm pheromones. And Taki couldn't predict how the haploids would respond if simultaneously confronted with the attraction of sex pheromones and the deterrent of alarm pheromones. Incineration seemed the best way to kill them quickly; the resulting ash should be relatively easy to clear before resetting the trap. Taki had considered an electric arc, but feared the haploids' electromagnetic senses would be put off by them.

Taki and Dieter settled on non-metallic flamethrower nozzles. The result was now in Taki's lab. It was too big to fit in any of their haploid enclosures, so they set it up in a classroom.

···

"Elke, they're ready to test the trap!"

Everyone gathered around the conference room table. The classroom was projected on the table. The trap sat in the middle of the floor.

"Taki's in the lab," George said. "He'll explain what we're about to see."

A moment later, Taki's voice could be heard.

"We're about to test Dieter's latest design. We've selected fifty haploids that we'll introduce into the enclosure. First, we'll flush the air in the classroom, then we'll introduce the first set of haploids, after which we'll turn on the pheromones. We'll start with five of our biggest haploids."

After a few minutes, they could see the classroom door open. A container was placed inside. Once the door was closed, the container opened, and five large butterflies emerged. They flew vertically, hovered, and opened their blossoms.

John exclaimed, "they're huge!"

George nodded. "About 6 kilos, about the size of a small dog."

Taki's voice returned. "I just activated the sex pheromones."

Within seconds, the hovering haploids turned their blossoms towards the trap. One by one, they flew towards it, slowly at first, then faster. The butterflies flew about the mesh, then rose, hovered over the opening, and descended into the trap.

"Well! That's a very good sign! Now, I'm incinerating them."

Suddenly, the interior of the trap burst into a flame that only lasted a few seconds. Then the trap was empty. Everyone waited with baited breath; finally Taki spoke happily.

"Very good! We're monitoring the air, and we haven't detected alarm pheromones. The haploids are now ash at the bottom of the trap."

The conference room erupted in cheers and applause. Over the next hour, Taki took them through additional scenarios. Even if alarm pheromones had not been produced, would haploids pick up on anything that might deter them from entering the trap? Taki released more into the classroom without flushing the air, and they were still drawn into the trap. Would witnessing the incineration of other haploids deter them from entering the trap? Taki released double the number of haploids into the classroom without flushing the air. When half of them were in the trap, he incinerated them. The remaining haploids still entered the trap. This confirmed deployed traps could cycle through luring and destroying haploids without concern that the butterflies would avoid the traps.

"Okay. Now we're going to introduce a large number of smaller, presumably least sexually mature haploids. The trap will run automatically, incinerating occupants whenever there's at least five haploids in the trap. There's a lot of haploids in the room, so, rather than relying on ourselves as observers, we're going to have room monitoring track individual haploids."

As they watched, haploids entered the trap and, periodically, the trap incinerated its occupants. Over time, the rate at which haploids entered the trap declined until, finally, a few small haploids flew about the classroom, ignoring the trap completely. When ten minutes lapsed without any of the remaining haploids entering the trap, Taki ran an analysis.

"Post testing analysis reveals a correlation between size and response to the pheromones. The bigger the haploid, the more attracted it was to the pheromones."

George opined, "That makes sense, given sexual maturity usually correlates with size, so the bigger they are, the closer they are to sexual maturity, and the more compelling they find the pheromones." He paused, then added, "y'know, size also correlates with hunting success. So, if the largest individuals are the most aggressive hunters and are the most effectively lured and destroyed, we are killing our biggest problems first."

Elke thumped the table. "I'll take it. We'll need to destroy the rest of them, too, but this will be a huge leap in the right direction!"

She returned her attention to the conference room table. "Nikko? Can you bring up that projection of the primary and residential domes?

Nikko muttered "sure" while summoning the projection. Compromised doors were red. A lot of them were red.

Elke swore. "Worse than I'd feared. And I'm not really seeing a pattern. Nikko, work with Bhavia. See if you can discern any kind of pattern so we can prioritize deployments."

Again Nikko mubled "sure," then scanned the room.

Bhavia wasn't there.

"Where is Bhavia?"

Elke stood, her height allowing her to quickly scan the room.

She inquired with the computer. "Where is Bhavia?"

In the projection, a figure appeared, walking through one of the main corridors of the base station.

"What the *hell* is Bhavia doing?"

Elke and the rest watched Bhavia walking the hallway.

Elke established a communication link. "Bhavia? Where are you going?"

Silence.

"Anyone know what the hell is going on?"

Nikko, noticing an active display, walked over to it. After a moment, he muttered, "oh, shit!"

"What? What is it?"

Nikko pointed at the display. "It's a casualty display. Bhavia must have used his credentials to circumvent security. He found Nur."

Elke walked over. There it was. Nur's remains had been recovered, but couldn't be identified without DNA analysis. She'd been turned into a host. Elke sank slowly into one of the chairs by the displays.

She pictured Nur injected with those things, those monsters chewing through her conscious, immobilized, agonized body. She imagined butterflies hatching out of Nur, just like with Pete.

Memories flooded her, memories of Daniela Wu, crushed by a kraken diploid, holding her hand as she died, all those years ago.

Elke closed her eyes tightly, forcing herself to set aside the emotion. She reopened to look at Rajiv. Nur had been Rajiv's lead foreman. Rajiv's eyes glistened, a tear on his cheek. She could only imagine what Bhavia was feeling.

She collected herself and cleared her throat. "What is he doing?"

"Well, apparently, he left here about fifteen minutes ago. He went by a weapons locker. He took…well, he took a *lot*. Flamethrower, scattergun, lots of ammunition!"

"So, what, he's going to try to hunt down the haploids that impregnated Nur?"

Nikko grunted. "I don't see how Bhavia could track down the haploids that hatched from Nur or even tell if those haploids are still alive! But, if I had to guess, I'd say he's looking to kill some haploids, and he may not care which ones."

"Alone? What are his odds?"

"He may not care at the moment."

Elke swore. She didn't want to lose Bhavia; she didn't want Bhavia throwing his life away with an emotional outburst. But sending anyone to intercede meant taking those resources away from protecting other colonists. Bhavia was a key asset, but Bhavia was one individual. Was she pragmatically prioritizing a key asset or selfishly prioritizing the life of a friend?

"Any guesses where he's going?"

Nikko pondered a moment, then snapped his fingers.

"He left here, went to that weapons locker, and now, if he takes the next turn…"

He whistled.

"Yep. He's headed for Taki's lab."

"What the hell for?"

"Taki and George have haploids there. I think he's heading to the lab to kill the haploids being held there."

"But that doesn't make any sense! Those butterflies are in cages!"

"I don't think Bhavia is entirely rational right now!"

Elke swore again.

"Guido, I need you to address this. Reason with Bhavia. Maybe send the squad from that breakroom to meet him."

"Understood; I'll take it from here."

She nodded, then said, "Nikko, use your best judgment regarding deployment, but get those traps out there ASAP!"

■ ■ ■

Bhavia strode through the corridor, his face a mask of grief, his heart filled with rage.

He had ignored Elke. Now he was ignoring Guido.

It didn't matter. None of it mattered.

Nur. Poor, precious Nur!

He couldn't stop picturing Nur lying in their quarters, in agony, those things moving through her, sprouting out of her. She didn't deserve that! Bhavia should have been there to protect her!

Their last conversation was an argument. Nur pressed to start a family, Bhavia resisted. Now, Nur was gone. She wanted a baby so badly. Now her only "birthing" experience was these things erupting from her body. Bhavia flogged himself for refusing to start a family, for ignoring her messages, for not leaving to find her.

*Why? WHY?!*

All Bhavia could think of was those butterflies. He needed to kill those things. He needed to see them burn, suffer, and die. He needed to see them break, see them explode as his bullets pierced their bodies, shredded their wings. He needed to grab them, stomp on them.

His mind was filled with different notions about how to kill those little monstrosities.

■ ■ ■

"Guido, any progress?"

"Ignored me completely. Elke, I care about Bhavia, too. And Nur. But I don't think we can redirect squads to rescue him from himself. Not right now."

Elke paused, then nodded. An alarm went off. Elke could see, on the display, a door flashing red.

"Holy shit! That's the lab!"

■ ■ ■

The teaching lab was a large complex. The main entry opened into a shared workspace used by technicians to prepare samples and equipment for a suite of classrooms. It also served as an impromptu kitchenette. One classroom held Taki's haploid enclosures. Another was being used to test haploid traps. Two were filled with bunk for the grad students and lab technicians supporting research.

George and Taki stood at one of the enclosures, surrounded by graduate students, engaged in lively debate about the various behaviors they were observing. Beyond attraction to the kraken sex pheromones, they just weren't seeing anything suggesting sexual maturity. George struggled to maintain his composure given his increasing sense of urgency. Part of him knew creativity cannot be rushed, but part of him was all too aware of the lives at stake.

He bristled as he noticed Taki staring past him; then George heard one of the grad students scream.

He turned. In the shared workspace, a young man flailed on his back fighting off three haploids. One was perched on his chest, its blossom pressed against his face; the other two tore at his legs as his kicks became less and less vigorous. Most backed away, but two onlookers stepped forward, grabbing at the butterflies. They struggled to pull the haploids away as their claws dug deeper into the young man's body. Then more haploids hit the two onlookers, taking them down, pressing their blossoms against them as well. No one else gathered the courage to intercede.

The young man went limp as the venom took effect. The haploids folded back their blossoms, opened their beaks, and began to feed. The other two that tried to help fell victim to venom themselves. More haploids entered the space, their blossoms opened wide.

George stared and started raising his wrist to hit his computer's alarm. He suddenly became dizzy. He couldn't think. He broke into a cold sweat and felt a tremendous pressure on his chest. He turned to see Take staring at him.

Haltingly, sinking into a chair, he ordered Taki to sound an alarm. Instead, Taki helped him take his seat.

"Are you alright, George?"

George sat, clutching his chest, unable to speak. He heard Taki yelling.

"We're in the lab! We need help! Haploids are in the lab! I think George is having a heart attack!!!"

A cluster of grad students, backing away from the door, stood between them and the haploids. George, squinting, could see others in the classrooms on the far side of the workspace, also backing away.

The haploids followed the grad students. Their blossoms continued to move from side to side. Suddenly, the butterflies unfurled their wings and launched themselves into the crowd, taking down many as the frightened group scattered about the room.

George watched in horror as the students fell, struggling against the predators. Then, a ray of hope emerged as an armed squad ran into the workspace. They quickly started triage on the fallen students, then ran to victims that were still struggling. They pulled haploids from their feasts, threw them against walls, and incinerated them with flamethrowers.

One of the squad members was Bhavia! Bhavia struggled to pull a haploid away from one of the students. He threw the haploid against the wall, pressed the muzzle of his scattergun against its flank, and pulled the trigger. He screamed as it exploded, then turned and bent to pull another away. He threw that one to the floor and kicked it hard. One of the butterflies' wings broke and silently fell to the floor. Bhavia dropped his scattergun, unslung his flamethrower, and hit it. Bhavia's blood curdling cries filled the teaching lab.

Then a haploid hit Bhavia in the ribs, sending him careening sideways. He held the trigger of the flamethrower as he fell, setting one of the squad members aflame. The hard impact stunned Bhavia temporarily. The haploid pressed its blossom against Bhavia's face as he screamed in pain and rage. He released the flamethrower and tried to push the thing away as it dug its claws into his chest. Then his movements slowed. The haploid folded back its blossom and opened its beak. Three tongues reached out to caress Bhavia's face, then took hold as the beak spread wide and snapped down to bite deeply into his head.

Bhavia's body went limp as the butterfly fed.

The squad continued to fight and destroy haploids, but were overwhelmed by their number. Students were down, scientists were down, squad members were down, and Taki was struggling to protect George. No matter how many butterflies they killed, more poured into the workspace. One by one, the whole squad succumbed to the onslaught. It was only a matter of time before the swarm reached Taki and George. There was no escape, no way to get out except through that doorway.

# ▪ DAY 8: 00:12
## *DEUS EX MACHINA*

"Nikko, what's happening at the lab?"

"It's not good! This is the biggest haploid swarm we've seen. Grad students are down. Squad members are down. Bhavia rushed in, and now he's down. There are just too many haploids. Taki reports George is having a heart attack and John wants to send an emergency team."

Elke pointed at another red door under the residential dome.

"What's that?"

Nikko rushed up to the table as two more doors turned red. "We have two, no, three haploid attacks underway under the residential dome! Squads are rushing to assist!"

Elke bit her lip. *George…*

There was nothing more she could do. Her best squads were deployed; they'd do what could be done. She stepped away, then tapped her wrist computer.

"John? How urgently does George need help?"

"I won't know until we see him. We could lose him if we don't get to him right away.

"And we could lose your paramedics if they encounter haploids on the way," Guido interjected. "And I don't have an armed escort for you."

She could almost hear John shrug. "I have volunteers ready to go anyway. I'm going with them."

Elke started, catching John's words. "Send your volunteers. Not you, though! You stay put!"

"Elke!"

"That's *not* open for discussion!"

She grunted and looked towards the window. They were losing. So many people were already gone. Squads were being decimated all over the colony, trying to intercede, trying to kill the damned haploids. And they *were* killing haploids, just not enough!

All the butterflies seemed to be within structures now. There weren't any left outside for the scoops to catch. The traps were steadily reducing the butterfly population, but they were cumbersome, taking too long to build and deploy. There were just so many butterflies! And every trap deployment was another opportunity for haploids to attack her crews.

She didn't need to run a simulation. She knew their losses were horrendous, and that many, many more would be lost despite the traps. At the rate they were going, it was only a matter of time. If they couldn't come up with another way to kill the haploids, the colony would be decimated.

She swore. Then, she noticed that the group around the table had gone silent. She turned, cringing, wondering what was happening now.

"Nikko?"

He turned, looked back at her, his expression impossible to read.

"What is it?"

He looked at her incredulously. "They…stopped! All over the colony! I'm getting reports from all over the colony that the haploids have stopped attacking. They're just…flying away!"

# ▪ DAY 8: 00:42
## BIOLOGY

*Pop!*

The butterfly alpha paused as it felt a "pop."

*Strange…*

The butterflies were feeding. It was glorious! The prey were delicious. The butterflies were hungry, *always* hungry. They fed and grew, and as they grew, so did their hunger. If they could, they would feed constantly!

So they fed until the prey were consumed, until every morsel was drawn from their bodies. Then they flew through the strange canyons, probing for the magnetic signatures of prey.

Not all prey were readily accessible. The butterflies could sense them through the walls of the strange canyons. There was *so* much prey to choose from! They could afford to be a little picky, to wait for large groups. Some groups were too small. Others weren't near a magnetic field, so there wasn't an obvious way to get at them. So they flew, probing through the walls, searching for the right opportunities.

When the butterflies sensed a large cluster near a field, they hovered. They aimed their blossoms at the field and 'talked' with the field until they found the right thing to say. The field would disappear, and they would fly through and it would be absolutely wonderful! The prey would turn and run and shriek, and the butterflies would follow, digging their claws into the meat of the prey, pressing their blossoms against their flesh. They pressed and tasted until the prey slowed, stopped, and fell. The butterflies buried their beaks into the meat; blood pulsing as they sliced through the flesh. Their tongues tore away little morsels as they relished the fear and pain and anxiety of the prey. It was so, so good!

But now, a "pop."

The alpha was feasting when it felt the "pop." Its beak bit through the flesh of the prey when suddenly the meat lost all its taste. The butterfly perched on the prey, reveling in the experience one moment and completely indifferent the next.

*How strange!*

Something was happening. It felt movement in its back, almost like a tear. The alpha felt two new limbs it didn't know it had, stretching and flexing from its back. One of the limbs splayed its tip, and it felt an exquisite pleasure as something misted into the air around its limb.

And then there was hunger. A *new* kind of hunger, a hunger it had never felt before. It resented this new hunger! All of its brief life, the alpha felt a hunger never fully sated, that drove it constantly, incessantly, filling every moment of its existence with a need to to feed, and to grow. It *understood* that hunger; it knew how to satisfy it.

But now, a new hunger replaced the old. It was a confusing hunger. And the butterfly resented it!

Then the chemoreceptors of its blossom detected a new flavor, an amazing, alluring flavor, unlike anything in its experience. The flavor was delicious, and it could not be ignored.

*Follow it...*

Without thinking, the butterfly loosened its grip, the prey forgotten. Its wings beat as it rose. The flavor was *everywhere*! It began to realize that the intensification of the flavor increased with the electromagnetic signatures of other butterflies. Not its siblings, no.

*Other butterflies!*

It sensed its siblings also hovering, also pivoting. It moved in the direction of the most intense flavor, and sensed its siblings flying alongside it. They flew through the strange canyons until they came across the other cohorts of butterflies. They were beautiful!

Its blossom was saturated with the flavor coming from their bodies. Its electromagnetic senses tingled and aligned. It approached one, hovering so their blossoms were almost touching. After a few moments, the two butterflies settled, then walked past each other until the limbs on their backs lined up.

Each butterfly reached with their forward limb towards the rearward limb of its partner, placing the cupped tip of its limb over the pointed tip of its partner. Pleasure exploded in their bodies. They felt warmth squeeze through their forward limbs, and felt their hindward limb drink in their partner's warmth. The sensation was nearly beyond their tolerance. After a few moments, it was done.

They detached, and moved away from each other. Their blossoms sought more prospective partners. They lined up in pairs. They lined up in rings, each extending its hindlimb to one side and receiving a hindlimb from another.

In pairs and rings, they mated.

They mated, then detached, changed partners, and mated again, ignoring all else.

They mated and mated, again, and again, and again…

# DAY 8: 03:24
## NUMB

Three hours now.

Three hours without a haploid attack.

Secmeds and their squads reported from all over the colony. Everywhere they looked, haploids were mating. Sometimes the butterflies mated in pairs, sometimes in groups. Sometimes the mating rings blocked the corridors completely. They found butterflies mating inside, outside, coupling and uncoupling, changing partners. It was a leisurely, ongoing orgy of alien sex with no signs of stopping.

The butterflies did seem to sort themselves by size; but now, even the smallest ones that were not responding to the trap's pheromones at all were mating. They didn't seem the least bit interested in nourishment. Was it a reprieve? For how long? Would they eventually resume hunting?

Elke gave orders. Every surviving secmed and every surviving squad went to the nearest weapons locker and helped themselves to whatever was left: rifles, scatterguns, flamethrowers. Secmeds with smaller squads sent some members door to door, summoning every able bodied person they could find. They armed the frightened survivors and sent them to destroy as many butterflies as they could.

Ronnie, Badru, and their squad walked through a corridor. They didn't speak. They were totally exhausted, wrung dry. Ronnie, barely holding her flamethrower, drifted past a smoldering pair of butterflies. There were more butterflies ahead of her.

More, and more, and more.

Their mating behavior brought back painful memories of the kraken. Some deep, analytical part of Ronnie's mind thought she should find this cathartic. But she was too numb. She walked to the nearest couple, pausing a meter away from them. She aimed the wand of her flamethrower lazily, pulled the trigger, and watched them catch fire and burn.

They simply didn't care.

Behind her, the fire suppression systems activated. Per Elke's orders, Nikko adjusted the sensors to delay fire suppression long enough to let the damn things burn, but not long enough to risk fire spreading. It was working well.

Ronnie stood impassively as the butterflies smoldered. For a while, she'd periodically looked up to see how the others were doing. But there was no need.

After all the battles, after all the valiant struggles, the victories, the losses, it was reduced to this. A chore.

It should be a relief.

It should be cathartic.

But it wasn't.

It was a chore, and nothing more. Like sweeping a floor or raking leaves.

Ronnie stepped past the charred butterflies and came across a ring of them. Seven individuals, each reaching to the partner on one side and accepting the partner on the other. She'd seen them pause, then reorganize themselves in order to exchange sex cells with multiple partners.

She didn't care.

Ronnie walked up to the ring of silent horrors, pointed her flamethrower, and pulled the trigger. it burped a small fireball before dying. The fireball singed the nearest two butterflies, but they didn't seem to notice.

She checked the fuel gauge.

*Empty.*

Ronnie checked for the location of the nearest weapons locker, then waved to Badru to get his attention. As he looked over, she tapped the fuel gauge, shrugged, pointed in the direction of the locker, then pointed at the ring of butterflies.

He nodded slowly. He understood.

As Ronnie walked away, Badru finished incinerating them for her, then went on to the next pair.

# ▪DAY 8: 11:12
## REPRIEVE

George was very, very groggy. His eyes fluttered open, then closed. He struggled to stay awake. How much time passed between his eyes closing and opening again, he did not know. He heard strange sounds, noises his sluggish brain began to process.

*Medical equipment…*

George heard a distant voice say, "doctor! I think he's waking up!" He opened his eyes and squinted hard. He was in the colonial hospital. A nurse fussed over him for a moment then left the room in a hurry. The equipment displays beside him chirped methodically.

"What happened?"

Nobody replied, so he asked again, more loudly.

"Hello? Hello??"

He saw movement to his right, and turned to see John smiling at him.

"You're fine, George. You had a bit of a scare, that's all. But you're fine!"

"What happened?"

John breathed a big sigh. "You had a good, old fashioned heart attack. Nothing serious. We brought you back here and fixed you all up. And, since you haven't been listening to your doctor's advice about getting some rest, we kept you under a while."

"How…how long?"

"Oh, it's been a few hours now. But, my boss wants to talk with you, so I really can't justify keeping you under any longer. Your heart's fine now, there's nothing keeping you here except that you need a lot more rest."

"Can I get up?"

"How about we sit you up, for now. I've got a tray coming with some food, and some people that are anxious to talk with you. Feel up to that?"

George's mind was clearing. Suddenly, he remembered!

"The lab!" He grabbed John's hand. "What about my lab?"

John lowered his eyes, then raised them to look at George.

"We lost a lot of people, George. I'm sorry. I'll get you a list later. But it's over. The butterflies flew away."

George stared at him, puzzled. "Flew away? What do you mean they 'flew away'?"

"Well, that's what they want to talk with you about."

With a reassuring nod, John released George's hand and stepped back as Taki appeared.

"George! How are you?"

"A little out of it, but John here assures me it'll pass."

John, now with another patient a few meters away, glanced over. "You *will* be fine! I want you in that bed another hour or so, and I don't want any crowds in here. Taki will catch you up on what's been happening, and then Elke and the rest will appear virtually to pick your brains. After that, I'll do a final check and we'll let you go. Alright?"

George nodded, then turned to Taki and raised his eyebrows.

Taki cleared his throat.

"The butterflies have stopped feeding, George. They just…stopped! All over the colony! At the field sites, too. All at the same time! They stopped hunting, stopped feeding, and started releasing sex pheromones. Now, they're mating everywhere."

George digested this information. "Do you have any theories?"

Taki nodded vigorously. "Yes! Yes. You know I've been sacrificing butterflies, doing dissections, trying to find signs of sexual maturity. We know what glands kraken use to generate sex pheromones, so I've been checking those glands in the butterflies, thinking we might get a head start synthesizing them. But they've remained sexually immature! They're attracted to kraken sex pheromone, but they weren't producing any sex pheromones of their own. But *now*! Now, they're sexually mature! They're producing sex pheromones and mating! Sexual maturity is not related to size! Not at all! Suddenly, they're *all* sexually mature!"

He leaned back, then continued. "Then it hit me. Their tidal sensors! I checked, and, sure enough, their tidal sensors tripped! As the lunar alignment progresses, they're programmed to produce offspring to capitalize on the squirts. Then, as the alignment wanes, they're programmed to all reach sexual maturity at the same time. I presume this allows them to maximize the number of partners in order to secure genetics for whatever they'll encounter at the next alignment forty years later."

John, looking over and couldn't help but smile at the childlike fascination on George's face. Not only was he recovering from his heart attack, he was becoming himself again.

He checked the time, then walked over and said, "George, Taki, it's time. Ready?"

■ ■ ■

George and Taki appeared at the conference room table.

Elke smiled and observed, "you're looking well, George!"

"Feeling well! John runs a good shop!"

She nodded and added in a sarcastic tone, "I'll bear that in mind at his next performance review. In the meantime, can you two help us understand what's happening out there?"

George looked at Taki, who repeated what he just explained to George.

Elke took a long, deep inhale. "So, what happens now?"

George shrugged. "They're now focused on mating, obviously. We can't know how long this will last. Could be minutes, could be days. And, when they're done, we can't know whether they'll resume feeding. The kraken certainly continued to feed after reaching sexual maturity.

On the other hand, they're not kraken. We know that, at some point, they will settle as pineapples. If we're lucky, I mean really, *really* lucky, that's what they'll do next. But we cannot know for sure. I know this may not be a particularly useful insight, but it seems our best option is to continue destroying as many of them as we can as quickly as we can. Don't ease up, not at all!"

Elke leaned back in her chair, pleased. "Nikko's continuing to deploy traps as fast as Dieter can make them. The traps consistently draw butterflies and incinerate them. Guido's secmeds and squads are also walking through the colony, destroying every butterfly they can find. Apparently, they ignore you as you walk up. You can hit them with a flamethrower, put a scattergun to the braincase and pull the trigger, and they don't seem to care."

George pursed his lips. "Suggests to me, at least, that in the field there aren't any predators capitalizing on this opportunity to feed on them. We can ask Diedre to take a look."

Elke's eyes fell and she taped the table with her forefinger thoughtfully. "We're destroying a lot of them, George, but we can't get them all. Not all of them are accessible. Some of the mating groups are perched high on structures where we can't reach them. I've directed Dieter to divert some fabrication resources from traps to rearming drones with flechettes."

She leaned forward, then continued, "We have to assume we won't be able to get them all. I need you and your team working on what the next phase might be, and what our options are."

# ▪ DAY 8: 14:09
## SETTLING

The haploids stopped mating.

As suddenly as they lost interest in feeding, they lost interest in sex.

They uncoupled, spread their blossoms and their wings, and took off.

Armed personnel and rearmed drones could no longer touch them. Deployed traps stopped attracting them. They flew higher and higher, exploring the boundaries of the domes, exploring the external structures of buildings. For what, no one could tell.

Taki, pondering as butterflies flew back and forth along the lids of his enclosures, was inspired. He worked with a lab tech to put together a set of small troughs filled with soil. They put the troughs into one of the enclosures, and watched the haploids settle into them. One by one, they used their hind limbs to grasp the edge of their trough and pushed their tails into the soil. The butterflies spread their wings, then spread their hind legs, and opened their blossoms.

Over the next hour, Taki marveled as the butterflies steadily transformed into pineapples. When the transformation seemed complete, he pulled one from the soil and took it to a workbench.

▪ ▪ ▪

An hour later, Taki and George walked into the main conference room, and all conversations stopped.

Elke walked over, reached out, and clasped George's hand in both of hers. She smiled wearily and said, "you look much better!" With that, she walked back to her place at the table. As everyone else took their place, she leaned forward, reflecting on how it hadn't been that long ago that George and Taki called an emergency meeting in the middle of the night in this very room. She looked around the room. They'd been through hell, and every face reflected it.

Every face except George and Taki. She realized that they looked relieved. *Why?*

"Okay, you've brought us back together. Can you help us understand what's happening?"

George smiled, then pointed at Taki.

Taki cleared his throat. "Well, I uh, I was watching the haploids in our enclosures, and noticed they seemed to be looking for something. Well, not that they can 'see', mind you, but they seemed to be searching."

He cleared his throat again and started over. "Uh. Sorry! Anyway, they were flying about the enclosures, trying to get out. I worked with a tech, and we installed some troughs. Troughs filled with soil. As soon as we did, the haploids settled into them. Dug their tails in and began transforming into pineapples."

"What does this mean…is it over?" Rajiv asked hesitantly.

"All the haploids seem to be searching for something," George answered. "And the ones in our enclosures are physically transforming in ways that would seem to preclude any ability to resume hunting."

He nodded to Taki, who said, "in the enclosures, as they settle, their claws fall away. The flaps of skin between their toes are broadening as their feet turn into leaves. Their hindlimbs and wings are locking into place. I dissected one, and I found that the joints of their wings and hindlimbs fused to support these leaves. They're stiff, like branches now, and they can't move them any-more. I suspect that their muscles will atrophy over time."

Nikko looked unconvinced. "That sounds like quite a transformation!"

"Not as much as you might initially think," George answered. "I believe I've explained before that on Earth barnacles are crustaceans that start life free-swimming, then settle. Imagine a crab that glues its head to something, and spends the rest of its life spreading its limbs to snatch food out of the water. As for the transformation, well, the wings are already broad and green, filled with an Eden equivalent to earthly chlorophyll. The hind limbs are also green and steadily broadening. In no time at all, they'll look just like the pine-apples Pete and his people were harvesting until, what, just last week?"

"And it's not that unlike things we saw on Earth," Taki added. "For example, a number of fish, like flounder, start life swimming in open water, then essen-tially lie on their sides. They live the rest of their lives on the seafloor, with one eye actually moving from the side of the head pressed against the seafloor to join the other eye on the other side!"

George snapped his fingers and pointed approvingly at Taki.

"Yes! Yes, an excellent example! It's easier to accept these profound morphological shifts if we remember that there are earthly examples of all of them. Even the cannibal morphology! It was in the North American southwestern deserts, I believe, that we saw amphibians do this. Tiger salamanders and, I believe, spadefoot toads. Yes; that's right. When ponds dried too fast, the tadpoles would develop enlarged heads and extra rows of teeth…"

Exasperated, Elke interrupted to ask, "but, why? Why, now? They were winning. Why did they suddenly stop?"

Taki looked at George, who took a deep breath before answering. Despite his hours of rest, he was still technically recovering. And he felt like it too.

"As we discussed last night, it's the tidal sensors. The building alignment of the four moons tripped the sensors of the pineapples, so they fertilized their eggs and began gestating the diploid generation. The waning alignment tripped the sensors of the butterflies, so they shifted from feeding to mating and now from mating to settling.

From an evolutionary perspective, it ensures they're all ready to mate at the same time. Even though they found kraken sex pheromones compelling, they didn't produce any sex pheromones of their own. This synchronization allows each individual to maximize its reproductive potential by mating with a wide variety of partners, which provides enough genetic diversity to deal with whatever environmental conditions they might encounter forty years later. Natural selection favors the individuals that optimize their ability to contend with an unknown future."

John smiled and observed, "George, I was sure you were going to cite divine intervention, *deus ex machina*!"

George laughed heartily, but pulled back to avoid a coughing fit. "John, machinations of the gods? I am a man of faith. And, sure, I prayed for inspiration to help us reason our way through this. But, no, I'm not one to call for, or count on, divine intervention." He tapped a finger to his temple and added, "The good Lord gave us the tools to solve our problems, and God helps those that help themselves."

He turned back to Elke. "You said they were winning. For the butterflies, it was never about winning or losing. They're just living things, creatures living their life cycles, not good or evil. Just life forms, living their lives, like us."

Elke held his gaze. "Respectfully, George, they were as close to evil as ever I've come. We've lost a lot of people, and we're incredibly lucky any of us survived this."

"I can't argue with that."

She slapped the table, stood, then said, "people, we live to fight another day. But, now, right now, we have a hell of a lot of work to do."

She looked around the table. Everyone looked awful, and justifiably so. She could only imagine how their squads were doing, or the colonists.

There was a lot of work to do, indeed. And a lot of healing…

# ▪DAY 8: 15:42
## EPILOGUE

Elke walked wearily back to the residence she shared with John. She didn't expect to see him any time soon. He and his staff would have their hands full for quite a while. She let herself in and walked to the minibar. She took a generous pour of Irish whiskey to her favorite chair. It was a custom chair, provided years ago by Moira and her team, designed to accommodate Elke's height. Until recently, it was in their quarters aboard the orbiting platform. But when she and John decided their main home should be here on the surface, she'd asked Nikko to bring it down. Now, it was perfectly positioned by her window, great for appreciating the mountains in the distance. She loved that view. She loved this place.

*Dear God, for all its horrors, this is such a beautiful place!*

Elke sipped her drink. She held the sample in her mouth to enjoy the complexity, then closed her eyes and swallowed. The warmth felt good! It was from a distillery under the primary dome. They offered a number of spirits, and she was told they were all excellent, but their first was an Irish Whiskey, christened *Elke's Elixir* in her honor.

She reopened her eyes and looked at the Garcia Mountains. More clouds rolled past the peaks. Soon, the rains would come, and the desert would flush green again, albeit briefly.

Just a few weeks ago, she was discussing the rains with Rajiv, Dieter, and Nikko. The settlement was designed to capture and sequester as much rainwater as possible, and, of course, they recycled that water as efficiently as they could. But, given their population growth, they would need more, soon. At some point, they'd need to tap some of the water collected by the Garcia Mountains, but that would be a massive project with significant environmental impact. Planning needed to start soon. Elke was looking forward to worrying about things like water again!

But first, she needed rest. She knew the rest of colonial leadership did, too. There were a few pressing issues that required immediate attention; everything else could wait a day or two.

Elke smiled, daydreaming. John would, at some point, be satisfied that his hospital was in good hands, and he'd come home to join her by this window with a glass of his current favorite cabernet in hand. Well, she had a surprise for him! A few months ago, a few bottles of real cabernet from one of the inner colonies finally arrived. It cost a fortune! But the real bottles were so much better than the algal derivatives they were limited to here. She'd ordered the bottles years ago, then tucked them away for a special occasion. Well, this wasn't the special occasion she'd envisioned, but she'd give him *one* bottle. He didn't need to know about the others, not yet…

Elke took another sip, then sighed deeply.

In a few days, Guido would be ready for after action reviews. It would take weeks, perhaps months, to work through recommended actions, so waiting a day or two wouldn't matter. She hadn't realized the degree to which their preparations presumed another relatively large predator like the kraken. It nearly cost them everything. The secmeds have been through hell. She knew these things took their toll. She'd need to confer with Ronnie, gain some insight into how all of this was impacting her. The heroism and commitment of the secmeds could not be overstated.

They needed acknowledgement. They needed care. They needed *rest*.

The colony also needed to step up research. Elke doubted George knew how much heat she took for the funding she allocated for his research; but, unlike any other colony, their very survival depended on understanding Eden's life forms. She enjoyed a level of autonomy regarding funding allocations, as long as she met her mineralogical and organochemical targets. But this near disaster convinced her they needed even more research. They couldn't afford another surprise.

Elke paused mid sip. She thought about George, and Taki. She could see this past week had taken a toll on George. She wouldn't be surprised to hear him announce retirement soon. He needed a successor. Elke knew Deidre was George's doctoral student and protege, but she'd also been impressed by Taki. Between them, Elke was confident they'd be in good hands.

That reminded her that she also needed to talk with George about the dual hub proposal. She was afraid to read her messages. Naturally, she sent updates as she was able, but she hadn't read any responses. Elke could imagine what was waiting for her. If the promoters of the dual hub model were calling for the extermination of kraken before, she could only imagine their reaction to the pineapples. They were probably voting for mass exterminations of Eden predators, if not actually terraforming the planet.

She recalled George's observation of the retreating butterflies. She completely understood George's point that the creatures weren't evil. They were amoral, not immoral. Right and wrong, good and evil were irrelevant to them. The butterflies were just wild creatures living out their life cycles, and all the tragedies and atrocities of the past week were the result of human greed and her own shortcomings.

Elke didn't share George's devotion to his faith, but she shared his passion for good stewardship. For her, it was a secular thing. What right did humanity have to nearly destroy Earth's biosphere, let alone Eden's? She didn't have George's grounding in ecology, but she understood that Eden's biosphere was a complex web. Attempting to selectively exterminate species like the kraken or pineapples would reverberate through that web, just as attempts to selectively eliminate Earth's wolves, sharks, and other top predators did.

And the prospect of attempting to terraform Eden, especially with only a sliver of understanding what Eden's biosphere offered, wasn't just economically foolish. It was *wrong*.

She remembered talking to John about all this just a few days ago. She told him she couldn't bring George into the discussion. Well, just imagining what was waiting in her inbox was enough to change her mind. She needed an ally, and George's research was popular. He complemented his research with a series of publications tailored for popular consumption and had a devoted following across known space. In a day or so, Elke would sit him down and explain what was going on. They needed to start making plans. And if the DSS leadership didn't like it, well…

She went to take another sip, but realized she'd already finished her drink. After a long pause, Elke poured herself a little more. She stared down at the swirling, deep brown liquid.

Elke confided in John that she was considering resigning. His attempts to reassure her that she wasn't at fault were hard to reconcile with her sense of responsibility. But he also reminded her that Elke also had an important role to play in the responsible development of Eden's resources.

Rajiv would be fine. He just needed to appoint another lead foreman. *Poor Nur! Poor Bhavia!* But Rajiv was a proficient leader and Elke had every confidence he already had candidates in mind. They'd be able to resume construction projects soon. And Dieter! Dieter had done amazing work! Moira was right about him. Even after all these years, Elke still missed Moira. They had a lot of deployed equipment to reclaim, but that could wait. Nikko would be busy another day or so. He needed to oversee the release from lockdown and estimate the immediate needs of surviving colonists. But he, too, at some point, would be satisfied that his senior staff was ready to follow through so he could get some rest. Mitch, Nikko's second, was doing a great job.

Earlier, before Elke left the conference room, Mitch told her about a stray interplanetary craft. Apparently, it went out right before the alignment, heading for one of the asteroid belt mining projects. A member of the crew brought a damn pineapple with her, and their intense acceleration triggered it to hatch. The captain was lost. Mitch showed her the craft's course. It had gone way off course before the surviving crew member regained control. Now, the survivor was in a chamber and heading back on an optimized course, with an automated distress signal. He figured it would be close enough to intercept in about eleven days.

Elke tried to imagine what the survivor went through, whether she'd even be alive.

Elke took another sip; her eyes glazed over a report. Nikko had provided preliminary estimates of their losses. He needed a few days to finalize, but his estimates were bleak. Last week, the colony's population stood at just over 17,000 souls. Nikko could account for just under 2,000 deaths, with another 500 or so missing. And the odds that any of the missing would be found were poor, very poor.

From a purely practical perspective, the senior staff needed to do a skills assessment. They needed to see what their losses were, see what they could do from a cross training perspective to rebalance the colony's skill sets for a functioning society. But more than 2,000 gone? Would there be enough people to perform all the tasks required to keep the colony running? Two of the agricultural domes were lost. The crops were still there, but the farmers and their livestock were gone. The farmers in the remaining domes might be able to handle the fields. But it would take time for livestock populations to recover.

The people would need some sort of ceremony, some way to acknowledge and process grief.

*Oh, damn! That's right!* That reminded her that she still needed to organize a memorial for the *Lucky Strike*. And *that* reminded Elke that she'd seen some urgent messages coming in from Alexandria.

*Sigh.*

Elke didn't want to process any messages from DSS leadership about the dual hub proposal, not yet; but she really couldn't ignore those messages from Alexandria any longer. Elke stood and walked to her communications console. She applied a filter to highlight messages related to Alexandria and the *Lucky Strike*. Probably something to do with processing salvage claims. She knew they could get complicated when cargo and personal effects were involved.

Elke paused, trying to remember if she'd ever heard about salvage claims involving a deep space vessel. After a moment, she shrugged. She couldn't recall any precedents, but this couldn't be the first time it's happened. She'd have to research it. Elke could understand why they'd want *her* involved in claims against the cargo that could be her colony's property. As for the personal effects, well, she'd be honored to have that custom coffee mug monstrosity Moira made for Sri…

Elke returned her attention to the console and started scrolling through the messages, initially irritated that they'd started marking them "urgent." Didn't seem appropriate, given everything she'd been dealing with these last few days.

*Not that they know anything about that, of course…*

She sighed, began reading, and dropped her drink.

# ACKNOWLEDGMENTS

I'm grateful to my family for putting up with me locked away in my office for so many hours of writing and rewriting (and, of course, re-re-writing).

In particular, I want to thank my wife for encouraging me along the way. I also want to thank the folks at Paperclip Publishing who were fabulous to work with, particularly my editor, Abigail. In addition to catching my typos and corralling my run-on-sentences, she made numerous suggestions that made it a better book.

Hours were spent working through the underlying science for *Tides of Eden*. A big part of the fun (for me and hopefully for readers) is exploring Earthly biological examples that inform what might be possible on an alien world. And of course, the outdoor experiences like George's diving or Ronnie's reaching the crest of a mountain range are based on my own adventures.

I hope you've enjoyed reading the story as much as I've enjoyed writing it. Thank you!

# ABOUT THE AUTHOR

George Moakley started his career studying biology, with dreams of doing fieldwork and ecosystem modeling. To make ends meet, he took a data entry position with a precious metals company. Throughout his long career in the tech industry, George gained an inside perspective on various scientific and business practices, including designing Edge Intelligence solutions and conducting strategic planning workshops. He owns several patents, and holds prestigious advisory positions with ASU's School of Business and UCI's Customer Experience Program.

A fan of science fiction since childhood, George remains fascinated by the hard sciences. He feeds his passion for nature through photography while traveling the world; he also regularly partakes in hiking and scuba diving. Such travels have brought great joy, but also great concern about the fragility of our ecosystems. He has witnessed devastation caused by climate change, invasive species, overfishing, and other environmental issues. George is a long time member of the Nature Conservancy; a meeting with a conservancy representative in 2019 inspired a strategic thought experiment, regarding how the twenty-first century is likely to play out. The results were sobering, but provided the real-life inspiration behind Kraken of Eden.

Today, George makes his home in sunny Arizona with his inspiration, Diana. Between them, they have seven kids. When he's not locked away writing, he loves to visit his children and grandchildren, and can often be spotting driving back and forth from various sports activities.

EDEN WILL RETURN...
2026